THE TWELVE TRIALS OF DOUG

THE TWELVE TRIALS OF DOUG

JEREMY BRUNDAGE

Cursed Dragon Ship
PUBLISHING

Cursed Dragon Ship Publishing, LLC

6046 FM 2920 Rd, #231, Spring, TX 77379

captwyvern@curseddragonship.com

Developmental Edit by Kelly Lynn Colby

Proofread by S.G. George

ISBN 978-1-951445-55-3

ISBN 978-1-951445-56-0 (ebook)

For those who have forgotten how strong they are.

Contents

PROLOGUE

It was a quiet day up on Mount Olympus. The king of the gods was enjoying the sun from his son out on the balcony.

Zeus waved up at the chariot driven across the sky by Apollo. Apollo nodded back in acknowledgment of his father.

Zeus called out, knowing his boy could clearly hear him. "Dinner tonight? I'm firing up the BBQ to smoke a couple racks. I've got a new version of *Pournari Drys* I just made,[1] and I want to try it out and see how the wood enhances Ambrosia. I might roast some acorns and smoke some goat cheese too, as appetizers."

"Sounds good." A hearty, home-cooked meal always got the sun god's attention. Apollo let the chariot drift just a bit off track to the north because he was distracted by the offer.[2] "I love it when you're wearing the apron at the grill, Dad! I'll be there!" He flicked the reins and tugged the horses slightly to the south and back into the correct path across the sky.

Dinner plans were set. His boy was going to be there. That was good.

Zeus went inside and plopped down on his easy chair, kicked his

1. *Pournari Drys*, also known as a Holly Oak. Zeus loves to experiment with local woods to enhance flavors on the grill because he hasn't heard about mesquite yet.
2. Crete had a sudden, unexpected cold snap in the middle of the day. Not noticeable enough to hurt anything, but the cold blast of air fortified the grapes on the vine and made for an excellent wine later in the year.

feet up on the *hupopodian*,[3] and stretched back against the chair, linking his fingers behind his neck to relax a bit.

Curled up on a rug by his side, the aged dog Kyon Khryseos raised his grizzled old head from his paws.[4] "Woof," the dog said, then his voice fell into a low, rumbly growl.

"What is it, boy?" Zeus reached down and put a restraining hand on Goldy as he sat up and looked around. "Is someone here?"

Only one person ever managed to get Goldy's dander up anymore because the dog was so old. "Hermes?"

The messenger god was seen in an instant because he'd already been there anyway. He simply coalesced from the shadows. "I don't know how the damn dog does it. Every. Single. Time." Hermes glared down at the hound, undisguised disgust on his face. He held a sheaf of papers out for his father. The correspondence was the reason Hermes was in his father's den in the presence of the dog.

"Oh, he's a good boy, aren't you, Goldy?" Zeus leaned over and ruffled the dog's ears, ignoring the outstretched hand of his messenger son. Zeus continued to scratch the dog between the ears.

Hermes fidgeted and squirmed with the unacknowledged correspondence dangling from his grasp.

"Your dog," Hermes huffed. "I don't like him one bit."

"And he returns the sentiment." Zeus chuckled.

Hermes glowered.

"Oh, don't be like that," Zeus said. "The beasts don't mean anything from it. It's just in their nature." He scratched the old dog on the side of the cheek, and Goldy, exhausted from the high level of activity, laid his head back on his paws.

The dog spared a low growl and bared his teeth once more in Hermes's direction.

---

3. The Greek term for foot stool.

4. The name literally translates to Golden Dog, the animal left as protector to Zeus when he was an infant. Kyon is getting a bit long in the tooth, and even though losing his loyal companion pains him, Zeus isn't going to wait much longer before putting the dog in the heavens. Once again literally. Kyon becomes the constellation Canis Major.

The messenger glared right back at the dog. "I'll take care of you, dog, just you wait," Hermes said in a voice so quiet you almost couldn't hear it.

"What was that?" Zeus asked, pretending he hadn't heard what Hermes said.

"Nothing," Hermes said. His eyes drifted from the dog and hit the king of the gods without changing expression before the hate flickered off his face and was replaced with a forced smile.

Zeus was still looking at the dog with love, blind to anything else in the room. "I'm firing up the grill and smoking some dinner tonight. You're more than welcome if you'd like to come."

Hermes arched an eyebrow as if to consider. "I'm busy."

"Fair enough," Zeus said. "You're always welcome, though, if you have a spare minute."

"Why wouldn't I want to be here to watch you fawn over your other children while your dog contemplates clamping down on the dangling bits between my thighs?" Hermes sounded a bit perturbed. "Have a nice dinner," he said in a flat voice as he took the messages for Zeus and tossed them on an end table. Then he was gone.

The abrupt exit finally got Zeus's attention. "Was it something I said?" Zeus sat forward, his fingers raking furrows in Goldy's fur.

"The boy's trouble," the dog said with a breathless huff.[5]

"Hermes? No," Zeus couldn't even contemplate it.

Yet, he didn't like his children being upset with him. "I'll make that fruit salad with the marshmallows and cherries.[6] Hermes loves that. It'll make him feel better, and he'll know I was thinking about him."

"What is he, a three-year-old?" the dog scoffed.

"He loves it. It's his favorite dessert," Zeus defended his decision.

"If he comes to dinner." Goldy arched a disbelieving brow.

---

5. Ancient Greece. Dog of the gods. Of course he talks.

6. Yes, I know what that particular type of fruit salad is called, and no, it isn't the ambrosia Zeus is going to be throwing on the grill.

"Slimy marshmallows, mandarin oranges, and pineapple chunks aren't enough to fix the problems happening with that boy."

"Oh, hush," Zeus said. "Hermes is a good boy."

"If you say so." The dog shook his head and closed his eyes. After a few minutes, he quietly began to snore.

CHAPTER 1

LOVE AND YOGURT

TRAFFIC IN THE FOOD COURT HAD WOUND DOWN AFTER THE lunch rush in the ancient Greek city of Larissa. The crowds left the area for the most part, and the whole of the catering and fast-food district would be calm were it not for the impromptu entertainment attempted in their midst.

A few in the crowd covered their ears, ready to be done with the performance just underway. "I am fond of it. I am exceedingly fond of it . . ."[1] The spoken word poet paused,[2] waiting for the crowd to pick up the rest of the phrase. They didn't, and he was forced to continue. "I desire more of it!"

"Shut up, you unemployable philosopher," one of the annoyed patrons said in a desperate tone just loud enough the band might hear and be thus encouraged to wrap up the terrible set.[3]

The lead poet continued to elucidate in a cracking voice and play his instrument out of tune, much to the chagrin of those who listened.

---

1. A translated interpretation of this poem was refined, paired with compelling music, and popularized by Tim McGraw. "I like it, I love it" was the song. The popular belief is that Tim wrote the lyrics to his song while he hung out in his backyard in the process of consuming half a case of beer. Not so. McGraw was just the performer. His songwriters, however, were accomplished history sleuths who expertly translated the lyrics from a 3500-year-old chamberpot unearthed from the rumored lost city of Troy and were duly inspired. *The more you know.*
2. Think William Shatner's cadence and tempo in the song "Mr. Tambourine Man" from his 1968 album *The Transformed Man.*
3. "I'm going to sit around and think of things, and you should pay me for it." You had to be a pretty good philosopher to earn a livable contract.

Those in the know and within earshot took some small consolation that sound amplification systems hadn't been invented yet.

The performing troupe finished butchering a verse when a well-aimed souvlaki, dripping with a generous helping of tzatziki, slapped the drummer in the neck. The slightly spongy pita was probably the best pay they'd get out of the gig, so the lead poet cut the whole set right there. The meaty wrap was split between the two, and the musicians picked up their lyre and bongo drums and left the stage.[4]

Doug—tall, earnest, with a mop of curly hair corralled by a paper hat—was all eyes and ears into the pretty young lady sitting across from him in the booth. If he could figure out how to use his other senses to get more into her, he was all for it.

Larisa, the young lady in question, returned the attention given with a fevered intensity.

I think she really likes me! Me! She's so pretty! And I'm, well, me? Doug couldn't believe he'd talked to her. He looked across the table at Larisa, and she blushed and smiled and batted her eyes right back at him. The eye-bat was enough to flip his brain.

What was I thinking about?

Brain spasms, a small price to pay to gaze upon such beauty. Doug would do it without a blink if he could, but after the first half hour he noticed his eyeballs were dried out, and it affected his vision. He was also aware this sort of prolonged, unblinking stare could be considered kinda creepy.

Larisa didn't seem to mind.

They'd been locked in each other's eyes for a long time, way longer than the fifteen-minute break from his job Doug had intended to take. Doug thought he had to get back to work. Every time he was about to force himself to leave Larisa's presence, his manager, Asklepios, would silently indicate it was okay for Doug to sit there with the pretty lady and he, the manager, would pick up the slack.

---

4. Perhaps the troupe had more skills than I realized. How do you play bongo drums out of tune?

Asklepios was like that. He always looked out for the physical and mental health of those around him. The guy was way too understanding and supportive for his own good.[5]

Doug would usually have objected and got right back to work. But the girl was right in front of him, and it would be rude to leave, right? And business was slow today, so taking a bit of extra time wasn't hurting anybody, especially if Asklepios felt he had it under control.

The line of people looking to purchase yogurt was non-existent at the moment. Doug wouldn't have noticed if there was a line or not. He'd been vaguely aware of the lunch rush around him when he'd worked the crowd earlier, but they were just nameless faces to him. Doug had been distracted by the girl in the hooded cloak with a smile that dazzled as she waited for the crowd to leave so he could serve her an order of fig ripple personally. He tried to be professional, to focus on the customers right before him, but by the time he could bring himself to pay attention, almost all of the people had been served and were gone.

Most who'd wanted a dairy treat during their lunch break had asked the manager what was wrong with the server, who messed up order after order and slopped clabber hither and yon, all while he stared intently at the pretty girl in the corner booth.

A couple of the old women who'd been in the line had thought the young lovers were cute and had excused Doug in his dereliction of dairy delivery duty.

The majority of those inconvenienced did not share the same sense of understanding. A few even got so flustered, they yelled at Doug.

---

5. That quality would later get the man in trouble. Asklepios dabbled in medicine and was really good at it and brought a few people back from the dead. The gods were offended by him overstepping his bounds, and Zeus fried Mr. Do-gooder with a lightning bolt. Asklepios was actually a bit relieved when it happened. He'd always had a hard time saying no to anybody, and being dead was the perfect excuse to let go of the constant pressure, sense of responsibility, and guilt so he could finally get a bit of rest.

Doug just nodded, his eyes still on the girl, which only angered the patrons further. "You're absolutely right," he'd said. "Talk to my manager." He pointed at Asklepios.

Asklepios sighed and pulled out a couple of blank complaint forms for the aggrieved patrons to send to the franchise's corporate offices.

"I'll deal with this paperwork," Asklepios said to Doug as the disgruntled customers walked away. "Go spend your break with your girlfriend."

No one had ever called Larisa Doug's girlfriend before. Doug liked how it sounded. "Thanks, boss!"

Asklepios went out back for something, so Doug and Larisa were the only ones there. An apparent straggler who'd missed the lunch rush appeared out of nowhere, slunk up to the counter, and loudly cleared his throat. The man wore a deep hood that hid his face. When the manager didn't return quick enough, Doug pulled himself away from Larisa and forced himself to the counter.

The man, who wouldn't show his face, tipped a finger in the direction of the pretty girl. "You normally take personal time with customers like that?" The man asked in a dark whisper.

"Uh, not usually." Doug had no idea why the man would care. "Would you like to place an order?"

"I got it, Doug." Asklepios patted Doug on the shoulder. "Back to your girl."

"Thanks, boss!" Doug vaulted over the counter, and Larisa giggled in response.

The customer grunted, his voice still guarded and hushed. "Quite the work ethic."

Asklepios defended Doug. "He's actually quite the hard worker. One of the best I've ever had. Just a bit distracted right now."

"Good help is hard to come by," the customer whispered, unconvinced.

Doug paused halfway back to the booth. "If you think there's a problem, sir, I can totally take care of your order."

"I told you I got it." Asklepios waved Doug away and addressed the customer. "He really is a hard worker. I'm gonna ask him to close tonight to make up for his long break, and he won't even grumble about it." Asklepios stifled a yawn as he finished scooping yogurt into the waxed paper cup. "You want nuts with that?"

The man nodded and placed his coin on the counter. He took his purchase and once more appraised Doug and Larisa from the shadow of his hood as he turned to leave.

The man was almost out of eyesight when Doug watched him drop his wholly uneaten snack in a trashcan at the edge of the food court.

"Must not have been hungry," Asklepios said.

Doug returned to his seat in the booth, just a little rattled. He wasn't sure why, but the man who skulked away with the pomegranate swirl with almond topping unnerved him. Maybe the man's gaze lingered just a bit too long on Doug and Larisa. Maybe it was the way Doug felt like he was being weighed or judged by the man. It wasn't the way the man threw away his food. That was fairly normal. A lot of people had buyer's remorse after purchasing pretty much anything from the food court.

Maybe the man was just jealous of two young people in love?

Love?

It was amazing how one word distracted Doug from the thoughts about the strange customer. Doug hadn't held Larisa close yet, or kissed her even. Not that any of that mattered. She was the girl he was meant to be with.

Doug felt like he needed to say something to her. "You haven't touched your yogurt."

Larisa looked at the curdled dairy product as it proceeded into the later stages of evolution under the hot Grecian sun. "Silly me." She shrugged. "I'd totally forgotten about it."

The angelic sound of her voice temporarily wiped any trace of intelligence from Doug's brain. "Forgotten about what?" His mind tumbled. *Wait. I just asked her a question, didn't I? What did I ask her about?*

Larisa looked as if she knew why Doug found it hard to concentrate on anything but her, and she took it as a compliment. She also seemed to be able to read what he currently stumbled over and pointed at the center of the table.

Doug's mind blipped again as he watched the grace and fluidity of motion of Larisa's arm, hand, and fingers. *She's pointing at something?* His eyes followed the line down her arm to the fetid mess she'd indicated on the table.

The yogurt burbled and writhed. The accelerated transformation and evolution of the dairy treat into a higher life form was impressive. A fermented bubble burst from the surface and spewed warm clabber in a beautiful splatter that covered a good portion of the table.

The image suppressed the appetite, and a whiff of the accompanying smells gifted Doug with a renewed ability to speak. "Oh, yeah. Your triple fig ripple." Doug watched as the confection did its best Vesuvius impression. It was going to be a pain to wipe down the table later. "I don't know if I'd eat that if I were you."

"I wasn't hungry anyway." She patted Doug on the back of the hand.

The physical contact was almost too much. Doug had to look away before he lost what little control he managed to maintain. While doing so, he caught a flash of plumage and red silk as it peeked out from behind the olive tree a few paces away.

The majordomo of the king of Larissa pulled back behind the trunk of the olive tree where he'd hidden but could peek out to see the young couple if he needed to. He'd been there the whole time Larisa had.

Doug knew the man was sent to spy on them by the king. Still, Doug found he'd developed a certain respect for him. The official looked as if he tried his best to be nonchalant and not stick out. It would be a very hard thing for anyone to accomplish after having spent hour after hour observing two young people as they wooed each other in a public place. For any person dressed in full palace court robes, silly hat with plumage denoting his station included, in the middle of the city market under the hot Grecian sun in the early days of summer? That took stamina, determination, and a lack of self-awareness anyone would have to be impressed by.

"Your dad's man is still there," Doug said to Larisa. "I thought he'd get sick of it and leave, especially after those two old ladies beat him with brooms for watching us."

"Dad's been a trifle overprotective as of late, almost as if I was a piece of property. He wasn't always like this," Larisa sighed and shook her head. "It's only been lately that I noticed him change, so he's probably instructed Daphis to follow me for some reason. It'd take more than two noble-hearted, experienced old grannies to beat him off."

It was an odd turn of phrase. Well intentioned, lauding the dedication and protectiveness of the pair of venerable matriarchs, yet it still came across a trifle dirty. Doug tried not to laugh at it. He stifled a giggle in his throat before he lost it and snorted.

"What are you laughing at?" Larisa's eyes went wide when she realized what she'd said about the old women and Daphis. "Ewwww, gross! I didn't mean anything like that!" She laughed and slapped playfully at the back of Doug's hand. "I meant Daphis is nothing if not dogged and loyal. If Dad asked him to follow me, he'd do it 'til he died or Dad told him he was done."

"I don't blame your father or Daphis or those old ladies. You're worth being protected." Doug was unaware of how syrupy he sounded.

"Those grandmothers were thinking you're the type of boy they want to introduce to their granddaughters," Larisa replied.

"I'd have to tell them sorry, but I'm already spoken for." He beamed at her.

"Ah, to be young." Doug overheard Asklepios say as the manager shook his head and started wiping down the counter.

Doug and Larisa twined fingers across the table.

Asklepios wasn't the only one paying attention to them. The majordomo flipped out behind the olive tree. "Me holding your hand got Daphis's attention." Doug was not remotely interested in letting go. "He's scribbling notes like mad now."

Larisa tightened her fingers on Doug's hand. "Do I need to go ask him to leave?"

Doug shook his head. "That would mean you'd have to get up, and I'd not have as much time with you. Just let him be."

"You're so sweet." Larisa turned her head and flipped her braid off her shoulder.

You are so, so very pretty, Doug thought. Doug felt the pressure from each of her perfectly manicured fingertips. He wanted to let go for a second just so he could feel the electric rush he got when she touched him again, but he didn't want to pull away. *I can't believe I'm holding her hand!*

Larisa consulted the stylish sundial strapped to her wrist. "Oh dear! Father will be furious if he finds out I've been gone this long." She pulled her hands from Doug for a moment.

It was devastating.

"Do you really have to go?" Doug's heart ached at the thought of her leaving.

Larisa reached across the table, took Doug's hand in hers again. "Oh, what's a few more minutes going to hurt?"

A little while later it was finally time that Larisa *had* to go.

Doug watched the path she took long after she was gone.

Asklepios whistled to get Doug's attention. "Hey, Eros, how 'bout you wipe down the tables?"[6] He threw a wet bar rag at Doug.

Doug caught the towel even though he hadn't looked in his boss's direction. He twirled it round in his hand and incorporated the spin into scouring the top of the table he was closest to.

---

6. A cute nickname to jibe Doug with but a terrible person to emulate when it comes to work ethics. Eros was the original pretty boy, and he never learned to do anything for or by himself.

Doug continued to wipe down tables when the patron who'd questioned Doug's work ethics earlier slithered behind the Gearloose Gyros food wagon at the other end of the court fast enough his presence couldn't be verified.

"Hello?" Doug called out, not really expecting an answer. After a pause with no response, he shrugged and got back to work.

CHAPTER 2

A NICE DAY FOR A STROLL

A DAY OR TWO LATER IN THE CITY OF LARISSA, DOUG LED HIS adoptive brother, Modifixeus, through the midday crowds of the city marketplace.

The huge square in the center of town was filled with just about every sight, sound, and smell available in ancient Greece. A chaotic collection of things bought and sold, deals made in whispered voices or yelled at the top capacity of lungs. Housewares, farming implements, livestock, cheeses, vegetables, wines, entertainments, and practical everyday necessities passed from one hand to another in a pattern played out day after day in a manner that felt fresh and new, eternal and unchanging.

Doug didn't really care about any of the things he passed by. He was intent on being somewhere.

The two young men walked along a path that wound through the livestock pens. To one side of Doug and his brother, goats screamed in stupid abandon as they did their best to climb on top of one another. On the other side of the path, ducks stared glumly through the bars of their cages.

Modifixeus hunched over and fiddled with something in his hands as he walked.

Doug led on. Modifixeus followed Doug on a sort of ethereal tether. There was a delay in Modifixeus's directional recognition response, but aside from that, he usually arrived at the intended destination. They'd worked out this system a long time ago, Doug in front, Modifixeus trailing, and it worked for the most part.

Doug paused as the hackles on the back of his neck stood up.

Modifixeus bumped into the back of Doug before his brother could turn around. "What was that?" Modifixeus didn't even bother to look up.

"Dunno." Doug scanned the crowd behind him. He was almost certain he saw that same hooded, cloaked guy from the other day following him. "Maybe nothing." After a bit Doug gave up and tugged on his brother's shoulder to get him moving forward again.

Doug needed something to distract his mind from the sense he was being followed. "The ungulates are rather chipper today, don't you think, Mod?" Doug said to his brother as he pointed out the animal perched precariously atop a writhing goat pile.

"I currently identify more with the ducks' view of things, myself." Mod looked up briefly before he turned his attention back to whatever he held in his hands. The odd, shiny, spherical mechanism twisted and spun. Mod prodded and poked at the metal plates of the device. He paid more attention to the gadget than the crowd.

Doug knew Mod was like that, at least in public. His brother didn't like being out in the middle of things. Mod would much rather see how something was built or take the same thing apart to put it back together again. Or study a scroll. Anything that wasn't social or out in public, really. Doug was glad Mod loved him enough to follow him, and Doug really wanted Mod to come with him today.

Mod only acted like himself when he was at home or in his shop or in a small group of people he loved or cared for.

Doug really understood and did his best to shield his brother while still keeping him a part of things. He continually reached over to redirect Mod before he crashed into this or that. Directing Mod was only difficult sometimes, like when Doug was distracted by the feeling he was being followed.

The crowd grew thicker.

"All the crazy, loud weirdos must be out today," Mod said as he twisted a knob on the side of the device. He still hadn't looked up. "Is it a festival or something?"

Doug spun around. That feeling was back, like someone was right behind him.

Mod walked right into Doug, took a step to the right, and continued forward.

Doug was almost sure he'd seen someone before Mod stumbled into him. Almost.

"Dang it, Mod. Would it hurt to just look where you're going?" Doug risked another look behind them.

Mod exhibited excellent timing, choosing that moment to plow into an incredibly large, overly muscled man who wore a lion skin as a cloak.

The machine fumbled from Mod's hand. "Awe, man. You made me drop it."

The guy Mod bumped was half the size of Olympus and looked to have the temperament of Lyssa with a toothache.[1] Doug's stomach dropped, and he tried to steer Mod into the anonymity of the crowd. Instead, the crowd split around them, like two giant, invisible hands pushed the people to one side or the other, leaving Doug, Mod, and the burly titan in the center of an impromptu arena.

An air of quiet descended over the entire area.

Even the goats stopped screaming.

It was the sudden silence from the goats that really drove it home for Doug.

Goats were notorious spectators and facilitators of barnyard brawls. They most likely get that peculiar trait from the faun side of the family. Doug was pretty sure he saw a couple of nannies placing bets, with a big billy acting as a bookie.

This is bad. Doug gulped. *Of all the times to get distracted, Mod.*

The big billy winked at Doug. "Go down in the second round.

1. Lyssa: the Greek goddess of mad rage, frenzy, and rabies. She sprung from the blood spilled on the ground by the castration of Uranus. Not the person you'd want to be on the bad side of.

It'd be worth your while."[2] The goat then sized up Doug and Mod's competition one more time. "If you can last that long," he added.

The nannies looked skeptical, altering their bets for the two young men to go down in the first.

Hoping the goats were wrong, Doug risked a glance to see how he stacked up against the competition.

Maybe if I had a Phalanx, of say, three hundred Spartans? Doug considered.

The giant straightened, the muscles in his back rippling.

Better make that two phalanx. Doug corrected.

The giant stiffened and turned slowly toward Mod, veins in his forehead humped out, his face a tachycardic red. "You dare?" The question was punctuated by a spray of angry spittle.

Mod wiped at the moisture on his cheek as he bent down and picked up the machine. "No harm done. Just watch where you're going. You could have busted it."

"And with a clueless mutter, my brother kills us both." Doug gaped at Mod. He rapidly prayed for a bit of luck,[3] something like an unexpected hero to come to his rescue.

The gambling goats upped the ante.

A tufted duck from across the way waved his bill as he tried to horn in on the action.

With a palpable tension in the air, the billy stopped accepting bets.

The big vein on the giant's forehead pulsed like an overinflated

---

2. Yes, the goat talks. We're in ancient Greece. Animals, rocks, grass, the wind, and pretty much anything or everything else might just pipe up and give their two bits at any given point. It was a very disconcerting, schizophrenic time.

3. Tyche, goddess of luck, didn't excel at answering off the cuff pleas. Contrary to her supposed nature, she was not spontaneous and liked to have things planned out, weighing all options before she carefully committed to anything. Nemesis, on the other hand, listened to pretty much all the pleas meant for Tyche, and answered them readily, usually placing warring bets on both sides of the conflict. Nemesis loved a good smackdown.

balloon and his eyes bulged fully out of their sockets. "Have I seen the two of you before?"

Doug recognized Mod was lost in an engineer's daze, so it was up to Doug to quell the anger of someone he assumed had to be a titan. "Forgive us, my lord, for interrupting your peaceful midday stroll. It's quite possible you've seen us before, though we've only been here, local, for a little while." Doug gulped and continued. "I have a job selling yogurt. My bro—my frien—this guy here hangs out by my stall sometimes. You may have chanced upon either of us in that vicinity. But you," Doug made note of the man's rippling biceps and swallowed again, hard, "don't seem to be the yogurt chomping type."

"No," the man replied.

"We're originally from Iolcus, if you've ever been that way before," Doug offered. "It's a place much beloved by both of us, that we'd really like to see again, sooo"—he grabbed Mod by the shoulders and attempted to steer him away from the situation—"by your leave, my lord." Doug scraped and bowed and pushed his brother to do likewise.

Mod, not understanding why his brother shoved him, planted his feet and fiddled with the contraption. He fumbled it and dropped it squarely on the giant's exposed toe. Apparently, the device was heavier than it looked.

The giant's eyes rolled up and steam poured from his ears.

Mod, oblivious, bent over, picked up the device, and began poking at it again.

Doug, now fearing for their lives, pulled Mod back and gave an uncomfortable explanation. "Apologies, kind and gentle sir. My friend is haunted by furies. They attack if he looks up, so he pays attention to the gadget in his hand to distract himself from madness."

The giant seemed unconvinced.

Doug reached into a pouch at his waist and pulled out an ostracon. He really didn't want to do this, but it was probably the best way to ensure he and Mod didn't end up eating yogurt through straws for the foreseeable future. "My father's name is written here. Show him this pot shard if you happen to be around Iolcus and I swear he'll make it worth your while."

"Huh." As he read the name, the giant's temper cooled. "Your father's name is very familiar to me. The great and powerful men of Greece honor and respect him. Why are you so far from home?"

"Just trying to find my own," Doug replied, a little embarrassed he couldn't defuse the situation without bringing up his father's name.

The giant nodded in acknowledgement of Doug's answer, then growled and snorted. "Your friend doesn't realize how close he just came to losing his head."

Doug grinned sheepishly. "He probably wouldn't have noticed if he had."

The response made the giant laugh. He punched the support post for a nearby merchant tent, and the thick piece of wood broke neatly in two. The roof sagged, groaned, and dropped on the vendor and patrons inside.

"For the gift of mirth, I'll let you and your friend live! Watch the path you tread from this point on. I won't be so forgiving a second time." With that, the giant turned and disappeared into the crowd.

"Mod, gods love ya, you gotta pay more attention." Doug breathed a sigh of relief. He glanced over as arms and legs wriggled free of the collapsed building. "Sorry for the mess."

The vendor popped his head up out of the rubble. "I'm pretty sure that was a son of Zeus.[4] It could have gone a lot worse."

Doug slung an arm across Mod's shoulders and steered him to a less bustling and dangerous path through the market. "Why don't we take the road over by the potters and mudslingers. Nothing exciting or dangerous ever happens over there."

Mod nodded and walked in the direction indicated as he

---

4. The sons of Zeus weren't particularly known for their social graces and benefits to society. They were heroic, gifted, and usually ranked on a destructive level with the same category scale used to rank hurricanes.

continued to fiddle with the thing in his hand, unaware anything had just gone on around him. "Just a bit more . . ." He stuck his tongue out the corner of his mouth as he turned a small rod inserted into the gizmo. The outer shell of the thing clicked sharply as the skin unlatched so it was only attached by hinges at the top. The newly released blades spun and whirled until the machine rose from Mod's hand and began to gain altitude.

"Ha!" Mod gave a small fist pump. "I told Hephaestus I could make it work!"[5]

"Not so loud about us dealing with him." Doug tried to shush his brother. "He told you to keep it quiet."

They stopped and watched as the flying gadget rose higher and higher. "You introduced us," Mod pointed out. "When I told you about the classified ad, you said you'd go with me. Dad deals with old Heph all the time, and Heph actually seemed a little impressed when he realized who we were." Mod poked at Doug. "You and Dad deal with gods on a regular basis. I just do a little bit of haggling from time to time."

"Dad's just Dad," Doug said. "Everybody who knows him respects him."

Doug wanted to be someone like his father. How do you create a name for yourself without thinking it was handed to you by the legacy of your parents? He'd find a way to prove himself someday, but the question was how?

Doug didn't have an answer yet, so he just waved it off. "You can't rely on name-dropping Dad forever. Talking about badgering a god into low-priced, shady dealings is bound to have repercussions if people hear about it."

The hackles on Doug's neck prickled. Again.

---

5. Hephaestus had a problem with impulse purchases. His wife had a problem with the pile of crap collecting in the garage. Aphrodite suspended marital bed privileges until the problem was resolved, and that really motivated Heph to find a solution. Enter Modifixeus. Mod had a love of gadgetry equaled only by the god of the forge, a large empty cave to store junk in, and a weekly allowance to help offset Heph's costs.

Someone repeated the phrase about badgering a god in a whisper.

Doug's head swung around as he searched for who'd just spoken.

Someone else in the crowd with exceptional hearing also overheard and cast their eyes about. "God? Gods? Are we in the proximity of deity?"

Distracted, a potter stopped pedaling his spinning table, bumped the top with his knee, and twisted his palm in the wrong direction. The side of his hand brushed against the unfinished vase, and the thing shifted and collapsed in on itself, ruining an hour's worth of work.[6] The man swore and looked up.

The potter caught sight of movement in the air above and squinted to see it a bit better. He pointed a mud-caked finger skyward. "Truly, we are in the presence of something divine!"

More heads angled skyward.

Mod's gadget, now far above everyone's heads, picked up speed. It rose faster and faster, the light of the sun reflected off it so brightly that everyone in the marketplace became transfixed on it.

"Helios! Come to shower blessings on us!" someone shouted.

"Nay, 'tis Apollo!"

"That's an awful small chariot to carry a god."

Doug stopped searching for who followed him and tracked the path of everyone else's gazes instead. He realized what they were watching and started to panic. "Oh, for Pallas's sake—" Leaving before someone backtracked the gadget's trajectory to find out where it originated was the best option. Doug grabbed his brother by the shoulders and steered him through the crowd while everyone was distracted.

Doug noticed one man watching him instead of the object in the sky, but the man ducked behind a pallet of roofing tiles. It was too quick, so Doug didn't really get a look at whom it was.

---

6. I have it on good authority that a skilled potter can throw a pot in a matter of minutes. This guy was obviously not a skilled potter.

Doug kept pushing Mod out of the area. This was not the time to sleuth out a phantom.

The machine sputtered and wobbled. It lost altitude as it careened off to the east. It made several erratic loops in the sky then crashed with a brilliant explosion just beyond the horizon.

"Apollo is dead!" someone screamed. "The bright god has died this day!"

"Or maybe it was Helios?" someone offered helpfully. "Nobody cares about him, right?"[7]

7. People do actually care about Helios, it's just with the same devotion we of this current age now reserve for celebrities like Wayne Newton or Mel "The Velvet Fog" Tormé.

CHAPTER 3

LOOKING FOR LOVE

"YOUR STUPID TOYS ARE GONNA GET US INTO TROUBLE ONE DAY, Mod," Doug said.

Mod pouted over the loss of his gadget. He stuffed his hands in his pockets and kicked at a rock in the road. "It would have been fine if you just let me work on it in the shop. What did you drag me out here for anyway?"

Doug tugged him along faster. "I told you you'll see when we get there."

Mod finally looked around. "We're in the market district. Are we heading toward the palace?"

Doug smiled and moved a little quicker.

They came into a large open area in front of the royal palace. There were hundreds of people crowded into the space. A large contingent of guards ringed the area, the bulk of the soldiers positioned at the base of the palace steps to keep the people at bay. Every so often the majordomo, Daphis, now dressed to the nines in turquoise and blue ensemble capped off with a stunning new hat, would consult with the angry looking man sitting on a huge wooden armchair flanked by two smaller stools situated on a landing two-thirds of the way up the steps.

Doug squinted at the majordomo's new outfit. "He has a peacock feather in his hat now. Pretty daring."[1] Doug grinned.

1. The peacock was sacred to Hera, queen of the gods. Messing with one was like

"Who's that?" Mod asked as he pointed at the Liberace cosplayer.[2]

"Daphis, majordomo of the king," Doug said. "If he's here, it means she is too."

"She who?" Mod asked.

No response.

Doug's attention was focused on something other than Mod.

Mod tried not to take it personal, but it annoyed him anyway.

Bereft of his mechanical distraction, Mod tried to pay attention to what happened around him. Up near the palace, after whatever words were exchanged between king and official, Daphis would descend the steps to the guards, who would then admit one of the subjects of the king to pass only to have the guards grab the person and throw them into a pit just off to the side of the steps.

As the person dropped into the pit, the crowd would go wild. They cheered and hooted and pumped their fists in the air.

Everyone angled to get a good view into the pit. The crowd pressed close.

"Too cramped for me down there." Mod liked wide swaths of personal space. Someone brushed up a little too close and bumped into Mod. He shied away from the stranger and pushed closer to his brother. "I hate crowds."

"Just give it a minute," Doug said.

The same hooded, cloaked guy that bumped into Mod circled around and bumped into Doug. Doug didn't notice. Mod would have pointed it out, but the guy had already disappeared into the crowd.

Mod watched his brother scan every visible part of the palace. Doug took long enough Mod grew bored and turned his attention back to the crowd near the pit.

After several moments a pattern established itself: selection, pit,

---

asking the goddess for a smackdown. If Daphis did garner a beating, he would deserve it. Poor peacock.

2. The minor god of flamboyance and sequins. He has long since retired, ceding his powers and principality to Ru Paul.

cheer; selection, pit, cheer; selection, pit, pause, cheer; selection, pit, cheer. It was an exceptionally easy pattern to follow, and Mod had no idea what it meant.

"Seems to be a little harsh on the constituency here." Mod nodded his head in the direction where the crowd was thickest and people jostled for position in the foreground. "They're all pretty eager to get to the front of the group, which means they want to be the next to be thrown into the pit." Mod scratched his head, thinking. "When has it ever been a good thing to be thrown into a pit?"

"Uh, huh. You're absolutely right." Doug's eyes scrutinized the areas behind the guards. Doug clearly wasn't finding what he hoped for.

And he ignored Mod while he searched.

Well, this is perturbing. Mod turned his gaze from his brother to the group pressed close around them. The unruly masses assembled were made up entirely of young men.

"Hey, Doug, why are all these guys being thrown into a pit?"

No response.

"Is that guy on the big chair up there the king?"

Mod sighed, grabbed Doug by the arm, and pointed at the man sitting on the throne on the raised dais. "Big nasty tempered looking man with the crown? King?"

Doug stopped his searching and looked where Mod pointed. "Uh, yeah. Teutamides, king of Larissa."

"Yeah, I kinda thought he might be the king, you know, throwing his subjects into a pit and whatnot." No reaction. Doug hadn't heard what he'd said.

Mod put his hand in Doug's face and snapped his fingers. "Yo! Residents of the surface of Gaea to Doug. As entertaining as it is to see guys that bullied me during academy being thrown into a pit, I just have to ask—hopefully with an answer this time—why we are here?"

"What? Oh, that's easy." Doug smiled. "We're here to see Larisa."

Mod was confused. "We're standing in the middle of Larissa. We saw most of the good stuff on the way in."

Doug's fist clenched. For an instant Mod thought his brother was going to hit him, then the tension eased from Doug's face.

"Not Larissa the kingdom, Larisa the princess," Doug said.

As if on cue, Larisa walked onto a palace balcony fronting the square.

"Wow." Mod's eyes went wide as he took a step back and nodded his approval. "From the yogurt shop, right? She's the princess?"

"Yeah." Doug laughed. "I'm impressed you recognize her."

"I pay attention in public. Sometimes," Mod huffed. "With exceptions for most men, women, and the occasional natural disaster."

Doug laughed and nodded. "She sneaks out of the palace in disguise once a week to pick up an order of fig ripple."

Mod stared at his brother. "That's why you changed your work days at Amalthaea's.[3] So you could see her. I wondered why you'd passed up that assistant manager position."

Doug blushed. "She's nice. Really smart too. We hung out after closing and talked a bunch. I like her a lot."

Mod looked at Doug's face, then followed his gaze to the girl, then back to his brother. "I've never seen you like this before."

Doug sighed. "I've never met anyone like her before. Mod, I think she's the one."

"Oh, that's nice." Mod managed. He suddenly felt decidedly uncomfortable, and it wasn't from the crowd.

---

3. Amalthaea's: named for the foster mother of the king of the gods, Amalthaea is the best-known franchise for yogurt and kefir in the Peloponnese with over three hundred locations. For franchise information, send a herald to HermesCorp™.

Chapter 4

Not in Public, Dear

Larisa's eyes were drawn to the commotion below. As she glanced down, her face fell. "Father!"

The man sitting on the throne hunched over to present a smaller target, then halted the action before he could embarrass himself or appear weak. He rose up regally to address his daughter's impropriety. "Greetings, Daughter. It would be best if your tone were reserved for more private settings, or better yet, not used at all. Addressing your father in such a way might incur the wrath of the gods." He subtly indicated the crowd and mouthed, "Not in front of the peasants, dear."

Larisa nodded curtly to her father. "Fine. I won't talk to you that way," she said through a forced smile. She turned from her dad and pointed at the majordomo now frozen halfway up the steps. "Daphis, I swear, if you've helped him throw so much as one young man down to the crazed old monoceros,[1] I will sow dragon's teeth in your undergarments!"

"But it's rodeo day," Daphis exclaimed. "Good for the spirit and wellbeing of the kingdom."

"I don't approve!" Larisa said. "The danger! What has the poor old monoceros done to deserve such treatment? Besides, he's an endangered species! He might be the last of his kind!"

---

1. Mono: one. Ceros: horn. Most would translate this to mean unicorn, but they'd be wrong by about a ton and a half. The animal in the pit is a Grecian Wooly Rhino, a leftover from the last glacial period in the area.

"Oh, he's fine." Daphis looked over the side of the pit. "Looks like the young men are in the most immediate danger. I mean, what if they drop on the horn, and what if Mr. Horny were to step on them?"

"A good point!" Larisa said. "What if Mr. Horny got them?"

"Then we get the scars of battle with a near-mythical beast, or should we best him by a successful ride, we are awarded a T-shirt!" one of the young men in the front of the crowd answered.

A chant of excitement started in the crowd. "T-shirt! T-shirt! T-shirt!"

"No honors as of yet!" Daphis yelled over the sound of the others. "No one has ridden Mr. Horny for more than twenty seconds!"

"Then there's still a chance to win!" One of the young men in the front launched himself over the barricade of soldiers and into the pit. "Yeehaw!"

The crowd went wild.

"Daphis!" Larisa cried.

The king sighed, looking as if he were trying his very best not to pinch the bridge of his nose. "Count to ten," he whispered. "Breathe in. Breathe out."

Daphis nodded an acknowledgement to Larisa, descended the stairs to the pit, had the soldiers throw a rope ladder over the side into the blackness, then returned to stand by the king as if nothing were amiss.

Several bruised and battered young men scrambled up from the black. Instead of fleeing, they immediately rejoined the group of young men near the pit.

"Gotta give the people what they want," the king said to his daughter.

Larisa fumed, but knew she was beaten on this point. "Fine. Let them ride the beast, but if Mr. Horny steps on them, don't let them come running to me."

Several of the young men took this as a cue to resume the rodeo. Three or four pushed past the guards and leaped into the pit. The last one did a blind, backwards cannonball.

The last guy missed the target, or rather, he was right on point.

"Ooohhh, gross!" The crowd gawked and gasped collectively. "That's got to hurt!"

"Too bad we have no way to replay the action to really get the full effect," the king mused.[2]

"Sire, the masses are engaged and entertained. If I might suggest retiring to the palace's inner courtyard to discuss the other business of the day?" Daphis said.

"Much as I love the rodeo, that would probably be for the best." Teutamides took several steps closer to the crowd and raised a fist to the assembled young men. "Yee! Haw!"

"Yee! Haw!" The jubilant crowd went wild.

Larisa leaned over the balcony, looking down at her father and his man. "There has got to be something better for the young men of the kingdom to do, Father."

The smile slipped slightly from Teutamides's face. "Willful, frustrating girl. Take your outburst inside!" Teutamides shook his head from side to side. He pinched the bridge of his nose, and his shoulders slumped just a fraction as he walked toward the door leading into the palace. "When the ones we are waiting for arrive, send them to the inner courtyard."

"As my lord wills it." Daphis bowed, his feathered hat brushing the king's face. Then the palace official turned, raised a red kerchief in the air, and waved it about.

Daphis signals for something, but what? Larisa wondered. She went inside, looking down at the inner courtyard from her upper walk to see who was waiting in the room.

Teutamides entered the royal receiving area on the floor below. He rubbed his eye as he walked.

Daphis's stupid hat must've caught her dad in the face. Larisa

2. I, for one, think instant replay ruins a bit of the magic. Sure, it's great for catching a bit of the action that you might have missed, but pretty soon all you do is watch highlights and you miss the point of the game. But I mostly played chess in high school, so what do I know?

smirked. Dad deserved it with how much of a butt he'd been lately. Her attitude shifted as worry took over. *Could a peacock feather scratch his retina?* She didn't want her father hurt or anything.

The king walked up to a guard, said something, leaned in close and held open his eyelid with both hands. The guard shook his head, but the king insisted. The guard leaned forward and blew a puff of breath into the king's eyeball.

Teutamides blinked hard a few times and gave the man a nod, his eye obviously feeling better. The king stepped hesitantly into the center of the room.

Curious about what had her dad so on edge, Larisa surveyed the rest of the room. There were attendants, servants, guards, and a spattering of officials and nobility mingling about. None of the young men from outside were present, which was odd because her father loved bestowing honors upon the successful rodeo riders.

Her dad hadn't been telling her a lot lately, and there was definitely something big in the works today. Then it dawned on Larisa what her father was doing. *Time for me to make my entrance*, Larisa thought. She rushed to clarify what was going on, and hoped she was wrong in her assumption.

She headed for the hall and stair that would enter the throne room just behind her father's chair, arriving just before the king.

Teutamides continued to look back over his shoulder as he made his way up the steps to his throne where at least the large arms and solid back of the chair offered the illusion of protection. He ascended the steps and curled up in his seat as if he feared he was about to be struck, which was quite the possibility. Larisa resisted the urge, however, as she stood board-straight next to his throne.

Daphis appeared a few moments later. "We will be informed the moment the guests arrive. I'm sure the princess will be pleased."

The king nodded somberly before he whispered something meant only for himself, "I know being proactive is going to come back and bite me."

"Oh, it's gonna bite, all right." Larisa leaned over and whispered to her father.

The king gave a startled jerk. "When did you get there?"

"Just a moment before you. You would have seen me if you weren't still paying attention to the rough riding crowd outside," Larisa said.

"Would that I could pay attention to the riding today," the king said. "But other matters have been brought to my attention that must be dealt with."

"Your spy told you about my boyfriend." It was a statement, not a question.

The king narrowed his eyes. "You keep much from me, it seems."

"I do not," she said. "I told you I was seeing someone."

Teutamides narrowed his eyes further.

Larisa didn't like the look he gave her. "I'm seeing someone. I like him a lot, but I feel it's a bit premature to be talking about marriage."

"You're seventeen. Practically a spinster," the king said.[3]

"You did not just go there?" Larisa said.

"People are talking. I need an heir. A worthy, male one," Teutamides clarified. "In case I don't live forever."

The last bit made Larisa pause. She'd never heard her father talk about his death before. She wondered what brought that train of thought on. She pushed it aside for now and focused on the more pressing matters.

"If I have told you once, I have told you one thousand times, Father! I will not have you barter me away!"

"A king must provide for his daughter and his kingdom!" Teutamides jumped from his chair and spun to face his daughter. "The gods demand it! I am merely swept along with their whim!"

Larisa glared at him with her hands propped on her hips.

---

3. Typical marriage age for ancient Greek women was fourteen to sixteen years of age. The typical age for men to marry was thirty or so. No judgment here, just stating the historical facts.

"Really? ''Bout time that girl of yours got hitched' was what the oracle said. The oracle who, I might remind you, had just returned from a hard week of partying with Dionysus."

"That is a little hardcore and out of the norm for an oracle," Daphis noted.

"You really want to participate in this?" The king threatened Daphis. "The monoceros could always be graced by a little cultured company."

"How is throwing your adviser into a pit doing anything that the oracle said?" Larisa asked. "We'd discussed this, and I will marry a man of my choosing when I choose to do so."

"But that's not the way things work."

Larisa arched an eyebrow and stared down her father.

Teutamides hunched down in a sulk. He turned from his daughter and dropped back down in his chair. "Stupid new aged feminist ideals. I never should have allowed you to go to that Amazonian Summer Camp."[4]

"Spartan women run the kingdom when the men are at war and do quite a bit when the men are home too. More places should be like that. Women are people too and should be treated as such. I'm not a pretty trinket to be bartered off to the highest bidder."

Teutamides attempted to feign shock at her assumption. Larisa wasn't buying it.

"There might have been a numerical value attached to your hand, but I assure you I am looking for the absolute best fit of a husband for you that I can find," the king said.

"Using *your* criteria?" Larisa asked.

The king nodded.

"So, my boyfriend has to be the son of a god and nephew of Midas?"

"Midas is a total miser. We'd never get anything from him." The

---

4. Another fine idea from HermesCorp™. Actually, Hermes started this one as a joke, but it made money and was wildly popular, so he went with it.

king managed a disinterested shrug. "I would accept a son of a demigod and maybe someone related to Croesus. Those Lydians spend money like crazy, always eager to impress everyone."

Larisa held her hands at her sides in cold rage. "I like Doug. I swear if you have bartered me away, I'll—"

"Who? Is that his name?" The king held up his hands in a placating gesture when she glared at him. "I just want to talk to the boy. See what kind of prospects he has. I have an adviser coming to help me sort out details on if this lad might make an appropriate husband for you." The king ordered the main doors opened. He held his hand out to the side as if something miraculous were about to be revealed.

Nothing.

The king sat there in his throne for a moment, his hand pointing toward the open door until the position became a bit awkward.

A breathless page ran into the hall and then up the steps to the king's throne.

"My lord." He bowed to the king. "Your advisor approaches!"

"Aha!" Teutamides stood and walked to the edge of the dais the throne rested upon. From that spot, he could make out the crowd gathered outside the palace through the broad arch of the open doorway.

"Where?" the king demanded.

"Back of the crowd," the page clarified. "On your orders I've left word for him and those chosen to be brought forth with all haste."

"Now, where could you be?" Teutamides acted as if he saw what he hoped for and brightened, which was impossible. No way he could make out an individual that far away.

Larisa was already tired of the little theater act being put on for her benefit today.

Some new commotion, big enough the effects could be seen and heard even this far away, started outside.

The king looked pleased. "Excellent timing, Heracles."

Chapter 5

Dog Barks and a Demigod

The ancient hound by the side of the king's throne raised his head and gave a solitary, weak woof.[1]

Everyone in the chamber turned and looked at the dog.

"Thank goodness. That's the most I've seen old Ergos move in weeks," Larisa said as she went round to the other side of the throne and petted the dog.[2] "I was worried he was dead."

"He half smells as if he is," the king said.

"I wonder what has roused him from his sleep?" Larisa asked.

Teutamides looked about uneasily.

Drawing on some unknown reserve of strength, Ergos managed two more barks.

"He's really riled," Larisa said.

It was all the energy the ancient dog by the side of the king could muster for today. After another menacingly cute huff, Ergos laid his old head on his paws and loudly started to snore.

"He must be barking at Heracles," the king said as he scanned about the room. "I wonder the last time he sent the Nemean lion out for dry cleaning?"

---

1. Long ago, Daphis said it lent an air of sophistication to the chambers of the king to have a canine present. The king initially put up with it because he thought the dog might be good for protection. A king could never be too sure. That was a long time ago, and the dog in question is old and does certainly lend an air to the throne chamber. But most everyone is too polite to mention it.

2. A gift to Teutamides from the king of Ithaca. Ergos came from the same litter as Odysseus's dog, Argos.

"I'm not marrying Heracles, or anyone else unless I want to." Larisa grumbled as she let the sleeping dog lie. She returned to the other side of the throne, folded her arms, and leaned against the side of her father's chair.

The comment brought Teutamides up short. He obviously hadn't expected that line of thought from his daughter. "What? Oh, no. No. The son of Zeus will be attending us in more of an advisory position this day." His eyes narrowed and he brushed his upper lip with a finger while he thought. "Although—"

"Please don't even entertain that as a possibility." Larisa shook her head. "You asked Heracles to come and advise you about my boyfriend? Really? Heracles?"

The man in question appeared at the top of the palace steps. He turned and posed for the crowd before he entered the hall, going from one flex to another while he was framed in the doorway. Heracles was making a show of it.

From the sound of the roar outside, the crowd was eating it up.

"He entertains the masses almost as much as the rodeo," Teutamides said.

Larisa watched Heracles flex and pose, growing more nauseous by the moment. It was the one where he stretched up on his toes and clenched his buttocks tight that finally did it. Larisa didn't know what he looked like from the front right now, but his oiled, toned backside poking out between the Nemean lion's back feet and tail was a little too much. "You'd think he could afford a slightly longer chiton." Suddenly she was very glad she couldn't see him from the front.

Mercifully, the guards on either side of Heracles closed the big doors, ending the spectacle.

"Who better than a verified son of Zeus to vet a hero for my daughter to marry?" Teutamides quietly voiced to his daughter.

"Doug is not a hero; he's just a polite young man," Larisa sighed and pinched the bridge of her nose. Apparently pinching the nose in resigned frustration was a genetically inherited trait. "Heracles doesn't really have the best track record when it comes to relationships."

"You won't be dating or marrying him, so his history with women is irrelevant. Besides, son of a god!" The king gestured wildly. "Son of a god! What could go wrong?"

Heracles ascended the final steps to where the king had risen from his throne to greet him. The overly large man opened his arms wide and bellowed. "King Teutamides! My wise and noble and wise friend! How does this day find you?"

"Very well." The king beamed. "With you here, the day is certainly a day that promises rich reward." The king rubbed his hands together and cackled. "Heracles!" Teutamides threw his arms around the giant.

"My king!" Heracles picked the king up off the ground and hugged him until his bones creaked.

"Get a room, you two," Larisa whispered. "This isn't Sparta."

"What?" The king managed to wheeze.

"What?" Heracles cast about to see who had whispered. "Ah, I see, little Larisa makes a joke at our expense. What mirth!" He swung out and good naturedly punched the arm of the nearest guard, who spun around from the blow, teetered on the edge for a bit, then tumbled off the throne platform.

It was a small drop, but the tumbled guard was still.

Larisa leaned over the edge. "You all right?"

The wide-eyed guard nodded without getting up and gave a pained little whine.

"Ha! Did you see how he fell down? Of course he fell! Who could resist the might of Heracles? Who would like to see me do it again?" Heracles eyed the guard standing on the other side of the royal platform.

The guard shifted nervously and tried not to make eye contact.

"How does losing a palace guard figure into the expense account, Dad?"

"Quiet, you!" Teutamides hissed at his daughter. The king

straightened out his rumpled robes, righted his crown, then hobbled over to the throne and gingerly set himself down. He gestured to the bench on the right side of the throne. "Come, my friend. Sit. Let us get on to the business of the day."

"So we shall! Let's do this!" Heracles posed and flexed as he surveyed the inner courtyard. "Not many people here to judge from. Is she to marry one of your officials or a guard?"

"No. She's supposed to be betrothed to a young man," Teutamides said.

"Father! *No*!" Larisa cried.

Teutamides ignored her.

"Young man?" Heracles questioned, clearly not seeing anyone here that fit the bill.

"You passed them coming in." The king pointed at the closed door, looking somewhat perplexed.

Heracles squinted and tried to look outside the giant entrance, only to be thwarted by the solid boxwood planking of the door. He still concentrated for a minute. "Ah, yes! Quite the crowd. I remember them all fondly! They were all quite taken with me. She is to marry the crowd, then?"

Teutamides gaped at Heracles for a second, before he shook his head and waved to his majordomo. "Daphis. Do you have the young man prepared?"

Daphis's peacock emboldened headgear tipped in the affirmative. "The spy has singled him out."

"Then show him in." The king motioned to the door.

Chapter 6

The Chosen

Daphis emerged from the palace and raised a handkerchief in the air. All the soldiers in the square snapped to attention.

Something sharp poked Doug in the butt. He turned and smiled at the soldier jabbing his backside with a spear.

"Move." The guard motioned with his weapon.

"Where are you taking my brother?" Mod demanded.

The guard glowered at Mod. "He is marked in blue. I was instructed to take the one marked in blue forward." The guard indicated the large blue stripes adorning Doug's chiton.

"When did that happen?" Mod asked. "You have blue chalk all over your back."

"Somebody bumped up against me. It's a crowd. I didn't think anything of it," Doug said.

Then the guard looked at Mod. "You are also marked in blue."

Mod started to panic. "It's a crowd. I hate crowds. The same guy must have bumped into me too, or I bumped against my brother and some of the blue chalk rubbed off."

"Does this alter the fact that you are marked in blue?" the soldier asked.

"He's got you there," Doug said to his brother.

The soldier angled the spear at the brothers. "Why am I explaining this to the two of you? Move!" The soldier punctuated the statement with a stabbing motion directed at Doug's groin.

Doug gulped. "I suggest we do as the reasonable and polite young man requests."

Doug and Mod made their way deeper into the crowd as the guard followed close behind. All of the soldiers converged in the center of the square.

"Up the stairs and through the main entrance," the soldier directed.

"Well, at least we aren't bound for the pit," Mod muttered.

Several of the other young men close by gave the brothers looks of pity. "No yee haw for you today? That sucks."

"Whoa, man. If I don't get the pit, it'll ruin my whole week," said the young man closest to Doug.

"You guys are all insane," Doug said to the group of young men.

"It's all for glory, man!" one of the other young men said. He had a tattoo that read *kavalíste í pethánete* on his forearm.[1] "If you earn the shirt, you get noticed. You might just get inside the palace or even marry the princess!"

The guard poked Doug in the butt with his spear. "You'll have to excuse me, gentlemen," Doug explained to the young men around him as he moved toward the palace steps. "I have to go into the palace, where I just might have to marry the princess."

The young men around him gaped. "He's got to be pulling our legs, man!" one of them said.

I'm probably off to be executed for seeing Larisa. Doug grimaced as he trudged up the steps. *Worth it, but maybe I should have kissed her when I had the chance.*

The soldier marched Doug and Mod into the palace courtyard, and the huge doors closed with a sense of finality behind the two brothers. Mod clung onto Doug's shoulder. Doug knew his brother was scared, so he patted his brother on the back of his hand. Doug

---

1. *Kavalíste í pethánete* is supposed to mean *ride or die* in Greek. But I'm probably getting the translation wrong. It could just as well mean something like *You are cavalier and scurrying* or *Which way to the water closet?*

turned and thanked the guard for escorting him and his brother inside.

The guard blinked hard, nodded an acknowledgement, then stepped to the side with a smile.

Now Doug and his brother stood alone.

Doug recognized the majordomo and was a bit panicked when he saw the lion skin wearing bodybuilder that had threatened him earlier up there as well. Doug could hazard a guess that the man must be Heracles. The muscle bound man let his gaze wash over Doug as if he didn't remember him at all, but then he stopped, focusing on Doug as if seeing something familiar.

Doug could feel a flush of heat as Heracles stared at him. Then the ancient old hound laying beside the demigod made a sound, and Heracles glared down at the dog.

From the way Heracles wrinkled his nose, Doug was pretty sure it wasn't a whimper that had escaped from the dog.

Heracles isn't the one I have to worry about anyway. Doug shifted his attention to the man on the throne who must be Larisa's father, Teutamides.

Doug caught Larisa's eye. It gave him quite the boost, and he forgot his discomfort for a minute. Doug winked and gave her a shrug. "Not quite how I imagined meeting your dad, but here I am."

"Two?" Teutamides gave his daughter a sidelong glance.

"Doug's the one who just spoke." She pointed out the one on the left. "The other one is Modifixeus, Doug's brother. They pretty much do everything together."

Her father continued to scrutinize Larisa.

"What?" Larisa said.

The king said nothing. He arched a questioning eyebrow instead.

"Doug is the one I've been seeing," she said after a quiet moment under her father's eye. "I'm only dating the one guy."

"I had wondered why there were two young men brought before me," Teutamides said. "Lots of funny things happen on the dating scene in Greece, and I don't want my daughter getting caught up in any of it. We don't want a Leda and the swan scenario playing out in the kingdom."[2]

"Ewe, Dad. Gross," Larisa said. "Why would you even go there?"

The door opened quietly behind Doug, and a man with the cloak and hood came slinking past Doug toward the throne.

"Hey, you're the guy who's been following me the past couple days." Doug pointed after the figure. "In the food court. Through the open market."

The figure stopped short. "You truly detected my presence in the market? I hid only because I was being cautious."

Doug nodded.

"Curious," the man said as he shed his hood and cloak.

"Now you let me see your face?" Doug asked.

"After today, you having knowledge of my face won't matter," the man replied.

"Well, that was ominous and threatening." Doug held his brother's hand a little tighter, and Mod gave a little squeeze back.

"Aesimus, my father's spy," Larisa explained to Doug despite the scathing glare given to her by the man. "What? He knows your face now, but he can't know your name?"

Aesimus narrowed his eyes at the princess but said nothing. He went and took his place near the throne just to the side of the sleeping ancient dog.

Ergos let out a little fart and whined in his sleep.

The spy wrinkled his nose in distaste.

Teutamides turned to face the young men, and he leaned to the side to ask a question of his spy. "What can you tell me of this youth?"

Aesimus spoke softly. "He is modest. Odd for one of his possible strengths. He works at a job most menial. Again, odd for his potential.

---

2. Zeus turned himself into some crazy things to sleep with the women of his choice. The crazier thing is that a bunch of women went for it. "It's a swan," "It's a bull," "It's a ray of golden sunshine!" But maybe the most insane thing about the entire scenario is that Greek society just kinda shrugged and went along with it.

But there are very strong signs. His father, whose identity we have not been able to so far deduce, is said to be respected far and wide. The youth's minions deal regularly with the pantheon of Olympus and are blessed to access sorcery and magic from those interactions. The youth's name is said to be rather short and odd for a Greek. And he is known to come from Iolcus."

"Short, odd name. From Iolcus?" The king puzzled for a moment before he looked over his shoulder at his daughter.

"I told you his name is Doug," the princess said.

The spy ignored the princess. "Your daughter is very good at keeping secrets," Aesimus stated. "She didn't even write the young man's name in her journal."

"You read my journal?" Larisa didn't look very happy about that.

He'd listened to the whole exchange thus far, even the bits whispered by the spy—they were in the same room, after all. Doug's stomach was tying itself in knots, and he wasn't sure if it was fear or excitement. He didn't think he could put up with what he was feeling much longer.

Best to just get it over with.

Doug raised his hand. "Uh, your highness? Excuse me? I'm Doug, and I've been dating your daughter."

Aesimus turned toward the young man. "By his own mouth, he confirms it!"

"Hmm, bold enough to speak before being asked?" Teutamides scanned over Doug. "Used to princely rights, perhaps? The King of Iolcus is my cousin Aeson, and any son of royalty would have to prove his worth by leaving and taking on a quest. There are reasons for such a quest. Seeking to prove his own worth, a test set by his royal parents, or compelled by a godly nature, perhaps?" Teutamides said.

"It's the first one," Doug confirmed, but the king apparently wasn't much into listening either.

"But then, if he is the son of Aeson, he couldn't be the son of a god, could he?" Teutamides questions. "Still wouldn't be a bad thing. A marriage of Larisa to Iolcus would be greatly beneficial to my kingdom. Son of Iolcus or son of deity, I swear to the gods I would have such a son-in-law to succeed me."

Larisa stood by, wide eyed, as the men discussed a future she clearly hadn't agreed to. "Listen, guys. I like Doug. I like Doug a lot. But I'm not quite ready to have a group of men decide I need to start birthing little Greeks just on their say-so."

Doug was a bit shocked by the turn of the discussion as well. "Shouldn't Larisa and I be involved in this discussion a bit more? Aeson isn't my father, but if you'd like to meet my family that can be arranged. I do feel it's a bit premature at this point in the relationship."

Doug got no response from anyone surrounding the throne.

"I can answer any questions you have," Doug said. "I mean, I'm right here."

"I'll call Doug up here and introduce him to you, if you'd like," Larisa said.

The men on the throne platform ignored both Doug and Larisa.

Heracles's face screwed up in deep concentration.

That can't be a good sign, Doug thought.

"Perhaps you could have an alliance with Iolcus *and* deity as family. My father has been known to take a myriad of guises to partake of the favors of the fairer sex. Appearing to any woman as Aeson would not be much of a stretch," Heracles said.[3] "But I'm sure a son would know if he was sired by a god or not." Heracles put his hands on his knees with a loud clap and rose from the bench. "So let us get to the bottom of this." He pointed a commanding finger in Doug's direction and bellowed. "Raise your hand if you are the son of the great god, Zeus?"[4]

---

3. Zeus never took on the form of Aeson to seduce anyone. He did, from time to time, appear as Odysseus, but not for the purpose of wooing any women. As Odysseus, Zeus would find and attend the nearest academic symposia. People always paid attention to whatever Odysseus said, and Zeus just liked the feeling of being important and listened to.

4. Pretty much all mysterious births were blamed on Zeus. If you're gonna say you

Doug didn't raise his hands. A couple of the guards did, though.

And they weren't the only ones.

Doug looked over at Modifixeus. "Something you need to tell me?"

Mod smirked and slowly dropped his hands back down to his sides. "Sorry. Got caught up in the moment." He coughed and dropped his gaze and stuffed his hands in his pockets.

The king leaned closer to his spy. "Doug didn't raise his hands." The king looked disappointed yet slightly intrigued. "Not a son of Zeus, then?"

Aesimus frowned. "No, it would appear that he is not. He does have the bearing, confidence, and regal manner of a king or godling," Aesimus said in a whisper to the small group around the throne.

The spy continued, "Are you the son of a god?"

"Didn't raise my hand, did I?" Doug answered the question with one of his own. It was a little bold to respond like that, but Doug was replying to a spy, not the king. Anyway this was getting a little ridiculous, and Doug was getting tired of it.

The spy asked the next question. "Is your birthplace the royal palace of Iolcus?"

"I already told you, I'm not the son of Aeson," Doug repeated.

Larisa shook her head. "This is dumb."

"Hush, girl! The men are talking." The spy snapped at Larisa.

"Hey!" Doug took a step forward. The soldiers looked conflicted, not knowing if they should stop the visitor or let him proceed.

Teutamides held up a hand to stop Doug, and then reprimanded the spy. "Careful how you address the princess, my spy."

"In the frustration of the moment I forgot myself." The spy dipped his head in a quick nod of apology before he addressed Doug again. "Are you possessed of princely riches? Do you have experience leading men?"

---

were sired by a god, make it the *Big One*. Go large, right? Oddly enough, many sons of Zeus often grew up looking remarkably similar to the local milkman.

Doug indicated his clothes. "Only robe I got. I assume you can deduce my financial status from that."

The king slumped a bit in his chair.

"As to my experience leading men," Doug continued, "Modifixeus has followed me around since we were both three."

"He usually has pretty good ideas about stuff to do," Mod said. "And I'm usually not that busy."

"Which one are we talking at?" Heracles asked.

Aesimus gave the demigod a sidelong glance as he explained what should have been obvious. "We are talking to the one who has been answering my questions."

Heracles shifted his gaze from the left to the right. "The tall gangly one or the myopic eunuch servant?" Heracles pointed at Doug then Mod.

Anyone could see Mod looked a little put out at being called a eunuch.

"That wasn't very nice," Larisa said to Heracles.

"Cruel, but good word usage," Mod said.

"I'm impressed he knew the word *myopic*," Doug said. "But I agree, the eunuch bit was a low blow. Anyhow, can we all get back to the matter at hand?" Doug suggested.

All eyes focused back on Doug.

Heracles clued into who the others had been talking about. "The lad on the right?" Heracles pointed to Doug on the left.[5] "I just realized where I'd seen him before. I've got his information right here."

He remembers me now, Doug thought. *Great. If Teutamides doesn't kill me Heracles might still get his chance.* Doug tensed up like he was about to be hit and shut his eyes. Nothing happened. He opened one eye and dared a glance at the gathering round the throne.

Heracles didn't look like he was going to rush Doug. The big man

5. They knew which youth Heracles was talking about. Directional dyslexia is a hard trial to overcome, and it can affect demi-gods too. It took me 'til the age of twelve to distinguish between left and right.

fumbled for the pocket in his cloak and pulled out the ostracon and handed it over to the king.

Teutamides snatched the pottery shard from Heracles's hand. The king read the writing on the pottery and then read it again, slowly. "Why did you hide this information from us?"

"I haven't hidden anything," Doug said. "If you wanted to know my father's name, you could have just asked."

Teutamides read the shard again, out loud this time. "Doug, son of Aoug of Iolcus." The king looked up from the ostracon and glared at the youth. "Aoug of Iolcus, as in Aoug the pig farmer?"

"You've heard of him," Doug stated.

The king glared harder.

"Finest smoked pork in the Peloponnese," Doug continued.

"Fine hams," Heracles noted.

"Glad to have the conversation turned to a subject you're knowledgeable and comfortable with?" Larisa asked the giant in what was a not-so-subtle dig.

"Of course!"

"Wasted effort on my part," Larisa said of her attempt.

"Everyone wants some of Aoug's pork on their table," Heracles continued. "Hephestus always has a haunch on his desk and a loop of his sausage by the forge."

"The son of a pig farmer wants to marry my daughter?" Teutamides clenched his fists.

Doug was offended by Larisa's father marginalizing his.

"What's wrong with being a pig farmer? Besides"—Doug raised his hand and pointed up at Larisa—"you guys are all fussing over stuff you don't understand, trying yet failing to figure out what's going on, when the person with all the answers is right behind you. Ask her."

"I'm pretty close to done on this subject," the king said. "Not a god. Son of a commoner. What's the point of you pursuing this with my daughter anyway?"

"I think I love her," Doug whispered so softly only Mod could hear it. Doug shook his head and spoke up. "My king, I may get in trouble for saying this, but I will anyway. All that really matters here, in this instance, is what Larisa thinks."

The king did not look happy to have someone question his judgment.

"Well that certainly calmed things down," Mod whispered to his brother. "What do you want me to tell Mom and Dad at your funeral?"

Teutamides gaze stayed on Doug, his eyes burning and intense. Slowly, the king turned to look behind the throne at his daughter.

Larisa tried to hide her emotions. It might have tricked some, but not her father.

"This interview is over. Throw him into the pit," the king ordered as he dismissed Doug with a wave. "Give him a T-shirt as a prize or whatever, but I don't want to see him again."

"No!" Larisa jumped forward. "All the other morons outside want to rule a kingdom and lord over a bit of arm candy. They're all only after cheap thrills.[6] Doug is the only guy I've ever met who doesn't care about those things. Not even you"—she glared at the men closest to her—"my father and the people who should know me best, will listen to what I'm saying, but he . . ." She looked at Doug and she flushed a bit. "He really cares about me."

The guards hesitated as they looked between the king and princess.

"Pit." The king growled at his guards.

Well, I managed to screw that up pretty well. Doug wasn't sure how to backtrack from here, or if it was even possible. He might have just lost the love of his life.

"Son of Iolcus or son of deity, I swear to the gods I would have such a son-in-law to succeed me," Larisa quoted her father. "That statement by my father sounds pretty binding to me, wouldn't you say, Heracles, demigod advisor to Teutamides the king?"

---

6. The song by Lady Gaga hadn't been written yet, but I'm not sure the crowd outside would have liked it anyway. They strike me as more of a Luke Bryan crowd.

Heracles cocked his head to the side. "By Zeus's beard, I believe it is."

Larisa, you brilliant, beautiful girl, you! You might have just given us a chance. Doug grinned up at her, hopeful.

She looked back at Doug and winked.

Her father still didn't look convinced.

"Pit," the king squeaked. Teutamides cleared his throat and continued, "Pit!" He glared at his guards. "Does no one listen to me? I'm the king! Hades's filthy knickers,[7], you are all so, so . . ." The king clutched at the air, his fingers hooked and clawing, his muscles straining. He slapped his face and doubled over in the chair, breathing heavily. It took several minutes for him to calm down enough to speak again. "So what we have is the son of a swineherd who works a menial job shilling kiefer who wants to marry my daughter and take over a kingdom." He glared down at his spy. "You said he was from Iolcus. You said his father was respected of the gods. That his minions have dealings with gods. You said he would be exactly what we were looking for."

Aesimus put his index finger and thumb close together. "Missed it by that much."

"Enough out of you!" The king spat. "What am I to do? Pledged to the gods, I have to do something."

There was a brief lull in the air, as if the ability to think and speak had been momentarily halted.

Ergos, the dog, woke long enough to give a weak growl in Heracles's direction.

The giant was beginning the process to scratch his nose when he cocked his head to the side, as if a thought just occurred or someone whispered into his ear.[8] "Not that it matters much, but the girl seems to like him." Heracles looked down on Doug. "Have him prove his

---

7. A curse. A dirty, dirty curse. The king should be ashamed for using such language in front of his daughter.

8. Stranger things have happened.

worth. Have him prove he is a worthy successor and suitor," Heracles suggested to the king.

"How?" The king demanded.

There was a pause as Heracles leaned in like he was trying to hear someone better.

Doug strained, inching closer to Heracles, but he couldn't hear anything. He did feel a presence though, something menacing and hidden. *I might really be in trouble, and not just from my girlfriend's father.*

A look of understanding crossed Heracles's face, and an evil glint grew in the demigod's eye. "I think I have an idea."

CHAPTER 7

MISGIVINGS AND SUPPORT

Heracles's idea turned out to be twelve tasks. Most of them as of yet to be determined. The first task involved aiding or subduing a beast in the land of Elis. It was an almost annual act that somehow hadn't been performed the last couple of years and was long overdue for accomplishment. There weren't any clarifications given beyond that, almost as if the king and his advisors were embarrassed to discuss it. Doug was told he would get further instructions from the master of the beast when he arrived. The details were still sketchy, but at least Doug knew the place he needed to go.

Doug was good with animals. He hoped he could accomplish the task without killing the thing or vice-versa.

The king and his advisers were gone. Doug sent Mod home. That left Larisa and Doug sitting on the grand steps outside of the palace with a couple of discreet guards watching over them from a distance.

Doug's legs were dangling over the edge of the monoceros pit. The ancient wooly rhino glanced up at Doug while he contentedly chewed on a stalk of celery.[1] Doug thought the presence of the vegetable being masticated was appropriate. He was contemplating jumping in and letting the monoceros chew on him too.

"Holy crap," Doug said. "What have I gotten myself into?" He

1. Celery was used heavily in ancient funerary rites in Ancient Greece and was often used to cover the graves of the dead. The deceased were sometimes buried with a crown of celery placed upon the brow. Contemplate that the next time you're drinking a vegetable smoothie with a celery stalk garnish. It helps you feel like a bad ass when you finish the drink and end it decisively as you munch down on a symbol of death.

paused a second, a scowl appeared on his face before he amended the statement. "What has Mod gotten me into?"

Larisa patted him on the shoulder, trying to comfort him and defend Doug's brother at the same time. "He meant well. He just got caught up in the heat of the moment."

"Twelve," Doug grumbled. "I don't think even Heracles would be dumb enough to agree to twelve tasks to prove his worth."[2]

"He's in the midst of accomplishing the ten trials assigned to him now." Larisa pointed out.

Doug glared at her.

"Not actively working on them, mind you," she clarified. "He took a break to visit my father."

"Heracles probably can't count past ten unless he uses his toes," Doug said in a pout. "He probably only got the task idea because it was already happening to him. He doesn't strike me as a fount of originality."

"What goes around comes around." Larisa said. "We'll just have to wait and see how forcing this fate on you pans out for Heracles in the end." She sighed and looked down. She waved at the monoceros staring up at them from the pit.

Right now Doug was having a hard time standing his brother. It might have been all right if Mod hadn't gotten swept up in the fervor of the moment. It was the same feel of an auction, with bids being cast on Doug, and Mod just kept negotiating the price higher and higher, not realizing he wasn't the one who was going to have to pay in the end.

Doug tried to stop his brother, but once Mod got fixated on something, it was hard to turn him aside.

---

2. Heracles is exactly that dumb, except he only agreed to ten tasks, but the king in charge of it all wouldn't accept two and insisted Heracles accomplish two more. Peisander wrote about it in one of his lost epics the *Heracleia*, a poem twelve rhapsodies long, with one rhapsody for each of the labors described. The lost epic is not to be confused with Peisander's other shorter poem that was not lost, *Bohemian*, which is only one rhapsody long and very well known to this day.

He'd have to address that with Mod later.

Right now he had a brief amount of time with Larisa, and he wanted to make the most of it, but he just couldn't get over the impending sense of doom that hovered over him.[3]

Most of the guys in these types of stories came back on their shields—if they came back at all. He assumed there were plenty of idiots that wound up being incorporated into some pile of droppings after being eaten by a monster or a titan or such. Being chewed and digested didn't sound so enticing. Just outright dying was the far better option.

"I don't even have a shield," Doug bemoaned. "I am so gonna die and there will be nothing to carry my body on."

"I'll get you a shield, if it'll make you feel any better, if such a thing matters to you," Larisa said.

"The only thing that matters to me is you," Doug said. It was an oversimplification, because a lot of things mattered to him, but Larisa and her happiness and safety was way and above every other concern he had.

"They'll never let me near you again if I don't achieve whatever it is they come up with," he said, resigned to his fate. Doug covered his face with his hands. "Twelve impossible things, and I don't even know what they're going to be. How do you prepare for that?"

"Am I not worth twelve impossible tasks?" Larisa asked.

Doug dropped his hands, his face a mix of shock and apology. "Of course you are! I didn't mean—"

She smiled back at him teasingly. Larisa started laughing at him. "Oh, Doug, sweetie. You could conquer the world if you set out to.

3. The Greeks were the first ones to write about a sense of impending doom. They even had a doom cheerleader in the form of the god Moros, who had a fun little party trick of allowing people to foresee their own death. Moros has since fallen on hard times, and now does appearances at small gatherings and special events to make ends meet. I made the mistake of booking him as a replacement for a child's birthday party when the magician I'd hired came down with covid. It was horrifying. Moros's balloon animals aren't very good at all.

You could save all the Greeks if you needed to." She looked deeply at him, her eyes intense. "Nothing is impossible for you."

He wasn't so sure he could save all of Greece if he was asked, but he'd certainly try if she called him "sweetie" again.

She reached out and took his face in her hands, pulling him close enough he could feel the warmth of her breath on his face. Her lips were so enticingly close, and it would be so easy to move that small distance to kiss her.

"You seem to have more faith in me than I do," he said. "Why?"

Her lips split into a dazzling smile, tears welling in her eyes. "I see in you what you don't see in yourself. Look into my eyes and see what I see."

In her eyes, he could see it. In her eyes, whatever he was asked or set his mind to do, he could accomplish.

"Doug, if you decide you don't want to go through with the challenges it won't change a thing I feel for you. If you accomplish everything asked of you by my father, it won't change anything either." She tilted his head down and kissed him on the brow before rising to her feet and taking several steps backward as she headed inside.

"Then why should I do it?" he asked.

"You're finally catching on," she said. "I think it'll probably only take you twelve tasks to really figure it out."

CHAPTER X

THE PATH OF REFLECTION

"TWELVE, MAN." MOD LOOKED AT THE SCROLLWORK BOX WITH the first task concealed inside. The box was meant to reveal only one task at a time, with new scrolls delivered if the current scroll's worth of tasks ran out.

Doug could see his brother was already working out the mechanics of the container. The box was made to be non-tamperable by the brightest minds and engineers in the kingdom. Doug gave it about five minutes until Mod had the thing pulled apart.

"Should you be messing with that? Isn't the box supposed to send a flare up or something every time one of the tasks is completed?" Doug asked.

"This is just the prototype. The real box is supposed to be delivered after the first task is completed, so I don't think this one has the flares in it yet," Something clicked in Mod's hand. The unopenable drawer in the front of the device popped open.

A flare shot up in the air.

Pop!

"Whoops! Guess I was wrong about this being loaded! I always wondered how Greek Fire works![1] Guess you're obligated to finish the first task now for sure. Sorry about that." Mod laughed. He looked to be having a great time now that they weren't surrounded by crowds

---

1. Not actually Greek Fire. Mod got excited and used the wrong term. Greek Fire was a naphtha/quicklime-based gel that burned on the water and was used as a weapon in naval engagements during the Byzantine era. The rocket Mod just shot off was a party favor bought by Daphis at a fly-by-night, illegal roadside fireworks stand.

or in a social setting and a clever device was falling apart at his will. Mod was more relaxed, easygoing, and quick-witted.

Mod pulled the first scroll out of the drawer and tossed it to his brother.

Doug caught it and pushed the thing in his pocket. The scroll was just a formality. He knew the general area he was supposed to be heading to and the name of the keeper of the beast.

Doug looked over his shoulder. "By the way, who are these random people following us?"

Doug and Mod glanced back at the six Greeks following close behind. The men and women were of varying shapes and sizes, but something seemed to connect them to each other aside from the close grouping. The lead woman stopped in her tracks when she saw the brothers looking at them. The others bumbled into the first, tumbling them all to the ground. The sound of them falling was akin to a bunch of anvils and bowling balls being dropped from the back of a wagon.[2]

"That sounded heavier than expected," Mod observed. "I have no idea who they are, but I know why they're following you." A grin spread across Mod's face.

Doug stopped on the path. "Please, enlighten me."

"You, my brother, are now a man of destiny." Mod punched Doug lightly on the shoulder. "Men and women seeking to make names for themselves will be drawn to you. The gods are probably watching and choosing champions to assist you and villains to oppose you in your quests."

Doug looked at the limbs sticking out of the pile of rumpled chitons. "How blessed am I to have such minions." Doug could see Mod was pretty excited to have people following them.

"Pretty cool, right?" Mod said. "Minions appearing is a sign the

---

2. You totally thought I made up the thing about bowling, didn't you. Sure, anvils have been around since the invention of metallurgy, so you didn't question that, but bowling? Hah! I got you! Depictions of bowling were recorded on the walls of Egyptian tombs possibly dating as far back as 3200 bc!

quest is blessed by the gods. Which gods? No idea. Still, it's a good sign."

"If you say so." Doug felt the people following were probably just doing it for the entertainment possibilities, but he kept his opinion to himself. "Time's a wasting. We should probably get to it."

Mod nodded, patted the quest box, and pointed his chin in the direction of Doug's pocket.

Chapter 4

Pondering Over a Drink

Zeus, king of the Greek gods, in a very exclusive club high atop Mt. Everest in the Himalayas,[1] watched Doug and Mod walk down a dusty track on their way to find Helen. He was drawn to them by the multiple lines of fate that suddenly became crossed around them. He smiled as he saw them and knew immediately the hearts of the two young men were in the right place. He'd never paid much attention to them before, but here were two young men he liked and felt a fatherly relationship with immediately. Focusing a bit more, Zeus divined a fair idea of what they were about. The first few tasks they had before them sounded simple enough, but a dark pall hung over the lines of destiny farther out in the future. These possibilities weren't firmly in place yet but looked more and more certain with each step the young men advanced.

Zeus searched through the nut mix on the bar until he found a grouping of macadamias, scooped up the bunch, and absently started chewing on a few as he turned his attention back to Greece.

He cast his eyes about until he focused in on Teutamides and Heracles in one of the lower rooms deep in the palace in Larissa. Heracles was his boy, and although not the brightest fire in the night, he always intended to do right. Teutamides, especially as of late, was selfish, greedy, misogynistic, egotistical, intelligent, and a sore loser,

---

1. Right. Not Olympus. I know the Greek gods reside on Olympus and that Olympus is not part of the Himalayas. The best bar for a god to unwind just happens to be nestled in the saddle between two peaks in the Himalayas.

all qualities the king of the gods seemed to find more and more in the kings of earth. Teutamides hadn't always been like that. Something had changed. Zeus would figure out what was going on there later. Right now he focused on several strings of fate that passed close to Heracles and then onto the boys, but the really dark threads, the ones that hadn't really coalesced yet, seemed to have originated from the king. Actually, they seemed to be originating from a point beyond the king, as some shadowy influence directed them. Odd that Zeus couldn't parse out who was doing it, but odder still the aura of the influencer seemed so familiar. Teutamides was being played, but to what end?

"Teutamides." Zeus drug his hand against his forehead. "What am I to do with you?"

"You look a bit concerned, Mr. Z," Isaac, bartender of the gods, said while he wiped a glass with a bar rag.[2] "Anything I can do to help?"

"Have you thought about drowning them and just starting over again with a limited breeding stock?"

Zeus looked over to the other end of the bar. "You always seem to suggest that, Jehovah."

"It worked for me that first time around." Jehovah took a long sip of his wine. "For a while, anyway."

"While there are several of my children I am frustrated with, offing the lot of them just to start again seems a tad extreme." Zeus sighed. "I just wish I could make some of them behave with a bit more kindness one to another."

"I could make them behave," another voice chimed in.

"Really? None of your ideas have ever panned out." Zeus glared at the other man. "Get thee behind me, Satan."

---

2. Isaac, bartender of the gods, is a constant, central, and unifying thread in many mythologies and pantheons of gods. The supportive and wise one. The one you can talk to about any problem. He appeared briefly to share his wisdom with mortal men in his actual guise starting in 1977 through 1990 in the scriptural episodic drama *The Love Boat*.

Satan, scowling, picked up his Shirley Temple and moved over to a dark booth in the corner.

Jehovah swirled the wine around in his glass for a bit, thinking. "Have you given them a guide for how they should be acting? Any kind of scripture or instruction manual?"

"I've always hoped they would figure it out on their own," Zeus said.

"Kids need rules. Something to help them toe the line when they aren't sure what to do." Jehovah emptied his glass. Isaac reached for the empty, but Jehovah waved him off. Instead, Jehovah reached for a carafe filled with water, refilled the wine glass, and swirled it a couple times. The clear liquid turned red and rich and aromatic.

"Neat trick," Zeus said.

"I'm teaching my kid to do it." Jehovah grinned as he took a sip. "It's amazing how good it is."

Zeus was impressed. "I'd ask you how to do it, but I'm a bit of a traditionalist." Isaac filled a clay mug from an amphora and passed it to Zeus. "I'd miss it if I couldn't taste the dirt on the fruit or the feet that squished the grapes." He took a deep swig and smacked his lips. "A bit funky, but it sure grows on you." Zeus nodded his approval to Isaac.

"I understand your frustration." Jehovah considered his wine for a moment. "I've given my kids rules before. Narrowed it down to ten. Ten is a nice, small number. Should be easy enough to remember, but they always want clarification. Thousands and thousands of pages of clarification, and then they latch onto something in the clarifications that didn't mean what I said or got misinterpreted and start killing each other over it."

"Kids."

"Yeah. Whacha gonna do?"

The two gods drained their cups.

"I'm watching a couple of boys I have high hopes for, but someone is placing obstacles in their path," Zeus said as he examined the rim of his mug.

"Not very sporting," Jehovah answered.

"I have faith in the boys, but they're young. They might need someone to help see the traps laid ahead."

"So they could avoid them?"

"What good would that do for them?" The king of the Greek gods pursed his lips and shook his head. "No, they won't know who they are until they have to make the hard choice and follow through. But a bit more detail on what lies ahead probably couldn't hurt to get them where they're going." Zeus stood and put some gold on the bar top. "Isaac, excellent as always." He nodded to the barman. Zeus picked up his lightning bolt from the corner and headed to the door. "Good to see you again, Jehovah."

Jehovah tipped his glass in Zeus's direction. "Let me know how it goes."

The door closed and Zeus was gone. Gone, but still focusing a bit on what was going on behind him. Zeus found you could learn quite a lot if you paid attention to what happened after you left a room.

"That's a tough one for Mr. Z, isn't it, Mr. J?" Isaac asked.

"He'll figure it out," Jehovah said. "We all have our problems, but at the end of the day, we wouldn't trade them for anyone else's."

"Ain't that the truth, Mr. J?" Isaac said. "Ain't that just the truth?"

Chapter 10

Snickers

Doug contemplated whether or not to even look at the scroll. "Why wait now?" He sighed, pulled it out of his pocket, and felt as if he'd just committed to something larger than he expected.

Doug looked at the note written on the linen scrap, referring to a small map Aesimus had drawn in the margin to get them started. "We're in the right spot. The first quest should be around here somewhere." Doug looked at the scroll, scanned the surrounding countryside, looked back at the scroll, squinted, then flipped the map upside down and repeated the process.

"Do you need me to look?" Mod asked.

Doug handed the scroll to his brother. "We're to aid a great beast. 'Ask for Helen,' it said. Let's put it away for a bit, Mod. We're close. Someone living here will know this Helen. Let's just ask one of the locals where we need to go."

Mod balked at what Doug just said. "Have you lost all your senses, man? We're living smack dab in the middle of the age of heroes. No man asks for directions."[1]

Doug—far from being the normal man—had no problem asking for directions. He turned at the first driveway he came to, moseyed into the courtyard, and surveyed the place before he cleared his

1. Odysseus is a prime example of this almost hard and fast rule. After ten years of the Trojan War, he tried to get home quickly, but it wound up taking another ten years. If he had actually stopped and asked where he was heading, his epic journey recorded in *The Odyssey* would have lasted seven weeks, tops.

throat. "Hello? Is there someone here that can give us directions? We're looking for someone and appear to be lost."

A voice replied from inside the home. "Who are you looking for?"

Doug tried to peer into the dark interior of the house. "Helen? She's supposed to live somewhere around here. She's the protector or guard of a great beast, if that helps at all. Do you know her?"

The voice inside the dark house suddenly seemed more attentive, if a trifle suspicious. "And why do you seek this Helen?"

"My name is Doug. I've been sent on a quest by Teutamides, King of Larissa."

"You actually have a reason for finding Helen?" The curtains in the front window parted and several sets of eyes studied the young men and women gathered with Doug.

The curtain closed again quickly. "Could this be about the curse?" Another feminine voice in the house said in a hushed voice.

"There's one sure way to find out," the first woman's voice replied. The curtain opened again. "I thought you were a salesman or dramatic performer or some such undesirable person."

"But they're not wearing tights. And they don't have masks," another of the women noted.

"So they aren't salesmen, but they could still be entertainers." The myriad eyes scrutinized Mod and Doug from the dark recesses of the house. The curtain closed as an intense discussion happened within. A tentative hand parted the curtain once more. "The King of Larissa sent you?"

"Yeah," Doug said. "He's being advised by Heracles in this matter."

The hand disappeared back within the curtain as the first speaker addressed them once more. "That sounds pretty important, so I should probably talk to you after all. I must warn you that I will not be alone, and I will have the companionship of my dog, so don't go thinking about any funny business."

Several pretty, dainty women exited the house to form a semi-circle around the door. A small, commanding woman exited last, closed the door behind her, and occupied the position of authority on the step as she took stock of the men and women in Doug's group. "Adventurers, no doubt?"

"Careful. You know what they say about adventurers and heroes." One of the other women, the slightly mousy, wary looking one, reminded.

The woman on the step nodded and scrutinized Mod and Doug a bit more intensely. "Still, you seem a strong and capable looking group."

"Group?" Doug questioned.

"You and your minions." She pointed behind the brothers to the group that had followed them on the road.

Mod smiled at the mention of minions, like it reinforced his suspicions about the quest being blessed by the gods.

"Anyway, I'm Doug." Doug gave a little bow then indicated his brother. "This is Modifixeus, my brother."

"Call me Mod." He bowed.

Doug turned and looked at the group behind him. "And these are . . ." The lead woman of the group smiled brightly and waved at having Doug acknowledge them. Doug gave a weak smile back and continued. "These are my hangers on and support crew."

The whole misfit group of Doug fans beamed.

"And I am Helen." The woman on the step formally introduced herself. "These are my friends, Hypoallergenia, Erato, Suppositoria, Callianassa, and Debbie." The women all curtsied slightly as they were introduced.

Helen rattled off the names too fast for the young men to catch them all.

"Nice to meet you," Doug managed.

There was a great crash and the sound of something heavy shattering inside the house. A beast, titanic in power, ran into the wall and the whole building shook on its foundations behind the women.

The violence of the sounds and tremors from the impacts vibrated and rattled Doug and his entourage, but the women from the house looked on, unmoved, as if they were entirely used to the destruction about to be unleashed.

Doug and Mod both took tiny, involuntary steps back as they braced themselves for whatever was about to emerge from the door.

The small, previously unseen, flap on the bottom of the door was flung wide open, and a mop of fur and chaos burst forth from beyond the door jamb and whirled amongst the newcomers. The dog immediately commenced a thorough and blurringly fast investigation of the assembled outsiders.

Doug tried to visually follow the small, yapping whirlwind of activity as it bounded here and there. He had little success. The thing was a flash of energy that stayed in no one spot long enough to yet ascertain its nature.

The dog paused in her frenzied whirling, sidled up to Doug and rubbed her crotch urgently against his ankle.

Doug tried to not look aghast as the dog inched further into intimate space.

The dog took the ankle rubbing to a new level when she wrapped her legs tight around Doug's leg as passion increased in speed and frenzy.

Helen smiled. It was clear the animal could do no wrong in her eyes. "Tis a new type of dog. A wonder from the West and gift to me from heroic Paris. He called it a Poottool, but I call it my precious Snuggy-wuffins. Most Poottools are majestic, savage beasts, long of leg and swift in the hunt. Not so with Snuggy-wuffins, she is challenged by the gods with a minute stature to cage and encompass her oversized spirit. The frenzy of spiritual energy cannot be contained by her diminutive bodily vessel. See how it spills out of her?"

"I must admit, I'm afraid to look and see what has spilled forth." Doug tried to ignore how warm his leg was becoming. "Snuggy-wuffins, you say?"

Helen nodded then clarified. "Snuggy-wuffins is a title bestowed upon my beloved companion by me that speaks of my undying love for her, and she responds with glee when she is addressed. She has another given name to which she may answer. Paris told me it when he gave her to my trust. Her given name is Snickers."

Doug tried to shake the horny dog from his leg. "Snickers is tenacious."

"Tis the blood of nobility that runs hot through her veins." Helen looked at the profane dog lovingly. "Her lust for life will not be constrained."

"Uh, yeah." Doug shook his leg harder, trying to dislodge the dog before it melded to his flesh. "She's going at my calf fur so urgently and thoroughly that I fear I'll break out in a rash soon."

"Oh, that twill not happen!" Helen beamed. "Snuggy-wuffins is hypoallergenic!"

Doug looked perplexed. "Hypoallergenic? What the heck does that mean?"

"Do you men of the far country know nothing?" Helen laughed lightly and turned to the lady-in-waiting standing next to her. "Tell him what it means, Hypoallergenia."

Hypoallergenia batted her eyes, breathed seductively, and pushed out her chest to accentuate her assets. All the men in the group but Doug took a step closer to her.

"Hypoallergenic means everybody likes you." She let out a sexy sigh. "And you like everybody."

Staring at the dog humping his leg, Doug cleared his throat. "Can we get to the point of me being here?"

Hypoallergenia's face fell when Doug wasn't bowled over by her looks.

"Don't mind him," Mod said to the pouting woman. "He's in love. He only has eyes for Larisa."

All the women, Hypoallergenia included, melted a little and looked at Doug with more fondness. "Awe. So sweet." They all sighed together.

Doug missed the looks as he concentrated more on his present assaulter. He gave several hard kicks and cleared his throat to distract everyone from what he was doing. It didn't work. Everyone was looking at him and the dog. With a final kick, Snickers flew through the air and landed behind some bushes. Then Doug noticed all the women staring intently at him. "Uh, sorry," Doug said sheepishly to Helen.

"You wouldn't have been able to dislodge her had she not wished it," Helen said matter-of-factly. "Perhaps she requires a brief respite to garner and replenish more strength to show her desire?"

Doug worried the dog might be back for more. "Anyhow." He hoped getting the task done quickly might deflect that possibility. "We're here for a divine purpose. I have a task, given me by King Teutamides and approved by the very gods themselves, that I must be about."

Helen stared at the bushes where Snickers landed. A bark emanated from the deep foliage, and a growl, then the bushes started to shake. There was a high-pitched chittering from a squirrel, followed by a screech as the bushes' tremors increased. "She has found another onto which to slake her lust. Such an indomitable spirit." Helen shook her head in awe and wonder and turned back to Doug.

Helen saw Doug's shin and suppressed a giggle.

"My apologies for the unseemly way I forced Snickers to dismount my, my . . ." Doug looked down at his leg. The hair on his right shin was rubbed away. The corner of his eye twitched as he looked back at Helen.

"Your task is about a girl, isn't it?" Helen asked. The question distracted Doug from his depilated leg.

"The aforementioned Larisa," Mod explained.

The women all sighed in unison again. "So sweet."

Doug blushed. "It's very important."

Helen smiled and nodded. "Tell me the task and we shall see what we can do to help you achieve it." She leaned in toward Doug and winked knowingly. "Mustn't disappoint the gods."

Doug cleared his throat again and glanced at the ground. "I was tasked to give the healing medicine to the Great Beast of Elis. They said you, Helen, would know of the beast's whereabouts."

Helen's eyes brightened. "You are truly here to give aid to the Great Beast of Elis?"

"So I was charged. Do you know where the beast is?" Doug stood up straighter.

Helen jumped up and down and clapped her hands. "Long has it been that the beast has needed to take her meds! You are truly here in our time of need, Hero!"

"Her meds?" Doug's masculinity deflated a little at the thought of besting a female beast to give her medical aid, but a task pledged to King Teutamides and the gods must be done. "I must confess. I don't know what the beast is or of the medicine it requires, or even how I'm to achieve this task."

Helen reached to the small satchel that hung from her waist. "I actually have the medicine here. I carry it with me on the off chance someone so heroic and daring might come to our rescue." She opened the drawstrings and pulled out a small round ball. Helen extended her hand toward Doug. "Here, Hero, one of the necessary pieces to your task is now yours."

Doug reached out and took the large pill from her outstretched palm. "So, part of the mystery is solved, but where am I to find the beast?"

All the women tittered at the clueless man. "You've already met the beast." Helen giggled. "And I believe the beast is fond of you, or at least fond of your manly shins."

Confusion slowly faded into unbelieving recognition. "Snickers is the Great Beast of Elis?"

Helen nodded. "Even so."

Doug looked at the pill in his hand. "Kinda big for poor Snickers." He tossed the pill in the air and caught it in his fist. *Getting a dog to take her meds. How hard could that be? This first task was going to be a breeze.* "Right. Let's get this done." He stomped off toward the bushes.

Helen raised her hand as if to stop him. "Doug?"

"There you are, Snickers. Come and get your num-nums." Doug bent down and searched the bushes. A frazzled squirrel ran from the scene. The flailing of the bushes stopped as barks and snarls filled the air. "Open wide."

Helen waved a bit more frantically. "Uh, Doug?"

Somewhere in the bushes, Snickers bit Doug. His confidence in this task being quickly and easily resolved rapidly eroded.

"Son of a . . . Come here, you little"—Doug looked up to Helen watching him—"you little sweetheart. It's only a pill."

"Doug!" Mod called out after his brother. "Helen has something important to tell you!"

"I'm busy!" Doug called back. "Is it important?"

Mod looked at Helen who nodded.

"Yep! Pretty Important!" Mod replied.

Snickers snarled and snapped. Doug stumbled and fell into the bushes. A sandal arced high above the foliage as bits of tunic sprayed the air like confetti.

"Sweet mother of Hades!"[2] Doug's hand waved frantically above the twisted branches for assistance. "To me, my minions! Snickers is too powerful for one alone to tame!"

"Doug is just a little antsy because this is his first task, so I apologize on his behalf for ignoring you." Mod started running toward his brother. He looked at Helen over his shoulder. "Uh, something we should tell him?"

Mod went down. The dog was after them both now. It was too late to tell either brother anything.

"Men." Helen shook her head. "Getting instructions before attempting to accomplish the task may have served them both better in this instance."

---

2. Rhea: mother of Hades. Of all the names in Greek mythology, Rhea actually was pretty sweet. She was kind and nice and always envisioned baking Kourabiedes (Greek butter cookies) for Dionysus and her other grandkids.

Doug's minions ran to assist the brothers. They too ignored Helen and her friends.

The bushes became enveloped in a cloud of dust. Soon the sound of the injured and the dying filled the air.

Doug and Modifixeus managed to drag themselves out from under the mangled foliage. They were bruised, battered, and torn.

Doug, concerned for the welfare of the people he'd quite probably just led to ignominious deaths, propped himself up and glanced back at the bush. "What about the others?"

Mod, usually more of the realist, surveyed the situation as he managed to look over his shoulder at the dust that settled behind them. "Did you catch any of their names?"

Doug felt terrible about his answer. "No."

"I didn't either." Mod shrugged as best he could from his half prone position on the ground. "I guess they weren't supposed to survive this test."

Doug looked shaken. "Uh, they'll be remembered."

"Not likely." Mod collapsed in the dirt.

Helen knelt down in the road next to the two heroes. She didn't look too flustered, as if she had seen this kind of activity play out before. "That was . . . It took great courage to . . ."

An uncomfortably long pause.

"Well, at least you tried." She smiled as the two men looked up at her. "The thing is, your intent was noble, but it was poorly executed and destined to fail." She looked over at Mod. "I tried to warn you."

"Poorly executed? How insensitive are you, lady?" Doug pulled himself up off the road and gestured wildly at the shrubs of carnage behind him. "We just lost five good people in there!"

"Six." Modifixeus corrected without raising from the dirt.

"What?" Doug looked at his brother.

Mod rolled his head so his brother could see him and hear him correctly. "There were two women and four men who jumped into the fray with us. We lost six brave souls there."

Doug counted out the minions in his head, trying to place each of those lost with a face. He hadn't paid enough attention to really visualize them and now felt guilty about that too. He turned back to Helen. "We lost six heroes to the beast."

"Snuggy-wuffins has sensitive gums," Helen explained. "She doesn't like people to touch her mouth. That is actually the source of many of the deaths surrounding her."

"Really? I hadn't noticed." Doug threw his hands up in the air then something occurred to him. "Many of the deaths? Who else . . .? You know what, never mind, just tell me how the heck are we supposed to get Snickers to swallow her pill if we can't touch her mouth?"

Helen winced and gave a pained smile. "That's the other thing I needed to tell you. It's not really a pill for swallowing. It's a suppository."

"A suppository?" He held the pill up and examined it more closely. "While this word seems familiar, I'm not quite sure of its meaning."

"Even if you know, you get tired of explaining it to people who don't." Suppositoria, the mousy one, the smallest of Helen's hangers on, got a sour, resigned look on her face. "Trust me on this one."

The other friends of Helen looked at Suppositoria with supportive eyes and nodded in agreement and solidarity.

None of them stepped forward to fill in Doug's gap of knowledge though.

"Do you know what they're talking about, Mod?" Doug asked his brother.

Mod blushed a bit. "I spend a lot of time in the library, you know, reading stuff. Kinda whatever catches my interest at the time, really. It's all pretty varied, and—"

One of Helen's friends, Erato, the tall one with a certain, slightly bawdy gleam in her eye, cocked her head to the side and smiled. "The adult section in the library?"

Mod's cheeks turned bright red. "Is it suddenly hot around here or is it just me?" He swallowed a bit and fanned his face while he continued, "It was just research. A combination of youth and curiosity–"

"And burgeoning hormones," Erato interjected.

"Uh, yeah. I'm sure that has to be a part of it." Mod looked thoroughly embarrassed. "Anyhow, I know the Dewey Decimal Classification pretty well. And I remember pretty much everything I read, even if I just read it once." He wisely rejected giving a full explanation. Mod leaned in close to Doug's ear and did his best to give his brother an understandable definition. Doug didn't seem to understand, so Mod followed up with an example he knew his brother would get.

"Athenian party?"[3] Doug looked at the pill in his hand and his eyes grew wide. He glanced over at Modifixeus. "This goes there?"

Mod nodded.

"Oh, I'm not sure if I can be a part of that." He held the pill out toward Mod.

Mod waved him off. "No way. I offered to help where I can, but I draw the line at helping shove something into the out door. This is your task."

Doug turned and held the pill out to Helen. "Snickers loves you! How come you can't do it?"

"Alas"—Helen shook her head sadly—"while I am a caring figure who would help any living creature were I able, I cannot aid my beloved companion in this instance. It was one of the conditions of the curse that only one unknown to Snuggy-wuffins may perform the task."

---

3. Doug, in one of his wanderings about Greece, happened upon a grove hosting a gathering of satyrs, several nymphs of dubious reputation, and members of the local chapter of Sigma Chi from the first Athenian university. Fueled by sleepless nights of rowdy partying, excessive use of cannabis and wine, and egged on by the satyrs and inebriated nymphs, the young Greeks were in the midst of a game called "hide the diples." Doug, never one to give into peer pressure and possessing a somewhat restrained and introverted nature, chose not to participate. The said "diples" in question and their supposed hiding place I shall leave to your own deduction or imagination.

"Don't you hate it when the gods get this specific in one of their punishments?" Mod asked.

Everyone nodded in agreement. The restrictions in this instance were a bit extreme.

Doug pulled the pill back and held it tight to his chest, resigned to his fate. At least after this he would be known to Snickers, and thus would never be able to render aid in this manner again.

Helen recognized the look of defeat and nodded. "It truly must be done." Then she reached out and grabbed Doug by the forearm. "But be forewarned, once done, the effect is almost instantaneous. Do not stay overlong in the path of danger." Then, as an afterthought, "Remember, Snuggy-wuffins is a gentle soul and delicate. Treat her as you would one you love."

"Perhaps we may be able to help in our own small ways." Helen's friend Debbie looked over at Callianassa, and her companion nodded. They both pulled out reed instruments and moistened their lips.

"We often accompany Erato to help establish atmosphere and feeling when she recites her newest limericks," Callianassa explained.

"Their music can truly sooth the savage beast," Erato acknowledged. "Trust them. They know what they're doing."

Debbie nodded to Doug as she and Callianassa brought their devices to their lips. "Whenever you're ready."

"Stupid Athenian rave," Doug mumbled to himself as he gave the flautists the go ahead.

A soothing harmony filled the air, Debbie taking the high, sharp notes while Callianassa hit some surprisingly deep, smooth tones.

"The music puts Snuggy-wuffins at ease and makes the whole medicinal delivery more pleasant for all," Helen said. "Is not part of the Hippocratic oath to aid the patient in any way you can?"[4] She signaled for the women to continue their serenade.

"Path of danger." Doug examined the pill again and closed his eyes tight. He approached the bushes. "Delicate. A gentle soul." Doug stepped over the severed limb of one of his crew while he tried not to focus too much on the implications of the task before him. "Right, let's get this done. Here, Snickers, sweetie, you're gonna love this—"

---

4. Actually the Hippocratic oath consisted of you stating a binding pledge of loyalty to your teachers, his family, and your colleagues. "Do no harm" only came about in the middle of the oath and has something to do with the diet you prescribe to your patients. It's right before the line that states you won't give your patient poison, which is pretty sound advice if you want return patients.

Chapter 11

Fertilizer Tsunami

"Done!" Doug leaped out from the midst of the bushes. He held his arm straight out so his right hand dangled.

Helen gasped. "Are you injured?"

"Only emotionally." Doug looked at his right hand with distaste. "This may cause some mental hang-ups for the foreseeable future. Anyone got a moistened rag or something I can borrow?"

Suppositoria handed Doug a dampened cloth. "You can keep it."

"Thanks."

"And my Snuggy-wuffins?" Helen clasped her hands in despair. "How fares she?"

"Actually, she was pretty good throughout the whole encounter." Doug was surprised to admit. "The music really helped calm her down."

"Told you so," Erato said.

Debbie and Callianassa gave each other high-fives.

Pained voices from behind garnered the group's attention.

"Sounds like athletes stretching after a particularly grueling Olympics competition," Mod noted.

Doug, Mod, Helen, and the others turned to find the previously slaughtered men and women righting themselves as they struggled to escape the foliage of Snuggy-wuffins's bush. One by one the butchered brushed off the dust and blood and stood until all were accounted for. The tall woman Doug assumed was the leader nodded in approval as the last of them rose.

Rising from the dead is one thing. Weird stuff happened in

Greece all the time. Resurrecting and reassembling oneself? This was a new one to Doug. He was too stunned to move. All the others observing the reassembling stood as frozen as he was.

"Uh, have you ever seen anything like this before?" Doug asked Helen, slack jawed and gaping at the sight.

Only Doug seemed to have regained the ability to speak. Helen and the others couldn't utter a word, shaking their heads mutely to acknowledge they'd never seen anyone pull themselves back together in this manner before. "That was quite impressive. Do you mind if I ask who you all are?" Doug asked.

The mechanical people all lined up and began to list off their names.

"I am One, the leader of my siblings," said the tallest female. She was strong, tall, broad shouldered, and big chested. One had the commanding presence and confidence of a firstborn child in a large family.

"I should have been the leader." The tall, dark, surly looking man standing next to One pouted.

Doug had to do a quick doubletake. The man looked remarkably like Larisa's father. "Must be the lighting," Doug muttered to himself.

"Our fathers decided, and we all agreed they knew best," One said.

"I didn't agree," the man said.

"Majority rules." One reminded him.

"They have this argument all the time," the second woman said as she bowed to Doug and the others and ignored her siblings. "I am Three." She was fit looking, energetic, and athletic. A perfect example of Olympic perfection.

"Number Four." The next man continued the introductions. He beat his chest with his fist as he spoke. Built like a brawler, the man was short, stout, no-nonsense, and looked capable of anything he was tasked to do.

"As the fifth child created, I am called Five. You can tell which one I am because I'm better looking than my twin." The tall young man punched the identical young man standing next to him in the arm.

His twin hit him back.

"And I am Six, and I'm not nearly as clumsy as my brother." He pretended to smack his brother with his right hand, only to fake him out and punch him really hard on the shoulder with his left.

Five winced and tried to grab his brother by the neck.

Six slapped the hand away.

"Don't mind them. They're idiots," One said.

The surly Teutamides look-alike stared at his two siblings as they grappled, fell to the ground, and started to try to wrestle each other into a chokehold. "They'd be better behaved if I were in charge," he grumbled.

Mod stood there for a second, mouth gaping, and then his eyes brightened and he jumped up in the air, clapped his hands, and giggled. "I'm so glad you aren't dead, and from what you just did, I think I know what all of you are!

"Ktesibios!" Mod was so excited he could barely talk. "I mean, the water clock he devised was the best the world had ever seen! So many tricks and gadgets and toys! I'm on his mailing list for his monthly catalog. He's my favorite creator! But this, this is a bit beyond what he's capable of doing alone. He had to have a collaborator."

"The nerd is wise," One acknowledged.

"Maybe the nerd knows what's going on, but I sure as heck am in the dark," Helen said to Doug.

"He's in a fanboy frenzy," Doug said. "It's best to just let it run its course. I'm sure we'll catch up eventually."

The reassembled men and women all turned and looked at each other, as if unsure they wanted their secret revealed.

"Tis all right," One said in reassurance to the others. "We reassembled in their presence. Our secret already dangles on their lips."

"These are mechanical persons," Mod suggested helpfully to the others. "Automata."

"Automata," Doug repeated, not sure he understood. "Living machines?"

"These aren't real people?" Helen asked.

"That's not a very nice thing to say. We have feelings, you know," Four said as the others grumbled their concurrence.

"Think of them like living dolls," Mod suggested helpfully.

"Action figures,"[1] Three corrected. "The term doll is a bit dated and derogatory."

Mod was too excited to contain himself, so he was going ahead without waiting for anyone's permission. "Hephaestus created a mechanical man to protect Europa in Crete. Talos the giant. Talos is amazing—or so I'm told—but as the only one of his kind, he's also probably incredibly lonely. I'd heard a rumor he and Ktesibios were working on something, but I never dared to hope it would be this awesome!"

The minions all started nodding to each other. "Our fathers."[2] They spoke with an air of reverence. "The nerd knows of our fathers."

Mod rushed up and inspected One. He stared intently at her face, her joints, her skin, hair, and everything.

"I see a seam." Mod squinted as he looked at her shoulder. "Can I touch it?

"Uh—I really don't feel we've reached that level in our relationship," One said as she shifted about uncomfortably.

Three arched an eyebrow at Mod and shrugged, exposing her shoulder and pushing closer to him. "I'm game."

Mod realized what he'd just asked and blushed a little before he

---

1. What you call your toys matters greatly, especially to the toys. Words can be hurtful.

2. *The Mechanical Man Has Two Daddies* was a moderately good seller in ancient Greece, though it did have opponents who felt it was too challenging to traditional Greek family values. It did sell well in Sparta, though.

cleared his throat and continued. "Pity you all pulled yourselves back together so quickly. I would love to see how you're assembled." Mod once again grinned from ear to ear. "Maybe next time you get ripped apart?"

Three shrugged again. "No objection here. You have my consent."

Doug cut off the chain of discussion right there. Mod wasn't very experienced with girls, let alone mechanical ones, and following through on any of this could lead to a whole mess of trouble. "Okay, this is getting a little weird, even by Greek standards." Doug gave Three a sidelong glance and addressed the group as a whole. "Why are you people following me?"

"Grandfather Hephestus said we should go out and learn about the world. He said the nerd and his brother would teach us the ways of men," One said.

"We've now learned what it is like to be dismembered." Five looked up from where he had Six in a wrestling pin. "Our knowledge and experiences are quickly developing under your tutelage."

"Wow." Doug shook his head in wonder. "This is truly amazing. You're all more than welcome to come with us. From this time forth we'll endeavor to lead you all in a manner that will give you knowledge and experience with a minimum of maiming, rending, and eviscerations."

"Where's the fun in that?" Six said as he tried to get his fingers between his neck and his brother's arm.

"Fun? I'm all for keeping my body in one piece, thank you very much!" Four shook his head at his idiot brothers. "Dismemberment is an event I'll cherish, but don't wish to repeat."

"Wait. I just realized you didn't tell us your name," Doug said to the surly looking man.

"My brothers laugh when I say it."

The other men snickered.

"See? I don't even have to say it. They mock me just for thinking of my name. I think I should have a new name."

Mod nodded in sudden understanding. "Oh, I get it."

"Well, I don't." Doug usually didn't care that Mod figured things out before him, but he felt this scene had gone on long enough.

Mod simply said, "He's the second one made."

A lamp lit up in Doug's mind. "Oh, I get it now."

"Well, I don't get it," Helen said, a bit perturbed at being out of the loop.

Doug continued, "His name is Number Two."

Five and Six laughed so hard they actually stopped fighting each other. Four guffawed and slapped his knee. Helen looked at them like they were all insane. One and Three nodded to her in confirmation, that yes, all men were indeed at least a half a bubble off plumb.

"Okay I get it, but I don't see why it's so funny," Helen said.

Doug turned to Helen. "You're not a guy, so you don't get it. It's wired into our gender to find the term funny."

The surly man grumbled. "I shall find a way to change my name!"

"Good luck with that." Five sniggered as he poked his brother in the ribs with his elbow.

Doug wanted to get back to the task at hand. "Speaking of number two, shouldn't something be happening by now with the Great Beast of Elis?" Doug turned around and searched the bushes for any sign of Snickers.

"The dog!" Everyone jumped at the unexpected shout from Two.

"Yes, the dog, you moron!" One looked over at her sister and they both rolled their eyes. "We're all looking for her now."

Two waved his hands in front of his face and shook his head to indicate they'd all misunderstood. "No! Not that dog. Another dog. One from our past!" he exclaimed.

Helen scanned the area. "I can't see Snuggy-wuffins anywhere."

"The dog is the answer!" Two continued. "We had a dog, much beloved, also named for a number. I could take that number as a name!"

"You can't name yourself after a dog," One said.

"I've got a lot of fond memories of that dog,"[3] Two said. "From now on, I am to be known as Number Nine!"[4]

"Whatever," the twins said in unison, leaning against each other and grinning moronically at their older brother.

"Not going to let it go, are they?" Doug asked One.

"Not likely," One replied.

Helen looked concerned. "The magic pill doesn't usually take this long to work, although Snuggy-wuffins has gone quite a while since the previous dose of medication." She whistled for the dog.

The response from Snickers was a drawn-out whine and a grunt.

"I've heard such sounds many times before!" Suppositoria shouted in warning to the others. "She's gonna blow! Run for high ground!"

What came next defied words.[5] Snickers must have really been backed up. A fount of unbelievable mass and power roared forth in huge plumes a thousand meters high and filled the lowlands of Valis in mere instants. Typhon the Titan never hoped to mete out such damage as was now dealt to the Peloponnese.

"Oh, dear lords above." Doug clamped his hand over his mouth and nose. "That is a lot of shit."

"Well I've already seen enough," Helen said.

Helen and the ladies in waiting seemed to be made of pretty stern stuff, but they immediately ran back to the house and disappeared inside, chased by waves of the fetid stench.

"And that," Mod noted, "is why you don't feed your dog cheese."

The mechanical men seemed unaffected. When Doug and Mod looked at them questioningly, One point at the center of her face.

---

3. *1989*. Popular movie. Great line. You can figure it out from there.
4. Growing up, my family actually had a dog named Number Nine. Ninth puppy born. Runt of the litter. We took pity on him and decided to keep him. In six months, he was the size of a Shetland Pony and going through fifty pounds of Gravy Train a week.
5. Crap, droppings, feces, fertilizer, guano, manure, night soil, ordure, poop, dung. They knew the words. It was the volume that was throwing them for a loop.

"Mechanical noses." She even gave a demonstrative sniff just in case Doug didn't know what a nose was. "Our dads never could get them to work right."

"What a blessing that would be." Doug tried to take his hand from his nose and gagged. His eyes began to water.

Mod pulled a couple of waxed leather ear plugs from a pocket and stuffed them up his nose. He handed another pair to Doug. "Just try to breathe through your mouth," he suggested.

"How that was a legendary task, I'm unsure." Doug wiped the tears from his watery eyes. The waxed leather earplugs shoved up his nose were doing their best at a job they were never designed for. "I think our actions in this matter just made life in this general area a bit more challenging."

The device with the tasks dinged. Mod already had it in his hands from rooting through his pockets.

It sent up another little flare.

Zing! Pop!

The drawer opened and another scroll popped out. Mod pulled out the new scroll and held it out for Doug.

"It's okay," Doug said, still unable to fathom the scale of the manure before him. "You can read it, Mod."

Mod put away the task device and unrolled the scroll. "Your trial period for accomplishing heroic tasks has expired. To continue to use our service please begin the second task listed on the scroll below."

Mod unrolled the scroll a little more and read in silence. "Crap."

"Observant as always, Mod. As you can see, we're surrounded by it." Even with the leather shoved up his nostrils Doug could still smell everything all too well. A huge part of what he was experiencing had to be psychosomatic. The impossible mountain of dung was imposing on his every sense. He wasn't looking forward to seeing what his dreams would be like tonight.

"No, no. Not that. Or rather, exactly that. Look at the next task." Mod held out the scroll for Doug to see.

"Well crap," Doug said. "Helen? You don't happen to have a shovel we could borrow?"

CHAPTER 12

POCKET FULL OF SURPRISES

"I've heard of things cursed by the gods," One said, "but I've never heard of a curse quite like this."

"Snickers must've taken a dump in a sacred pool," Doug said, still shocked by the sheer magnitude of the pile before them. "Whatever nymph or nature spirit she ticked off must have clout. I've never heard of an animal having this kind of ire of the gods brought against them before."

"And the meds we gave her definitely didn't work gently overnight,"[1] Four observed.

"It's fluffier than I expected." Mod noted as the explosion from Snuggy-wuffins's rear end continued to waft gently to the ground. "There's a certain, ethereal beauty to it, a snowfall in the darkest days of winter, if you will."

"I've known you all my life." Doug stared wide eyed at his brother. "And I fully believe I'll never understand how your mind works."

Mod scrunched his eyes close to shut. "Squint and flutter your eyelashes a bit while you look."

"Oh, yeah!" Three said. "I can totally see what you're saying!"

In the midst of the discussion about atomized fertilizer wafting in beautiful, awe-inspiring patterns in the atmosphere, Snickers made her reappearance.

Snickers was amazingly clean despite the condition of the field

1. Sorry, I just have to say this. They keep putting this line on laxative packaging. Dear pharma and naturopathic corporations, please, please understand that no one really wants to hear this. We know it's just a line you use to sell your product, but it conjures up some pretty disturbing mental images for a lot of us.

she emerged from, or what had just emerged from her. She trotted up to the men, plopped her butt on the grass in front of Doug and scooted in front of him with her hind legs raised high in the air.

All conversation stopped as the minute dog scratched her posterior over a good twenty feet of struggling lawn. Satisfied she'd disgusted everyone in attendance, the dog picked herself up and bounced briskly inside the house. She didn't look at Doug or any of his crew once.

"Apparently, we've served our purpose as far as the dog is concerned and are no longer worthy of her attention," Mod said as he stared at the doorway where the dog had disappeared. He turned to Doug. "I thought she might have at least acknowledged you, after you administered medicinal aid and all."

Doug blushed, somewhat embarrassed and unable to reconcile he had to be involved at all.

"The beast seems in good spirits," One said as she turned from the doorway and once again contemplated the mountains of manure. "A heavy weight has been lifted."

"A bit more spring in the dog's step now." Three observed as she stepped over the line of demarcation Snickers had gluteally scratched in the grass that separated the home of Helen from the carnage wrought on the rest of Greece.

Doug cleared his throat to get the attention of all the men and women staring intently at the vastness of poodle manure. "Back to the task at hand. How are we going to clear out the lowlands of the fertilizer they were just gifted?"

"Heracles diverted a river to clean out the Augean stables," One suggested helpfully.

Doug shook his head. "Creeks and such are close by, but any river large enough to divert is too far away. Besides, I don't have the kind of equipment necessary to move that kind of earth.

"Maybe Hephaestus?" Doug began. He paused and looked over at his brother. "Don't you have things in the shop that can excavate heavy things and move them?"

"Maybe. I've got lots of stuff I haven't shown you." Mod grinned. "Snickers's leavings are fluffy and light. With the last batch of toys I got from Hephaestus, I think I might have an idea."

Mod rustled in his pockets for a bit and pulled out a box and a loop of wire. He set the box on the ground and threw the wire up in the air above. The wire snapped into an oval shape, and the box began to hum. The humming stabilized and the air within the oval shimmered. Content with what he saw, Mod took a step forward and disappeared like he'd just stepped through a door.

"He carried that in his pocket? I want pockets," Three said.

"Just imagine what we could put in them?" Five and Six shared mischievous looks with each other.

Doug stared at the empty air surrounded by the metal oval where his brother had just been standing. "Well, this is new."

There was a grunt and the sound of something falling. "Oh, I've been looking for that . . ." Mod's disembodied voice came through the void. There were sounds of scraping as something heavy wheeled toward the gate.

Mod's head appeared briefly in the air. "Little help? I think the wheelbase is too wide to make it through the foot of the portal."

Doug nodded to the twins. They looked happy to be pressed into service. Six jostled his brother Five in the ribs, and the two men jogged into the ether.

"Yeah, grab it there," Mod directed, "and you, there. And if I just hold it here. Watch the handle as we go through." Five's head and shoulders appeared, then the first half of the contraption, then Six was there and finally Mod came through with the last of it.

"It's like the auto-furrower I used to plow Dad's fields last season," Doug said. "Two weeks work done in as many hours."

"I'm hoping we'll have similar results with this," Mod said. "The engine is powerful, a bit too hard for me to handle." Mod clapped Doug on the shoulder. "But you've got the shoulders and back to operate this kind of big equipment."

The contraption had two large, cleated chariot wheels, a massive steam motor, a large rectangular horn with a flat edge that scooped along the ground in the front, two arms with gear and drive controls in the handles, and a chimney with a directional funnel capping off the whole thing.

Mod picked the box for the gate off the ground, flipped the switch to off, collapsed the wires and stuffed the whole thing back in his pocket.

"I have so many questions right now," Doug said.

Mod slowed as he pulled his hand from his chiton pocket. He patted the bulge on his right hip and grinned. "Portal from Hephaestus. He made it for someone else, but they didn't want it.[2] It makes getting back and forth to my shop a breeze."

"Portal?"

"A gate between places," Mod explained. "Like a door that separates one room from another. You just have to walk through."

"The room you just walked to is one hundred and fifty kilometers away." Doug couldn't believe it.

"Not quite that far. It's in Iolcus, not Larissa," Mod clarified.

"You just walked through a gate from here into your old shop at Mom and Dad's?"

"Yep. That's the one," Mod said. "Caves are hard to move: organizing cyclopes to do the heavy lifting, making sure that super strong beings with no depth perception don't damage any delicate machines, unboxing everything after the move. Using the portal is way easier."

"I am officially at a loss. I had no idea, Mod," Doug said.

Mod took the compliment and gave a little bow.

"But what is this?" Doug indicated the big machine. "It has a similar motor and controls to the auto-furrower, but it obviously is something different."

---

2. Hephaestus created the portal as a labor-saving device for Hermes, reckoning that the instantaneous transport from point A to point B would be desirable to the messenger god. Hephaestus reckoned wrong. Hermes is like a dog in a car heading down the highway at seventy miles an hour—he has to stick his head out the window so he can feel the wind on his face. It's one of the things he lives for.

"Snowblower," Mod stated.

"It blows snow?" Doug asked.

"Yup." Mod nodded.

Doug pointed out at the pile of dung. "That isn't snow."

"No, it is not," Mod acknowledged. "You know, at festival how they take a cauldron with a screw on top, and they fill it with barley, and they screw the lid down tight, and they heat up the cauldron until it gets really hot and then the guy runs up to the cauldron really fast and he turns the screw and the lid blows off with a huge pop and the barley explodes out into that really fine netting and the barley is fifteen times its size and is huge and puffy and crispy and fun to eat because of what all the heat and pressure did to the barley?"[3]

"You're comparing this dog poo to puffed barley?" Doug surveyed the mound. Some of the smaller pieces were swirling in the dust as they danced with the gentle breeze. "Actually, that's not that much of a stretch."

"Pelletized, light, granulated, fertilizer."[4] Mod slapped the snowblower. "And this baby is going to distribute it to the greater Peloponnese."

"And it will handle the manure?" One sounded skeptical.

"Due to the intense pressure and rapid release from Snickers, it is light and fluffy and should pose no problem for the blower to deal with it."

"Well, my brave and noble friends, we have a plan." Doug stood behind the device and grabbed the handles. "Fire it up!

---

3. If you ever happen to be at a fair or country market where they do this, you have to stay and watch. It's awesome. The cauldron goes off like a cannon and the puffed rice/corn/barley/wheat/whatever that comes out is puffy, crisp, healthy, delicious, and probably overpriced but well worth it for the experience.

4. Dog manure shouldn't really be used as fertilizer. It can introduce some funky parasites into the soil. Helen, however, has Snuggy-wuffins on a very regulated, high fiber, high vegetable and grain diet with only occasional bits of cooked meat and cheese for variety, so it's okay. Probably. Plus, there's the curse. No parasite could survive that.

CHAPTER 13

AN IMBALANCE OF HUMORS

THE KING'S DOG, ERGOS, GAVE A SERIES OF WEAK BARKS. Teutamides glanced around at the people assembled in the hall, though the king knew he would see no reaction. The advisors and officials thought the dog was senile, but the king knew better.

Teutamides scratched Ergos behind the ears. "Good boy."

Ergos wagged his tail twice before the effort exhausted the ancient dog.

Teutamides furrowed his brow and glared at all his advisors. "Can you not see how your constant yammering is upsetting the royal hound? Be gone!" the king snapped.

Several of the advisors looked shocked to be dismissed in such a harsh manner, yet Teutamides was king. He still had one or two advisers approach until he finally had enough and waved them off. One by one they gathered their things and cleared the hall.

Ergos, worn out from all the excitement, passed out beside the king's chair. He still managed a weak, asthmatic growl at the memories of what had riled him a moment before.

Leaving the dog behind to rest, Teutamides rose from the cushioned throne where he'd been conducting official business in the now empty room. He walked to a corridor and took several turns until he was sure no one followed.

"Teutamides."

The voice was so soft Teutamides would have missed it if he weren't listening for it. The king advanced to one of the decorative stone archways built into the walls of the castle. He faced the wall and looked down the corridor both ways to make sure no one was present. He touched three stones in sequence, and a secret panel slid open to a darkened passageway beyond.

As the door pivoted shut behind him, the voice was already there.

"The boy fares well," the phantom said. "Two of the twelve tasks are completed."

The king was already well aware. "We could all smell it when he completed the second task, but then the crops began to really prosper, so the complaining went way down."

"The first tasks were meant to humiliate him." The phantom pointed out. "Instead the unpalatable undertakings have gained the boy fame and notoriety."

The voice came from what first appeared to be several directions at once, but as the king focused, he became convinced the voice moved around him so fast he just couldn't pinpoint it.

Teutamides searched about in the darkness as best he could without giving the impression of spying. The messenger made it clear when he'd first visited, the king was not to see him. So the clandestine meetings in the dark were called for as a matter of reassurance to the helpful stranger.

Still, it wouldn't hurt for the king to have something to suss out the mysterious messenger's identity. Such information almost always came in handy later, but thus far Teutamides had no luck in discerning anything.

"The first two were Heracles's assigned tasks." The king frowned. "The man's suggestions are infantile or crazed. I'm working on things more difficult for the boy to complete."

"Obstacles he can overcome are good for now," the phantom demurred. "Let him get a sense of accomplishment. The closer he gets to accomplishing the twelve, the more he'll vie to finish off the last, no matter how difficult or dangerous."

"I'm still skeptical," the king voiced his concern with no hesitation. "What if the boy succeeds? I have little desire to be forever remembered as the king usurped by a swineherd."

"Still, to be remembered as such would be a kind of immortality, would it not?" The voice joked.

"That's not funny," the king said.

The voice laughed. The sound echoed and repeated in the dark. "You amuse me, my king. I promise you this, at the conclusion of this experiment with the boy, you'll be remembered and compensated in ways you cannot even imagine."

"I can imagine quite a bit," the king grumbled.

"Then, my king, let your imagination have free rein." The voice slowly faded. "Remember to tell no one of our meetings."

"Remember your promise of payment," the king responded, but the voice was already gone.

Teutamides made his way back to the secret door in the dark. He'd have to find some leverage to use against his supposed benefactor. He'd already decided he would contact his spy, Aesimus, and see what might be done. How to eavesdrop on and blackmail a faceless wraith was beyond his kingly knowledge, but perhaps the spy would have some idea how it could be done with little or no risk.

The secret door had just sealed when the king was set upon by a frustrated Daphis followed closely by Heracles.

"You smell lovely today, your majesty!" Heracles said out of the blue.

"My king." Daphis scraped and bowed. "You left suddenly and had many of us worried."

"I was in the toilet," the king lied. "My humors seem to be off, and it is affecting my bowels."[1]

"You as well?" Heracles bellowed. "I all but destroyed the dung-shoot in the west wing of the palace. Using fragrant lavender to cover up the aftermath, quite the good call!"[2]

---

1. Black bile, yellow bile, phlegm, and blood. Hippocrates believed these four "humors" needed to be in balance for the body to properly operate. Teutamides's humors were fine, at least the types we just listed. The other humor, on the other hand? He really didn't have any to speak of.
2. Exactly what it sounds like.

Daphis gave Heracles a sidelong glance, clearly regarding the man as an uncultured faun or satyr or such. "Which reminds me, your lordship," the adviser continued. "The palace contractor would like to have a word."

Teutamides smiled through gritted teeth, all the while stuck on the thought that his daughter was going to have a field day with this one.

CHAPTER 14

DON'T KILL THE MESSENGER

ALL THE DOGS IN THE NEIGHBORHOOD, EXCLUDING SNICKERS, who was tuckered out from her recent experience, barked at and/or chased something coming into the valley. The automaton siblings had finished putting away Mod's equipment when a man wearing winged sandals raced past the chariot driveway with an innumerable clutch of dogs right on his heels. He found a way to ditch the pack somewhere down the line, swung wide to avoid reengaging the frustrated dogs, and made his way sweating and out of breath up the path.

His outfit came into clearer focus as he neared Doug and the others. The wings on the sandals were slick, embroidered imitations of the real thing, the shoes cushioned with arch supported. The man's chiton was obviously part of a uniform, bearing the double H logo for Hermes's Heralds™ emblazoned on the back.[1]

The messenger zeroed his focus on Doug. "Hey look"—Mod poked his brother in the ribs—"you've got mail."[2]

The messenger came to an uncontrolled, abrupt stop that sprayed everyone in the drive with gravel and grit from the road. He ignored

---

1. Originally registered by the son of Philippides as a messaging service to honor his late father. Hermes wouldn't allow it. Citing name recognition, trademark infringement, and half a dozen other infractions, Hermes easily won in court. The orphaned son of a foot soldier just didn't have the money, influence, or political clout to win a legal battle against a god.

2. In 1985, a sharp-eyed member of the America Online staff remembered this phrase from an ancient Greek text and suggested it as a salutation alerting whoever logged onto the service that they had a message. They went with it, and it went on to be one of the most mocked and reviled phrases in all of recorded history.

the discomfort and irritation he caused as he tiredly reached into the pouch at his waist to pull out a tiny scroll and noted his mileage traveled on it. Tucking the small scroll away, he quickly produced a package. He tried to maintain a sense of professionalism as sweat beaded on his brow and ran into his eyes. "Doug of Iolcus?"

Doug bowed slightly. "I'm Doug."

"For you." The man held out a box in one hand and a receipt with a quill in the other. "If you could just sign that the package was received whole and undamaged, I'll be on my way."

Doug looked from the proffered pen and paper to the box. The box wasn't in the best condition, squashed and mangled on one side. "There's no royal seal on this," Doug said.

"There isn't?" The man's calm sweating became a bit more panicked. "I coulda sworn there was."

Doug bypassed the paperwork and opened the box. The new task device was all flashy and slick, and half the size of the prototype, so Mod would have no problem putting the new device in one of his pockets. The right corner of the device, however, was dirty and dented right next to the slot where the message scroll would come out. "Looks a little damaged."

"Really? I coulda sworn this is the condition it was in when they gave it to me." The man's calm sweating became a bit more panicked. "I-I . . ."

The messenger's mouth worked up and down. He broke down and told the truth.

"I tripped running from a dog," the sweating man spoke with fear and pointed to his skinned knee.[3] "The only refuge I could see from the snapping jaws of the wolf intent on my shins appeared to be running through a flurry of what I can only assume was, well . . ." He

---

3. Dogs versus messengers. It's an old problem. The guy responsible for getting Fido his kibble is zealously worshiped by the four-legged sycophants. Anyone who tries to breach the barrier Fluffy has established is in for it, labeled and condemned as an outsider whether they bear the staff of a herald, mail from the post office, or your latest order from GrubHub.

shuddered in revulsion. "Actually, I'd rather not ponder on what it might have been. The unholy cloud blackened the sky and slapped my olfactory senses in a way I'm sure I'll never recover from. The hound ceased his pursuit, overwhelmed by the smell, so I persevered. Visibility was zero with the cloud, my eyes watering, filled to the gills with adrenaline due to the narrow escape from the hound of hell. I tripped. I tripped and I fell on the package and I smooshed the box. The royal seals fell right into oblivion."

"In such situations, I'd probably stumble about a bit too. Try not to focus on the stink. You get used to it after a while." Doug seemed satisfied with the man's explanation, though some of the others—Nine in particular—still looked wary. "Now the smell is not so much a slap to the face as a constant, irritating presence."

"Kinda like a tension headache in the nose," Mod suggested helpfully.

"The nose." Doug nodded. "And the mouth and the throat. And I'm actually a bit revolted by the gunk collecting in the corner of my eyes right now."

"Totally," Mod agreed.

"So you got distracted by a snarling beast chasing you into the black cloud, lost your footing, fell on the box. Stuff happens." Doug handed the package over to Mod. "Check it out, just to make sure it still works, will you, Mod?"

Mod nodded and started checking out the device.

"The messenger damaged the delivery. He should be punished," Nine grumbled.

Mod was through with his inspection. "Just a bit of surface dings and dents. Should still work fine."

Doug reached for the receipt to sign for the package.

"No!" Nine was suddenly in the messenger's face as he threatened him. "Confess! Think of the state of your soul, man!"

Doug pulled the automaton away from the now trembling man. "Volume control? Calm down. We don't need to give the guy a heart attack."

"He has all but admitted he damaged the device! He must be punished!" Nine shook with righteous fury as he stabbed a finger in the herald's direction.

Doug and Mod looked at each other in silence for a few seconds then they both burst out laughing. "He's a messenger," Doug continued.[4] "We can't do anything to him. It's like seven generations of bad luck."

Nine glanced about his compatriots and continued in a conspiratorial tone. "This device is very proprietary. I mean, just breaking a royal seal you're not supposed to is a crime punishable by . . ." He let the statement hang for a moment. "The man must be punished severely for his sin!"

"No," Doug looked the automaton in the eyes. "Absolutely not. What's with you right now? You eat too many of those Ethiopian bean treats Mod had stuffed in his pack?"[5]

"So, are you going to kill me or not?" The sweating man looked at a sundial strapped to his wrist. "I've got another message to deliver by noon, and I'm already going to be late."

Doug waved the man off. "We're all good. I think killing someone over denting a device that lists challenges concocted by Teutamides and Heracles is a tad extreme."

"Thank you, sir." The man looked relieved to return to his professional persona. "And before I leave, may I inquire as to one more

---

4. Messengers in ancient times had a sort of "diplomatic immunity" and most everyone went along with it. Not a hard and fast rule but generally followed. Especially if the messenger in question came from someone who could squash everyone around them like a bug. The messengers representing Genghis Khan are a good example of messengers you should leave alone. That one guy from the Khwarezmid Empire killed Khan's messengers that one time. Never heard of the Khwarezmids? After the Mongols were through with them, neither did anyone else.

5. An Ethiopian goat herder noticed that when his goats ate the berries on a certain plant, they gained supernatural abilities like parkour or being able to study without going to sleep. The herder mentioned the bean's qualities to a holy man, and the next thing you knew (a thousand years later), Starbucks franchises dotted the globe.

thing? How would you rate the level of service provided today? On a scale of one olive for poor to five olives being exceptional?"

"Uh, three olives?" Doug suggested.

The messenger looked a little crestfallen to get a lukewarm review. "That's justified, I guess." He shrugged and checked his list to see what other deliveries he had left to do today.

A new scroll rolled out of the slot in the front of the device.

Wizz! *Pop*!

"I told you it would still work." Mod admired the new device. "Slick. The flare and the scroll arrive at almost the same time." He handed the scroll to Doug.

Doug read the message. It immediately brought a flush to his cheeks. "The third entry in our impossible task countdown is obtaining Hippolyta's girdle."

Mod verified what was just read and grinned at Doug. "Should be no problem for you, brother, being the smooth talking, sophisticated, ladies' man you are."

"Shut up, Mod," Doug grumbled.

"Heracles definitely suggested that one," the messenger said as he tucked away his itinerary and bent down to tighten his sandals. He rose up to stretch. "He has a thing for Amazonian undergarments."

"And you know this how?" Mod enquired.

"Herald and delivery man." The messenger pointed at himself as he started running in place.

"I thought Hippolyta's girdle was a piece of armor." Doug sounded panicked in more ways than one.

"Not armor. Shapewear." The man in the uniform shook his head. "Heracles is on the monthly catalog list and is a frequent shopper. The packages he orders are usually wrapped in brown paper and marked 'personal.' Those Amazonian intimates catalogs are usually worth cracking the royal seal on for a peek or two, if you catch my drift?"

"Buying items for his lady friends?" Mod offered.

"Only if the items in question are sized for an extremely large, muscular woman." The messenger winked knowingly as he started jogging down the path. "You should check out one of the catalogs sometime. You can sign up to get them for free at any of the franchise locations in pretty much every metropolitan area in Greece. Good luck with the list." The man waved over his shoulder as he steadily power walked away.

CHAPTER 15

LIFTS, SHAPES, AND SEPARATES

"I HELP A DOG GO TO THE BATHROOM, THEN I GET THE CHARGE to clean it up. Now I have to obtain a female undergarment. Quite the legacy I'm building, aren't I?" Doug wasn't feeling too thrilled about this turn of events. Sure, there had been excitement to begin with, but if all the tasks turned out to be like these, he was wondering what the point was of any of them.

"It can't be that easy," Mod said. "I mean, you don't have to get the girdle off of Hippolyta, right?"

Doug checked the scroll again. "It doesn't specify," he said weakly.

"If braving aisles of merchandise is called for, I shall accompany you when you storm the door of the intimates store," One said.

"Unintentional rhyme," Five and Six said in unison. "Nice."

She ignored her brothers. "I'd love to visit a real store in person. I've only used mail order in the past and could really use some expert fitting advice."

Three concurred. "Our dads helped where they could, but there are quite a few intricacies of the feminine form they didn't really get. Designing a woman, sure, they did great, but dressing one?" She shook her head. "And One is a special case, anyway. When breasts the size of hers are made of tungsten steel, they need more padding than one might suspect."[1]

"I think I would have been fine not knowing that," Doug said.

---

1. For the protection of others.

"Just being honest. I need a couple of new things too, so I'm in," Three said.

Four, Five, and Six looked excited about the excursion too, but probably for different reasons.

"I don't like this talk of female undergarments," Nine huffed prudishly. "And to think that running man casually peruses bound periodical matter containing descriptions of such things? Scandalous."

"Where do we go to find the queen of the Amazons?" Doug wasn't looking forward to this. How was he going to explain wrestling a piece of intimate wear off of and away from a muscular, battle-hardened woman to Larisa? He was sure obtaining the garment would involve some kind of compromising positions if he could manage to pull it off—in more ways than one.

Mod pulled out the travel map of the whole of Greece and showed the map to everyone in the group. "The task with the girdle doesn't say anything about where we go. Is anyone seeing something we missed?"

"Is it a riddle?" Five said to the group. "Some play on words we must decipher?"

"Like you're smart enough to figure a puzzle out," Six said.

The twins started tussling with each other.

"Enough!" One shouted. "You two aren't helping anything."

"It shouldn't be that hard if the messenger is right and Heracles thought it up?" Mod shook his head as he addressed the question. "Then no. It's not something we should have to overthink."

"What was it the messenger said? You can pick up a catalog in pretty much any major city in Greece?" Doug didn't quite understand.

"Franchise locations." Nine frowned. "Dens of iniquity and radical indoctrination."

The last term was something Doug had never heard before. "Radical indoctrination?"

"'Buy our products' is their motto. Once they control how you dress, they can easily control how you think," Nine explained.

Doug and Mod gaped at each other. "The mall?"

"You will never find a more wretched hive of scum and villainy."[2] Nine's eyes narrowed. "We must be cautious."

It had shocked him a bit with the initial outburst Nine made a while ago, but now it was seeming to go to a new extreme. "What's with the sudden prudish and self-righteous attitude?" Doug asked Nine. "We're in Greece. Mountains, rivers, soil, pretty much everything around us came about because something somewhere got splashed with some form of bodily fluid."

"A proud tradition still practiced everywhere today," Three chimed in as Nine bristled. She laughed when she saw how it rankled him.

Doug glared a quick reproval to Three. "Not helping." He covered his face with his hands as he composed himself. Pulling his fingers down his face, he took a deep breath and turned back to Nine. "We're talking about a lingerie shop. Half of the population in Greece wears a bra."

"Tis unnatural," Nine said haughtily.

"You said bra without blushing." Mod looked impressed by his brother. "You might even make it to the register with your intimates purchase before you lose your nerve."

"Thanks for the vote of confidence." Doug deadpanned.

"*No!*" Nine grabbed the front of Doug's tunic and started to shake him. "Abandon your quest. Is it worth losing your soul?"

"I'm a young adult male who is trying to win the attention of the girl I really like, so, yes?" Doug turned to look at Mod and One as Nine continued to try to shake sense into him. "Has he got a setting

2. I'm not going to narrow this one down. If you can't place the words with the movie and the person who said it, you don't deserve the lightsaber or the seat on the council. And you will most certainly not be granted the title "master."

that needs a return to factory specs? Maybe he's flipped a switch that shouldn't have flipped?"[3]

"Let me check." One produced a club and whacked Nine upside the head.[4]

Nine blinked hard and let go of Doug's lapels. "Thanks. I needed that," Nine said as if nothing had been amiss.

"Awesome!" Mod clapped his hands and rubbed them together. "I can't wait to see what happens next. Let's find the Elis mall."

---

3. There are a myriad of moral settings in the automatons. Their fathers found it best to leave the gauge more or less in the center with the needle pointing just slightly toward *innocent and childlike*. Nine's gauge had been knocked off kilter and is currently stuck deep in the red between *radical evangelical* and *celebrity politician*.

4. The term "Percussive Maintenance" hasn't been coined yet. Ktesibios and Talos would have loved the term because it would've sounded so much better than the phrase "hitting the kids until they work."

CHAPTER 16

HIPPOLYTA'S SECRET

"Sure you don't want to come with me?" Doug asked his brother.

Mod shook his head. "I don't do well in normal social settings, and you think I'd be able to just step into this kind of store? You're on your own for this one, Bro."

"Just me and the girls, then," Doug looked at One and Three.

One nodded. "We shall not be far away should you require our assistance."

"You'll do fine, sweetie," Three said as she and her sister casually walked into the store.

Doug forced himself to follow them shortly after. *Did she have to call me "sweetie?"* He was sure Three meant the word as a comfort and reassurance. Probably. But now he was thinking of Larisa, and when she'd called him "sweetie."

One and Three disappeared into the store as if they knew exactly what it was they needed to look for. It was just as well. If two extremely well put together women hovered around Doug into the store, it would only make it more awkward for him.

He was out of his element enough as it was.

Doug had been in CornuCopiae™ with his mom before, [1] and it

1. CornuCopiae™ was the merchandising giant of Ancient Greece. A huge store where you could buy everything from barnyard implements to brassieres. It had toys, tools, footwear, clothes, and appliances. Think of it as sort of a primordial Sears, Roebuck and Co.

was the kind of store that had a lingerie section. How much different would an actual lingerie shop be?

Plenty, it would seem.

The first thing he noticed was there was no buffer zone. Once past the threshold of Hippolyta's door, nowhere was safe. In Cornu-Copiae™ when Doug had felt he was being exposed to too many feminine underthings, he could escape to the shoe section just across the aisle to wait for his mother to complete her search for the same yet newer set of mother's industrial-style undergarments that he saw every time laundry day came around.

This shop was not home to the same type of underthings Doug had been exposed to as he swished them about in a washtub with his father's striped socks and Mod and Doug's academy gym chitons. This was a whole different type of beast entirely.

He closed his eyes.

I do this for Larisa.

Then he stepped over the threshold.

He saw a couple of the sales force, and his eyes went wide. They had to be nymphs or sirens or such because he'd never seen this kind of beauty walking around while shopping before. Their goddess-like wiles would be too much for a mere mortal to deal with.

I'll have to find the girdle myself, without shop assistance.

Finding it himself meant more time. He was still in dangerous, unknown territory, and he knew it.

I'll need a mental distraction, to keep me from focusing on the cashiers. His mind stumbled over a good one right off the bat. *Uncle Pachysarkeos cleaning out the pig barn.*[2] Doug's stomach tumbled at the power of the thought. Pachy's image would be enough.

Doug had never seen so many lacy frills and soft padded things in all of his life. The shapes and fabrics suggested the garment's designa-

---

2. Pachysarkos means corpulent in Greek. That described Doug's uncle pretty well. Think of the out of shape gym teacher that follows the team around in a golf cart. Now imagine that same person mucking out pig stalls wearing nothing but a smock.

tion and duty for some, while other objects appeared to be simply ornamental. The ornamental ones made him stumble the most, their purpose obvious.

He stared at a particularly shapely teddy and envisioned how it would caress and drape a shapely woman's body. He couldn't help himself. It was right there, dangling from a hanger as it waited to fulfill its destiny.

Then his mind naturally drifted back to his girlfriend.

Doug slapped himself. "Come on, Uncle Pachy, do your magic," he whispered urgently, then thought if he talked to himself, it might make someone think he was a freak.

Don't talk to yourself. Find the girdle. You're on a mission. Remember the task. It was too late. His slap and the whisper drew the attention of one of the sales nymphs.

"Is there something I can help you find?"

The voice behind Doug startled him, and he spun around only to come face to face with one of the most perfect women he'd ever seen. She was slight, and her skin glowed faintly. Her visage and form were ideal, and her hair framed her face in silken waves adorned with the leaves of a tree.

"Fig leaves." Doug latched onto the detail hard. It was a good focal point to help keep him on task.

The saleswoman smiled and touched the leaves with her hand. "Yes, they are fig leaves. Most men who enter our shop are distracted by attributes other than the adornments in our hair." She laughed. "I'm Suke.[3] How can I help you?" Her voice was a bright, personable sound.

Her voice filled Doug's whole brain. Uncle Pachy wasn't strong enough to resist the force that pushed him hard out of Doug's consciousness.

Thinking and speech were compromised. Doug clung to his task

---

3. Nymphs were often associated with nature in some way. Rivers, lakes, trees, plants, and the like. Suke is the nymph of the fig tree.

like a drowning man to a sinking raft. "Need something . . ." He couldn't finish the thought.

"I'd be happy to find it for you." Suke smiled and came a step closer. "Do you need a bra?"

Doug took half a step back and shook his head. "No. No bar—Err, rab?" *What was the word again?*

Suke pointed at a brassiere on the rack next to them.

"No," Doug croaked. "Not one of those."

Suke nodded. "Panties, then."

Doug nearly choked on his spit. He shook his head in the negative. "Shapewear."

Suke smiled. "Cami or corset or—"

"Girdle," Doug managed to force the word out. "I need a girdle."

"See, that's not so hard," Suke said as she flashed a brilliant smile.

Hard? Doug was finding it hard to *breathe.*

"How big? Is she about my size?" Suke stepped back so Doug could see her better.

This beautiful woman just asked him to imagine her in underthings. Doug's already fragile mind went blank. Once again he was rendered speechless.

Suke pursed her lips in the long silence. "Maybe if I know who it is for? What's her name?"

"Their names," Doug's mouth operated independent of his mind now. He could hear himself speaking, but it sounded very far away.

"Their?" Suke's mouth twitched up in the corners as if she were surprised. "Way to go, Tiger. Who are they?"

"Teutamides and Heracles." Doug's eyes opened wide with horror in recognition of the names that left his lips.

"Awwww!" Suke cocked her head to the side and leaned forward to chuck Doug on the shoulder. "Well good for you!" she said. "You do what feels right to you, girl!"

One of the other nymphs on the other side of the store spoke up. "Did he say Heracles? You should totally give the young man Heracles's discount."

"That's a great idea." Suke leaned in and put her hand on Doug's arm. "It's against company policy, but if you won't tell, neither will I."

"Please don't." Doug felt like he was about to cry.

Three came up and stood behind Doug, too late to help avoid any of Doug's mental damage. "Isn't he adorable?"

"Oh, he certainly is," Suke said, then she waved to a couple of the other nymphs. "Carya, Ampelus, come over here, you just have to meet this adorable young man."[4]

"I'd just like to buy a girdle," Doug said in a haunted whisper.

Soon he was surrounded by all the women in the store, all eager to help him in any way they could.

Uncle Pachy fought his way back into the fringes of Doug's mind. *"Fight, boy!" he belched.*

It was just enough reinforcement to help Doug survive the ordeal.

One came to him after she'd finished her purchases. "You faced the challenge bravely, Doug. I would have intervened, but I could see you were determined to face your fears and come out the victor." She placed a hand on his shoulder. "A lesser man would have turned and run."

"Is that still an option?" Doug croaked as Suke placed a pink paper package in Doug's arms.

"I knew you were done with the task when the flare went off. I was lucky it wasn't in my pocket," Mod said. "Sure, they don't seem to do much, but in my pocket, they could majorly ruin my day."

"I'd hate for your day to be ruined." Doug hadn't stopped shaking from the last task yet.

"Poor thing." One stroked Doug on the back to comfort him.

---

4. Carya, nymph of the nut tree, and Ampelus, nymph of the vine. They aren't just pretty faces. The women are all dedicated and take their jobs very seriously. Carya is great at marketing, Ampelus does all the ordering and sales floor layout, and Suke does all the payroll and taxes. Their store has been recognized by corporate as the best performing location three years running.

"And thus you begin to reap the wages of sin." Nine's prudish persona returned with a self-righteous sneer.

"There was nothing wrong with Doug's interactions in the store. It was innocent and pure and endearing," Three said with a nod to her sister.

Mod clamped down on Doug's shoulder and gave it a playful squeeze. "You'll look back on this later and laugh, I promise. It may take several years, but . . ." Mod held out a small scroll to his brother. "Let's put the memory of the intimates shop behind you and see what the gods have in store for you next."

Doug handed the bag with the girdle to Mod, took the scroll, and unrolled it.

Mod peeked in the bag, then looked at the handwritten receipt. He let out a laugh and his face split in a grin back to his ears. The goofy smile stayed on Mod's face like it was threatening to become permanent.

"What?" Doug finally asked.

"There's handwritten personalized contact info for all of the girls in the store on the back of the receipt." Mod's cheek straining grin grew bigger, if that was even possible. "If things don't work out with Larisa, you might have some other options."

Doug ignored him and read from the scroll. "The next task is to find the enchanted apples atop Mount Gargantua."

Mod knit his brows together, serious now. "I know most places in Greece, and most of our history too, but I've never heard of Gargantua or the apples listed in the task."

"It says we need to go to Hermione," Doug clarified. "Well, at least we know the direction to head. I'm sure we'll find it on the way. It's a mountain, so how hard can it be to spot?"

CHAPTER 11

MOUNT GARGANTUA

THE TRIP TO HERMIONE WAS UNEVENTFUL, A RATHER pleasant and leisurely trek. Summer was in full bloom, the greens of the plants and colors of blossoms lusher than normal thanks to the huge profusion of fertilizer throughout the whole of the Peloponnese. Snickers's leavings had lost much of the olfactory potency, so you could take a deep breath to partake of the perfumes infusing the air, as long as you didn't make it a really, really deep breath.

All in all, it was a nice trip.

Mostly.

A bit of a pall hung over Doug, for the closer they got to the area indicated on the map to be the site of the enigmatic Mt. Gargantua, the more Doug was certain the fabled pinnacle could not be found.

Doug took the band all the way to the sea. The mountain the map claimed should be there was not seen.

Doug looked down the beach to the east as far as the eye could see. Nothing but some small, empty huts placed back from the shoreline. He turned to the west and squinted against the light of the low-hanging sun. There was an old man who slept with his back propped against a small dune topped with seagrass, but otherwise the view west was pretty much the same as the view to the east. Doug crouched down and rooted among the sand and gravel for a moment, selected a small stone and then pitched it as far as he could. It was an exceedingly good throw, and the rock broke the surface far enough out that he couldn't hear the splash.

"What do we do now?" One asked. She and the others milled about as they waited for direction on how to proceed.

"Maybe we walked too far?" Mod suggested. "Somehow we missed it on the way in?"

"How do you miss a mountain?" Three asked.

Good question. No mountain meant no completing his tasks. No completing his tasks meant no Larisa ever.

Doug looked out into the waves and searched for answers he wouldn't find out there and gave up a little.

He took a few steps into the sea, far enough out that the waves covered his ankles, and then sat down in the gentle water. He looked straight ahead, quiet as the surf lapped around him.

Mod watched his brother walk into the water. He hesitated for a bit, inching forward until his toes just touched the transition between surf and land. After a quiet moment of internal struggle, Mod waded out and joined Doug.

"It's pretty here," Doug said to his brother. "A good place to end a long trip."

"The trip's not over yet." Mod winced as a wave washed over his knee.

Doug noticed his brother's discomfort immediately. "You all right?"

"The ocean is still a bit hard for me." Mod trembled.

Doug knew in an instant what his brother was talking about. Mod had been his brother for a very long time, but he wasn't born as such. Mod was adopted. His birth mother died in the ocean, and little Mod had seen it all. "It never even occurred to me how this might make you feel."

He started to rise, but Mod pulled him back down.

"I'm assuming we'll have to be in a boat sometime later, so I might as well work out my feelings about deep water now," Mod said.

"How do you figure that?" Doug asked.

"Greece is a land of islands and waters. There's no way we won't have to get on a boat at some point," Mod said.

"You don't—" Doug started.

Mod killed the comment before Doug could finish. "Don't even think of saying I don't have to go." Mod's face burned with determination. He leaned closer to Doug and looked him in the eyes. "Doug, you are the best brother and best friend a man could ask for. I love you and want to be a part of this. I'm not going to let my fear of the water stop me from being there when you need me."

Doug hugged his brother. "I love you too. I'm glad you're here."

The brothers clung to each other for a long time before either felt they were strong enough to let go.

After a while, Mod started to speak. "Something cold and hard and terrible in my heart is easing away. The dark feeling I've held since I was a child is ebbing with the waves, not so harsh anymore. It's not gone, but bearable."

"Is there anything I can do to help?" Doug said, willing to do anything, maybe even let go of the thought of being with Larisa if he needed to. It would be hard, but he cared about his brother that much.

"You've already helped," Mod said. "You starting these quests made me realize I can't just have you stay with me and protect me forever. You know me better than anyone, but I know *you* better than anyone too. I could see how much it was weighing on you not seeing the mountain. I could see how much you were hoping for this to work out.

"It made me realize I was feeling disappointed too. I want you to succeed, to be with the girl you love, even if it means hard things are going to happen to me because of it."

Doug wiped a tear from his eye. "You'll always be a part of my life, Mod. No matter what happens."

Mod smiled at his brother and nodded. "I know, but things change. Things have to change, and I haven't stepped away from my safe places for so long that I'm not sure I'm able to."

Mod reached out under the waves and grabbed his brother by the hand. "You don't realize how much you're helping me. It's easier to deal with my own fears while I'm focused on someone else."

"I'm only really focusing on myself," Doug said.

"You're doing the right thing, what you should be doing, right now," Mod reassured Doug.

Doug still felt a little guilty.

"If it makes it any easier, you're helping me too. It's easier when you love the person you're helping," Mod said. "And maybe because I'm helping you, I'll end up in a place that's good that I hadn't expected or ever thought of."

Doug couldn't look away from his brother. "You're an amazing man, Modifixeus."

"Aren't I though?" Mod laughed, letting go of his brother's hand so he could bat some water at him.

"This isn't so bad." Mod sighed as he leaned back and pushed his legs out straight into the ocean. "I can see why so many people like the water."

"Perspectives change," said a voice behind the brothers. "A child doesn't see things the same way as an adult."

The brothers turned to see an old man that had been sleeping against the dune sitting on the beach a few yards away. He raised a hand in greeting.

Doug returned the gesture, a smirk on his face. "Sounds kind of wise. Are you some kind of wise guy or something?"

The man's face broke into a lighthearted grin. "I've been labeled as such a time or two."

Mod nodded toward the gentleman. "Is this your beach? Is it okay we're sitting here?"

"Not my beach," the man said. "And of course you may sit there. It is exactly where I expected you to be."

The two brothers looked at each other, still not quite sure what to make of the man.

"You expected us to be here?" Mod pointed down at the waves lapping around them. "Here? Sitting in the ocean?"

"In this general area," the man explained. "Somewhere right about this time."

Just enough was clicking together that Doug was intrigued. He waited for the old man to continue to see where this might go.

The Number Siblings had wandered closer as they overheard the conversation happening. "I've seen this scam before," Nine began. "Now he'll say something wise sounding yet vague in an effort to gain your confidence."

"It ends with him and his hidden confederates clubbing you over the head and taking all your possessions," Four continued. "We'll all wake up naked and broke behind an amphitheater somewhere, wondering how we got there."

The old man clucked his tongue and waved the notion away as ridiculous. "I'm here to help you on your quest."

"See? Vague and confidence building," Nine said.

"Hold tight to your purse." Four beamed as if he'd already figured it all out.

The man looked a bit perturbed. He waved it off and continued. "You are currently looking to complete the fourth part of a quest that shall ultimately have twelve parts. Yet you cannot complete the action asked of you because the location of the fourth part eludes you."

"That was a little less vague," Four noted. "Maybe this isn't a scam."

"See, he's already gained your trust." Nine clutched tightly to the bag attached to his belt.

"Enough dramatics, you two," Doug addressed the automatons and their assumptions. "So you're obviously here for us." Doug nodded to the old man as he picked himself up out of the water and walked closer to the visitor. Mod trailed right behind.

The old man rose to greet them more formally. He bowed slightly at the waist then righted himself. "Young masters. Visions from the gods have brought me to you. I will aid you in whatever way I can."

"My brother told me the gods would send help our way," Doug

said with a nod to Mod. "Well met, sir. I'm sure you've arrived at the perfect moment." Doug reached out to shake the man's hand.

The grip the old man returned was strong and sure.

"I'm Doug." He pointed at Mod with his chin. "My brother, Modifixeus." Then nodded to each of the mechanical people in turn. "One, Nine, Three, Four, Five, and Six."

"Automatons. I had heard of you and looked forward to meeting you." The man shook each of their hands in the order they were introduced. "Odd, that you should have a nine in place of number two," the old man said.

The brothers all grinned and snorted. "And you are?" Nine asked in a tight voice, clearly unamused by his brothers.

"Mopsus." The man bowed again. "At your service."

"Welcome, Mopsus." Doug turned to the land and surveyed it in the light of the evening sun. "I'll gladly accept help from anyone who can tell me where I can find the mountain I'm supposed to climb."

"Ah, about that." Mopsus held up a finger. "My direction from the gods is such that I may direct or interpret but am forbidden to outright tell anything."

"Great," Nine said flatly. "Typical soothsayer."

"A bit of background is all you need to find what you seek." Mopsus ignored the automaton and brought the attention of the group to a sparse gathering of small but serviceable huts nestled back from the beach. "Have you heard of Herodotus of Halicarnassus?"

None of them had.

Mopsus smacked his forehead with the palm of his hand. "Of course they haven't, Mopsus you idiot. Herodotus hasn't been born yet." Slightly flustered, he pointed out the huts again. "His family, his great, great grandfather to be exact, summers here with his mother and father."

"With Herodotus's mother and father?" Four asked, clearly confused. "So they've been born at the same time as the great, great grandfather?"

"I'm going to have to be more clear in the way I talk to people,"

Mopsus mumbled to himself. "The great, great grandfather's parents are the ones I was referring to."

Four looked as if the explanation now made sense, then his brow furrowed as if a new question had arisen.

"Ignore him. He's an idiot." Nine pointed at the closest of the small huts. "You're telling us that this Herodotus person's great, great grandparents live in that building right there?"

Mopsus shook his head. "Not grandparents. Grandfather, currently a boy aged seven. And he does not live in the hut you pointed at, but his family vacations in the one that is third from the left."

Nine looked like he believed none of it. "All of this is unverifiable. 'Dear sirs, you are looking for the great, great grandfather of a man who hasn't been born yet so he can give you directions to a mountain that doesn't exist. Please pay me handsomely for the brilliant insight and direction.' It's a scam. The thump on the skull and body cavity search for valuables will soon commence."

"I know someone who's about to get the club." One eyed Nine greedily.

"Is this a reset situation?" Doug asked.

"Possibly." The club mysteriously appeared in One's hand again as she stepped toward her brother. "Let me check."

Mopsus stepped between both of them. He held up his hands for them to stop. "Gentle sir and not so gentle lady, much as I'd love to see a naysayer get his righteous comeuppance, I must ask you to please bear with me for but a moment more." He glared at One until she lowered the club, scathed a suddenly mute Nine with a glance, and continued. "The boy vacationing in this idyllic place is named Dotus. Dotus is a bright child, full of wit and curiosity; he remembers what he learns and compares it with everything new he discovers. As a six-year-old, he felt the small point of land we now stand on was the whole world. He believed the hills behind the hut rose up until they breached Olympus itself."

"But they don't," Mod said. "These hills are hardly even hills.

There is no way they could be mistaken for Olympus unless you were so small . . ." He let the thought drop off as understanding widened his eyes.

Doug picked up where Mod was going. "So small that everything looked unscalable."

Mopsus was happy the brothers understood. "I was told you would be smart. This year, when his family comes to the seashore, Dotus will look at the hills and wonder why they're smaller. He'll go back to the places of grand adventure and see they're not so forbidding or dangerous or—"

"Gargantuan," Doug guessed correctly. "Impressive vocabulary and word usage for a small child. We're looking for what would seem like an immense, impossible mountain to conquer if you were a kid."

"Perspective," Mopsus said. "This will be a lesson Dotus will learn in his heart and pass down to his son, and he to his son, and he to his son until the lesson is learned by Herodotus who will change the way everyone sees the world."

"We're looking for an apple tree growing on a hill that would be hard to climb if you're a kid." Mod started to look around the area. "It can't be too far away, because a child wouldn't be able to travel too far."

"Already got it." Doug pointed to a neck of rock rising above all the others about two miles away. "I think I can see a tree on it too." With a way forward, Doug felt his confidence rise. "Well, my friends, let's go climb a mountain!"

CHAPTER 18

A SIMPLE CLIMB

SITTING IN A HUGE DEPRESSION, GARGANTUA WAS ACTUALLY twice the height of anything around it.

The mountain was far enough from the shore you could just barely hear the ocean. The ground around the mountain was scattered with cracks and crags. The hill's face was hard angles and steep drops difficult for a grown man to climb.

The trees adorning the crest were protected from ocean gales by a lip of stone atop the crown that hid them from view from directly below.

One side of the hill fell sharply into a small canyon, a split that worked its way back into the hill to form a shallow cave behind a small waterfall. The creek that fed the pool flowed along a gentle path that slowly wandered to the sea.

The other side of the mount was sheared away as if a giant sliced a portion of the hill with a knife. The cliff dropped down a rocky face deep enough the fall from where they stood was almost as steep as the climb above it.

"I would have loved a hill like this nearby when I was a kid," Doug said. "Though I'm not sure how I would climb it?"

"The invitation of the goddess makes the path appear to those she welcomes," Mopsus explained. "The way ahead will be made clear to you."

They all started forward, but the seer now barred the way. "Doug is the only one who may pass. Anthea is kind, but actions by man and god against her and her sisters has made her wary. That is why she prefers the company of children."

"I promise I'll be nice to her," Doug said as he moved to the base of the hill. He looked from side to side to find the best place to ascend. "It actually looks a little hard to climb. Not much to grab onto that I can see. The best choices are climbing up the cliff or following the creek. The water must come from a little spring up above, and it steps, falls, and pools a couple of times, but I don't think I can climb the water's path. The cliff side looks kinda sheer, but at least it won't be slick with moss or have algae slime to deal with."

"The goddess leads you forward. Put your trust in her," Mopsus said.

The cliff felt right. Doug made his way to the drop and searched for a handhold to start off with. He leaned around the corner and looked at the rock face. "Travertine. Lots of holes and notches to get a toehold. Seems solid enough, I guess."

There were indentations in the rock for handholds and footholds, but none of them were big enough for an adult to get his hand or foot into. A couple of fingers or a toe maybe, but not a whole hand or foot.

After several false starts, Doug took off his sandals.

Doug reached around the corner again and grabbed onto something, then swung his leg around and started again, this time, sure enough, he lost sight of his companions around the side of the hill.

Hooking fingers or toes in each divot of stone, Doug inched his way up.

Doug clung to the face of the rock. The thinnest parts of the rock crumbled and fell apart under his hands and feet. He pressed harder into the face of the cliff, trying to find holds where the rock was thicker. When that didn't work, he tried to suction onto the wall with his sweat.

The moisture from his hands and feet just made the stone he touched disintegrate all that much faster. This climb was going to be harder than he thought.

Hope I don't fall to my death.

And that was when the ledge of rock he was holding onto with both hands sheared away.

Doug fell about ten feet before he caught himself.

The sound of falling rock drew attention. Mod stuck his head around the corner and stared straight up. "How're you doing?"

"This is harder than it looks,"[1] Doug said. "How in the suffocating, dark, fetid bowels of Hades's musty closet do kids make this climb?[2] What parents would let a child try to scale this thing unsupervised?"

"Pretty much most parents would," Mod projected so the sound of his voice would reach his brother. "Especially after the kids partook of a healthy dose of sugar and participated in something overly stimulating."

"Heh." Doug grunted and moved up a couple more inches. "You're funny."

"That's why Mom and Dad like me better," Mod raised his voice again. "You know your big, poofy bed at home in Iolcus? The one with the pillows stuffed with goose down? Can I have it if you die?"

"We don't live in Iolcus anymore." Doug reminded his brother. "And you're allergic to geese."

"If your quest fails, I'm not going back to take over your yogurt job," Mod yelled back. "I'm going back home where Mom and Dad can dote on me as their only surviving child. I can always spring for some hypoallergenic pillows with my allowance."

"You're picking up new knowledge. That's good." Doug referred to Mod's use of the word *hypoallergenic* through gritted teeth as he trembled against the cliff face. "I'm glad this trip has been educational, 'cause I'm going to kill you when I get back down."

---

1. Writing this just made me think of the Man in Black climbing the Cliffs of Despair from *The Princess Bride*. Unintentional, but I like the vibe.

2. The outhouse in the land of the dead made that gas station bathroom on that deserted stretch of I-95 look like a marble and gold washroom from *Lifestyles of the Rich and Famous*. Doug came up with the swear on the spot. I apologize if you are now imagining Robin Leach perched on a toilet.

"Yeah, whatever," Mod yelled in retort before he pulled his head back around the bend. It didn't sound like he was too worried about violent retribution.

If Mod was trying to make Doug a bit angry and annoyed, he was doing a damn fine job of it.

Mod said something else, but with the distance and the blood pounding in Doug's ears, he couldn't make out what his brother had said.

I'm on my own now.

It was getting harder to hold on, and every time Doug let go with one hand or foot it felt like he wasn't going to be able to maintain his grip with only three points of contact.

A couple of things he would never say to his brother popped into his mind. *To hells with it, why not? It's not like Mod could hear him.*

"Mod is *kèpfos*," Doug giggled and could feel some of the tension that knotted his shoulders ease up.[3]

It was freeing to let go and not censor the thoughts that popped into his head.

"Mod, you *myrton, oinopìpes, moikalìs, gràson*![4] Bigger room at home if you switch and take mine, then you wouldn't even have to move the bed. Heck, why not use two rooms, one for your bedroom and the other to keep the current projects you're working on. Not like I'll be needing it."

Thinking up a curse to call Mod, Doug managed to claw ten feet higher up the cliff.

What other dirty words do I know?

"Mod is *kriòmyxos*."[5] That was a good one. He pulled himself up another foot.

Doug's right forearm locked up and he couldn't release his grip. He tried and failed to let go and jerked so hard against the rock that

---

3. Stupid. It just means stupid, okay?

4. A debauched, drunkard, two-timing woman, who stinks like a goat. None of these should be repeated in mixed company.

5. *Kriòmyxos*: stupid like a ram.

he feared he was going to lose his footing and grip with his other hand as he tried to let go with this one.

He finally managed to pull his hand free. His hand and arm were frozen in place, He shook his hand for a moment to loosen up the muscles, hoped it would be enough, then found another handhold.

Doug scraped his face against the rock wall and really let loose verbally. "Mod, you *pornoboskós* jerk employing *pórnos* and *pórnē* in a *porneîon* full of *kópros*! I always knew you were a *mētrokoîtēs*!"[6]

Oh, Mom and Dad wouldn't want me using this kind of language. His rate of ascension increased.

Doug was too tired to think of any more swears, so he repeated the one's he'd already used. Then he repeated them again.

He hoped his brother couldn't hear him. It might give Mod a complex.

The last thought actually struck a bit too close to home, and Doug suddenly felt guilty.

His hand touched the lip of stone ringing the top of the small mountain. His climb was almost finished.

He threw one arm over the edge, then the other.

As soon as he looked over the top of the mountain, he could just make out a stream with a little path running beside it. The path appeared well tended, with steps dropping down between arches and columns until the trail disappeared from his line of sight. There was probably an entrance to the stair hidden by the waterfall down below. He hadn't been able to see it because of the lighting before.

The goddess shall show you the way, Mopsus had said.

"Son of a *androkàpraina*!"[7] Doug swore as he realized what he was seeing. "The goddess either has a weird sense of humor or a poor sense of timing."

---

6. I know what I said, but I'm not going to translate it for you because my mother or one of my kids might actually read this book.

7. No, I'm not going to tell you this one either.

Too late to do anything about it now. Doug thought as he pulled himself to safety.

Chapter 19

The Apple of My Eye

Sweating and trembling, Doug pulled himself over the final lip of rock atop the cliff and tumbled gratefully onto the soft grass-capped peak. "I made it!" His brother and the others could probably figure out Doug's success based on him not falling as he flailed and screamed to his death.

I really hope I wasn't mistaken about the stairs. I really don't want to do that climb in reverse.

Doug didn't even know how he managed scaling the cliff the first time.

The climb would have been impossible if his brother hadn't poked at him the way he did.

Doug suddenly realized what Mod had done for him. The initial shock, the anger, and the shift in focus had saved Doug's life.

"Thank you, Mod." Doug whispered to the universe.

He sprawled on his back and stared at the sky. A blanket of blues and purples studded with stars thickened to chase away the last of the daylight. Doug, very content and completely exhausted, lay there and watched it happen.

A soft, sweet voice broke the evening silence. "It's pretty, isn't it?"

The speaker was a slight, elfin wisp of a woman, her fine hair and pale skin sparkled in the early starlight. Dressed in robes of gossamer that danced in the light breeze, she was perched on the edge of the drop. Her feet dangled in the ether. She didn't look at Doug, her head turned upward as she seemed to know and welcome each individual star as it winked into existence.

She was tiny and childlike, but also seemed ancient and incredibly wise. Just her being here stunned Doug for a moment, but the calm presence she radiated soon put him at ease.

Never one to easily let go of a discomfort, even in the presence of someone who might actually be some type of goddess, Doug brought forward his memory from just a little while before. He felt embarrassed for the language he'd used climbing that last bit of the cliff.

Can't take it back now.

He'd apologize later, sure she had to have heard something.

Doug propped himself on his elbows and looked at the girl for a second before returning his eyes to the sky. "It's beautiful," he admitted. "I like looking at the sky, but I don't think I've ever spent time really watching the transition from day to night before."

"It's my favorite time." She stretched out her hand to touch the substance of the dark. "Hello, Papa," the girl said.

Doug thought he felt something kind and loving respond to the nymph. For an instant, it seemed as if the night wrapped the girl up in its arms.

Doug didn't do anything to spoil the moment. It felt as if the right time to talk and interact with the vision before him would be revealed if he just waited long enough.

They sat in silence for a while as the last of the light from the horizon faded. Illumination from the awakened stars was bright enough to define and even cast faint shadows on the landscape and everything around them.

It was a good while before the girl broke the silence again. "Most of my visitors aren't patient enough to let me greet the Dark and watch the lights of Night be born. Thank you for sharing that with me." She smiled, comforting and brilliant, in the semi-dark.

To his ears it sounded as if she knew Night and Dark personally, like they weren't things or powers but people she knew and loved.

"You're the one I was supposed to come and meet, aren't you? You're the owner of the apple trees." It was a stupid question. Of course she was.

The girl smiled and tipped her head.

"I'm sorry if I intruded. Is it all right for me to stay here a moment to catch my breath?"

The slight nymph nodded that it was.

"Thank you for being such a gracious host, especially to someone who visited unannounced." Doug sat up in the grass and looked around the top of the hill, then stood and looked around the whole of the countryside. Here and there a fire twinkled in the night. Starlight traced the outlines of the hills and shore and waters surrounding them in silver. "You have a wonderful home. A home anyone would envy. This has got to be one of the greatest views in all of Greece."

"Oh, it's nothing special." She shied away from the compliment.

Doug was sure he could see a blush in the colors that radiated from her face. He smiled and bowed slightly. "I'm Doug."

"Anthea." She replied with a curtsy after departing whatever had supported her in the air. Maybe there hadn't been anything holding her over the edge of the drop, she had to be the daughter of a god or goddess after all.

"Would you like an apple?" she asked.

"I'd love one," Doug replied. "It's what I came for."

"I know," Anthea said. "I can see things that are going to happen. Or I remember them? In any case I know what is to be. I get that from Papa Erebus;[1] he could see things that would be, and I'm a bit like him. I knew you were going to visit and why." She walked in among the small trees, pressing to the center of the grove atop the hill as Doug followed close behind. "You're the first adult to visit me in what seems forever," she admitted. "I knew you were coming but wasn't sure you would behave."

---

1. Erebus: one of the five oldest beings in existence. The personification of darkness. People think him cold and uncaring because of their perception of his nature. They couldn't be more incorrect. He is kind, patient, and a loving father. He loves warm hugs and having babies fall asleep in his lap. He also loves making the sleeping babies' limp little arms and legs bounce and dance along with music. He can't stop himself from doing it. He thinks it's so cute it makes him want to burst.

"I'm sorry if I made you uncomfortable," Doug said. "And I apologize for the language I used earlier."

"Language used is not as important as the spirit it is used in," she said. "I saw your fears and how you fought against them. Your heart is kind, and the words are not as important as the love that drives you forward."

Doug stopped short, unaware that something so small and innocent looking could be so deeply philosophical.

The girl beckoned him to continue following. "Your heart is good, Doug of Iolcus, and I am very comfortable around you," she explained. "Papa said he would test you to see if you were okay. That's why he hid the gate and stair, to see if you were smart and brave enough to climb up the hard way. Papa hides the gate from people he doesn't like." Then she giggled. "It was funny listening to you and your brother talk to each other."

"I'm glad we could amuse." Doug shook his head in wonder, not realizing he'd passed a test just getting here. "We love each other, and I hope it shows."

"I have lots and lots of brothers and sisters. Sometimes I get to see them and play with them." She kicked her bare feet through the grass. "You and your brother love each other very much. Anyone with a sibling could see that."

Doug couldn't help but grin. "People don't always get me and Mod. I'm glad you understand."

The night actually grew brighter as they walked into the grove. The nimbus of light around the girl grew and the trees began to emit light as well.

Doug passed tree after tree, and yet it seemed they'd barely penetrated the edge of the treeline. "How many trees do you have?"

"Lots," Anthea responded. "Lots and lots and lots. Papa gave me the first one. He showed me how to make them. I made the other ones myself."

"You are very good at making trees," Doug said to her.

She giggled and blushed so hard you could see the color in her cheeks even if you walked behind her.

She talked and sounded like a child, but there was something ancient and powerful about her. It made Doug wonder. "Anthea, how old are you?"[2]

"I don't really know," she said as they finally reached the grand tree in the center of the orchard.

The trunk was wider and thicker than any of the huts down on the beach. The canopy spread before and behind them wider than any tree Doug had ever seen.

She turned to face Doug so she could better answer his question. "Time is funny after too long. I sometimes don't know if I'm seeing the future or remembering the past. I do know I am Papa's first baby. He gave me my mountain as a nursery and play place. It was much taller before it began walking to the sea."

She reached up into the branches and a handful of small, perfect fruit rushed to fill her hand. "Papa made this for me, my special tree. It always has fruit for me, so juicy, and crisp, and sweet. I know there are other apples now, but mine are still the best."

"I have no doubt," Doug said. There couldn't be anything else like Anthea, so it just stood to reason nothing else like her apples could exist either.

She reached out a hand to Doug and enticed him to take a few.

They were heavier than he expected. He pulled his cupped hands closer so he could see them better. Small and perfect of shape, skin such a dark red they were almost black. A mottling of white sparkled on the surface of the fruit. The white spots winked and flashed like stars in the night sky.

Doug held the apples close to his heart. He felt he was extremely

2. Someone once asked Hera this same question. It was an innocent enough inquiry, though poorly timed and executed. The questioner currently resides in the Fields of Punishment where an attempt to push an eggroll up a waterfall with their right nostril is and will continue to be underway.

privileged to participate in what must be an ancient and holy ritual. "I'm sure I'll never see an apple like this again. Thank you so much."

She looked at him with eyes innocent, far-seeing, and wise, as if she knew volumes more than she was able to tell. "You are very welcome."

There was the sound of a *fizz, pop*! somewhere down below, followed by Mod as he screeched, "Son of a motherless goat! It was in my pocket!"

"Your brother is in the stairwell with the others. He's fine, you know," Anthea said. "The sparkly shooting star only spooked him."

"I'm glad he's not hurt." Doug nodded his thanks to Anthea for letting him know. *Serves you right, Bro.*

Anthea grinned and looked at Doug. "He does deserve it, a little, I guess."

Doug laughed out loud, not shocked at all to have his private thoughts open and clear to Anthea. "I like you, Anthea. I hope we can become good friends."

Anthea smiled because she knew what Doug had said was true. "I'd like that."

Chapter 20

Nyxy Business

Doug was told by Anthea that she and her father invited all in his group to rest that night in the soft grasses that covered the ground between the trees atop Gargantua.

The hidden stair once revealed was very easy to climb—the passage obscured again once all were safely on the path.

Doug watched Anthea greet each member of his group individually and by name as they emerged at the top of the stair. He didn't know how she knew their names, but it didn't surprise him that she did. She talked with each of them briefly. He knew she somehow divined something special and heartfelt from every member of the small band, and shared her own heart and hopes in turn.

Once everyone was made welcome, the nymph retreated into her grove.

After she was gone, Doug could feel the presence of her father, Erebus.

Erebus placed a hand on Doug's shoulder. Once connected physically by the touch, the god's deep and ancient voice rumbled softly in Doug's head.

"Rest. I watch over you and your band. The dark and the night are mine, and I have power over all that are within them."

Doug looked around. No one else looked like they could hear the god. Unseen, unheard, but omnipresent, Erebus promised to watch over Doug and his crew just as Erebus would his own daughter. They would be safe until the moment Helios raised his golden brow above the eastern horizon.

"Thank you." Doug folded his hands over his chest and gave a little bow.

None of the men or women could remember a night when they'd slept more soundly.

The hosts atop the mountain were absent in the morning, but their charges to the visitors were not. Provisions were at the top of the stair for everyone in the group. Anthea even had little notes written to them individually placed atop each pack.

Doug's note brought a smile to his face. After he thought on it for a moment he knelt by his sack of provisions and started rooting around. He took one of the apples Anthea had given him and cut it into small slices before putting it between two plates he pressed together. Doug was raised to respect the gifts of the gods, and part of that meant giving back to them a portion of what had been given.

As Doug busied himself with the offering, he half watched the others in the crew to see how rested and ready they were for the day's travels.

Nine picked up his small scrap of linen and read the inscription. A small tear welled in the corner of his eye. "That is so sweet. It's nice to hear things like this once in a while."

"Are you crying?" his brother Four teased.

Nine quickly rubbed the tear away on the back of his sleeve. "Must be a malfunctioning tear duct from all those reset thumpings One is so eager to give."

Mopsus shook his head in gentle reprimand of Four as he read his own note. "Nine, you go right ahead and ignore your callous brother. Feeling loved by someone who you've only just met is a rare and precious thing. It should be cherished, not mocked."

"Her note to me was nice too," Four admitted a bit defensively. "I'm just not sure how to react to things like that."

Doug's odd little family seemed to be doing just fine. "I hope this is a good reaction." All the attention of the others turned to him as Doug angled the plates in his hands on their side and continued to press them together. A steady trickle of apple juice spilled into a strategically placed cup.

"You're squashing one of the apples?" One was aghast.

"Shush." Doug drained the last drops into the cup. He poured a bit of wine in with the apple cider until the small cup was brimming.

Doug rose carefully to his feet so he wouldn't spill anything. He held the cider in front of him and bowed his head. "Beautiful and kind Anthea, you've welcomed us to your home, given us rest and strength and friendship. You've given us what we need to advance closer to the goal we have before us. We have little to give to repay our debt to you. Please accept what we can give as a token of our thanks."

He walked to the fore of the grove and poured a small measure of cider at the base of all of the smallest of the trees.

As Doug walked around the trees, the light atop Gargantua began to dim, or rather, the shadows began to spread and grow until there wasn't as much room for the light. Transfixed on Doug and the grove, none of the others noticed.

"Why just the little trees?" One whispered to Mod.

"The big ones don't need it," Mod replied.

"By giving the offering to the small, he sows hope that they will one day grow to be as old and wise and grand as those that came before." Mopsus nodded his approval. "Well done, Doug. A very honorable offering."

Doug placed the final drops from the cup on the roots of a sapling. Each of the trees shimmered and grew ever so slightly.

"I'd say that was a sign of the offering being accepted," Mopsus said.

"Did anyone else notice the lights?" Four mentioned as the darkness descended around them.

Doug could feel the darkness take hold of him and could see the others being picked up as well, even Mopsus. Being picked up should have been terrifying, but it wasn't. *This is probably what it feels like when Erebus hugs his daughter Anthea tight,* Doug thought. It was a very comforting feeling.

"It would seem the gods have seen fit to have me continue accompanying you," Mopsus said.

"Glad to have you with us," Doug said in the dim light while they hung in the air.

They were all suspended weirdly weightless for some time before they were lowered gently down.

Doug could feel smooth wooden planking under his feet. The darkness pulled away and Doug's group, supplies and all, found themselves on a very fine boat speeding through the midst of the Aegean.

The sail of the ship was full of a gentle breeze. Oars were stowed against the railings in case the breeze failed. The ship seemed to know where it was headed.

"That was unexpected. I think Erebus has decided to aid us in our quest." Doug still had the cider cup in his hand. He tipped the cup at a particularly dark shadow under a cloud. "Thanks, buddy."

Mopsus didn't look that stable on the water. "A fine being to have on our side, to be sure." The seer acknowledged the god's help but squirmed as Doug spoke about it. "I don't know that I would call the embodiment of darkness 'Buddy.' I'm not sure Erebus would be okay with that."[1]

---

1. Erebus is totally okay with that.

CHAPTER 21

A SLIGHT FEAR OF WATER

MOD DROPPED TO HIS HANDS AND KNEES AND STARTED SHAKING in the middle of the deck. It was a bit of a shock to be plopped down in the middle of the ocean without an adjustment period, especially with his fears and phobias.

Doug rushed to his side. "Are you okay?" He looked really worried. "Is there anything I can do?"

"Don't have a bit of an isthmus or a jetty I can stand on, do you?" Mod teased as he clung to the deck for all he was worth. "On the beach, I felt as if I'd made some real progress. I thought I was ready to get on a boat, but I kinda expected to work up to it, you know?"

Mod struggled to raise his head high enough to see over the bulwark. As soon as he saw the ocean stretched all around them, he knew it was a mistake.

Mod dropped back to the deck.

"One, turn the ship to the nearest bit of land you can see," Doug ordered.

"Belay that order!" Mod choked out a harsh laugh. "Belay, Doug, nautical term. See? I'll be a salty old dog humping Poseidon's leg in no time," he joked through clenched teeth.

"Mod, what can I do?" Doug pleaded.

Mod looked over at his brother, attempted a smile, then focused hard on the pine boards beneath his hands. "I know you want to help, but I just have to work through this."

Mod paused, then managed to smirk at the deck. "Do you even know where we're going?"

His brother blinked hard. "With the apples and Anthea, Erebus and the ship I just kinda forgot about it," Doug admitted. "I assume Erebus must know because he put us on this ship."

"Now would probably be a good time to find out. Wouldn't want to spring a surprise on anybody," Mod said, bitter irony tinted his words. "Right pocket. I'd grab the device and pull out the scroll for you, but I'm kinda busy clinging to the vessel for dear life."

Doug looked unsure. He hesitated until Mod insisted.

"It'll be a distraction for my brain. That's got to be good, right?"

Doug nodded and took the device from Mod's pocket. The scroll was sitting in the message slot. "We're heading to Naxos to deal with a rogue flock of chickens."

"Ha!" Mod sounded a bit unhinged in his own ears. "At least I know we aren't supposed to be bobbing in the ocean forever."

It had been a long time since Mod had seen that intense look of concern on Doug's face.

"We have a destination. Knowing where we're going helps." Now Mod was trying to comfort Doug. Mod tried to rise again, only to just as quickly fall back to his hands and knees.

"You're really worrying me, Mod." Doug was right down on the deck beside him.

"Oh, I'm fine. Just admiring the joinery of the decking here in the middle of the boat," Mod said. His trembling hand took strength from the firmness of the pine planking beneath it. "This section appears to be particularly well made."

Mod could see Doug was still at a loss as to how to help him when Three sidled up beside him. "I've got this," she said.

Doug didn't look so sure, but Mod nodded that it would be okay.

"Look into my eyes," Three said to Mod.

Mod did.

Three was so sure and calm that a bit of it transferred to him.

Three reached out a hand, her fingers barely contacted Mod's trembling hand. After a quiet minute she had Mod's hand in hers, then got him up on his feet, then actually walked around with him a bit, her arm supporting him around the waist.

I'm standing on a boat in the middle of the ocean.

Three was so gentle in the way she handled him that Mod hadn't even realized she wasn't holding him up anymore.

"Thank you," he said to Three.

She took a step back, letting him stand on his own.

Doug looked at her, wide eyed and amazed. "I don't know how you did that, but I'm grateful that you did."

"Middle child," Three said. "We excel in supporting roles."

Mod gave Three another quiet *thank you* before he looked over at his brother. "I'm okay. Just was a bit of a shock is all."

"I've got this." Three repeated to Doug. She continued to stand close to Mod. "I'll be right here if he needs me."

Doug didn't argue.

The other members of the crew familiarized themselves with the vessel. Five leaned over the back of the boat, Six holding onto him so he wouldn't topple over the edge, so he could read the boat's name.

Mod turned a little bit green as he watched someone willingly go over the side of the vessel.

"*Nyxy Business.*" Five looked to the others after Six had pulled him back on board. "I don't get it."

"Wait until Florida," Mopsus said. "*Nyxy Business* is tame and coherent compared to what some of those morons will name their vessels."

Mod could see Doug kept looking at him just to make sure he was okay. Doug was like that, a hovering protector. *It must be hard for someone else to help while you have to stand back and let them?* The thought was a bit deeper and more poignant than Mod had expected, and he felt he understood his brother a little better because of it.

Now Three had Mod comfortable enough he could inch over to the side of the boat and look at the water rushing past. *I'm not freaking out.*

Doug and the others were still discussing the name of the boat, though Mod had missed some of the conversation.

"I think the name of the boat is sweet," Doug said. "Erebus named it after his wife."

Mod was stable enough now he could take it all in. The sea was calm, a gentle breeze blew the boat carrying the group quickly and surely on their way to the island of Naxos. Their destination rapidly approached.

It was amazing how quickly they'd all taken to the sea after being taken to the sea.

The Number Siblings had a natural rhythm when it came to rowing. They didn't need to row right now, with the winds and the sail doing all the work, but it didn't hurt to practice an unknown skill while the seas were calm. Five and Six worked as if they were one being and took up positions on either side of the boat. One and Nine were opposites of each other but that only made their rowing that much more in sync, as if one could only give their best on the left, while the other excelled on the right.

Four stood at the rudder, stout and stable as he adjusted the way forward true and steady.

Three eventually worked Mod all the way around the ship to the rudder.

"Could we try something?" Three asked her brother.

Four stepped aside as if he anticipated what she was going to do. "Of course."

Three took Mod's hand again and placed it upon the rudder. "I think you'll do well with this. Your mind is sharp and clever. You have the intelligence to be an excellent navigator."

"This will keep your mind occupied so you don't have time to freak out about being on the water" is what she really means to say, Mod thought.

Three squeezed his fingers again like she wanted to reassure him, then she took her hand away and left him standing by himself.

Having something to hold onto stabilized Mod on the deck and grounded him considerably. He realized he could read the currents and rivers and flows of everything in ways that were almost supernatural. Three might have meant putting him at the rudder as a distraction, but it worked. As soon as Mod directed the path of the craft his fear of water disappeared, or at least was pushed down enough for him to deal, as long as he didn't look at the water right behind him.

"I don't know how to thank you," Mod said to Three.

The mechanical woman looked pleased to have helped. "I'll be nearby if you need me." She then moved forward to the midships and took up position on one of the oars opposite her brother Four.

He looked at her a while, staring at her back as she pushed and pulled on the oar, unsure why she had helped him or what he was feeling, and he couldn't figure any of it out.

Confusion was better than fear, so he let his musings stay unanswered.

Mod checked out the position of the sun, looked at the visible land around them and figured out where they were from the memory of the map he pulled up in his head. It felt good to have a purpose. "Making excellent time. We actually should arrive at Naxos in about an hour."

"Erebus saved us a couple of days travel." Mopsus was clearly pleased. "And this boat moves far faster than that smelly little fish hauler I used to get to Hermione."

"According to the map, we swing wide around the isle of Paros and approach Naxos from the west side." Doug studied the instructions. "The chickens are running rampant all over that coast, so the supplicants can't even land their boats in an attempt to visit Demeter's temple."

"But they're just chickens? How bad can it really be?" One asked as they rounded the tip of Paros and Naxos came into view.

Fires burned up and down the coastline of Naxos. The visible docks and ports were in ruins.

"I stand corrected," One said as she gaped.

CHAPTER 22

REFUGE ON THE SEA

"Mopsus?" Doug asked for a bit of advice before he engaged in whatever you call a battle between mankind and the fowls that ran rampant on Naxos.

The seer shook his head. "No word from the gods on how to proceed. I'm at a loss."

Mod pointed to a bunch of fishing boats lashed together into a series of floating islands further south.

Doug felt that was a good place to start. He nodded for his brother to take them there. "Let's go ask the locals."

Mod steered in their direction.

The Mechanical Siblings stowed the oars as the crew pulled along one of the larger groupings of boats and threw out the anchor.

"Hello? How's everything going?" Doug called to the group of despondent people staring blankly at the turmoil ashore.

One of the men brightened as he saw them. "Hello, gentle travelers. Life is all just peachy. Thanks for asking."

"Peachy?" Doug asked.

"A peach is a wonderful fruit, firm and juicy," Mopsus explained. "Alexander the Great will bring some back to cultivate in mainland Greece in a few hundred years or so, though it appears the people of Naxos are already familiar with the fruit. The phrase the man just uttered can be meant to be taken as 'doing fine.'"

"So, you're doing okay then?" Doug asked the smiling man, certain that *peachy* was not the case.

The smile on the man's face grew more frenetic as the strain added tics and spasms to his expression. "Could be a bit better."

"Why are you all here in the middle of the water?" Doug asked as he stared at the shore. It was a pretty stupid question, now he thought of it. The chaos inland looked incredibly inhospitable.

A filthy woman sitting in the bottom of one boat had her eyes go wide with horrifying memories. "Roosters," she laughed and began to cry. "Buck*caw*!"

A mother with two small children reached out to comfort the sobbing woman. The small motion was enough the two toddlers thought their mother was attempting to leave them. Both of the children started to wail.

"It started with a gate," the smiling man talked over the sobs filling the air. "Someone said, 'Those guys by Demeter's temple sure rake in the dough with licensing and merchandising.'"

"Someone said," a wailing beggar agreed.

"Someone said, 'We could build our own temple. Get a piece of the action.'"

"Someone said." The wailing beggar wrapped his arms around his legs and curled into a ball, rocking back and forth.

"We built a gate! A gate with no door," the filthy woman cried.

"It was never supposed to open, but it did," the mother of the toddlers sobbed.

"We opened a door to the coup of Tartarus," another voice trembled.

"Buck*caw*!"

"So, I'm not understanding," Six said, looking at his twin who shook his head that he didn't understand either. "You built a gate and suddenly there are roosters everywhere?"

"Buck*caw*! Buck*caw*!"

"It was a small gate.[1] We had a modest budget for the temple. Big things from Hades couldn't pass through when it opened."

"We're dealing with *undead* roosters?" Doug asked.

The still smiling man shifted his teeth together so hard you could hear them grind from a dozen paces away. "There's the occasional duck or pheasant, but it's mostly the chickens."

"The poultry of Hell!"

"Grab an ax. Hack, hack, and the rooster is back!" The sobbing woman laughed hysterically. "Roast them, broil them, chop them into nuggets and they pop right up and start strutting around on your plate." Her laughter broke away in a staccato of chokes and sobs.

"I'm disturbed. This is disturbing." Nine pointed at the woman going crazy. "Is this kind of reaction normal?"

"I've experienced it before, from time to time," Mod said. "It doesn't ever go away, you just learn how to deal with it. Sometimes."

Doug knew Mod referred to the loss of his mother from when the pirates attacked years ago. He was impressed his brother could deal with the uncertain and debilitating mix of emotions the trauma brought on and knew because of what he'd gone through, Mod would understand any of these people better than he would.

Doug had never gone through any great type of loss, but he could see these people were frightened. He'd do his best to help and shield anyone feeling this kind of pain if he could. This wasn't just about finishing a task right anymore; it was about helping these people get back their lives.

Doug turned to the smiling man and his entourage. "I don't know how to take care of this, but I will. I'm sorry for what you and your people have had to go through."

"You're actually here to help us?" The smiling man's voice

---

1. The gate built for Apollo's Temple on Naxos is huge, comprised of four parts, each weighing about twenty tons apiece. The gate constructed by this band of locals of Naxos for the as yet unspecified god was smaller. Much smaller. Think of the Stonehenge replica from *This is Spinal Tap*.

faltered as hope threatened, only to quickly be dismissed. "But we made the gate. This is punishment for our greed."

"Some actions will always have consequences, but trying to build a better life for yourself by increasing tourism without hurting anyone doesn't seem to be worthy of a god-vetted demon rooster invasion," Doug said. "I don't think this is right, and I will try to fix it."

"We'll do everything we can." Mod backed up his brother.

Doug nodded it was true. A woman locked eyes with him. She seemed to expect him to look away, but he didn't.

Slowly, a sense of calm started to overtake the refugees.

They didn't know who the men on the fine boat were. It didn't matter.

The tasks given to Doug had been things with no impact up 'til now. As Doug looked over the people forced to survive on boats, their homes burning and their lives in ruins, he burned too. He needed to help them, so much he couldn't turn away. He had no idea how he would save these people's homes or rid the island of the threat it faced, but this would be a worthy quest.

The fiery look of determination in Doug's eyes let the refugees know that he was the type of leader and his were the type of people who did what they said they would.

CHAPTER 23

PURGATORY'S PURLOINED POULTRY

"HADES!" ZEUS BELLOWED.

"Yo." Hades skulked in and flipped his hair out of his face. He looked paler than usual, and it was a pretty fair bet he was wearing eyeliner.[1] "What up, bra?"

"Oh, lord." Hera covered her eyes with both hands. "I thought it was just a phase he was going through because he was dating younger women, but it's gotten worse." She dropped her hands and jabbed Zeus in the ribs. She gave a harsh whisper only Zeus could hear. "Do something about this."

"I'll deal with it later, dear," Zeus hissed back. "I have more important things to deal with right now."

"This is pretty important." She gestured at their oldest brother.[2] "The black paint on the nails? And does he have gauges in his ears?"

Zeus ignored her. "Hades, what in the hells is going on at Naxos?"

"Nothing's going on in Naxos, bro." Hades seemed to have no idea anything was amiss.

"Damned poultry walking the streets," Zeus hinted.

"A chicken can walk wherever it wants." Hades looked bored. "You called me up here to talk about rouge pullets strolling through the marketplace? I got stuff to do, man."

---

1. Hades was dressed and made up like a rejected extra in a Swedish Death Metal video.

2. Seriously. He's outfitting himself very weirdly. Hades is currently dressed as if he were auditioning for a spot in a biopic about the Cure or Nine Inch Nails.

"Damned chickens," Zeus reiterated and went on to explain. "Roosters that have crossed over. The poultry of purgatory. Birds that should be scratching dirt off the Elysium fields are now cawing good morning to Helios as he drives the chariot of the sun across the sky."

Now Hades looked nervous. He tried to change the subject. "I'd heard a rumor that Helios died." He let his attempt at a segue hang until Hera glared at him to continue. "I didn't believe it. If he'd kicked it, I'd be the first to know."

"Flaming undead cocks are running rampant through the towns of Naxos, you moron,"[3] Zeus fumed.

"Really?" Hades looked shocked.

"You just dropped a bit of your ill-conceived young-and-hip facade," Hera said.

"Um, yeah. Sorry about that." His brows knit in concentration. "I'm trying to focus on the animals in the afterlife. Poultry aren't intelligent enough to be bothered by the wards keeping smarter animals in death, but they usually don't wander too far. I guess one or two birds may have flown the coop. They're kinda hard to count sometimes."

"Try hundreds," Zeus said.

"Hundreds?" Hades gaped. "There's no way—I mean, I would have noticed." His head drooped, and he started hitting his forehead with the flat of his hand. "Stupid, stupid, stupid."

Hades was all business again. "Chickens normally make a big enough racket that I just listen to the whole of the afterlife to track where they're at and how many are there. But Persephone, she kinda likes this really loud music that focuses on dissonance and anger.[4]

---

3. The actual term for full grown males in the *Gallus gallus domesticus* family. You were possibly thinking of how the word is used in the modern-day vernacular? If so, get your mind out of the gutter. Also, Flaming Undead Cocks would make an excellent name for a Swedish Death Metal band.

4. Noise music, focusing on dissonance and shock, has been around since the very beginning. Persephone's current favorite band sounds very much like a modern Tuvan throat singing band named the Hu Band. Think Mongol warriors driving Harleys, wearing leather, vocalizing like non-terrestrial entities to a rhythmic and oddly

Ever heard of the term noise music? It's kinda like that, but it's not. Anyhow. I've been going to concerts with her."

"And?" Zeus urged.

"Hearing loss," Hades admitted sheepishly. "I should have worn earplugs, but I didn't want to seem like a square in front of Persephone and her friends."

"Then whatever you do, don't say the word 'square' in front of Persephone or her friends." Zeus sometimes had a hard time believing his brother could be so clueless. "Undead capons and cockerels?"

"Uh, I can't do much while they're strutting around topside," Hades admitted. "But I can see if I can find the hole to plug it to keep any other birds from popping up."

"I've got a man I'm watching at Naxos now." Zeus hoped Doug and company were up for the challenge. "I'll try to direct him in ways to send the chickens to their final reward." Zeus had no idea what those ways might be. He tried the connection to Mopsus and got nothing but fuzz and static. The seer must currently be tuned into something else or busy on another line.

"I just don't get it," Hades said. "It takes extraordinary measures for any being to cross the threshold from death back into life. Breaching the wards by one soul takes power of a magnitude that even my deaf ears should have perked up to. Hundreds of roosters? Small, I know, but it should have set off alarms from Elysium to Tartarus. It shouldn't have happened without me knowing it."

Zeus had a thought come to mind but wanted to confirm his suspicions. "Could I have done it?"

Hades was confused. "Wait. What?"

Blood drained from Hades's face. He already took pallid and wan

---

compelling multi-car pileup and repeating, "Thank you so much! You are awesome!" at the end of every song. Persephone loved the last concert. Hades liked it well enough, but he thought the music was so loud that all the nuance of the throat singing was missing, and it took a week after the concert for his heart to return to a normal sinus rhythm.

to new depths, especially with the goth makeup. Panicked, his complexion became the envy of Charon. He looked as if he might start to hyperventilate at any moment. "Did you do this? Is this some kind of test? I'm not due for a performance review for a while."

Zeus knew why that thought was worrisome to his brother. Performance reviews in the time of the Greek gods could result in some kind of demotion. A really bad review often resulted in shackles, relocation to the bowels or far reaches of the earth, and something eating your liver on a daily basis.[5] "I didn't do this, and I'm not testing you," Zeus dismissed the notion and clarified. "Could someone with the power of a god have done this?"

"Oh, you're trying to narrow down the culprit?" Hades let out a sigh of relief as Zeus nodded. "It would almost certainly have to be a god. A mortal couldn't pull it off without some major intervention from deity, but who? You could have done it, obviously. Me, I mean, my realm, isn't it? If I couldn't work something that simple, it would be time to think of retirement. Our brothers or sisters could have made it work, or their kids. Any of the notable gods, really."

Something clicked into place in Zeus's mind at the mention of "retirement." He walked over and lovingly brushed the hair out of Hades's eyes so he could see him better. "Thank you for your insight, brother. Watch your charges carefully. Please inform me if you notice anything else amiss."

"I'm sorry I got distracted. I'll let you know if anything odd or unusual happens." Hades bowed at the waist and took his leave.

Hera said something to Zeus, but he didn't catch what it was. He was deep in thought—about what he wasn't yet sure.

Hera had seen the look on his face before. "I know not what this is about, but you are wise and the answer you seek will come to you, my love." Hera ruffled his hair with her fingers and kissed him lightly

5. For an example, just look at Prometheus. The guy was only being helpful, but that's what you get when you fight against the current administration.

on the crown of his head. "By your leave, my lord." And she was gone.

"Retirement." Zeus pulled his finger absently across his mustache as he pondered. He tried to find a reason that word resonated with him other than the obvious. Try as he might, no other explanation revealed itself. "Seems like I should talk to a woman about some thread."

Chapter 24

An Island Full of Cocks

"The leader of the refugees said the gate is about three quarters of a mile inland from that point." Doug pointed out a small spire of rock and had Mod steer for the beach just to the west of it. The quicker they accomplished the goal, the sooner the people on the boats could return to their lives on the ruined island.

The Automatons pulled hard against the oars, pushing the ship as fast as they could along the top of the water.

The beach was the closest of all the open coastline. Doug figured beaching the vessel was the quickest way to avoid getting attacked immediately by the rogue fowl prowling the waterfront.

One and her brothers and sister scanned the shore with augmented eyes.

"The cocks are massing in groups to each side of our projected landing spot,"[1] One reported. "I think they're drawn to the motion and sounds of the boat. Many of the roosters I can see appear to be or have recently been on fire."

The island drew close. The automatons stashed their oars and braced themselves.

"Hold on to something!" Doug yelled. "This landing is going to be rough!"

The ship hammered into the beach, nose ram plowing a deep and

---

1. I had a running joke censoring the word "Cocks" and any other fowl names here. My editor didn't think it was funny. I took the joke out. Mostly because I know Kelly is just looking out for me, but partially because the woman just plain scares me.

nasty gash a dozen paces up beyond the waterline. One and Four were flung from the bow into the mass of roiling poultry swarming below. Four, despite his considerable strength, was faltering under the sheer weight of innumerable cocks. One rallied to her brother, adding her strength to his, and they flung the offending pile of roosters aside. One's reset club appeared in one hand and a piece of cast iron cookware appeared in the other.[2] The poultry gathered and charged, only to be thrown back, once, twice, and even a third time.

Doug and the others scrambled down from the boat and formed a defensive wedge right behind One. Mopsus dodged off to the left and pulled a slightly worse for wear Four into the relative safety of the group.

"To the gate." Doug rallied the crew, using oars taken from the boat they batted the pullets to the left and the cockerels to the right. The birds were brutal, but the reach of the crew with their wooden weapons were more than the poultry could overcome. Gradually the wave of attack from the most dangerous game birds began to falter, and the small band of heroes were able to advance.

The reach of the oars was long yet limiting. Some of the pullets dodged under the striking range of the oars to attack with beak and spur in close quarters.

"Out with the frying pans!" One bellowed as cookware materialized in all of her siblings' hands. "And into the fryers!" Fully armed, the automatons left a battalion of pancake shaped chicken patties in their wake.

The cocks were retreating in droves. Doug and his crew clearly outmatched the berserker rage of the unruly feathered mob.

"We're through the worst of it now," Four said. He flipped his pan in the air and caught it by the handle with a flourish. "The gate can't be far now."

---

2. Reset club. Frying pan. These tools, implements, and more are readily accessible within each of the automatons. The manufactured siblings are all multitools. Walking, talking, Swiss Army Knives, if you will.

"Do not let down your guard." Mopsus stumbled, one hand clamped hard on his temples and the other arm raised to point the way before them. "You've been fighting entities that have rudimentary mental capacity. Brains the size of a pea aren't noted for complex battle strategy. The roosters operate on base, animalistic urges. They're not in control. Another mind is directing the birds, a mind far more devious, cunning, and crafty." Mopsus's finger zeroed in as a thin shadow of a man appeared in the swirls of smoke that blocked their way.

"You didn't mention 'vindictive' in your description of me." A wicked, snaggle-tooth grin split the face of the thin, haggard man.

"Heinous?" Doug and Mod said in shocked unison.

"Hello, boys!" Heinous took a few steps forward. "Been a while, hasn't it?"

"I know not who you are, varlet." Three angled her avian-ichor encrusted cookware toward the man. "You are one and powerless against a force such as we."

"As bowel liquifying as you perceive that threat to be, I would be stupid to ignore it if I were truly alone." The man placed two fingers between his lips and loosed a piercing, painful whistle. Somewhere behind him in the smog there was an ominous sound as more than a thousand chickens started marching in unison.

"They've formed ranks." Three slowly let her pan drop to her side. "Forty birds abreast with columns ten birds deep."

"Four full phalanxes of four hundred birds apiece to the forefront, with two full phalanxes held in reserve," the old man cackled.

"Dude," Mod gasped, stupefied. "You have *got* to get another hobby."

"This is my hobby, my passion, and my life!" Heinous bellowed.

"The cocks in the forefront appear to be dressed in full armor." Three unconsciously took a step back until she was shoulder to shoulder with the others.

"Seriously?" Doug walked in front of everyone to talk to Heinous directly. "You got banned from running cock fights back home because you were strapping blades to the spurs of your birds and doping the feed of the opponents' fighters. There wasn't any contest involved, you were just orchestrating a slaughter."

"I wanted to win." The man sneered as the first ranks of pullets fell in behind him.

"To win by cheating." Doug took another step toward Heinous. "You took an already barbaric sport that served no purpose and made it more bloody and dangerous. For what?"

"I won." Heinous growled and took a step closer to Doug.

"Didn't you care about your cocks?" Doug asked. "They gave their all for you."

"And now they have the opportunity to do so again. And again. And again. You have to love undead minions that die and come back for more." Heinous grinned. "Because they will, for me."

Many of the birds looked far worse for wear. The injured or burned or smashed still moved forward on broken, baked, and twisted limbs at their master's behest. A rooster with a broken neck eyed Doug from a head pointing downward while a nearly severed foot scratched for purchase between its legs.

Apparently death had no hold on them, but they weren't healing from the damage done either.

Off to the side, a pullet saw an unlucky grub scrambling to get out of the way of the approaching army. The pullet broke ranks and snatched up the unfortunate larva in its beak. The group of birds nearest to him noticed he had something and immediately tried to steal it from him.

"*Back in line*!" Heinous bellowed. The birds all froze and returned to their position. The one with the grub swallowed the unfortunate bug with a quick series of bobs of the head.

"Huh." It all dropped into place for Doug. He surveyed the ranks of cocks who stood at attention and waited for their master's command. "Pea-sized brains. Basic animalistic desires." He looked up at Heinous and smirked. "Since you're certain about being able to send us to the underworld with your armored army of the unplucked, would you mind granting me a small favor?"

Heinous hesitated for a moment while he considered. "I must say, I'm intrigued." He waved dismissively at the thought. "But not enough to let you live longer than you have to."

"I expected as much. No matter." Doug turned to his brother. "Can you open a portal to Dad's feed barn?"

Mod pulled the gizmo out of his pocket and twisted a few dials. He threw the control box on the ground and fired it up. "Right next to the silos."

Heinous stared transfixed on the portal. "How odd. I never would have assumed there could be two." Heinous shook his head. "It doesn't matter. All ranks! Attack!"

"Five. Six. Come with me! You others, hold the line here as long as you can. Fall back through the portal if we need to retreat." Doug leaped to the door. He winked at the cock master right before he passed the threshold. "Be right back."

The chickens swarmed the area. The remaining crew managed to hold them back just far enough for there to still be a landing outside the portal.

Doug reappeared a few seconds later, a heavy bag over his shoulder. The automatons came through right after, a giant clay pot carried by each.

The battle, once so ferocious, halted at the unknown addition balanced on the cocked arm of the youth.

A hush fell over the battlefield.

Heinous shook, so angry he was unable to even speak.

"Here, chick chick chick." Doug threw a handful of grain onto the ground.

The front ranks of the rooster army vibrated as the thought of the scratch registered in all of their heads. A low murmur of clucks and trills ran through those closest to the grain.[3]

---

3. Translated from zombie avian: "Grains. Graaiinnnsss. Graaiiinnnssss!"

Heinous tried to intimidate those right around him. He screamed commands and went so far as to kick and strike out at those nearest.

Instead of scaring the ranks into submission, his actions had the opposite effect.

Once the cocks detected movement, they feared the other birds headed toward dinner without them. Discipline broke down, and Heinous was buried beneath a massive wave of chickens. He fought against the rush, appearing above the roosters time and again, only to be reburied or pushed aside by the unrelenting flow of fowl.

There was no way to even get to the man now. The best Doug could hope for was to lure the poultry horde away and see if Heinous survived.

Doug sidestepped the wave. He threw handful after handful of grain to the starving poultry as he indicated for the others to follow him. He gave the animals a wide berth and tossed another fistful of grain to the side every time the tide of poultry surged too close. "Heinous turned this direction before we lost sight of him. The gate has to be this way."

They walked inland for another quarter of a mile. Doug had them stop occasionally to replenish the bag's contents from the large containers being carried by the automatons. The army of poultry followed close behind, but the violent edge was taken off the birds as they depleted the provisions.

Doug happened across the gate just as Five and Six were just about to completely empty the second container.

The gate perfectly framed a portal just like Mod's.

"Isn't that an airhole to another place just like yours, Master Modifixeus?" Four asked.

"Not quite. This portal is smaller. And just call me Mod." Mod corrected as he knelt beside the gate and started to fiddle with the control box.

Doug knelt down beside him, a bit unnerved.

"The layout and controls are similar enough for me to operate it," Mod said. "Aside from the size difference, this is set for one way transport. The birds could walk through from Hades's realm, but they couldn't walk back again." Mod flipped a switch and crossed a couple of wires. "It'll go the other way now."

Doug picked up a rock to test his brother's work. He tossed the stone into the gate where it promptly disappeared. There was a resulting squawk from the other side.

The roosters paid great attention to the huge containers the crew carried with them, smart enough to realize where the sudden bounty of food had come from.

"Roll the amphorae through the gate," Doug instructed the others. "Both of them, the partial and the empty. We don't want any of the birds staying behind because they think there might be a stray kernel left in a jar."

Doug threw the bag through the gate for good measure.

The urge to follow the food was too great to resist.

The chicken army grouped and narrowed into a feathery torrent as they funneled through the gate. Before Doug's band could really register it, the last of the birds had passed beyond. Once the straggling partial and flattened fowl managed the door, Mod slipped forward, turned off the portal and slid the mechanism into his pocket.

"No!" Heinous wailed as he caught up to the group and saw them close the gate. He was bloody and bruised. The swarm had engulfed him with beak and talon and left the man's body and mind in tatters. He held his right arm tight over a bloodied gash in his belly, and his right leg no longer worked correctly. Heinous's face was swollen, scratched, and washed in blood. Physically hindered by the injuries, the man seemed unaware of them as he stumbled forward. "Don't take away my beautiful cocks!"

"To use anything Mother Gaea has given into our stewardship in such a way is horrendous," Doug said to the man even as he moved forward to help him.

Heinous brushed Doug's outstretched hands away. "I need those birds." Tears and rage, sorrow and desperation mixed on the man's face. Something inside Heinous broke. "The birds love me." He managed in a ragged whisper. "I love them."

"This isn't love." Doug took in all of the destruction around them, and wondered what the act directed by Heinous could possibly have obtained. He turned and looked at the injured man again, pity now filling Doug's eyes. "You're injured beyond what you realize. Please let us help you."

Doug's offer reignited the last vestiges of rage and hate in the man.

With a snarl, Heinous lunged at Doug and Mod, desperate to reopen the gate. Five and Six plucked him out of the air and threw him to the ground before he could do anything.

"Do we need to hold him down?" Five asked.

"No," Doug answered.

Heinous rolled into a ball. He sobbed and clawed at something in front of his face no one else could see.[4] The man started gibbering, his incoherent babble broken by unprovoked laughs and wails. It was clear to everyone the mind of Heinous—and the threat he represented—was gone.

Doug had known the man since he and Mod were children. Heinous had always seemed scary and mean and the boys never liked him, but Doug never wanted to see him like this.

Doug knelt down beside the injured man. He needed to help but was unsure how. "Heinous needs aid," Doug said to Mopsus.

"Your desire to help is noted, as is your forgiving heart," Mopsus said to Doug as he knelt to examine Heinous. "Your skills and heart are not what is needed."

Mopsus opened a satchel of herbs and medicines. He gave

4. Heinous is seeing images of primal goddesses called the Furies. Furies punish crimes by hounding culprits relentlessly. Depending on who you ask, the Furies are described as having snakes for hair, dog's heads, coal black bodies, bat's wings, or bloodshot eyes. They pretty much alter in appearance based on what will mess the most with the head of the one they're attacking. To Heinous the Furies look a lot like marshmallow Peeps in the usual assortment of colors.

Heinous a small sip from a vial that immediately calmed him. "I know some holy men on the island will be able to tend his wounds." The seer supported and coaxed Heinous up off the ground. "Mayhaps they will be able to ease the pains of his mind as well."

"We're actually going to help him?" Mod was aghast. "I mean, this guy is responsible for"—Mod just swung his arms wide to indicate the destruction around him—"I mean, just look!"

"It won't help us to see him harmed, Mod," Doug said.

"Do you remember how he tormented and scared us as kids?" Mod asked.

"Yes," Doug said. "It doesn't change what I think is right."

Mod didn't look convinced. "Saving Heinous. Never thought I'd see *that* day."

"Sorry, Mod, but this is the way it has to be. You'll see." Doug put his hand on Mod's shoulder, then turned to Mopsus and the injured man. "See to it that he is well cared for, if there is any cost involved, I'll find a way to pay for it," Doug instructed the seer. "I hope the men you speak of can help him to find peace."

Mopsus wrapped his arm around Heinous's slumped shoulder and steered the man inland.

"We're not going to kill him?" Nine asked, perplexed.

"No," Doug said. "I don't want to kill anybody, not even Heinous. Besides, what purpose would it serve?"

"Then the foe is vanquished and extended mercy. The mighty task is complete. Truly, this has been an experience to relish." One beamed at her brothers and sister then saluted Doug. "Inspired leadership, my friend. Never in the history of the world has an undead army been defeated by wheat germ and millet."

As if on cue, a chime came from the box indicating the task was completed.

Mod tensed up at the sound, then relaxed with an audible sigh.

"No flare?" Doug asked.

"Yeah, I disabled the flare function on the task device after that one went off in my pocket at Anthea's," Mod said. "No more surprises."

A wry grin tweaked the corner of Doug's lips as he looked at Mod's slightly charred right pocket. "I'd forgotten about that."

"Tis done!" the automatons shouted. "To Doug!"

"And to the awesome power of cast iron!" Five raised his frying pan toward the heavens.

"To the skillets of war!" Six echoed his twin's sentiment as he pumped his own frying pan skyward.

Soon all the automatons were doing the same thing as they hooted and shouted in the air.

Mod took a couple of steps back and scanned the ground.

"You all right?" Doug asked.

"Oh, yeah. I'm fine," Mod said. "I know you're worried about how I feel about Heinous, and saving him, but you're probably right about what you decided. It's something else."

Doug looked concerned.

"It's nothing. Really." Mod shrugged. "Uh, I feel stupid about it, really, especially with everything just going down. It's nothing." Mod dug his hands deep in his pockets. He pulled handful after handful of stuff out, sifted through it and then pushed it back where he'd taken it from. "I lost my nervous click-n-twist when we were running from the cocks."[5]

"Do we need to go look for it?" Doug would lead a search. He knew how much his brother liked the thing.

"No." Mod checked out a few more scattered objects that caught his attention here and there in the disturbed soil. He clearly didn't see any indication of what he searched for. "I haven't really played with it for a while, it just calms me down pulling it apart and putting

5. Mod created both the gadget and its name. The name might be simplistic, but the toy was amazing. Think of a fidget-spinner that spins in three directions at once, is made of a previously unknown brasslike alloy, and is complicated enough to confound Daedalus.

it back together." He sighed. "I've got other things I can mess with if I get desperate."

"You sure?"

Mod shrugged. "No big loss. I can always make another with Heph if I need to."

As Mod said the name, Doug wondered if they could trust Hephaestus.

Mod's brow furrowed when he saw the look on Doug's face.

Doug pulled Mod off to the side a bit more. The automatons were still lost in the moment, so Doug could talk privately to his brother. "I'm wondering right now something more important than your click-n-twist," Doug said softly. "Heinous looked at your portal like he'd seen it before, and we know he had."

Mod pulled the newly acquired gadget from his pocket and stared at it for a moment. He shifted his gaze from the machine to his brother. "Do you think . . ." He let the unspoken question hang for a bit. "I mean, he wouldn't, would he?"

Doug shook his head. "The workmanship on this portal is different from your other one. It's crude work. No finesse to it."

Mod nodded. "I already noticed the lack of craftsmanship. I'm not surprised you saw it too." Mod paused. "Maybe it was a prototype?" he asked.

That explanation didn't feel right.

They both looked at the machine in Mod's hand.

"Things are changing," Doug said. "I don't think it's Teutamides and Heracles we have to worry about now. Someone else wants me to fail."

Chapter 25
Goat Surfing

The next task was to find a violent cow destroying an island and milk her to calm her down. The ship was returned to the sea, and they headed southeast to Karpathos.

"Milk a cow? What kind of a stupid quest is that?" Nine scoffed.

"The last task was to subdue some chickens. Without Doug's quick thinking, they would have pecked us apart." One surveyed the scrapes and scratches that covered her arms and legs.

"Ah." Nine winced. "Point taken."

Nine made his way to the rudder where Mod piloted the ship. He was quiet and hesitant as he approached, but Mod smiled and invited him to come stand beside him.

Mod waited as Nine worked up the courage to talk.

Still tentative, Nine finally spoke. "You know your brother well." A statement, not a question. "The men and women of Naxos would have hailed him as a savior and a god. Why . . .?" Nine's voice trailed off.

Mod shifted the boat a bit more to port. "Why didn't he stay? Why didn't he take the money and supplies? Why didn't he accept any of the gifts they offered him? Is that what you want to know?"

"In a sense," Nine replied. "Other men would have used such a happening to their gain."

"My brother isn't other men." Mod smirked. "He doesn't care about wealth or possessions. We have enough to do the things we need to do, and it would have been a burden for the people of Naxos to give anything for us."

"Tokens of gratitude," Nine said.

Mod shook his head. "They gave thanks and were relieved to be heading back to their homes. It was enough for us."

"You and your brother don't seem to understand. Wealth could've been stored on the ship," Nine pointed out. "There's more than enough space for all of us to amass great fortunes on this journey."

"True. But none of that matters to me or my brother very much." He felt a change in the current and adjusted the ship into it. "My father offered my brother everything: the home, business, the status it would bring. Doug told our father how honored and loved he felt, and then said he couldn't take it."

"Why?" Nine didn't seem to understand.

"It's a bit hard to explain." It was simple yet difficult to learn. Mod had been given the years necessary to understand his brother's way of thinking. "Doug is smart enough to see things other people can't see, to see the traps others fall into. Money, things, power, he just doesn't care about them."

"Then what is there to care about?" Nine asked.

Mod's brother had just been splashed by the crest of a wave at the front of the ship. Doug laughed and kicked his feet out into the thick of the spray. "He's thinking of a pretty girl right now. Just the thought of her is enough to make him happy, so I guess that's a pretty good thing to think about."

Nine scratched his head. "I can't quite understand it. The thought of the girl seems nice and all, but I'd rather take the money."

At the other end of the boat, Mopsus offered Doug a towel.

That was when Mod saw the men standing on the water for the first time. "Doug, everybody, check it out!" Mod directed them all to a grouping of four men who quickly laid on their bellies on the water. As a wave passed by, the men would stand on the water, rising to the crest of the wave to attempt to ride the wall of water as it made its way shoreward.

"Why don't they sink?" One asked.

"When I see things that look like that and refuse to sink, it's a sure sign you need to flush again." Four wrinkled his nose in distaste as the others on the ship gaped at the sight.

"It is called surfing.[1] A sport where one tries to achieve great 'hang time' atop a moving wall of water," Mopsus explained. "A dance of patience, balance, and skill. In its true form, it shall not be known in this hemisphere of the world for a couple thousand years. In a place on the other side of Mother Earth called Polynesia, the activity is being perfected, becoming a significant part of their culture, religion, and society."

"Sorcery," Nine sounded appalled.

"Are these men before us Poly-knee-sians? Or some unnatural water spirits that dance upon the waves?" One asked.

"If you were to look closely, you would see these are not water spirits, but fauns, who appear to have washed out to the ocean on the tide. Drunk on their sleeping mats of woven reeds they awoke to see the ocean surrounding them and are now attempting to make their way back to shore," Mopsus surmised.

"And you don't need to see them up close to know Mopsus is correct. If you breathe deeply, you can smell the wet wool." Mod wrinkled his nose.

"Definitely moistened fauns," Doug agreed with Mod as the smell hit him.

"Ah, to experience such exotic perfumes," Three lamented. "But alas, the olfactory barrier."

The fauns were close enough now the crew could talk to them. They appeared to be wearing inflatable water wings.

---

1. Maintaining position atop water has always astounded. Japanese myth attributes the ability to the ninja. Christians deeply believe in the miracle performed by Jesus. Indian inventor Dwarka Prasad Chaurasia made shoes that allowed him to take a stroll on the rolling deep for a reasonable price. Design firm MSCHF made a pair of shoes cushioned with water from the River Jordan. The three-thousand-dollars-a-pair shoes don't allow you to walk on water, though for the price they totally should. They sold out in minutes. Neither Jesus nor Dwarka approved. The ninja could not be found for comment.

Doug called out. "Ho, friends. How fare you?"

The shaggy blond faun riding the crest of a wave closest to *Nyxy Business* flipped his dreads out of his face. He almost lost his balance as the wave tried to upset his raft. "Be better if we could swim." His face was slack, and his voice slurred as he said it. "The stress and tensions I'm going through are killing me, man."

"How did you come to occupy this space atop the water?" One asked.

Another faun answered, "Fell asleep in bed. Woke up in the big blue."

"Why were you wearing water wings when you went to bed?" Mod asked.

"Didn't drown, did I?" the first faun asked. "A little forward thinking can save a heap of tragedy, you know?" The first faun looked around. "Still, we may have lost one of us during the night." He tried to count the others. "There should be three of us. But I only count two."

"Totally bogus!" the second faun cried.

The third faun looked at the fourth faun. "We've lost a brother! This sucks majorly, dude!"

"Uh, I think I may have some good news," Doug spoke to the first faun. "There's four of you."

"Really!" Faun number one sounded excited. "We thought we lost Bucephalus last week!" He turned and finally noticed the exceptionally tight curled Bucephalus as he floated nearby. "Bo!"

"Yo! Bro!" Bucephalus bobbed his head. "Sup, man?"

"Nice to meet you and your compatriots, Bucephalus." Mopsus bowed in the faun's direction.

"I'm Larry." The first faun continued introductions as he pointed to the right and left. "And this is my brother Darrell and my other brother Darrell. And I see you are already acquainted with our cousin Bo."

Without continuing to drop on their bellies to lie on the sodden sleeping mats, the wool of the fauns began to dry out. Larry and his brothers were revealed to be towhead blond as their fur dried in the sun. Bucephalus was covered in black curls so tight and greasy he was the envy of the Assyrian Empire.[2]

"Bucephalus is a cousin?" Nine probed. "He doesn't look much like the rest of you."

"He's the lucky one," Larry said. "Me and Darrell and Darrell always have to be on the lookout because someone's always trying to skin us." Darrell whispered something to Larry. "Darrell says, 'Friggin' golden fleece,' Darrell says."

Both of the Darrells nodded as Larry continued, "Stupid Uncle Chrys.[3] Winged sheep my butt. He totally made his wings from paper mâché. He couldn't really fly. And his hair wasn't natural. He had to have it touched up every six months by a witch, Cosmetolia. It didn't look natural, but Uncle Chrys wouldn't listen." Darrell and Darrell ran their hands through their hair. "Me and Darrell and Darrell have natural tones and highlights. We can't help it we're so desirable."

"We'd love to give you a ride to shore—" Mod started to say.

"You hesitate because of the smell." Bucephalus nodded as if he empathized. "I wouldn't want it in my boat if I were you. We totally get it."

"The smell totally reconstitutes every time it gets wet," Larry said. "On a boat? Constant gnarly goat funk."

"Gotta rope?" Bucephalus asked, hopeful. "You could tow us in from a distance."

"I've a length of good cord." Mopsus dug in his pack. "It would be a pleasure to help you gentlemen."

Each of the fauns grabbed hold of the line attached to the railings

---

2. Assyrians loved tight black curls. Just check out their art. Bucephalus really fit the bill. He looked like he'd lost a fight between a Clarol home permanent and a bottle of Just For Men.

3. Chrysomallos was a golden woolled, winged ram that rescued Phrixus and brought him safe to Colchis, where Phrixus promptly sacrificed Chrysomallos to Zeus. No good deed goes unpunished, right?

of the ship. The automatons took up rowing positions and got into a rhythm that had the ship cruising along through the tops of the waves.[4] In no time they'd all safely arrived on the island of Karpathos.

"Home again," Larry said as they landed on a stretch of beach littered with trash. Apparently the wave was strong enough to wash the fauns out to sea, but not enough to clear the beach of their junkpiles.

"Uh, this place is really a mess," Three pointed out, as she flipped over a takeout package that showed signs of rot or signs of life or both. It was obvious the fauns hadn't had any nymphs over in a while. "How do you generate this much garbage?"

"It's not that bad." Bucephalus looked like his feelings were hurt. "Hey, we were totally gonna clean it up, but we been kinda busy."

"Chased out of the forest by that mad cow," Larry said as he dug around in the firepit for something to chew. He found a half-burned scroll and stuck it in his mouth as he continued to talk. "Fauns don't really like the beach and ocean, but the mad bovine is making it impossible to inhabit the groves and meadows."

One watched in fascination as Larry continued to chew the edges of the rolled menu. "Do you actually like eating that?"

Larry shrugged. "Paper's paper, man, but the glue they use on this is awesome![5] Familiar and flavorful."

"It's like the tenth menu we've eaten this week," Bucephalus said as Darrell and Darrell dug through the ashes for scraps. "They taste better if you toast 'em."

"Reheated mutton always tastes better than a cold shoulder," Mopsus whispered under his breath. When Bucephalus looked at the seer sideways, Mopsus coughed and excused himself.

"I miss the parties in the meadow," Larry said. "Stupid cow."

---

4. Behold the first instance of motor-powered water skiing. The fauns did well once they figured out to "keep the toes up," which is harder than you think when you have cloven hooves for feet.

5. Familiar glue? No one ever told the fauns what happened to all the parts of Uncle Chrys, and some mysteries are better left unsolved.

"So, what is it with the cow, anyway? Why's it causing problems?" Doug asked.

"The cow's got issues, man. Doesn't want anyone to touch her unless they drink her milk,"[6] Larry said.

"That's it?" Mod asked.

"What do you mean, 'that's it?'" Bucephalus had part of a gyro wrapper hanging from his lower lip. "Drinking milk is for babies and barbarians. Or, you know, weirdos?"

Larry, Darrell, and Darrell shook their heads in disbelief. "We may be fauns, but we have standards, bro."

"She won't let nobody milk her, and she's going crazy because she's overfull on milk," Bucephalus said.

"And there is no calf to suckle the mother?" Mopsus asked.

"She gave birth to twins, and both were transformed into glorious beams of light as they took their first breath," Larry answered. "Pretty sure some god was messing around in the cattle pen,[7] if you get what I mean."

"Well, I'm actually a pretty good milker. We had goats and used the milk to make cheese and soap. I wasn't too disappointed if there was a glass left over for me when I was done." Doug flexed his hands and limbered up his fingers. "Bucket." Doug held out his hand, and One put a pail in his grasp.

"The cow is going to want to see that you drink it," Bucephalus cautioned.

"That's not a problem." Doug patted the bag of snacks tied to his belt. "I have cookies. Cup." Three put a mug in Doug's empty hand. "I'll be back in a bit."

---

6. Actually a thing. Ancient Greeks believed milk was for making cheese and fattening up infants. I mean, yogurt and clabber were considered treats, but 100 percent whole milk? Anyone who drank unprocessed lactose was a deviant, a toddler, or a savage.

7. There's a ton of stuff like that in Greek myth. Don't try looking it up. Just take my word for it. It's too hard to scrub from your search history and will probably get you placed on several government watchlists.

Chapter 26

Cretan Reunion

The automatons ran back and forth in the surf with reed mats. They'd flop on their bellies at what they hoped was the right time to boogie-board the tops of the waves. The fauns shouted encouragement and suggestions on how the mechanical persons could improve their surfing technique from the dry safety further ashore.

Three gave a hoot as she crested a large wave and plowed her brothers Nine and Four under the surface. Nine bobbed to the surface of the wave and scowled before the wave broke and tumbled him onto the beach. Four dove under the wave and popped up in the trough on the far side. The others jeered and hollered and all of them showed signs of having a grand time.

Doug, Mod, and Mopsus let them all have their fun while they watched from the prow of the ship sitting on the shore. Adding the automatons and fauns into the current discussion would have been too much chaos to handle.

"So, I've been thinking." Doug sat on the bow of the ship and tossed pebbles at an empty wine jar lying on its side on the beach. "How are the task scrolls getting into the task device? Some look to be written in Teutamides's hand and the others in Heracles's scrawl, like perfect copies of their writing or something."

"A good question," Mopsus said.

"Totally off subject, but I was wondering. What did the cow think of you showing up with the cookies?" Mod asked.

"She liked them better than I did." Doug indicated the empty snack bag hanging from his belt. "Calmed her right down so I could get to milking. I'm glad I brought extra."

"You mean you're glad Mom sent extra," Mod corrected, then queried somewhat sadly. "None left? Even the plain oatmeal?"

"Sorry, Mod. I'll let you have first dibs next time."

"Care packages from home." Mopsus smiled. "Ah, the memory of deliveries received long ago. Always more appreciated than Mom realized." He paused, then added, "I should write my mother."

"Moms know everything," Mod said. "They must have a secret power that can sense when you are about to do something boneheaded or know what you need or . . . I can't figure out how they do it." Mod watched as Doug tossed three rocks in a row into the narrow neck of the small Amphorae. "Nice shot, by the way."

"Thanks." Doug tossed one more pebble, missed by a mile, and decided he should've quit while he was ahead. He dropped the remaining rocks onto the beach. "Mom's intuition aside, I feel as if someone or something is hand delivering these tasks. That means we're dealing with someone who can do things normal Greeks can't do."

"I can only think of four, maybe five, people I know of that could have made the portal that breached the netherworld." Mod exhaled as he leaned back against the ship's rail. "There are probably a few gods that could do it, but even adding them, the list is pretty small, say, six or so."

Mopsus waited in silence for a moment. "I'm unsure if I should speak my mind. My initial role and charge seemed I should keep much from you boys, but I'm rapidly altering my thinking."

"Well, I'm intrigued now," Doug said. "If you have any insight or clarification to share, feel free to do so."

Mopsus nodded. "The inclusion of Heinous, a man you both knew, in a place none of you had ever visited before, was no coincidence."

"Yep. Thought of that. We just don't know why." Doug was sure Heinous had been included in the task to unnerve him but couldn't figure out to what end. "Not worth wasting the brain power worrying about it right now. We'll figure it out, eventually."

They all sat in silence for a moment.

"Enough speculation about currently unanswerable questions," Doug changed the subject to something more actionable. "What have we been tasked by our benevolent Teutamides and his noble compatriot? I assume you took a look at the next task?"

Mod pulled out the scroll. "We thought it best to wait for you."

Doug took the proffered scroll. Mod and the seer closed in on each side to read over his shoulder.

"Uh, that might be a tad more dangerous than the cow," Mod said as he read the scroll.

"Your plea for easy tasks seems not to have been granted." Mopsus wasn't happy with what he read either.

"Release the Minotaur from the labyrinth beneath Minos's palace. At least Crete is close by," Doug tried to sound upbeat.

"What purpose does freeing the minotaur serve?"[1] Mod asked.

"I think this task is just meant as a danger to me. It eats people,[2] remember?" Doug was a bit unnerved but tried to make light of the situation. "No doubt our beloved king has instructions directing me to rub savory herbs and spices on my skin while repeatedly whacking myself with a meat tenderizer?"

Mod consulted the scroll. "No mention of that, but it does specify that you be accompanied by a gallon and a half of tzatziki and a sleeping bag sized loaf of flatbread."

---

1. Poseidon sent a white bull to Minos so Minos could sacrifice the bull to Poseidon. Minos liked the bull and decided to keep it. Poseidon got irked and made it so Minos's wife, Pasiphae, really, *really* liked the bull. Minos didn't want the resulting child but couldn't send the bull-headed boy away. He wound up living in his stepdad's basement subsisting on a yearly delivery of Athenian meals-on-wheels until Theseus took care of the problem.

2. Aegeus (king of Athens): "Hey kids? Who wants to go on the super special, super awesome, annual field trip to Crete? There's a boat ride, a fun maze, and snacks."

Kids: "We get snacks?"

Aegeus, ignoring the question: "I need seven boys and seven girls."

Doug picked up a blanket from the deck of the ship and whipped it around himself theatrically. "Oh, warm and toasty I'll be! Wrapped in a fresh-from-the-oven Cretan pita. A head of cool lettuce for a pillow."

"Cool pillows are the best." Mod grinned.

"Self-delivering main dish for a Cretan basement dweller. It's always been an aspiration of mine." Doug took a deep breath, held it for a bit, then let it out in a sigh. He threw the blanket back into the boat, jumped to his feet, and began gathering his things. "No sense putting it off, we should start prepping the ship to go to Crete."

Larry overheard the men discussing the island. "You're going to Crete?"

"We have to take care of something there," Doug explained.

An odd look, hopeful, yet braced for disappointment, appeared on Larry's face. "I know we just met, but would it be possible to hitch a ride with you?"

"You fauns were the ones that argued against us letting you board the boat," Mod reminded the goatman. "Why the sudden desire to go to Crete?"

"Oh, we got reasons, bro." He turned and called to the others further down the beach. "Hey, brothers! Doug and company are heading to our old stomping grounds."

"You guys are from Crete?" Mod contemplated for a second. "Not being fond of water, I would've thought you were from here on Karpathos."

Larry was silent until Darrell and Darrell moseyed up behind him. "Cousin Bo is a local boy, but we're not from around here. We'd like to visit our *madre*.[3] We haven't seen her in quite a long stretch." Larry looked pitiful, and his lower lip trembled when he said the word *madre*.

"Your mother lives on Crete?" Mod asked.

3. The Spanish Mexican word for *mother*. I don't know how a Cretan goat-man that speaks Greek knows the word, but it's obvious he misses his mother.

"Yep. In our hometown." Darrell and Darrell nodded vigorously as Larry wiped a tear from his eye.

"The fauns do smell better, or at least the smell doesn't carry as far, now that they're dry," Doug noted. "And it isn't that long of a boat ride."

"And they could ride downwind," Mopsus added.

"Next to me, by the rudder?" Mod looked suddenly unsure about agreeing to the boat ride.

Doug understood. Helping people out was one thing, and minor inconveniences were to be expected, but there were limits.

Desperation must have led to inspiration because Mod got a curious look in his eye. "You fauns still aren't entirely comfortable with being out on the water, are you?"

Doug knew a way to get the fauns to Crete. He opened his mouth to tell the fauns about the portal, thought about who his listeners were, and wondered how he could simplify it enough to make sense to them.

Mod beat him to it. "I have a magic door. I can open it when we get to Crete, and you can just walk through. No wet fauns."

Larry narrowed his eyes. "Not sure if I'm willing to believe what I'm being told. You mean to tell me that you have a displacement device that will fold space-time to allow an object to instantaneously transverse non-linier space?"

Momentarily stupefied, Mod somehow managed to respond. "Um—sure," Mod guessed.

Doug had never heard most of those words before. He was pretty sure even Mod, with his constant book reading and technical knowledge, hadn't either.

"I've seen those listed on the higher end emporia and emporoi message boards.[4] They're import items shipped from somewhere

---

4. Emporia(trade) and Emporoi(merchants) had to list the things they had for sale somewhere. Think Sharper Image for the high end, targeted, brand-new stuff. You can't sell quality, eclectic items—like this book—if you don't advertise.

back east. Sounds interesting, but I never ever knew anyone who had one." The faun brothers nodded in offbeat unison, clearly impressed. "Sounds good. We'll wait for you here, then."

With that, Doug and his crew gathered their things. The fauns helped push the boat out into the surf.

The winds were favorable. Doug would be in Crete in no time.

Chapter 27

Concerns of a Daughter

Something was rotten in the kingdom of Larissa.

Teutamides had taken the bulk of his daily duties and foisted them off on officials, Daphis in particular. Daphis coped as best he could, but it was clear the added responsibilities had started to take a toll. The majordomo no longer color-coordinated his wardrobe, and his dress and demeanor overall had taken on muted and increasingly gray tones. Daphis pulled upon some unseen wellspring of resolve, and business went on as usual in the kingdom. Or at least appeared to when looked at with a casual eye.

It was odd for Teutamides to shirk responsibilities like this, especially in times of peace and prosperity such as the kingdom of Larissa was now experiencing.

Teutamides often lectured his daughter that for a king to allow others to do jobs he should rightfully be doing was a sign of laziness and weakness, and an outward signal to nefarious forces that the kingdom was ripe for the plucking.

To the commoner, the kingdom appeared to be business as usual. To those more accustomed to the inner workings of ruling and protecting Larissa from opportunistic and hostile neighbors, the cracks had begun to show.

Larisa found her father in the library of the palace, sitting at a desk where he stared at a closed book.

He seemed distracted. Lately Teutamides hadn't been able to focus on any one thing in particular. He refused to look deeply at any subject as if afraid of what he might discover. When pressed on the matter of his attention, he grew irate and would send the questioner away or remove himself from the situation without an answer. All of his recent interactions had ended with a stomp and a turn. The angry king cursed at any who dared to approach him.

Was he distracted? No. Distracted wasn't quite the right word.

Fidgety? Larisa questioned wordlessly. That didn't seem right either.

He's frightened.

As soon as the idea popped into her head, she knew she was right. She'd seen her father in lots of stressful situations before. He was a king, and to be a good king one had to rule over things pleasant and painful. Pleasant things came along as momentary and rare distractions; it was pain, stress, and unpleasantness that were the daily bread and butter of the true monarch.

And Teutamides had always stressed upon himself and others to be true.

She tried to come upon him without startling him, at the same time she tried very hard to not appear to be sneaking around. She walked to him quietly and tried her best to project some aura of peace and calm.

He jumped when she approached. He looked down at the books and scrolls littering the desktop before him and pushed a few aside to obscure their titles.

"Daughter," he managed. A hesitant smile colored his face for a moment before it trembled and went away. "Do you need something?"

Larisa didn't know how to broach the subjects she would. Gentle and direct would most likely be best. "Father. I love you, and I know you love me." She walked closer to him and reached out and placed her hand over his. "Are you all right?"

The first emotion to hit his face was offense. For a second it looked like he might rip his hand away from his daughter's touch.

Teutamides appeared to fight the impulse. He shook his head as if to right his thoughts.

The more noble natures triumphed, and he gave his daughter a genuine smile. "Forgive me, daughter. Stresses and weights of a kingdom are not treating me well as of late."

It was the first true smile she'd seen on her father's face in weeks. He looked tired and weary, but his eyes were true.

"Of all the things I've seen you deal with time and again, the only thing unusual and out of the normal are the heroic tasks of Doug," Larisa said. She knew it was the source of the additional stress on her father, and she wouldn't avoid mentioning the one variable in Teutamides's life that'd obviously changed.

Teutamides's face darkened slightly. For a fraction of a second, he appeared to forget that Larisa was there. "Would that it were done," he whispered, almost to himself, then his eyes jerked about as if he worried he'd been overheard.

"Father?" She called his attention back to her. "As you say it, I wonder if there is wisdom in your words. What would happen if it were to be done? If you declared that Doug had proved himself. Would such a statement ease the burdens that weigh so heavily upon you?"

He looked at her for a moment as he judged her motives and intentions for saying such a thing. "You love the boy and would have him half-proven usurp me?" he asked suspiciously.

She leveled him with a look. "You know better. I love and care for you. I have desire and the beginnings of love for Doug. I see no reason to continue to press forward with something that will bring harm and pain to those I love if it serves no purpose."

A strange look crossed Teutamides's face. "Does it serve a purpose?" His eyes were lost, and he cocked his head to the side as if he tried to bring to mind something very necessary.

He looked at the mess of books and scrolls on the desktop before him. "I can't remember what it was I'd come to the library to find. There's a reason Doug's trial must continue, isn't there?"

Ergos, laying at the king's feet, raised his head and barked. It was an actual bark that carried a sense of urgency.

It made Larisa jump.

Teutamides flinched and cried out the second it happened.

His fingers stopped rummaging about the texts and papers as he pushed away from the desk and stood. "Gods have called for it. The boy must be proven," Teutamides said as if he were repeating something he'd heard or been told. If it hadn't come from his lips, Larisa would have sworn he hadn't spoken it.

"Are you all right, Father?" Larisa asked again.

"Ah, Daughter!" Teutamides said as if he just noticed her for the first time. "How wonderful to see you!" He patted her on the hand and leaned in to kiss her forehead. "I'm fine. I'm just fine. I must be off to find Heracles to put together the next list of tasks for that fine young man of yours. His strengths and abilities, once proven, shall make him a fine and noble successor to the kingship of Larissa." He kissed her once more on the brow then was gone.

She was sure what he'd just said was meant to reassure her. It had the opposite effect. It was as if her father was currently two different men, and someone had flipped a switch to hide the tired and worn Teutamides with one that was an outright liar.

The man that walked away from her wasn't her father. Or at the very least her father wasn't in control.

Teutamides was not an easy man to manipulate or fool.

Something must have clouded his thinking and ability to reason.

Larisa walked about and started rummaging through the pile of books and scrolls. Most of the books and essays centered around cultivating and clarifying thought. Hesiod. Thales. Anaximander. There were even scrolls by Aristotle and Plato.

Then a single scrap of parchment caught her eye. It listed the various deities linked to thought and the mind. There were six gods listed on the scroll, along with their realms and influences. She didn't know why, but she reasoned the list to be the most important document in the pile.

She rolled it up tight and slipped it into the neck of her clothes between her breasts.

The royal librarian might notice it was missing, but just being a list of several gods would probably deem it unimportant. And if interactions between the king and others had been like the conversation she'd just finished with her father, the librarian would probably avoid bringing the subject of the missing scroll up.

The parchment was sticking to her chest. It was itchy and uncomfortable, and she worried if she left the scroll nestled in her cleavage too long, she might start to sweat and cause the ink to resaturate and run or smear.

"I could get ink on my boobs." She mumbled to herself. "Not that there's anyone to notice."

That thought led to thoughts of Doug. And that led to thoughts of a man and a woman being together.

Larisa and Doug weren't even close to that kind of relationship yet, and Larisa was happy to wait for something grand and real and fully expected that Doug would ultimately be the one to fit the bill. Still, even the hint of such things gave her a little rush.

First things first. Larisa calmed her hormones and made her way to her chambers. "Dad must have thought something was up or he wouldn't have pulled out the books he did." She made it into her room and shut the door behind her, pulling the parchment out as soon as the door latched.

The name of the titan Ceous was first on the list.

Larisa pulled out a paper of her own and wrote the titan's name. She didn't know much about the titan, or half of the other names on the list either.

"Guess I'll have to do a little studying of my own," she said to herself.

Chapter 28

A Meet and Greet on Crete

The large island of Crete came into view.

The closer Doug drew to the island, the more ocean traffic they began to see. Within sight of the main harbor, the boats were so thick that running into someone looked less like a possibility and more like an inevitability.

"City traffic." Mopsus spat over the ship's rail in disgust. "Too dang many people trying to get to who knows where. Just watching it gives me a headache. That's why I live in the country."

Mod turned the rudder just in time to avoid breaking a small fishing vessel in two. The wake of the larger ship still made the smaller boat rock and almost tip.

Nine watched as the men on the other boat righted themselves. He waved at them then gasped at their returned acknowledgement. "Really? How rude."

"Gestures such as that are common in large cities," Mopsus noted. "Those who live here come to expect it. They feel it enhances their language and makes people take them more seriously."

"Is that so?" Nine turned back to the man who'd communicated with obscene signs. He flipped him off with one hand and waved goodbye with the other. "Have a nice day!"

The man shouted a response. It was just as well that nobody in Doug's crew could hear what the man said.

"People here seem to be a bit intense," Doug observed.

"It's all about the money. That's all they care about." Mopsus didn't sound impressed with the local way of living. "Minos makes money hand over fist, and the people living under his rule prosper, but at a cost."

"There's a line of boats over there." Mod inclined his head to a string of disgruntled merchant seamen who inched forward in a slowly progressing flotilla. Many of the men shouted and used gestures akin to the ones used on the nearly swamped fishing boat.

"Quite an extensive vocabulary." Nine took notes. "I wonder which gestures are most proficient in getting the message across."

"We won't be using any of the non-verbal language enhancers." Doug directed Mod to a spot at the end of the line. "We'll be patient and wait our turn."

An official sat under a shade where several slaves fanned him as he vetted each ship before they proceeded for unloading. A smaller boat with a slightly less impressive official darted back and forth among those waiting in line. It took a very long time for the smaller boat to make it to Doug and company.

When the lesser official finally pulled alongside Erebus's ship, he was drenched in sweat, tired, and clearly done dealing with people. He stood and addressed Mopsus, who he must have thought the captain. "Boat name?" he asked with a grimace.

"*Nyxy Business*," Doug answered, and the man did a quicktake. He'd obviously not expected the captain to be one of the younger men on the boat. "On loan to us from Erebus."

The lesser official jotted down the ships' name and started to scratch the owner's name onto the form in his hand. The man hesitated as the name registered. He arched his eyebrow and looked up slowly from his paperwork. "Erebus? The god?" Then the man looked at the ship. It was smaller than some in the harbor, but clearly of finer workmanship than any other boat in line. Finer than any boat the man had probably ever seen. The man straightened up and really looked at Doug. Intrigue dispersed some of the overworked man's fatigue. "Purpose of the visit? Business or pleasure?"

"On task from Teutamides, king of Larissa, to pick up something from Minos. So, business, I guess," Doug said.

"Figures. Who'd want to come to Knossos for pleasure," the man whispered under his breath, then Doug's statement connected, and he took a step back in the boat, almost losing his balance for a second. "You're here to meet with the king?"

"To visit the palace, at least," Doug said. "We're supposed to take something out of the basement for Teutamides."

The official stared at Doug for a few seconds, then bent back to his paperwork and checked off several boxes. "You'll need to fill out the necessary export paperwork then." He scratched a note. "One more thing, you aren't Athenian, are you?"

"From Iolcus. Born and raised."

"Good." The man nodded. "I always feel guilty about admitting people from Athens. I don't like knowing what could happen to them." He tore off a number from a perforated scroll and handed it to a servant behind him. The servant attached the number to a carbon-copy of the paperwork and tied them both to a weighted dart before he lobbed the blunted throwing device to Doug.[1] "Go to the end of the short line over there." He indicated the better kept dock where a smaller line of boats waited. "Wait to approach until they call your number."

"Thank you." Doug bowed in the official's direction. "We appreciate your help and direction."

"Wait, what?" The official almost fell out of the boat.

"Thank you," Doug repeated.

It took a moment for the words to register. "You're welcome." The man shook his head, and a smirk grew on his face. "You're truly not from around here, are you?"

"Just passing through." Doug nodded and raised a hand in friendship as the man's boat pulled away. The boat didn't continue through

1. Carbon-copy: special paper underneath the paper you are writing on that duplicates everything written. Used in duplicate checks, handwritten receipt books, and government paperwork. Abbreviated as "CC" on email. No one under the age of twenty-five knows what the abbreviation "CC" on the email actually stands for.

the waiting ships but turned back to report to the higher official lounging on the barge.

"What did he mean when he mentioned Athenians?"[2] One asked as they watched the previously reclining official jump to his feet and make his way to the palace.

Mopsus frowned at the knowledge on the subject he had. "Athenians have a habit of disappearing in Knossos, though not in a pleasant 'they might turn up just fine later' type of way. An Athenian killed Minos's son, and Minos has taken his vengeance out on Athenians ever since."

"Revenge never seems to benefit anyone in the end," Doug said.

"Trying to convince Minos of that is a losing cause. Many people, even some of the gods, feel he is one of the most enlightened men in the world. He does many good things for his people, but his hatred of Athens is hard to reconcile with the other good he does."

"I don't envy him his lot in life. We're not here to judge Minos," Doug reminded them all. "We're here to set the minotaur trapped under the palace free."

"What if the king doesn't want to let the beast go?" Three asked.

"We'll deal with it if it comes up." Doug noticed the official he'd spoken to earlier now waved them forward from the dock. "Looks like we're moving to the front of the line." They steered the boat past a banner proclaiming *now serving number seventeen.* Doug felt a bit guilty about it. The number he had in his hand was forty-three.

Mod directed the ship forward. He moved carefully around the others who waited their turn.

The looks received back were not the looks Doug expected. There was pity in the eyes of most of those they cut in front of, and others purposefully turned a blind eye. "As impatient as everyone

---

2. Officials had to fill out extra paperwork for Athenians:
   How long do you plan to stay on Crete?
   Do you exercise regularly?
   Can you outrun a bull?
   Do you consider yourself white meat or dark meat?

appears here, moving to the front of the line does not seem to be considered a good thing."

"How about being greeted personally by the king?" Mopsus pointed his finger to the shades being thrown up on the dock. A large red carpet rolled out as servants made hasty preparations.

The king, flanked by a dozen officials, stood on the dockside as Mod pulled the boat into its temporary berth. The spy from Teutamides's court, Aesimus, was one of those who stood closest to the king.

"Hey. That's Larisa's dad's spy," Doug said as he squinted. "At least, I'm pretty sure."

"It is indeed," Mopsus clarified. "I know him."

"That's good. I guess," Doug said. "What is he doing here?"

"On task for Teutamides, I would expect," Mopsus said.

Doug watched the spy closely. For the briefest of moments, the spy caught Mopsus's eye and flashed a series of hand signals to him. Then Mopsus stroked his beard and scratched the side of his left cheek deliberately.

"That guy sure gets around," Mod said to Doug.

"Uh huh," Doug said, watching the man and Mopsus out of the corner of his eye to see if they had any more interactions.

Mopsus leaned in close to Doug and whispered so only he could hear. "Aesimus has warned me that Tuetamides plans to set you at odds against Minos. Be on your guard."

"Do you trust him?" Doug whispered back.

Mopsus nodded. "I do, but he must also act as his king commands. Be wary."

Minos took a step forward and searched the faces of the men on the boat until the official pointed out Doug. The king had a slight, possibly permanent, scowl on his face as he addressed Doug directly. "I am told you wish something from my basement," The king said brusquely.

"Yes, your majesty. You've been correctly informed." Doug bowed to the man.

Minos arched an eyebrow, and continued, "You may be unaware, but the basement under my palace contains only one thing."

"Great King Minos, I was made aware of the basement's contents in the details of the quest given me by King Teutamides." Doug bowed again.

"Fair enough." Minos threw Doug a large metal ring holding one key. "You'll find the beast at the end of the tunnel on the south side of the palace proper. Unlock the gate that bars the way, load him on your ship, and get him off Crete before the sun sets."

Doug looked at the key in his hands. "My thanks, King Minos."

"Your thanks?" The king scoffed. "You rush headlong to your untimely death. Give my regard to the god of the damned." He turned to walk away, already done with the whole situation.

"This is not the end of it," Mopsus said to Doug. "The spy informed me that Teutamides did not wish for this to be so simple a challenge."

Aesimus barred the way. He lowered his head and whispered in the king's ear.

Minos turned around abruptly, calculation on his face. "My kataskopoi tells me that you are men of some means? Men of determination, yes, but also men who possess devices that give you powers envied by gods?"

Minos called Aesimus his spy? Curious. Whose side is Aesimus on? Doug couldn't ponder on it too long because Minos stood waiting for an answer. "We have a few things that are special, I guess." Doug indicated Mod standing at the rudder. "Most of them belong to my brother, Modifixeus."

"Mechanical men and women? A ship from a god? These aren't deemed special in your eyes? But you're correct on one point, the thing I desire does belong to your brother." Minos sneered, turned to Mod, and got directly to the point. "The portal. Give it to me."

Doug watched Aesimus making tiny little jerks and symbols with his fingers meant only for Mopsus to see, and then Mopsus returning the communication in kind.

Mod stared at the king for a moment. He didn't shy away as the leader's gaze bore into him.

Minos punctuated his demand as he forcefully held out his open hand. "I do not have time for your internal debate. The portal. Now."

Mopsus exchanged a few more hand gestures with the spy as he joined the brothers at the back of the ship. "Be strong, lads," he whispered so only Mod and Doug could hear it.

"I grow weary of waiting." Minos raised his empty right hand. The royal guard all took a step forward and brandished their weapons.

The implied threat had the opposite effect on Mod than the king likely expected.

"No," Mod stated simply.

The response gave the king pause. His hand lowered slightly.

"Fulfilling an oath you already made will expose Minos's weakness," Mopsus whispered to the boys. "You hold the key to what he fears most. A key he now asks for," Mopsus hinted. "Do what you feel is right."

Mopsus couldn't come right out and say it, but Doug could sense the solution was close. He just needed time to think, to figure it out, there just wasn't any time. *I'll have to stall.*

Mod stood tall, but the hand that held the rudder shook.

"I got it, Mod." Doug stepped in front of his brother. Doug spoke directly to the king. "For a man to show such force to another is either a sign of intimidation or an acknowledgement you see those in opposition as your equal. I take the gesture as I am sure it was meant, so from this time forth I will no longer refer to Minos as king, for he clearly sees me and mine as his equals."

Minos bristled at the words but said nothing.

Doug continued as he hoped Minos might reconsider. "You've made your intent clear. We've clearly answered. Do you intend to accept my brother's answer, and let us be about our quest?"

Minos didn't look amused. "Are you playing, boy? I'm a king addressing a swineherd, so no, I'm not inclined to acquiesce."

Minos's response was expected. The swineherd bit was meant to bait Doug into a misstep, but he didn't take it. "The battle about to ensue will be brutal, though the outcome is close to a surety. The mechanical men and women who fight with me are fierce and can take injuries that would kill a dozen men and still fight on."

Minos's warriors didn't waver.

Doug didn't waver either. If anything his presence and the power he held over everyone assembled grew. "Erebus may take issue with the forceful boarding of his ship, of the attack on those blessed by his good graces, and no one should dare lightly the wrath of so powerful a god."

The soldiers kept their stance at the ready, but many of the officials who surrounded Minos began to shrink and squirm. Doug spoke and acted the part of a hero vetted by the gods, and any opposition presented to him could have long reaching and unforeseen consequences.

"Sheer numbers are on your side." Doug gazed steadily at all the guards assembled. "I know this is but a fraction of the fighting men you possess, and more will surely be called upon should the tide of battle turn to our favor." Doug spoke as if he could see the outcome. Minos's soldiers didn't flinch though they likely felt death approach with each breath that passed.

"We will fight bravely, but in the end we will surely be overcome." Doug narrowed his eyes and locked his gaze with Minos.

The king of Crete was the first to look elsewhere.

The power of Minos lessened somewhat. Royal advisors whispered among themselves as Doug continued, "There will be repercussions as the gods judge such a slaughter and why it was committed. Can your intentions for the portal justify the actions to obtain it? Will the portal give you the power and prosperity you vie for, or will it prove the catalyst that earns you the ire of the gods?"

Minos seemed able to see the untenable and tenuous nature of his position. He lowered his hand and the soldiers stood down. "We are at an impasse then. I still desire the portal, but if you are intent on defending it, the cost would be very great indeed."

In the ensuing tense silence, Doug stumbled upon the solution Mopsus hinted at earlier. "I've no desire to die, so I propose this. Allow us to come ashore. Allow my brother to open the portal to fulfill a promise he's already been sworn to, and once that's complete we'll discuss what will be done. You'll see the portal in use and be able to decide more fully if it would be to your benefit or not to own such a device."

Minos clenched his jaw. "Fair enough."

Mopsus put one hand on Mod's shoulder and his other hand on Doug's. "Well done."

"I don't see how bringing the fauns home will save us. We'll most likely be dead within the hour," Doug said quietly to the man. "And if the king doesn't kill us, there's a good chance the minotaur will."

"Have faith, boys." Mopsus clapped them both on the shoulder. "I've a feeling things will turn out favorably as you set about what you've sworn to do."

Doug had One and Four run a plank out. Doug, Mod, and Mopsus walked ashore to stand before the king and his councilors while the automatons stayed on the boat to make ready defenses for a possible hasty retreat.

The hoop of the portal snapped into place and Mod turned the portal on. Mod looked from Mopsus to Doug then stepped through the void.

Larry's voice, muted and unclear, could be heard on the other side. "Dude, you totally were good to your word! Awesome!"

At the sound of Larry's voice all the color drained from Minos's face.

A woman with blond, wooly curls walked up behind Minos just as Mod disappeared. "What's this, dear? Have we visiting dignitaries we should make welcome?"

More color disappeared from Minos.

"Pasiphae, wife of Minos," Mopsus whispered smugly to Doug.

"Now almost all the players are here. Do the queen's golden ringlets look familiar?"

Doug's eyes widened slightly with realization. "You've got to be kidding me."

"Watch," Mopsus said. He sounded as if he was enjoying the unfolding drama immensely.

At this moment the king appeared to be carved of the finest white marble. "Close the portal," he croaked. "The portal is dangerous to me."

The portal stayed open.

Larry, Darrell, and Darrell stepped through the doorway. Darrell and Darrell both took a deep sniff of the air and Larry basked in the sun on the dock. "Feels different from the sun on Karpathos. Helios must radiate more here. I've missed the Cretean sun." Larry looked over, noticed the king for the first time and bobbed his head. "Hey, pops."

"*SQUEEEEEEEEEEEE!*" Pasiphae squealed and raced forward toward the fauns.

"Shit. It's over now." Minos held his head in his hands. "She's seen them."

"Oh, my precious, precious boys!"[3] She grabbed the three round the necks and pulled them all close as she proceeded to choke them with her overly enthusiastic love. "How I've missed you! How I cried when I thought you were dead! Mwah! Mwah! Mwah!" She smothered the brothers in kisses. "But you're alive! And you're here! And I love you so much!"

The mouths of all of the automatons dropped open at the sight. "You three are all sons of the king?" One asked.

"Step," Minos muttered. "Stepsons. Not my boys."

---

3. Pasiphae got around. But it was ancient Greece, so it wasn't really a reason to be judged by society though she was somewhat judged by the resulting children.

Pasiphae plus Marathonian Bull equals Minotaur

Pasiphae plus Panera the Goat equals Larry, Darrell, and Darrell

Pasiphae plus Papia the Duck equals Donald

"Your father said you boys had been out on a boat." Pasiphae looked at them and smiled. She was an unsettling sight. Her makeup had run and tears and snot streamed down her face.

"Pops took us out on the boat," Larry said. "We were excited because he really didn't do much with us. Father and sons bonding. It was nice."

Pasiphae sobered up a bit. "He said you were lost in a storm."

"Clear seas," Larry said as one of the Darrells tapped him on the shoulder and whispered in his ear. "And clear skies. Was a nice day, really."

Pasiphae stopped burbling and turned to look at Minos. "He said you fell overboard."

"Nope. Tossed. After we got in our sleeping bags," Larry explained. "Pops tucked us in by tying the tops closed. He said it would be warmer that way, which was odd, because it was the middle of summer."

"Really?" The word was drawn out and cold. Pasiphae glared at her husband and pulled the fauns closer to protect them.

"A miscommunication," Minos tried to explain. "Now rectified. We welcome you boys back home. We are so glad to see you." The king, for all his rumored skill in diplomacy and reputed intelligence, was a terrible liar. "We'll have a party, pull out all the stops, kill the fatted calf."[4]

Larry's ears perked up at the mention of a bovine. "How is Taury anyway? I'll be glad to see the little tyke."

"Taury?" Doug asked Mopsus.

"The faun's younger brother. The minotaur," Mopsus explained.

"Ooohhhhh," Nine said from up on the boat. "The fauns and the minotaur are brothers. Everything makes much more sense now."

"Our quest just said we were to free the minotaur but made no mention of where he had to go after that." Doug walked over to

4. Pretty good deal for everyone but the calf.

Pasiphae. "My queen, here is a key to the basement. Go get your son."

"All the boys can stay in the basement. There's plenty of room." Minos attempted damage control. "Plenty of space down there."

Far too little, far too late.

"Oh, there'll be someone staying in the basement." Pasiphae eyed Minos from the corner of her eye as she held onto her sons protectively. "Mark my word."

Chapter 21

Ladies' Night

The three women sat in an intimately lit booth at the back of the bar. Atropos (the inflexible) was dressed in a fine peplos. Kali Maa (Hindu goddess of destruction) was naked, blue-skinned, and four armed. Ethel Rosenbach (Secretary of Education for the greater state of New Jersey) was dressed in a no-nonsense gray business suit and skirt with lines and edges so hard and sharp the outfit was apparently carved from granite.

The king of the gods approached the booth. "Ladies." Zeus indicated the open space at the front of the booth. "Do you mind?"

Zeus knew Atropos and Kali Maa both enjoyed his company, but they waited for Ethel to give permission for the king of the gods to sit. Ethel took a slow sip of her drink, nodded her acceptance of the proposal, put her drink back on the coaster, and folded her hands in her lap.

"My thanks." Zeus turned a chair backward so he could rest his arms on its back when he sat down. "I don't plan to stay overlong. I apologize for interrupting, but I needed to speak to Atropos about some odd happenings."

Atropos narrowed her eyes and glared at the god. "Are you the one messing with my yarn?"

"I never mess with the weavers of fate," Zeus said honestly. "People ask me to alter destiny all the time, but I trust your judgment over mine in the matter."

"So it's not you?" Atropos looked confused. "If it'd been you, I'd feel some relief. Someone's messing with the pattern of the grand tapestry, and I could only think of one or two who could do it. If you aren't the one . . ." She screwed her eyes tight and pressed her palms over them. "This is all so very frustrating."

"I'm not sure how you do it all," Zeus admitted. "I know the basic principles and concepts, but the mechanics and magnitude of how you trim all the threads eludes me."

"It's severing threads. What's hard about that?" Kali Maa pushed her straw to the side and took a large nip from the ice on the top of her drink.

"There's an art to it, Kali, my dear," Ethel said. "Your technique is ending things in one grand flourish. Efficient, but not very precise."

Kali Maa nodded. "A valid assessment, I admit."

Ethel continued, "Atropos keeps track of every living thing, their actions and interactions with others, and severs the line of life at the exact right moment."

Atropos pulled at her hair. "Thousands and tens of thousands and hundreds of thousands of threads a day. Tiny threads of gossamer and silk for the insects and such. Fine thread for the animals, growing in girth and resilience with the size of the beast. A thicker, substantial cord for men and their kin. I keep them all organized and in their proper place, never losing them in the weave, never tangling them with the lines spooling out by the yard next to hundreds of thousands of adjacent threads."

"But lately?" Zeus probed as he guessed there was more to come.

"Lately?" Atropos grabbed her drink, drained all that was left in one large gulp, and slammed the empty down on the tabletop. "Someone's doing something, I'm sure of it. I've never had a tangle or a knot, and all of a sudden I have an entire wall of threads that should've been cut that aren't!"

Zeus looked rather concerned. "Chickens?"

Atropos's eyes went wide. "How the #%X@# did you know?"[1]

---

1. I can't repeat it here or the book would burst into flames. Five letters. Starts with a Q.

The uttered word made all the glasses at the table burst into shards.

Zeus nodded like he deserved the harsh rebuke.

Kali Maa caught most of her fruity cocktail in her hands. She almost did a spit-take on everyone at the table.

Somewhere across the bar, Hel laughed.[2] "Nice one," she said as she raised a glass in their direction.

Ms. Rosenbach placed a large napkin atop the remains of her drink. "Atropos, dear," Ethel reached out and patted the younger woman's hand. "We must not let our frustrations bring us down to a primal level. Never give your lessers the satisfaction." Ethel cast a disapproving look at Zeus. "I'm sure Mr. Zeus was just about to explain himself."

Isaac appeared just over Zeus's left shoulder. "Here, let me clean that up and refresh your drinks."

"I think we're good on the drinks for now," Ethel said.

Kali Maa looked disappointed, like she'd wanted another round.

"But if you would be kind enough to give us a minute and come back with a towel?" Ethel continued.

Isaac smiled and took a step back. "You take your time and finish whatever business you need to. I'll take care of everything once you're through." He bowed and smiled at each of them. "Ladies. Sir." And then he was gone.

"My apologies." Zeus looked suitably sheepish and humble. "I meant no distress. I was only trying to figure out why some things are defying the natural order. I noticed a flock returning topside and talked to Hades about it."

"A flock? A *flock*?" Atropos sounded a little maniacal. "Two-thousand birds is one heck of a flock of chickens."

Zeus nodded and gave her a kind smile. "It was enough of a gathering that even my blind eyes couldn't miss it. I've no doubt that's a

2. Hel: Norse goddess of, well, Hell.

bigger anomaly than you've ever encountered. If I can find out how it happened, I can try to make sure that it will never happen again."

"Two-thousand threads reknotted and restrung." The Fate drug her fingernails across the tabletop in frustration. "Someone came in and attached all of those severed lines in my workspace. *My workspace*! And I have no idea who."

"You were there when it happened?" Zeus said. "If you were, any information you have could help me in finding out who's responsible."

"Of course I was there. When was the last time I took a day off?" Atropos said.

"It's not like you do nothing but work. You're in a bar now," Kali Maa pointed out.

She shot Kali Maa a glare, then Atropos sighed and shook her head. "Sorry. That came out a bit harsher than I meant it. I couldn't see anyone, but I watched the thread rise up like it was being held between someone's fingers. Then the phantom picked up the other end and tied the two together."

"While you watched? And you saw nothing?" Zeus tugged on his beard as he thought for a moment. "Did you feel anything while it happened? Anything out of place or odd?"

"Someone was violating my sacred space, of course I felt—" Atropos stopped suddenly.

"Go on, dear," Ethel coaxed. "You stopped in the middle of what had potential to become an epic tirade as if something just occurred to you."

Atropos nodded. "It's always a bit dim in the room, and calm, but it was darker that day, and for the first time I can remember there was a bit of a draft. I remember because I could hear a dog barking, and I thought someone left a window open." She blew out her breath and sat back heavily in her seat. "Darker and breezy? I was probably just tired."

Zeus reached across the table and gently turned Atropos's chin so she was facing him. "Look at me. I want you to really hear what I have to say."

She scowled and rolled her eyes but settled her gaze on him.

"You don't make mistakes. Of all the things I can count on in everything I watch over, I can trust you to do things right. Someone is messing things up for you and you care so much you feel you're responsible." His gaze intensified as he leaned in closer. "You are not responsible for this, and I will find who is."

"I don't—I don't know. It shouldn't have ever happened. Maybe I'm just getting old and it's time to think about quitting and doing something else."

Zeus sighed and shook his head as he leaned back. "You're the second one to talk to me about stepping down in as many days."

She looked at him like the statement shocked her.

"Hades is taking it rough too," Zeus clarified. "Atropos, you and my older brother are among the most talented and dedicated people I know. If someone can be so subtle as to be sowing uncertainty in the minds of the two of you, take a guess what they might be doing to those possessing lesser wills?"

"Everything being told at this table sounds very familiar to me," Ethel said. "Sounds to me as if someone is prepping for a change of administration." Ethel looked as if she now weighed Zeus's resolve and capabilities. "You be careful, young man. I think someone is gunning to be your replacement."

"Astute as ever, Ethel. I shall be on my guard." Zeus nodded to the others at the table as he rose. "Ladies. Thank you for your time. Please let me know if you see anything else amiss. Whoever is doing this is playing in the shadows and will have to stop if their efforts come to light." Zeus glanced over his shoulder. "Isaac, I'm taking care of the tab for this table."

"You most certainly are not," Ethel told the god. "I told the girls it was my treat today, and I'll not have you rob me of my promise."

Zeus inclined his head to Ethel. "I only offered as a way of expressing my gratitude. I meant no disrespect. Have it as you will for today, but if the next excursion for you women were on me, would that be acceptable?"

Ethel nodded curtly, and Isaac gave Zeus a thumbs up.

"My thanks." Zeus put his hand to his chest and bowed to the ladies before he made his way to the exit.

Zeus knew the women in the bar watched him intently as he left.

"I always enjoy seeing him walk away," Ethel said in a slightly bawdy voice.

A grin spread over Zeus's face as he stepped outside. *Still got it.*[3]

3. Is it inappropriate to notice the attention given to you by the opposite sex in a time of crisis? Probably. But Zeus *is* a guy. Give him a break.

CHAPTER 30
GORGON PICNIC

THE TEMPLE SAT ON A SMALL, ISOLATED ISLAND TO THE EAST OF the isle of Lesbos. Not exactly secret, but not really on the main tourism circuit. Most of the Gorgon[1] Medusa's victims were people the gods wanted to off, so the unfortunates were unwittingly directed to the spot of their ultimate demise. These people, by and large, deserved what they got. A notable exception was Atychos, one of the mainland yokels who got really, really lost while trying to deliver a wheel of cheese to a fall festival.

The wheel of cheese was not immune to Medusa's curse either. It was the perfect size to be a fairly comfortable stone stool. Atychos's chiton had billowed in the moment he dropped the cheese, so now it was somewhat like sitting on a stool under the shade of a beach umbrella as long as you didn't look up to see what the billowing stone skirt had once concealed.

"Comfortable?" Three asked.

Nine rested smugly on the block of petrified cheese. He obviously hadn't paid attention before he sat down.

---

1. Gorgon: a name most often associated with Medusa, who was a beautiful young woman sworn to celibacy during her service to the goddess Athena. Poseidon saw Medusa going to Athena's temple, was driven mad with lust, and forced himself upon her. Athena felt the violation was a personal offense, but instead of going after Poseidon, she accused Medusa, and placed upon Medusa one of the most horrifying of all curses in Greek history. The takeaways from this brief explanation? Medusa is a victim. And gods are often jerks.

"Don't turn around too quickly or you'll likely put out an eye," Three challenged.

Nine didn't know what she was talking about, so he turned around anyway.

"Oh, you are a foul, foul woman!" Nine spat at his sister as he rose up and searched for another, less offensive, spot to sit.

Three sat down on the petrified cheese, gave Atychos's underskirt topography a quick evaluating glance, and nodded her approval. "Not half bad."

"Doug! She's mocking me!" Nine cried, poking a finger at his sister.

"Oh, just let it go." Doug saw nothing wrong with Three's good-natured teasing. It lessened the tension for everyone except picked-upon Nine. "So, is everything set up the way I asked for it to be?"

"Took care of it all before Three offended the prude," One confirmed.

"I'm still not sure of this," Mod said.

Doug shrugged. "It's simple. Impress the Gorgon with my gift and convince her to give me her bow."

"The task says you have to obtain the bow, not how you have to get it," Mod said. "We could steal it. Sneak in under the cover of night."

"The direct approach is kinder and endangers less of my family and friends."

Doug had talked to Mod and the others about it. Mod hadn't found the dangerous solution Doug had come up with amusing. He'd said as much to Doug multiple times.

"Trust me," Doug reassured Mod.

"It's a different approach, a really different approach," Mod said. "But still, this is Medusa we're talking about."

Doug patted his brother on the back. "It'll be alright. I've got a good feeling about this." It still wouldn't hurt to get some divine information to back him up, though. Doug turned to Mopsus. "Any insights on this one?"

"The gods are silent," the seer said.

"Do you realize how often you say that?" Doug teased Mopsus a little.

"Tis not normally so." The seer shrugged. "I wonder anew why my inspiration, my connection to the gods, usually so reliable and free flowing, is of recent so still. I'm hoping in this instance you blindsided them with the idea just like you blindsided us. It's either that or they're choosing not to say anything."

Doug could see Mopsus was frustrated. "I didn't mean to stress you out over it." Doug squeezed the seer on the shoulder. "You've done a great job with what they've given you."

Doug's lips twisted up into the lopsided grin that fit his face so well. "Nothing more to it then. Remember to stay back, even you mechanicals. No sense anyone taking any risks they don't have to."

Doug took a long, thick strip of cloth and tied it over his eyes. He tilted his head this way and that to see if the blindfold would remain in place and secure. Satisfied, his grin grew. "If you gentle people will point me in the right direction, we can get this started."

Doug caught Mod's hand mid-reach because he was expecting his brother to try to stop him. "I know you're worried. We'd be stupid not to think this is, well, stupid. But it feels right. It'll work because no one, not in all the history of the world, has tried something like this."[2] Doug gave Mod's hand a squeeze.

"Fine." Mod turned Doug a half turn to the right. "You're set."

Doug moved into the shadows of the ruins.

Doug wound back and forth through the tumbled marble columns of the entry court, then began to count steps in an attempt to avoid the statuary. He stopped and readjusted whenever he ran into something.

---

2. There's direct ways of dealing with a monster or perceived threat, and then there are unorthodox methods. The wild man in the Sumerian legend of Gilgamesh, Enkidu, is tamed in the wilderness by a temple prostitute. An inventive use of the missionary position to achieve a goal. Doug does not plan on subduing Medusa the same way. And I was talking about proselytizing, not the other thing. Get your mind out of the gutter.

Doug made it to the steps of the main hall where he stopped. He knew what he'd planned, knew what he intended to do and hoped to accomplish, but here, in this moment, he had a harder time moving forward than he'd expected.

"Hello?" His voice cracked so bad he cleared his throat and repeated himself. "Hello? Medusa? Are you home?"

No response. It was absolutely silent.

Doug was about to call out again when a quiet, harsh reply echoed from the darkened room beyond. "Go while you can, boy. I've no desire to add to my garden of effigies today. I'll be compelled to do so should you linger."

"I don't really intend to be turned to stone. I just have a few things to ask of you, if I may?"

There was a resigned sigh, and the sound of someone moving forward. "I did try to warn you," the voice lamented. "Pity. You sound young. You still could've had much to look forward to. Tell me what you came here for before my curse seals it behind stone lips forever."

"I did come here for something," Doug admitted, "but I'd like it to be in a manner of a trade. I'd like to give you something I hope you'll like, if you'll allow me."

"I can take whatever you brought for me from your lifeless fingers. With ease," the voice sounded wary but intrigued. "What, of all the items in the realm of Uranus above or the depths of Gaea below, might I possibly be willing to trade for?"

"Won't be the same if you just take it from me," Doug said. The footsteps of the Gorgon were very close now, but oddly enough, Doug felt better and better about what he planned.

Doug heard the sound of the footsteps stop at the top of the steps.

She must be looking at me, judging my intent. Doug waited for her to address him.

"Standing right here in the open," she noted. "You're either more confident or stupider than most. At the moment I really have no idea which."

"I could easily be both," Doug laughed. "Do I have to choose one over the other?"

"I have before me a youth, happy and strong and healthy, and endearingly dumb," she said. "You should leave."

Doug could hear it in her voice. She was glad to have walked out to see him, but fearful of what might happen. "I can't leave. I haven't shown you what I wanted to yet." He leaned forward in a formal bow and held out his hand.

Medusa scoffed. "What in Eros's twisted fantasies are you expecting me to do?[3] Take your hand? I'm not some girl going with you to the summer festival. I'm a monster who's been responsible for the deaths of hundreds."

Doug held out his hand, insistent. "What I have set up for you isn't the same if I don't escort you," Doug explained. "Just trust me for a second, okay?" He stretched his fingers out a little farther.

Medusa's voice fell into a whisper. "I desperately want to trust you, but there's no way I can." Her voice gained a little strength before she continued. "You'll die just by being here! Flee while you still have a chance!"

Doug shook his head ever so slightly and let his outstretched hand creep closer. "It'll be worth it."

Doug had always been a good judge of the level of trust someone or something else had in him. He could feel that Medusa was conflicted. She wanted to send him away, but her curiosity was piqued.

Her fingertips brushed against the palm of his outstretched hand.

Doug twined his fingers with hers and rose from his bow. His face beamed. "I know I have clammy hands, and I might be a bit sweaty, but if you hold my hand tighter you don't notice it as much."

He tightened his grip, and she let him.

---

3. Eros's twisted fantasies were actually pretty tame. Being from a family with a reputation, he really only wanted to participate in a few normal, everyday things. Like splitting a milkshake with someone using two straws or going on a double date to prom or just hanging out and having a pizza and sodas.

"I'd forgotten how good it was just to touch another person. Boy," she said softly, "you should go while you still can."

He squeezed her hand just a bit to reassure her. Then he backtracked the path he'd used to find her. "Call me Doug."

Doug concentrated so he wouldn't veer off the memorized path. Every time he stopped to say something he'd have to count how many steps he'd taken to reorient himself.

He walked headlong into the petrified outstretched arm of some overly muscled creature. Doug gave the statue a quick once over with his fingers. The statue's hands ended in the claws of a crab. "He must have been pretty scary to deal with."

"Achaeus," Medusa answered.[4] "All he cared about was money. He thought I had a stash of treasure somewhere."

"Fat lot of good greed did him." Doug felt around to the points of Acheaus's claws. They were still pretty sharp. "Glad I didn't walk into that; it could have blinded me." He pointed at the blindfold and let his mouth gape.

Medusa didn't respond to his attempt at a joke. "You didn't ask if there was a treasure."

"I'm sorry. Was I supposed to?" he asked.

"You don't care about riches?" Medusa pressed the issue.

"Not really." Doug sidestepped the petrified monster, recentered on his intended path, and was off again.

Medusa gave a little surprised snort.

Her questions had made him lose his orientation. Doug could feel the sun, bright and pleasantly warm, leading him on. A light breeze brought perfume-laden air from an orchard somewhere nearby. "I'd have you lead, since you can see and you know the property better than I do, but it would ruin the surprise."

"I'd forgotten I live in the midst of beautiful things," Medusa said.

---

4. Think of a cross between the real-life versions of the characters Mr. Crabs and Larry the Lobster from *SpongeBob SquarePants*. Doug was lucky he couldn't see it. The sight of Acheaus was *terrifying*.

"I'd love to take it all in, but . . ." He pointed at the blindfold and grinned. Doug paused for a moment to get his bearings. He took a deep breath and caught a faint hint of something delicious. "I think we're almost there. Stone wall and an apple tree off to the right?"

"Just a few yards away," she responded.

"Great." Doug said. "We're close enough. Will you close your eyes for a second?" He knew Medusa was cautious, but she'd come this far.

"My eyes are closed," she said.

Doug moved her forward a couple yards. The wonderful smells were much stronger now. "It might not be perfect," he said. "I'm judging the direction we're facing based on the warmth of the sun on my face."

"It will be fine, I'm sure." Medusa sounded a bit excited.

Her being excited was good. Doug was sure she hadn't looked forward to anything in a very, very long time.

"A little to the right, maybe?" Doug inhaled deeply and nodded. "We're probably close enough. Okay. You can look now."

She gave a little gasp.

Doug knew what she was seeing. He'd set it up just a while before.

A lovely little blanket sat partially in the shade of the fruit tree, the other end of the blanket cushioned by a carpet of blue-green grass. There was fruit and wine and fancy little sandwiches. There were even those little desserts made with berries and fresh cream layered with some kind of cake.[5]

"It's a picnic," Doug said.

Everything was quiet for a moment as the reality of the scene sunk in.

Doug really had no idea what was going to happen, and then Medusa gasped and began to cry.

---

5. Parfaits. I used to live for a good parfait. Doug didn't know what to call it because the dessert didn't get a name until it showed up in some French cookbook in the 1890s.

"I thought—well, I thought you probably haven't been out for a while, and you might like to just sit down and have a nice meal and feel normal for a bit." Doug listened as the Gorgon continued to weep. "I'm sorry if I did something wrong."

"No." Medusa choked back a sob. "You didn't do anything wrong at all."

Doug gripped her hand a bit tighter. "Are you going to be okay?"

Medusa latched onto Doug's forearm to steady herself. "Yes, Doug." She stifled a sniffle and gave a little laugh. "I think I'll be just fine."

"Whew. I am so glad you're okay with this." Doug swept his arm out to indicate the meal. "If the lady would like to take her seat, I have many fine things prepared for her culinary enjoyment."

"It would be my pleasure." Medusa giggled.

Chapter 31

End of a Curse

The conversation was pleasant and lighthearted, the food delicious. They spoke of why Doug was here, and he told her of Larisa and his twelve-part quest. He asked about her, and finally got her to open up enough that she spoke of memories long buried, and how she wished things could have been so much different. The pleasantness of the situation made it clear to Doug just how overwhelming the reality of life was for Medusa.

Every so often she just broke down and cried.

"Are you all right?" Doug sat aside the pita and cheese he'd just taken a bite of.

The gorgon blew her nose on a napkin. "Oh, I'm fine. This is just an emotional day," She sniffled. "I never thought I could feel this—Normal again, you know? And then when I actually forget for a moment what I am I realize this is temporary, and it'll all go back to like it was before when you leave." She was silent for a moment. "Bittersweet."

"I've been thinking about that." Doug leaned a little closer. "Would you mind terribly if I were to try something?"

"In my recent memory, by the time I've been in someone's presence this long, I've either been injured or am watching the last earthly movements as my attacker slowly turned to marble. Most often both."

"Odd segue, but it has been an odd day." Doug didn't waver. "Do I need to point out how I'm bucking the trend?"

She didn't answer the last question. Sounding tentative and fearful, Medusa managed a slight whisper. "What would you like to do?"

Doug scooted a bit closer and raised his hand just a bit. "Could I touch your hair?"

"What a ridiculous request!" She snorted. "No, you idiot. It might bite you."

"I don't think it will." Doug really meant it. "But just to be on the safe side, your hair isn't a bunch of adders, is it?"

"Asps." Medusa corrected him, then chuckled. "I'm not sure what kind of snakes my hair is? Are?" She paused. "There aren't any asps in Greece? Are there? What if I told you my hair wasn't poisonous and it wound up killing you?[1] Wait, let me grab a strand and look at it." There was a pause and a hiss. "It doesn't look like an adder or cobra or such."

Doug grinned at her like an idiot, the number of teeth exposed grew larger the longer she debated.

"You're teasing me?" She couldn't help but laugh along. "Oh, gods, I can't believe you have me joking about that. I don't think my snakes are poisonous, but no one's ever gotten close enough to find out before."

Doug sat in silence, sincere and earnest.

"I don't want to hurt you," she said.

"Do you want me to sign a waiver?" His grin cocked off to one side.

"Oh, Pan's hairy back,"[2] she swore. Doug felt Medusa leaning closer. "Go ahead, but don't say I didn't warn you."

With her permission, his hand brushed the nape of her neck, and his fingers combed the hair at the back of her head. His fingers glided along her temple next as he brushed the hair out of her face so he

---

1. If it was the kind of snake that killed with a bite, it would have to be venomous. Poison has to be ingested. A small distinction easily forgotten or misunderstood. We can't blame Medusa for misunderstanding this insignificant bit of trivia.
2. It really was. You have no idea. He had a back like an unruly yurt wall.

could tuck it behind her ear. "This doesn't feel like snakes to me." He leaned back and dropped his hands to his lap.

Medusa said nothing.

"Would it be alright if I touched your cheek?" Doug pressed.

She was crying again.

"Medusa?" Doug asked.

"Sorry. I nodded, but then I remembered you couldn't see me," she said. "You can touch my cheek if you want to."

Her skin was smooth beneath his touch. Warm and soft in contrast to the coolness of his fingertips. He wiped away tears from her face the best he could without seeing. "Medusa, I don't believe you're cursed," Doug said.

"Well, you're an idiot then." The words came harsh and clipped. She pulled away from his touch. "I'm pretty sure I'm the definition of cursed."

"Fair enough," Doug said. "You are and have been cursed, but I think it's time the curse is broken."

"Like you get to decide that." Medusa scoffed.

"Let's find out." Doug turned his head skyward and raised his arms to the heavens. "Zeus, king of the gods and protector of us all, I think this woman has been unjustly burdened with a weight she has no right to bear. She's suffered this without recourse or hope for redemption. It has brought horror to her life and denied her the beauty in the world around her. Hear this plea and give her, your mortal child, a respite from the pains she's endured." He bowed his head and folded his arms to his chest.

"Please, hear me, my lord. I believe this deeply, so deeply that now I seal my resolve." With the final words, he pulled off his blindfold.

"*No*!" Medusa screamed and screwed shut her eyes. Sobs wracked her slight frame. "Oh, Doug, you stupid, sweet, idiot child! Why did you have to do it? Your girl will never see you again because you looked at me." She wept and beat her hands on the ground, not caring what treats and foods she mangled and scattered. "Stupid boy!

Why in all the realms of the gods would you do something so, so grand?"

Medusa was crying so hard she almost didn't feel the gentle hands on her shoulders that shook her to get her attention.

"Medusa," Doug said softly. "It's all right. I'm fine. I'm fine and so are you. We're all right."

"This isn't real! If I look, you'll be stone!" she screamed and refused to open her eyes.

Doug scooted in a little closer, ignoring the mess of the picnic she'd made as she flailed about. He put his arm around her shoulders, and she collapsed against his chest. "It's all right," Doug soothed. "It's all right."

"You feel of flesh, not stone," she managed before she began to blubber. "What if it's me looking at you that turns you to stone?"

"Please open your eyes?" Doug asked softly.

Medusa shuddered and managed a weak nod.

"What do you see?" Doug asked.

"A fuzzy pair of knees." She hiccoughed.

"Not the first sight of your new life I would have chosen but revealing of my un-petrified existence nonetheless." Doug helped her sit up straight and took a soft cloth as he wiped away the tears that blurred her vision.

Medusa looked into his eyes, and the still-living Doug looked back.

She threw her arms around his neck and broke down again. "You stupid, sweet, moron! How could you take such a reckless chance?"

"Your curse"—Doug stroked her hair and held her tight—"is gone."

Doug watched as she examined herself, wonder in her eyes. She gaped at her arms and legs. "The scales that covered my skin are gone!" She grabbed a handful of hair and pulled it in front of her face. "This is hair, not snakes. Hair!"

She looked like she was going to be sick. Doug caught her before she could fall. He laid her gently on the grass beside the picnic blanket. "Are you all right?" he asked.

It took a moment for her to answer. "Never, in my whole life, have I felt as right as I do right now. Is this real?

"Oh, Doug, I feel so fine." Medusa pushed herself up and shook her head in wonder. "And look at you, hero with the kind eyes who sits so wonderfully colorful and alive before me."

"Yeah, look at me." There had been no hesitation in the moment. Yet now, as he realized what he'd just done, Doug began to understand the ramifications of the situation. He'd just done something reckless to save someone he'd never met before. It had been done on impulse and could have turned out far different than it just had.

And I'd do it again in an instant.

That was a pretty deep truth to realize about himself.

He must have been quiet for a bit too long because now Medusa looked worried about him.

"How do you feel?" she asked.

"My joints feel a little stiff." His impish grin grew brighter.

She slugged him hard on the shoulder.

Then she gave him another hug.

CHAPTER 32

MISOGYNY AND JUDGMENT ON THE BACK OF A BOAT

MEDUSA GAVE DOUG THE BOW HE'D COME FOR.

Task completed, the next task was given.

"Subdue the behemoth that rends the populace of Assos and causes them to flee," Doug read.

"That sounds vague and threatening." Mod had just barely come down from the panic he'd gone through as he worried and waited on his brother.

"At least we know where we're heading," Doug responded.

They left the island with the turning of the tide.

All of them.

Doug had insisted.

Medusa sat on the railing of the ship at the front of the boat, her eyes turned to the ship's wake, the physical prison she'd been confined to for so long was being left behind.

Mod watched her from a distance. He was a bit in awe of her. She was beautiful, and it contrasted so much with the mental image of her he'd started with that it short-circuited his brain. As the rolling of the ocean took hold of *Nyxy Business,* he finally found his mind and set to getting the ship to the next island they were summoned to.

It was all good until Mod heard one of the automatons rumble to the others that something was amiss in having a woman on board a ship.

Mod watched as One grabbed Nine by the front of the shirt and picked him up off the deck. "Hey, moron, if you haven't noticed, there were already two women on the boat before."

Nine narrowed his eyes at Three who lazed against the rails of the boat and then turned his attention back to One, who held him suspended in the air. "You're not women; you're sisters. And, as is so often pointed out, you aren't women born and bred, but machines manufactured and made."

One snorted in disgust and dropped her brother to the deck.

Four, Five, and Six shifted about nervously.

Mod could see the ill-intentioned cogs that slowly turned in One's brothers' heads.

"And you lot? You have a position on this?" One asked.

Five and Six looked like they'd lost the ability to speak, so Four spoke on their behalf. "Nine has a point."

"Are you kidding me?" One scoffed.

Mod caught some of the interaction and tried to ignore the rest.

Until Nine finally took it too far.

Nine puffed himself up and sneered. "Up until an hour ago, she was a monster who posed a danger to mortal and god alike, and all of a sudden we have her onboard with us? She shouldn't be here. I think that women and seamen don't mix!"[1]

The ship was large enough that Doug, Mopsus, and Medusa couldn't hear what was being said at the back of the boat, but that would change if the exchange got any more heated.

Mod had heard enough. "Have you guys got a problem with Medusa?" He wanted to bring the conversation out in the open where he could squash it.

Five and Six looked away.

Four cleared his throat and said nothing.

Three got a disgusted look on her face as she studied her brothers. She shrugged. "Nope. No problem at all."

Nine looked disgusted at his brothers' sudden lack of courage, sparing a particularly nasty glance for Four. "What, you guys

---

1. Phrase revived and delivered perfectly by Weyland Smithers, *The Simpsons*, season four, episode five, "Treehouse of Horror III."

suddenly became suffragettes?" He pointed at Five and Six. "You guys just said you didn't want damaged goods onboard."

"I said who are we to question what the gods have cursed." Five shot back at his brother. "Testing the will of the gods doesn't always go well for those who do it."

"I was so excited when I first met all of you. This is the first time I've ever felt ashamed to know any of you." Mod glared at the male automatons. None but Nine would return his gaze. He met the automaton's stare and rose up in righteous anger. "And you? How dare you? Damaged goods? Says the guy whose factory settings are glitchier than a Popiel invention?"[2] Mod fixed his icy stare at Nine. "Medusa suffered more than anyone should ever have to bear, and she's been granted a new life free of her curse by Zeus himself. No more questions as to her worth or value. From this point forward, you will speak kindly of her or you'll have me to deal with."

Nine did a spooky finger wave at the engineer. "Oooh. Mystery of mysteries! Suddenly the nerd is tough. The monster girl brought out the courage in him. Are you in love?" Nine started making kissy sounds.

Mod's hands gripped the rudder so tightly you could hear the wood creak, his knuckles white. "I have access to all the bits and ratchets necessary to make sure there could be another woman on board."

Nine pulled away, shocked. "Are you suggesting what I think you're suggesting?"

"Neutering a mechanical. No more plug and play." A cool smile

---

2. Popiel of Imbros was a hack. His Mutton-O-Matic was responsible for more than its fair share of household maimings, and his combination Rotisserie Cooker and Mosaic Polisher single handedly destroyed the last vestiges of the Neolithic civilization that centered around Gobekli Tepe in modern day Turkey.

"But wait, there's more!" Ron Popiel, not to be confused with the flimflammer of the Persians, was a savvy businessman and talented creator. Inventor of the Chop-O-Matic, the Ronco Pocket Fisherman, and the 5-in-1 Turkey Fryer & Food Cooking System. The modern day Popiel was a gift and blessing. R.I,P. Prince of invention. Late night infomercials will never be the same without you.

spread across Mod's face. No humor touched his eyes. "We could use the spare parts as a trolling lure for fishing."[3]

"My special friend being gobbled by a fish? Never!" Nine gasped and protectively warded his groin. "You wouldn't dare!"

"Speak bad about her again to find out." Mod then hinted emasculation would not be the only course of action taken. "I have Allen wrenches."

Nine sucked in a hard breath.

Mod continued, "A few twists from the hexagonal bar would be more than enough to bring on a myriad of plumbing problems, and the service calls to fix such problems are hard to schedule and expensive."

A high pitched "*gleep*" escaped Nine's lips. Still cradling his crotch, he hop-skipped away from Mod, through his jeering brothers and sisters, to the front of the boat.

The remaining repentant mechanicals seemed to accept that their leaders made it clear Medusa was welcome. They'd already had their fun at Nine's expense, and that was the end of the discussion.

Mod *hoped* that would be the last of it.

It had been hard for him to stand up for someone like that, but it had felt right.

Doug would have done the same thing.

---

3. Brings a whole new meaning to the name *Pocket Fisherman.*

CHAPTER 33

THE BEAR OF ASSOS

THE SILENT CITY CAME INTO VIEW ON THE SOUTHERN SHORE.

"And the slave king, Hermias, shall welcome thinkers from across the Mediterranean to converge in this place to think mighty thoughts." Mopsus looked on solemnly as the boat drew closer. "Three-hundred and fifty years before the meridian of time, Aristotle will begin his academy here. Assos shall be one of the great pillars establishing western philosophic foundations that will spread to influence the entire world."

"Sounds like an enlightened king." Four nodded as if he approved. "Course, being a slave, I assume he'd have a different outlook on the importance of free thought than those born to nobility. I'm glad this will all work out for him."

"Wouldn't that be nice," Mopsus said with a pained smile. "The dream only lasted a few years. Things will heat up when the Persian Empire starts moving in next door. Aristotle, the great thinker, will see the writing on the wall and skip town. Hermias will try to balance relations between Macedonia to the north and Persia to the east. It will end about as well for Hermias as you'd expect."[1]

---

1. Persian general torturing Hermias. "So, let's just start with what we have. What did this do to you? Tell me. And remember, this is for posterity, so be honest—how do you feel?"

You know what movie this footnote is from, right? Wallace Shawn. Robin Wright. Carol Kane. Cary Elwes...?

No. Not *Flubber*. Guess again.

The city was unearthly quiet as Doug and his crew pulled into the harbor.

"Not the most reassuring of signs." Mopsus pointed out the empty docks. "This is one of the main ports accepting goods from all the cities ringing the Sea of Thrace. There should be boats loading and unloading items to and from Asia. The silence is—"

"Wonderful!" came a call from high above in a watchtower overlooking the large open square abutting the docks.

"We were finally able to think," another voice from up above chimed in.

"Quiet and safe," the first voice said. "No sailors. Or seamen. Or bears."

"Sailors and seamen and bears, oh my!" The second voice laughed with a shudder.

Mopsus shielded his eyes with one hand as he scanned the windows and balconies of the tower high above the open area. "Hello? Kind sirs, might we inquire as to where all the people are?"

"More fodder for the bear?" the first voice asked. A round faced man with a mustache peered over the top of one of the highest porches on the watchtower.

A thin faced man with bushy eyebrows and a huge nose joined him a second later. "Special guests."

Round Face laughed. "Should we warn them?"

"What? And miss the show? We didn't pay for these seats for nothing," Big Nose said.

"We didn't pay for these seats at all," Round Face retorted.

"Is this your tower?" Nine asked. "Did you build it?"

Big Nose snorted. "No, the Trojans built it for our protection."

The surface of the tower had an intricate pattern of rises and dips running from the base to the balconies. The tower was the most visually stunning architecture in the area by far and matched nothing around it. "Does the ribbing and banding on the outside of the tower have a purpose?"

"Doesn't do anything for me," Round Face said.

"Neither does anyone else," Big Nose retorted.

A distinct, unpleasant smell wafted off the square. Doug was the first to notice it, but the others who could smell quickly wrinkled their noses at the stench.

"The odor of death permeates the air," Mopsus said to Doug.

"And no one is about except these two in their high tower." Doug pointed out warily.

Now everyone on the boat stared up at the two men on the balcony.

"We have nothing to fear from the men in the tower," Mopsus said. "This progressive form of punishment is reserved for the wealthy upper class. Imprison them in a high tower where they can observe and reflect on their poor choices while they watch life happen around them, unable to participate, unable to really live."

Big Nose put a finger on his wrist. "No pulse. He's right. I must be dead."

"He didn't say you were dead. He said you had no life," Round Face clarified.

"What's the difference?" Big Nose hacked.

"Are they expecting some sort of reaction?" One asked. "We haven't been here but a minute and they're already getting on my nerves."

"If this were a few years in the future, one might think this is a bad comedy routine," Mopsus said.

Doug arched an eyebrow and studied the two men.

"What's a comedy routine?" Four asked.

"Comedy was just recently invented," Mopsus replied. "At the moment the fledgling art form is mostly defined by political satire, with liberal sexual innuendo and scatalogical references."

Five jabbed his brother Six in the ribs. "Sounds like something right up our alley, 'cept for the political stuff."

Six nodded in agreement.

"If it's anything like what we're hearing right now I'll pass," One said.

"We are a company on a gods given quest," Doug said to the men on the balcony. "As no one else is here to guide us, we would wish to gather information from you two gentlemen. May I inquire as to your names?"

"Having this knowledge will do you any good," Big Nose replied.

"Knowing our names will give them something to scream while they're dealing with the bear," his companion replied.

"That's an unsettling thing to say," Nine observed. "Anybody else freaked out a bit by what they just said?" He looked around to see if he'd garnered any support for his opinion, but nobody was paying attention to him.[2]

"Clearly, they've gone mad. Something terrible must have happened here and they were unable to flee from it," One said as she let her gaze sweep the square.

Scraps of fabric drifted about here and there in the slight breeze. There was an odd coloration to the ground and lower floors of the buildings around them.

"Those who could flee have not returned, including the ones I must assume are the caretakers of the men trapped in the tower. The resulting isolation of this place must have been too much for their fragile minds to take," Mopsus said.

"I was alone for years," Medusa said. "Under worse conditions than this, and I didn't go to pieces."

"You'll get a chance to see the audience go to pieces soon enough," Big Nose said.

---

2. When Odysseus was trapped by Polyphemus, he got the giant drunk, told the huge man that his name was Nobody and promptly gouged out Polyphemus's one eye. The neighbors heard the ruckus, asked if Polyphemus was okay, and left when he replied, "Nobody just poked me in the eye! With a burning stick, even!" While the neighbors thought Polyphemus's answer to their enquiry was oddly specific, they weren't really concerned enough to undertake a casual investigation.

Just to clarify, Odysseus isn't there. The nobody referred to above means everybody in Doug's crew. After being stuck on a boat with Nine and putting up with his crap in close quarters nobody, meaning everybody, just kind of mutually and simultaneously agreed to ignore him.

The two crazy men laughed together.

The passenger and crew of *Nyxy Business* threw down a plank and crossed to stand on the dock under the tower.

"Part of the show now. No going back," Round Face said with a hint of sympathy.

Nine looked disgusted as he kicked a piece of cloth off the dock. The tattered fabric rolled away to reveal part of the human thigh bone it'd concealed. "Uh, guys? Are we sure we want to be here? There appeared to be a lovely little beach we could have stopped at just a way back."

"Where was that?" Four asked, clearly annoyed to even be talking to his brother.

"Crete," Nine said as he took a step back from the fleshy bone.

Doug looked down at the femur. It had claw marks on it spread wide enough apart that whatever made them was bigger than any animal Doug had ever run across. He didn't say anything about it. If the beast was close, it was probably too late to do anything to avoid it.

Something large and loud snuffled down one of the streets that led from the open area. A musical chiming, so soft Doug almost thought he imagined it, could be heard with each of the beast's steps.

"As I just foretold, the main attraction is here," Big Nose's voice quavered above.

"I can't watch another show!" Round Face cried as he tried to hide his eyes behind ineffective, puppet-like hands.

Another loud whuff from somewhere closer, accompanied by the sounds of immense claws as they scraped and rasped along the cobbled streets.

The author of the sound inched into view. Its nose and ears rounded the corner first, followed by the rest of the head. The dog-like face was set in the middle of a skull the circumference of a chariot wheel. Then the rest of the bear came into view.

Doug had never seen an elephant before, but if you lost the tusks, trunk, and oversized ears, covered the remaining gray body in well-worn yellow shag carpeting, and added ten-inch claws to the ends of its feet, you might have a pretty close approximation of what just walked into the square.[3]

The bear shook its head from side to side, a musical note accompanying the movement. A thin golden chain with two little bells at the clasps was tightly wrapped around the great beast's neck.

Medusa looked the animal up and down. "I'm somewhat impressed but not overwhelmed. I've seen my share of monsters in the past. Let's assume this didn't come from the same place as the chickens you told me about."

"That would require a bigger gate than the ones we've encountered," Mod said. "I don't even need to do a quick calculation."

Doug nodded. The bigger, better gate purchased from Hephaestus wouldn't be capable of letting this beast through. "Improbable at best. Besides, this animal doesn't look like it's been to Hades's realm, it just looks massive."

The pans of war sagged limply in the warriors' hands. "Our standard form of attack may not suffice in this instance," Three noted.

Doug held up his hand. He had an obscure memory that teased his mind, something about the beast he recognized or understood, but he just couldn't quite place it. "Give it a second. We really have no idea what it will do." He tilted his head and looked at the thing standing in the entrance of the square.

The thing tilted its head and stared back.

The great bear's front paws beat the ground with a thump that made the water under the dock splash. It hit the ground again and pushed up to stand erect on its back legs. Its head and shoulders easily cleared the roofs of the single-story buildings built next to the tower.

Doug watched the bear and his crew, hoping their reactions to

---

3. You know, like the tan carpet everyone had in their home in the 1970s. It was either the dirty, mottled tan or avocado green or a vomitous orange color. Those were your choices. I think it was required as part of the universal building code.

the beast might trigger his memory and lend insight as to what they might be facing.

Speechless, Mod and the others inched away from the awesome beast.

Not much to be gleaned from my crew, is there? Doug was catching all of the tension from his friends on the peripheral, while most of his attention still silently focused on the bear.

The bear nodded in acknowledgement of the group on the dock and swept its large paws to the top of its head to grab what must be a hat. It held the tattered cap to its chest with both hands, shifted its weight from one foot to the other, and stood as if it waited for something.

"He's just figuring out which of you is the softest, so he can eat that one for dessert," Big Nose said from high above.

"We've seen this performance before," Round Face tried to warn the people on the dock.

The bear glared up at the men in the tower, a burning frenzy ignited behind its eyes. It launched itself at the tower, huge arms almost circling the base of the structure. It tried to climb but the texture of the surface somehow made the bear's claws lose purchase. And as the bells at its neck chimed, the bear seemed to lose track of what it was doing, almost as if the chain and bells were sapping its will and desire to move forward.

Or enraging it.

The bear sent its anger toward the men up above. It began lashing out at their tower, striking the base with blows that shook the surrounding buildings with aftershocks like an earthquake.

Five got a mischievous look in his eye. He pushed Six toward the great swinging arm of the bear.

Six figured out what was happening too late, but still quick enough to grab Five by the sleeve to take his brother along for the ride.

"Well, that wasn't well thought out," Five declared as they both tumbled forward.

The backswing of the great bear's arm took apart both brothers, sending detached limbs and parts flying akimbo all across the open area beneath the tower.

The bear hadn't even noticed it had dismembered the brothers. The beast scrambled to ascend the tower for several minutes, all to no avail. Time and again it rose only a few feet off the ground before the bells would ring and it would slip and fall back to the cobbled streets.

The bear's fury spent, it finally saw the strewn body parts littering the cobbles. It looked panicked for a second, his eyes locking with Doug in desperation.

Doug wasn't going to dismiss the mangling of two of his crew, but he knew the attack on Five and Six was unintentional. It wasn't the bear's fault. Doug held up his hands, and in a clam voice, said, "It's all right."

Nine gaped. "All right?" he hissed in a whisper. "That monster just smooshed my brothers into jelly!"

Six rolled over and grabbed a leg he assumed was his. "That was a terrible joke, Five! I wish I'd done it to you first."

Five stretched and put an arm back into his right socket. "I was going to have you describe what it felt like for me, but I have a pretty good idea."

"See?" Doug indicated the two brothers to the bear. "No harm done."

The bear looked perplexed, yet much calmer as Five and Six put themselves back together. The bear shook its head in wonder and snarled, irritated as the tinkling sound of the chain could be heard again. As soon as the bell went off, it turned its attention back to the tower.

Doug motioned for all of them to be still to not recapture the bear's interest. "No more pranks you two," he said to Five and Six.

Five looked repentant. Six didn't.

"I'm serious," Doug said to both brothers. "Not all of us can be put back together so easily.

"All right. I guess." Six looked at his feet. "Hey, am I supposed to have two left feet?"

Five chuckled. "As it should be, you uncoordinated loser."

Five and Six started tussling again.

The others ignored them.

"You gotta say this for those Trojans, they sure know how to build a bear proof spire," Medusa said.

"I think the bell has more to do with it than the tower. The chain must be enchanted." Doug suspected, but he wasn't sure how to test that hypothesis as of yet. Magic bell notwithstanding, the massive claws of the beast hadn't even scratched the tower. "I'm fairly certain fortifications built by Trojans would be unbreachable by pretty much everything."

"Well, not everything." Mopsus shook his head. "Knowledge of the heavens only seems to be popping in at the most inconvenient and pointless of times, yet now I feel the weight of seeing future and past events regarding Troy fully, not that it helps us as anything but a diversion. Blessing or curse, the knowledge is just there."

"Fair enough," Doug said, willing to embrace a little diversion from the danger looming before them. "What can breach a Trojan defense?"

"A hollow horse and a dash of Trojan self-righteous gullibility," Mopsus answered.

"Who would scoop out a horse?" One asked. "Once again I realize just how much about organics I fail to comprehend."

"Right?" Three said. "I mean, really? Who in their right mind?" She looked from mechanical sibling to mechanical sibling. "What purpose would that even serve?"

"I'll explain later," Mopsus said. "If we get the chance."

Nine stumbled back away from the others as he tried to get to the boat. "Uh, guys, not to change the subject, but we have more immediate concerns than equine excavation."

The bear had given up on its contemplation of the tower, its attention now fully on the crowd gathered on the dock.

Doug looked back at the group to reassure them, a particular warning glance given to Five and Six. "No sudden moves," Doug said to everyone in a deliberately calm and steady voice. "Let's see what all of this is about before we do something that might get anyone else ripped apart."

The bear looked unsure, and nervous, as if it realized it had already lost its chance to make a good first impression. He snatched its cap off the cobbles where it'd dropped before the unsuccessful attempt to scale the tower. Standing on its two hind legs, it held the hat tight to its chest and looked Doug right in the eyes. Then it wiggled its ears.

Doug pursed his lips, unsure as to what he just saw.

The beast bent over double, its center of gravity lowered as it balled up into a crouch. With no warning it uncurled and launched itself into the air.

Nine, Five, and Six all screamed, high-pitched and girlish.

Everyone in the group but Doug took a startled step back.

Something clicked in Doug's mind. He held up a hand to stop his crew from retreating any further, because that was the opposite of what the beast wanted. "Look!" he insisted.

The bear hadn't launched itself at them. Rather, it shot up in the air, almost to the height of the tower balcony, performed three flips on the way up, and another three flips on the way back down. It hit the city street with the force of a meteor strike, its feet firmly planted on the ground.

The bear stood tall, wiggled its ears again, clasped the tattered hat between its lethal claws, and took a bow. The bear's ears flapped in punctuation.

Doug took a step closer to the beast as he ignored the warnings of those behind him. The bear singled its focus on the man, a palpable tension in the air. Doug shook his head from side to side, whispered "I can't believe it," and started to clap.

The face of the bear split into a good natured, although terrifying, grin.

"The traveling acrobats." Mod started to clap along with his brother. A smile grew on his face. "I'd totally forgotten about them."

One by one the others clapped along, until even Nine struck hand to hand and cheered at the beast's antics.

Doug explained over his shoulder, his eyes on the bear. "Many trained animals are taught that to fail to entertain a crowd means a punishment after the performance. Despite his great size, it seems the same training was employed on this big guy. Maybe the trainer took it too far and the big bear finally snapped?"

"He just wanted people to like him?" Mod asked.

"The look on his face is your answer," Doug replied.

The bear looked extremely pleased with the attention. It did a series of somersaults, tiptoed around the open square while it zigged its head from side to side, and wiggled its ears furiously.

Mopsus took a step forward to be closer to Mod. "Acrobats?"

"I didn't remember until Doug started to clap," Mod explained as he continued to applaud. "Once, when we were very young, our father happened upon a group of travelers the likes of which we'd never seen before. They came over huge tracts of land and bodies of water in search of the wild and exotic. Performers from a place far, far east. From a people called the Liangzhu,[4] I think it was? They had a bear with them that would ride a one-wheeled pedal cart or a huge leather ball around in a circle. The bear came from a place beyond even their home, farther to the east and impossibly far north. A place of freezing cold and evergreen trees.

"I have heard of such a place," Mopsus said as he clapped along, "but have never seen a bear from there before."

Doug silenced his hands. "I don't think this bear is from

4. A lost civilization from the area of the Yangtze Delta. Advanced in culture, society, and technology for agriculture and aquaculture, they nevertheless disappeared over four thousand years ago. They told the neighbors they were just stepping out for a bit, and asked if they could water the plants and feed the dog.

The neighbors thought the question incomplete. "Feed the dog to whom?" They wondered.

Liangzhu. It's not a normal bear, so I don't see why it performs and entertains unless it is compelled to do so. Perhaps it has something to do with the chain around its neck?

"Only one way to find out." Doug carefully approached the talented showman.

The bear kneaded the already threadbare hat with razor sharp claws as it nervously watched the youth approach. The young man dropped his gaze just slightly to the side of the animals' eyes and let a toothless smile spread across his face. He held his right hand up, palm down and waited, an open invitation for the animal to be the one to close the space between them. The bear hesitated as it judged the situation. The huge beast shuffled forward until its forehead rested against Doug's open palm. Doug gently brushed the ruffled fur of the animals' brow, scratched its ears, and circled the beasts' head in a warm and playful hug.

You could hear the false teeth of the two tower-dwellers hit the floor of the balcony high above.

Doug scratched the bear down its neck and across its shoulders. He teased its fur into furrows while the bear chuffed its happy approval to be touched. "Wonderful! The best act I've seen in a while. You are a very good performer!" The bear snuggled against the youth and playfully hugged him back.

"The bear is a vicious killer," Nine hissed. "How is Doug able to bewitch it like that?"

"I think the rampage started because someone punished him when a performance didn't go right, and then it got out of hand. This is not just a bear or an entertainer, he's more," Doug said. "I can feel it."

The bear looked at Doug as if it wanted to verify what Doug thought, but was kept from doing so, most likely because of the chain.

Doug leaned against the bear as the beast lay down on the road. "Once he decided I was okay and that I really liked his performance, it was all good."

"So we're done, and the rampage is over?" One asked.

The device in Mod's pocket dinged. "Well someone certainly thinks it is."

"Over for now," Doug said as the bear rolled over and Doug leaned in to scratch its belly. "If we leave him here, he's just going to go bonkers all over again. He really doesn't like the guys in the tower."

The bear cocked its head in the direction of the balcony, saw the two old men who stared through the slats in the railing, and let out a slow growl. The men squeaked and dropped out of sight.

"The horrible critics of the bear in the tower will be left," Doug said. "They seem safe enough there, and they can be dealt with by the returning populace of Assos, since I assume they're the ones who put them there."

"But what about the bear?" Nine asked in a trembling voice.

"That depends on him, doesn't it?" Doug replied.

The bear returned his gaze to Doug, a smile creasing its face.

Carefully, Doug slid his hands in the direction of the chain. "Do you mind if I take a look?"

The bear gave a slow nod, a hopeful look in its eyes.

Doug found the clasp that held the chain around the bear's neck. It was fused somehow, and the chain seemed rooted to the spot so Doug couldn't slide it up and over the bear's head.

"No luck, I'm afraid," Doug said. "The chain's enchanted."

The bear nodded as if he suspected that was the case. He looked disappointed yet grateful Doug had tried to help.

Four furrowed his brow. "If the bear is in his right mind now, why did he rampage amongst the citizens here? Is this a god or just an animal?"

"I think whatever the chain's enchantment does, it pushes our friend right up to the breaking point," Doug said. "He's smarter and stronger than the average bear, so he's fighting the effect of the chain. He's doing fine now, but I would suggest no one do anything to upset him until we can find someone to help get the chain off."

"Then why did the bear try to attack the men in the tower unprovoked? They didn't say anything snarky or upsetting about him or his performance to set him off," Four asked.

"I think the bear just hates them," Doug answered.

The bear nodded.

Four turned to Nine. "You probably should stay away from the bear."

Nine laughed nervously and moved back a couple more steps.

"So did we finish the task, or not?" One asked.

"The box dinged just a bit ago," Mod pointed out.

"I guess if the box thinks so, the task must be done," Doug said as he smiled at the bear.

The bear smiled back, reassuring and terrifying.

Mod fished the task device out of his pocket and took out the scroll. He handed the next task to Doug.

Doug read the scroll, nodded, and handed it back to his brother.

"So what do we do?" Nine asked. "We can't leave the beast here and we can't take him with us."

"Oh, we can take the bear to someone who can help deal with the chain binding him." Doug scratched the bear's ears, and the bear nuzzled Doug's face. "It just so happens to coincide with where we need to head next."

"Our next task says we're off to visit Hephaestus so we can put out the fires in his forge. Old Heph will know what to do about the bear's chain."

CHAPTER 34

THE CHAINS THAT BIND

A MOLTEN GLOW EMANATED FROM MULTIPLE POOLS OF liquified rocks and ores. The light tinted the depths of the huge pit in a hellish glow. Ominous red and gold illumination cast harsh shadows and backlighting among the tortured rock formations. Great gouts of heat and steam blistered the air with gasses that choked and fumes that poisoned with a breath.

Deep in the bowels of the huge crater, a giant welcomed an unexpected guest.

"Oh, that is just so adorably precious!" Hephaestus tittered and clapped his hands. The god that commanded the molten ores, heat, and steam that filled the huge caldera, a god gruff, tough, and manly, baby talked every time he looked at the bear.

"Uh, Heph?" Doug raised a finger to try to get the attention of the god. "He's not a puppy, and I didn't really bring him here to be a pet."

It appeared to Doug that Hephaestus hadn't clued in yet. Or he was being willfully ignorant. *Wouldn't be the first time.* Doug folded his arms and waited for the god to tire himself out.

"Who is my pwecious, widdle baby? Does widdle fuzzy baby want to stay with Pawpaw? Hmm? Does he? Does he, pwecious?" The forge god giggled and tickled the giant bear under its arms and the bear promptly bit him.

Maybe the bear can hold its own. Doug thought as the rest of the crew watched slack jawed at the interaction before them.

"Oh, how cute! He's teething!" Hephaestus beamed. He held the bear at arms' length with both hands and drank him in with his eyes.

The god almost swooned before he pulled the bear close and nearly smothered him with kisses.

"You know," Mod watched as the god played with the bear and the bear made a halfhearted attempt to get away, "I'm almost inclined to be worried about the hairy creature."

"Which one? Hephaestus and the bear are both rather furry," Mopsus said, confused.

"I was referring to the welfare of the bear," Mod clarified.

Doug had a slight sense of trepidation when he asked if the god could come to pick the animal up. Hephaestus, big in everything he does in life, always showed a tendency to be a tad over the top in making a first impression. He also didn't make friends easily, so he might misread the reason Doug brought the bear to him in the first place.

Doug's fears faded the longer the bear and the giant interacted. Hephaestus's true heart and good nature became apparent, and now the bear reveled in the fact it could interact with someone without accidentally dismembering them.

"No, this is perfect," Mod said to the seer. "Heph is just a bit over-excited at the thought of a new friend and will be proud as punch when he figures out the bear can do tricks."

"The bear can do tricks?" A look of absolute delight dawned on Heph's face. "Fuzzy widdle puppy can do jumps and rolls and play dead?" He held the bear up and looked at him again as he sniggered in a high pitched, excited staccato.

Doug gave Mod a reproaching glance. "Did you have to bring that up?"

"What?" Mod asked, clueless.

Doug signed and turned to the god. "The bear was probably compelled to perform. Most likely through force," Doug said. "If he wants to continue doing any such thing it will really be up to him."

"How will I know if he wants to perform or not?" Heph asked.

"Take the chain compelling the bear off of its neck and then we'll see," Doug said.

The bear nodded to Doug then turned back to the god of the forge, craning his neck to the side to expose the chain. His fur was so thick nothing but a link or two of the gold was even visible.

"See?" Doug said. "He wants it off. That's part of the reason I came to you."

Heph looked hesitant. "I like him. I kinda want him to stay. If I take off the chain, he might leave."

"We do a thing because it is right, not because of what we want at the time," Mopsus said.

Heph looked appropriately chastened by the words from the seer. "Fine. Show me the chain."

The bear turned his head further in a futile attempt to expose the chain. He tried too hard, and a slight tinkling of bells could be heard in the caldera.

The bear shook his head and got a dazed look in his eyes.

Now Heph was paying attention. "The chain is powerful."

"It seems the chain dulls his higher reasoning. He's in an unfamiliar place, and just recently introduced to us. Give him a moment." Doug said in a quiet voice.

The bear backed away and bared his teeth.

Doug signaled for everyone to wait a moment while the power of the bells wore off.

After a few moments, the bear blinked hard and looked at Doug, desperation in his eyes.

"It's almost too much for you, isn't it?" Doug raked his fingers through the fur of the bear's neck as he searched for the chain. The jewelry acted like it was trying to hide. "It was so easy to see when I first met him."

"The enchantment works against you." Heph narrowed his eyes as if something sinister about the chain occurred to him. "I've dealt with such compulsive spells before."

"The chain doesn't want to leave?" Mod asked. "Like it can think?"

"Malevolence gains power the longer it exists." The god tugged at his beard. He now looked worried.

Doug's fingers brushed against the chain hidden in the thick fur. It fought against his efforts for Doug to get his fingers under it, but he persisted and managed to pull it up so everybody could see it.

Hephaestus drew in a sharp, shocked, gulp of breath. "Steel of my blood and rock of my bones, how in my holy name did you get snared by that?" the god asked the bear.

"You know what the chain is?" Doug asked.

"Know it?" The god looked embarrassed. "I'm the one who made it!"

Everyone looked to the god, waiting for an explanation.

"I was in a righteous snit. Ares and Aphrodite . . ." The light in the caldera dimmed, all of the air took on a more menacing tone as the god's mood darkened. "Relationships are complicated. Not even a god is free from harsh emotions and hurt feelings."

He sighed, shaking his head at his folly. The lights in the caldera began to turn back up, the anger in the air fading. "Well, stuff happened, and I wasn't very elated. Instead of taking it out on the ones responsible, I made something to punish the resulting child. Bad of me, I know.

"What the bear has round his neck is the Necklace of Harmonia."[1]

"I've heard about it," Mopsus said. "Compulsion. Unbreakability. Misfortune. You poured a lot of bad juju into it."

"I was heartbroken, not to mention more than a bit pissed. I got drunk, made the thing, and put all my ire and anger into it," the god said. He didn't look proud of what he'd created.

"Can you remove it?" Doug asked.

---

1. A necklace wrought by the hands of Hephaestus to bring misfortune to the lineage of those who wore it. It granted eternal youth and beauty as enticements to keep on using it while everything around the user went to @#$%. Greek gods, man. They're like the Maury Povich audience of the ancient world. "Da baby a' your baby momma din't do nuffin to you! Take it out on your baby momma, but you leave da baby alone!"

The god looked sheepish. "Maybe? I was really, really mad, and the power of the thing seems to have grown since I made it." He turned to the bear. "I'm so sorry. Will you allow me to take a look?"

The bear cocked an eyebrow. After a short moment of consideration, the bear raised his head, exposing his neck and the tight chain of gold ringing it.

"Thank you," Hephaestus said. He knelt down and took the chain in his large hands. What Doug had taken for a pair of bells were actually the heads of two serpents, the tinkling chime sounded every time they gnashed their teeth against each other.

The clasps tried to bite the god.

"Oh, behave!" Heph thumped the little golden serpent heads with his finger.

That just made the snakes even less compliant.

"Oh, for the love of me," Heph swore.

"Here. Let me try," Medusa said.

She leaned in close, whispered something dark and powerful, and the snakes screeched in response. The two heads hissed at her.

Medusa narrowed her eyes. "Try me." She dared the snakes.

There was a whimper, then the caustic smell of sulfur and burnt gold filled the air.

The chain slid free.

"I'm impressed," Heph said to Medusa. "I didn't even know snakes could whimper."

"Sometimes a curse can be a learning experience," Medusa said as she backed away from the bear.

The air around the bear shimmered as he stretched and rose up on his hind legs. Suddenly larger and grander, the power surrounding him was undeniable. "Aye, yes," he said with a slight Celtic accent. "My situation has much improved!"

"The bear can talk?" Nine gasped.

"Of course it can," Mopsus chided in a reverent whisper. "Age of gods and myths, remember?"

Everyone in Doug's crew felt compelled to take a step back and bow. The bear wasn't a Greek god, but he was a god of someplace nonetheless.

Heph looked to the bear. "If I'd known I made something that could snag someone like you, I would've thought twice before making it."

"A thing made in anger, meant to punish, and employed by another for a nefarious cause," the bear explained. "I was bound by the chain by one unseen, but he let slip his reasoning for my capture." The bear inclined his head in Doug's direction. "My captor hoped in my unreasoning state that I would lash out at the youth and his crew, and further hoped that Doug would reach out to one for help, you being the closest friend of the youth's that might deal with someone of my level of power."

"Someone planned to use my own creation to hurt me?" Hephaestus said, shocked.

"To hurt both of us," the bear reasoned. "I was of the impression my captor cared not who he hurt, so long as chaos ensued."

The chain dangled limply from the hands of the god of the forge. "Sorry I made such a powerful weapon for another to wield," Heph said.

"Your apology is accepted." The bear inclined his head slightly to Hephaestus. "Ironic, that the chain brought us together anyway in a manner my captor never intended. Doug's intelligence, patience, and kindness were not factored into my captor's plans."

Everyone turned to look at Doug, and he shied away from the admiration focused on him. "I didn't do anything, really. I couldn't deal with the chain causing the problem."

"Hmmm." The bear arched an eyebrow at Doug and considered. "You shouldn't be dismissive of your part in this. Malicious intent toward many was thwarted by you being who you are. But you're correct about the chain." The bear turned to Hephaestus. "Please destroy the chain or hide it away so it doesn't hurt anyone from this point forth."

Heph looked at the chain, considered for a moment, then tossed it into one of the glowing vats of molten ore.[2] "Easiest and simplest way to deal with it really."

The bear tipped his head to Hephaestus. "My thanks. I hold no ill will toward ye for creating the snare which bound me, though I would ask ye to consider the ramifications and consequences of your creations once they've fulfilled their intended purpose."

Heph nodded. "I will, indeed, be more careful in the future."

"Aye. That'd be fine," the bear said. "I like ye well enough, and if the invitation to stay still stands, it'd be lovely if I could abide a while and get my bearings again."

Hephaestus looked more than happy to oblige.

"As to what to call me, I go by the name Arktos,"[3] the bear said.

"Pleased to finally be properly introduced, my lord Arktos." Doug bowed. The rest of his crew followed suit.

Arktos objected. "No, young master. Ye will not bow to me. I was bound, trapped, and silenced, and you have freed me. I bow to ye, as the one in debt." The bear bent deeply at the waist, holding the position until Doug tapped him on the shoulder and bid him to rise.

"It's all good." Doug smiled and deflected the praise to the god of the forge. "I only connected you to the one who could free you. I'm glad it worked out."

---

2. How hard was that really? If the jewelry is evil, just pitch it. Isildur from *The Lord of the Rings* could have saved a lot of people a lot of pain if he'd just tossed a certain ring into the fire when asked.

3. While Arktos is the ancient Greek word for bear, you can tell from the bear's accent that he wasn't from ancient Greece. He's from a small grouping of green islands just off the coast of mainland Europe, where he is a god to some, and the once and future king to others. You can extrapolate the rest from there.

Chapter 35

Have You Tried Turning It Off and Back On Again?

"Well, that's taken care of, so now to the real reason you're here," Heph said to Doug. As he asked the question, Heph reached out, his hand hovering near his new companion as if to give a loving scratch to Arktos.

The bear considered for a moment, then leaned into the god's outstretched hand.

Hephaestus scritched Arktos under the chin.

"Aye, that feels fine," the bear said.

Hephaestus continued to scratch Arktos as he turned back to Doug. "This quest from Teutamides needed you to do what exactly?"

"The scroll from the king states we have to put out the fires of your forge," Doug explained. He had Mod hold up the scroll for Heph to look at to confirm the instructions if he wanted to, but the god dismissed the idea.

"Doug's understanding of the task is good enough for me to go on," the god said.

"I don't know exactly what putting out the fires entails," Doug admitted.

"Do the fires have to stay out?" Heph asked. "Because that one thing could have huge consequences."

"It doesn't specify," Mopsus interjected. "There's been an incredible lack of detail in how or why certain things are supposed to be accomplished." Mod handed the completed tasks to Mopsus without having to be asked. The seer unrolled several scrolls and looked at the tasks and instructions. "I'm not sure how much thought was actually given to the tasks before they're assigned to Doug. Any forethought on completing them and the ramifications that entails seems to only be done when our part comes to play."

Mod agreed with the seer. "Putting out the fires permanently would have a disastrous effect on Greece, and I find it hard to believe any god or king in the service of our land would vet such an action. Hard enough to live here as is, but take away our ability to utilize iron and bronze and existence would become downright barbaric."

"I for one think that a reset of the machines every once and a while is good for everything." Hephestus nudged Mod in the ribs. "Have you tried turning it off and on again?"[1] The god laughed.

Mod didn't get the reference.

"Ctesibius!" Hephestus bellowed.

The Greek inventor known as the Father of Pneumatics was in the shop while he completed a service call on the auto-bellows attached to one of the big forges.

"Yo!" A wild-haired man wearing safety goggles popped up from the guts of a half-assembled machine fifty yards away. He was clad only in a leather apron studded with belts and hoses that ran to and fro from a dozen machines. The largest contraption was a compressed air canister strapped to his back. He glanced at a pressure gauge on his wrist frequently and pumped small bellows at his waist every time the needle dropped past the red line.

"The number three furnace is still down?" The god asked.

"Vacuum lines are shot, and we don't have another shipment of reinforced tubing coming in 'til the end of the month," the man

1. "Have you tried turning it off and on again?" is the main catchphrase of the show *The IT Crowd*. Hephaestus empathizes and identifies with the characters on the show because he feels he's an underappreciated nerd too. *The IT Crowd* came out way after our story takes place, but one of the perks of being a god is not being constrained by linear time. All the grand ideas from history and the future are laid out to be perused and utilized as needed or wanted. Think YouTube without the ads and a thousand channels filled with only things you actually want to watch. Heph is the only one in the shop that can watch it, though. Password sharing with mortals is really looked down upon in the god community.

explained as he cleaned the dust and grime from his goggles so he could see better. "I've got spare belts and hoses from an older model that should limp us along until the new stuff comes via messenger."

"Place the order. We'll keep this machine down until we get the right parts." The men all nodded at the god's insight and wisdom. Heph was a stickler for keeping to a maintenance schedule, and he only operated his machines the proper way. "And as for the rest of the operation . . ." The god of the forge waved at the cyclopes wearing a monocle and porting a pocket protector in the control and observation booth up over the work floor. "Telamon![2] Shut it down!"

Telamon reached out to press the button. The cyclopes looked puzzled for a second. He pressed the intercom instead. "Hey, boss, someone messed with the controls. If I press the emergency shut down button, I don't think we can bring everything back online."

"Who could have done that?" Hephaestus glanced around at the others in the shop.

"It's okay. I've been working on a work around, just in case." Telamon twisted and knocked someone's coffee onto a control panel. The introduction of brown, sticky liquid to delicate electronics sparked a fire and electrocuted the technicians sitting on either side of him. The fire set off the suppression system and a burst of high-velocity foam blasted a single corrective lens onto the interior surface of the protective glass surrounding the booth.

The power in the shop snapped off. It was silent except for the distant bark of a dog somewhere high up above.

"That was the workaround, right?" Doug asked.

---

2. Three cyclopean brothers were known to work with Hepaestus. Arges (bright), Brontes (thunder), and Steropes (lightning). There was also a fourth brother, Telamon (helper). Smaller and less physically imposing than his siblings, he nonetheless was valuable in the execution of most of their creations. The larger brothers had the strength and skill to create, but Telamon was the one who told them how best to make everything work and come together. An ancient version of our modern-day tutorials and "how to" videos on the internet wrapped up in a myopic package with no depth perception.

Hephaestus nodded. His eyes wandered left, up, right, and then did a full three-sixty. "That went smoother than last time."

The only illumination was the deep red glow emanating from the vats of liquid metal and cisterns that glowed in the deep crater.

A door burst open in the control room. The formerly bespectacled cyclopes dragged his unconscious coworkers out of the foam-filled control booth and onto an observation platform, his two-eared monocle clamped in his teeth. Once he finished rescuing his coworkers, he straightened up, pulled the earpieces of his glasses from his mouth, and tried to clear the foam shrouded lens with a clean spot on his smock.

Hephaestus waited long enough for a rime to form on the cooled surface of some of the molten alloys.

The task device in Mod's pocked dinged.

The signal another task was accomplished made Doug smile. "That'll do it. Thanks, Heph!"

The god waved the thanks away as if he'd done nothing. "Telamon!"

The cyclopes froze at the mention of his name.

"Good job on the improved efficiency of the shutdown procedure. And that was the backup? I'm impressed."

"I'll figure out what happened to the main switch, but yeah." Telamon grinned stupidly at the praise and shuffled his feet. "The boys and I have been running drills. I'm glad you noticed. Thanks, Chief."

"That's wonderful. Congratulations. And don't call me *Chief.*"[3] Small words of praise delivered, Hephaestus was all back to business. "Now bring 'em all back online but number three."

The cyclopes finished cleaning the foam from his corrective lens and hooked the earpieces back in place. Head down and shoulders

3. Phrase uttered by Daily Planet editor-in-chief Perry White in the varied *Superman* franchises. The definitive delivery of the line was given by Jackie Cooper when he took the role in the Richard Donner productions.

set he pushed back into the suds-filled room. There was a series of pops. Something sizzled followed by a muffled explosion. The corrective lens and frame once more tried to embed themselves in the protective glass that surrounded the booth.

The bellows roared to life. The lights blinked on. The heavy machinery all jumped back into production.

Barely visible behind the semitransparent plexi, a hand trembled as it rose above the level of foam in the operations booth and gave a thumbs up.

Heph returned the thumbs up salute with gusto. "Great job, my boy!"

Hephaestus looked around the shop, a broad grin on his face and his fists planted on his hips. "A new pet, err—" He looked at Arktos and repented of his word usage. "Correction. A new *compatriot* to dote on."

The bear smiled and nodded.

Heph continued, "I was able to do a favor for a friend. Everything looks to be running just the way I like it." He planted his hands on his hips and smiled. "A good day! Glad we could get everything taken care of."

"Actually," Doug put a hand on Heph's arm and pulled him off to the side. "If you've got a minute, there's one more thing I'd like to discuss with you in private."

Doug sent the others off for a moment to get ready to leave. When everyone but his brother and Heph were gone, Doug told Mod to pull Heinous's portal from his pocket.

CHAPTER 36
A WORD OF WARNING

HEPHAESTUS KNITTED HIS BROW AND CHEWED ON HIS LOWER lip for a second as he looked at the portal. "Well isn't this interesting?" he whispered angrily. "And you got this where?" he asked Mod.

Mod told him.

Hephaestus straightened up. "Telamon!" the god called over his shoulder.

The cyclops was there in an instant.

Heph jotted down a list of items on a greasy note sheet and handed it his helper. Telamon looked confused, so Heph put out his hand and beckoned for the device from Mod.

Mod handed it over.

Telamon squinted at it and scoffed. "Amateurs." He took the list from his boss and walked away.

"He'll be back in a minute," Hephaestus said. He held up the portal to look at it a bit more closely. "So this let the chickens out of Hades's coup. Definitely not mine, or the work of the cyclopes either."

"We expected as much." Doug was relieved to hear it from the god's mouth. It gave a bit more piece of mind to know he wasn't mistaken about his friends. "The workmanship was too crude for even a prototype."

"It was crude, all right," the god agreed. "The problem is, I think the bulk of the materials came from my shop."

Telamon walked up behind the god and handed him a clipboard with a materials list.

"Thanks." Heph took the printout.

"Do you want me to check security footage to see who might have messed with the main shutoff switch?" Telamon asked.

"You can, but I suspect you won't find anything on the tapes." Hepheastus shook his head. "Whoever is messing with things is too sneaky to get caught. Go ahead. If you can't find something, no one will."

Telamon brightened at the praise. Now he looked determined to find something.

Heph scanned over the materials list Telamon had handed him. "Controller chip and power supply went missing from the stockroom. And the wire for the frame of the portal itself? Pulled right off the roll over there." They all looked in the direction the god indicated to where a large wooden spool hung suspended on a rack by the wall.

"But the frame for the portal looked much cruder on the device we took from Heinous," Mod said.

"You're right. The frame looked like it was made of Typhon fewmets.[1] It's the sheathing on the wire. The surface coat looks like they just glopped it on," Hephaestus said. "I have a machine that coats wire in a flexible plastic sheath accurate to one tenth of a micron. Uniform and exact every time."

"What did they use to cover their wire?" Doug asked.

"Oh, their stuff was really primitive! They used a naturally occurring tree sap that has to be hardened through the application of sulfur and heat." Hephaestus sounded aghast. "I'm amazed anyone should have to use technology so outdated. I didn't even recognize the coating at first. I had to have Telamon look it up for me. They call it vulcanized rubber."

"Vulcanized? What a stupid thing to call it," Mod said.

"Oh, don't get me started," Hephaestus agreed. "Their application process was all globby and uneven, like they painted it on with a brush. It worked, I guess, but it sure didn't look nice." Heph straight-

1. If you don't know, don't ask. Trust me. It's disgusting.

ened up and handed the clipboard back to Telamon. "Watch your back, boys. Someone who can snatch a scrap from my shop unnoticed is a sneaky bastard, to say the least. I don't know what they'd be up to, but it can't be good."

At the upper ring of the caldera, a dog started to bark.

"There he goes again. Always barking at the delivery guy. But it's early." The god shielded his eyes as he looked up to the open sky above. "What the devil is that mutt going on about? Telamon?"

The smaller cyclops pivoted on his heel as he heard his name.

"We couldn't possibly have gotten that delivery for the stuff Ctesibius ordered yet, could we?"

The cyclops shook his head as he consulted his handheld. "The order has been placed but hasn't been packaged yet. We aren't expecting the delivery man for at least three days."

"I thought as much," Heph said. "I wonder what's making the dog go off this time?"

"The dog was barking earlier too, right before we did the reset on the machines," Telamon said.

"Quite right, boy. Didn't see any visitor then either, did we?" Hephaestus pondered.

The cyclops pushed his eyeglass up a bit more snugly on his nose. "No, sir. No sign of anyone. I just made note in the logbook that the dog was barking at the time."

"Thank you, Telamon. That'll be all for now," Heph said. "And good job today. I'm proud of the work you're doing."

The cyclops held the clipboard close to his chest and gave a shy smile. "Thanks, sir," he said as he turned back to his tasks with a little more spring in his step.

"I think I may have the boys go through and do a quick inventory, just to be sure everything is where it should be and nothing else has been tampered with," Hephaestus said. "I'll let you know if we find anything." He picked up a hammer and a sewing kit from a workbench and turned to take his leave. "In the meantime, I'm gonna go make Arktos a guesthouse while I think. Something custom and comfortable for his visit."

"Always good to take a moment, isn't it?" Doug said.

"You'll have to come by and see it when I'm finished." Heph chewed on his lip a bit as a suspicion bounced around in his head. "Take care, boys. Something strange is afoot, and I don't want you kids in the midst of it, though"—he leveled his gaze at Doug—"already too late for that, am I right?"

Doug didn't know how to answer, so he just said, "Thanks."

Chapter 37

Larissa and Athena

Her father was getting worse.

The men the king tasked to help administrate the duties of the kingdom had all gone into hiding. Their tasks were still being done, just not in the presence of the king. None of them wanted to be around Teutamides. He'd become obnoxious and illogical. His advisors would turn the other way if Teutamides approached and hoped the king hadn't seen them. If he did see them, they pretended not to hear him screaming after them as they quickened their step and made their escape.

Even mighty Heracles, usually not quite so quick on the uptake, decided there was a monster in the hills close by that needed to be dealt with, and he took his leave.

The last time Larisa had seen her father, he'd yelled at her.

It wasn't playful banter where he teased and she poked back.

It wasn't even an argument. She'd had plenty of those with her father and had learned to recognize when the battle could be won or lost.

This hadn't been any of those.

He'd been mean.

For no reason.

He'd lashed out at her simply because she was there.

She rubbed an errant tear from her cheek and inadvertently smeared the corner of her eye with ink from whatever she'd just read. She almost didn't know why she was still in the library where she studied and searched for who knew what.

The chief librarian fled like the other important people of the kingdom, so at least Larisa could rifle through scrolls and histories without being questioned about what she was doing.

What was she doing, anyway?

Searching. She answered herself. She started to lose hope that researching the list of gods responsible for thought would lead her to anything. The more she studied the more she just felt lost.

She looked at the titles spread before her: Aristotle, Plato, Herodotus. No one school of thought or single philosopher led her in a direction she felt was right.

She was just grasping at straws right now.

The next name on the list was Athena.

Athena was her hero.

Larisa had studied Athena all her life, so she doubted any new insight would be forthcoming.

I feel like I'm doing nothing but wasting time.

She'd been in the library for a couple of days, no closer to the answers now then on the first day when inspiration struck. She placed her face down on the desktop, draped her arms over the back of her head, and cried her frustration into the unfeeling wood of the desk.

Someone sat down opposite the table from her.

Larisa looked up.

The woman was tall, regal looking, and carried herself in a manner that bespoke of being more than a mortal. She also had a huge bronze spear, wore a horsehair plumed war helm, and had an owl perched on her shoulder.

What were the odds that Athena would show up when she was doing research on Athena?

Not very likely.

The simplest explanation was probably going to be the correct one.[1]

---

1. We call this principle Occam's Razor, after the 14th century friar William of

I'm hallucinating.

Larisa decided to go with it and see if the hallucination had any insight to offer. "You're Athena, right? I know all Greeks love good theater, but isn't the costume just a tad over the top?"

The woman smiled, leaned her spear against the arm of the chair then reached up and took off her helmet. Eyes the color of amethyst regarded the sleep-deprived princess before her.

"Hello, child." The goddess studied Larisa. "Have you learned much in your studies?"

"Ha!" Larisa meant to laugh ironically. Instead she croaked and regretted her laugh as soon as her voice sounded.

Larisa grabbed the cup she'd sat on the edge of a shelf nearby and drained it. It was just enough to wet her mouth and return her voice somewhat.

"I haven't found a thing," she admitted. "I'm running in circles and not getting any closer to the point."

Athena nodded as if the answer had been expected. "Distracted?"

"Like you wouldn't believe or understand," Larisa admitted. It was nice to have someone to talk to that didn't cower in fear or fly off in a rage, even if it was just in her imagination. "Too many things have been turned upside down. It's hard to concentrate and form a coherent thought."

Athena appeared to ponder this for a moment, her unblinking gaze boring into the younger woman. "Such a thing is not normal for you, is it, Larisa, crown princess of Larissa?"

It took a second to realize the woman just called her by name and title. *My hallucination, why wouldn't it use my formal name?* "Do I know you?"

Athena deflected the question with an observation and then a question of her own. "For one so sure and inquisitive as you are,

---

Ockham. He obviously hadn't been born in Larisa's time, so she didn't know what to call it.

muddled thoughts must be a terrible burden. Have you prayed to the gods for clarity of thought?"

"I have." When she'd done it, she'd reasoned it to be the right and proper thing to do.

"Ah," Athena said as if things now suddenly made more sense. She reached up and grabbed the shaft of her spear. She swept the weapon over the top of the desk and pushed aside all the books and scrolls that littered the table.

The priceless and rare documents and essays fell to the floor, and the woman looked as if she gave not a one of them a second thought.

Larisa was shocked at how this imaginary Athena threw knowledge on the ground like garbage. "I've been looking through those! Do you know what it will take for me to find my place in all of those different texts again?"

"I'm helping." Athena indicated the pile of documents on the floor of the library with the tip of her spear. "Distractions and misdirection, child. You were on the correct path before you doubted yourself and turned the whole quest into something much more convoluted." She pulled the tip of the spear back around and pointed it in the center of the desktop again. "You began with your quest so close to the mark that someone simply had to come along and throw you off center."

There was just one document left on the desk.

It was Larisa's list.

"It was frustrating, child, seeing you spiral farther and farther away from the truth, when you were so close to begin with."

Larisa picked up the sheet of paper. "But this doesn't answer anything. It's just a list of names of the gods responsible for thought in the hearts and minds of men."

"Some men think with their hearts." Athena pursed her lips and narrowed her eyes. "Some with their mind. A large section of men think with"—the woman looked down at her lap and sighed before she continued—"other parts. Most rely on false inspiration from gods or others so when something goes wrong they can foist the blame onto someone else. They think it simpler. Laziness compels them to do so."

Athena trained her eyes back on Larisa. "Are you lazy, child?"

"What? I—no!" Larisa sputtered. She hadn't expected the question.

"I already knew as such." Athena indicated the note in Larisa's hand with a slight nod of the head. "You thought, surmised, and reasoned. You. With the help of no man or god to assist you. The information was seen and stood out to you. It registered. You used your brain, and you came up with a possible cause for the current troubles that plague you and you began to search.

"Only you were going in the wrong direction." Athena rose, picked up her helm, and placed it back upon her head.

"How can I be going in the wrong direction?" Larisa was exasperated. "I found the gods who were responsible for thought and looked for clues in the words of those who came after them!"

"Ah. Quite so," the woman said. "Gods act within the powers and principalities they're bound to. Things become complicated the more you add into the mix. Man has further complicated things by breaking the laws of the gods into smaller rules that are easier for them to follow, yet all of these spring from a common root. You search the branches spreading away from the trunk of the tree when you should be searching for the acorn that begat the oak."

"Am I a squirrel?" Larisa said. "And there's no nut to search for. By its very nature, the acorn nut becomes useless once it's sprouted into the tree."

"Does it now?" Athena mused. "You're so close, and your mind tries so hard it's making it difficult for you to see. Step back. Reflect *back* on what you've already discovered. Reflect on what you've just said, and the path forward will begin to become clearer to you."

"I'm looking for a nut?" Larisa felt she might actually be looking at a nut with the woman. It wasn't what she thought when she first saw the woman, but first impressions can be wrong. *My hallucination, right? Maybe I'm the nut?*

"Don't overcomplicate things. The correct answers can be found at the beginning." Athena's mouth twisted to one side in a smile, like she was somehow privately amused by the princess comparing either of them to a nut. Whatever it was that really amused the woman was something she chose not to share with Larisa.

"What are you, a friggin' oracle?" Larisa was getting angry. "Spouting off wise-sounding and cryptic phrases that get me no closer to the truth?"

"Days ago you were very close to the truth." Athena looked a bit frustrated that Larisa hadn't grasped her point yet. "You found a point of truth and wandered in the wrong direction."

"I started with a list of gods! Then I studied the myths that came from those, and the men and women who were inspired and wrote the history that followed!" Larisa waved her arms in the air and started stomping around the room. "I mean, I've studied everything that came after the gods put thoughts into man!"

She caught herself. "After." Larisa took a few halting steps as her mind shifted gears and spun out as it headed in a different direction.

Larisa's eyes grew wide. "Oh! I certainly didn't think of that!"

"And now you have." Athena nodded and walked through the closed door, passing through the wood and gold as if they weren't even there.

On the list in her hands, one of the possibilities for who was behind everything crossed its name off the list.

Athena.

What had just happened had really just happened.

"Well, holy *deisa*."[2] Larisa swore. She was tired and full of adrenaline at the moment, so she forgave herself for language inappropriate and unbecoming a royal this one time.

---

2. *Deisa*: ancient Greek word for excrement. You just learned a new word. Now when you're frustrated and in mixed company or in the presence of children you can swear, and no one will be the wiser, as long as the people in question aren't from the Mediterranean.

She rushed to the door, pulled it open, and called out even though no one was there. "Thanks for the help, Athena!"

No reply.

Larisa looked down at the list in her hands. She didn't know if it was wise to take a god at her word when the other names on the list were gods as well, but somehow, she couldn't see it as possible to be lied to by the goddess of wisdom like this. Anyhow, having Athena off the list felt right to Larisa, and it was the first progress she'd made in answering her question in days.

The goddess made it clear that I should trust in myself, and I do.

She was finally heading in the right direction.

Larisa looked down at the paper in her hands. Athena's name was obviously crossed out, so that just left five possible suspects on the list to go.

"Next up, Ceous, Titan of the inquisitive mind." Larisa walked through the library until she came to the section on titans and sorted through it until she had several scrolls that looked promising.

"One down. Five to go."

CHAPTER 38

PIG

THE NEXT TASK BASICALLY SAID, *KILL THE PIG*. THE PERTINENT details were listed underneath the execution order. Should be a simple enough task, though Doug hated the thought of killing anything for no reason.

As soon as Doug saw the animal, he knew there was a problem.

He explained the dilemma to Mod and the others. None of them were very quick on the uptake.

"Dealing with a pig. The boar is big, but so what? Does Teutamides not know who our father is? Of course he does." Mod shook his head. "Was this task really supposed to be this easy? I mean, it's just a pig."

Doug knew he was seeing things the others didn't, so he explained a bit more. "You need to read the scroll again."

Everyone looked at the scroll a second time. Mod understood what Doug was getting at first. He looked at the pig and balked. "Great shades of Elpis![1] That's not—"

"No." Doug shook his head. "That's not the pig we've been sent to deal with."

Doug explained a bit more.

Mopsus furrowed his brow. "So, kill the beast before you and you offend a god and it could be argued that you didn't accomplish the task. Do what is listed on the scroll and you risk offending another

1. Greek god of Hope. Not to be confused with the hip swinging crooner that scandalized your great-grandparents.

god and it can also be argued that you misunderstood and still didn't accomplish the task set before you."

"You're being played," One said.

"It's a cheat," Four agreed. "I don't see how you win this."

"I win by not playing, or at least not doing the things they expect me to do. They think I'm so eager to be done I'll just rush in without thinking and cause a bigger mess in the process." Doug looked tired. "Mod, can you open a portal back to Heph's place? I need him to contact someone for me."

Mod set up the portal then paused, "How in Hades—"

"Exactly." Doug turned to go back into Heph's shop. "If Hades agrees to come and see, we'll get his take on what to do. He owes us for taking care of all those chickens."

The meeting was set, and Doug and his crew made ready for the god's arrival.

They didn't have to wait long. Doug had the appropriate offering ready on the advice of Heph. Hades accepted the offering, and followed Doug as he led the god down a canyon track.

Hades stopped in the middle of the path and looked over his shoulder. "So, what's this about?"

Doug motioned for the god to follow him. "This way. We penned it in a small box canyon."

"Penned? Did you drag me from my kingdom to come and see some little animal you trapped?[2] I couldn't be less interested in what you think you need to show me than just about anything else in the world. I wouldn't have even come, but I"—his voice dropped to an embarrassed whisper—"sort of owe you for the chicken fiasco."

"You're welcome," Doug said.

Hades still looked as if he contemplated leaving right then but was reluctant to commit to that course of action.

---

2. It's summer, so Hades is with his wife visiting his mother-in-law's house. He was a little relieved to have a legitimate excuse to leave.

Mopsus bowed down low before the god. "You'll be most interested in what we have to show you."

"Doug recognized what we trapped right away and knew you'd need to see it, so Hephaestus got a hold of you,"[3] Mod explained.

Hades took another bite of the mint-chocolate-coated cracker in his hand.

"What we've captured is important to you," Doug said.

"You sound pretty sure of yourself," Hades said. "While Hephaestus argued it would be worth my time, I remain unconvinced."

"Just a bit longer, I promise," Doug said.

One, Four, Five, and Six moved an awning to keep Hades in the shade, one to a corner with the god dead center. Hephaestus told Doug it would be a good idea to have one prepared, and he was right. There was a sizzling sound every time a direct ray of sunshine hit any of Hades's exposed skin.[4]

Hades settled into a defeated mope and shoved another cookie in his mouth. He motioned for Doug to lead on.

They followed a game path a short distance and rounded the bend. A large, newly erected stone wall capped off the end of a small box canyon. Sounds of a huge beast could be heard from behind the distant barrier.

"A familiar tone, I'll admit." The lord of the underworld's pace slowed. "Where have I heard this animal's utterings before?"

---

3. Calling upon the god of the dead does not involve some convoluted ritual involving incantations, a blood sacrifice, and candles made of grave wax lit under the light of a full moon. It involves an order for the ancient Greek equivalent of Girl Scout cookies. You just have to find a deep crack in the ground where you can whisper, "Hey Prince of Darkness, we have Samoas." The cookie currently being devoured is the historical inspiration for Thin Mint.

4. There was more exposed skin than you might have guessed. Hades is currently clad in sneakers and a goth wrestling singlet. When the request for his presence came, he was in the middle of a cardio routine with Persephone. Hades thinks the exercise program is a crock, but seeing Persephone doing stretches in yoga pants and jumping and running in a sports bra is more than enough for him to see the wisdom in keeping his mouth shut.

"You'll see soon enough," Doug said.

Off in the distance, a dog started to bark. Another dog, somewhat closer, soon joined in the call of its cousin.

Hades looked over his shoulder. "Have you told anyone else of what you found?"

To Doug the god appeared uncomfortable and exposed. "Didn't even give the details to Hephaestus, just asked how I could get a hold of you," Doug reassured the god. "He trusts me enough if I ask for something, he figures I probably have a good reason. I asked for your contact info, and he just handed me what he called a roll-a-dex card.[5] He was really distracted and wanted to get back to playing host to Arktos. I'm surprised he gave me the right card."

"Telamon would have caught any mistake before you left," Mod said. "Heph's probably just happy another god is as hairy as he is."

"They're becoming pretty fast friends,"[6] Doug said.

Hades looked a bit confused.

"Arktos is Hephaestus's new furry friend,"[7] Mod gave a brief explanation. "He's a god of some island kingdom to the west."

Hades didn't look like the explanation cleared up any of his confusion, yet he didn't ask for additional clarification.

They continued onward. The sounds of a great beast became more distinct.

Hades focused, his brow knitting in concentration. He grew even paler as suspicion gave way to knowledge. "I've most definitely heard the noises coming from this animal before." The god seemed to recognize the bristle-covered mound of the beast's back rising above the barrier Doug and his crew had erected to corral the animal.

Hades took the last few steps forward and peered over the top of the stone wall.

---

5. Ancient contact list device. Cutting edge for its time.

6. You know that person you just met but you clicked with immediately? Same sense of humor? Same sort of challenges and trials? Same body hair frustrations? Arktos and Hephaestus, man, they get each other.

7. Not that kind of furry. What is it with you?

The huge pig lifted its snout from the feed trough and stared right back at him.

"The Calydonian Boar," Hades said. "I feel I should be surprised. However . . ." The god frowned.

"I knew you would want to know," Doug said.

Hades looked down at the giant boar as it buried its snout back in its lunch. "How in the world someone managed to slip this particular behemoth past the gates of hell without me noticing is beyond me." The god looked frustrated. "I can't begin to explain. Why in the world is this dead killing machine back up here on the surface?"

"Because someone made a mistake or someone is getting sloppy. I don't know. All these tasks seem to make less and less sense to me." Doug was a bit tired, or irked, a mixture of the two emotions, really. "The challenge given to me concerned killing the Erymanthian boar, which I, or anybody else couldn't do without ticking off Artemis. Getting me in trouble with a god or goddess may have been the point."

He climbed up on the wall and watched as the animal happily chomped its lunch. "Anyway, whoever set the whole thing up decided I might get in more trouble if I cut down the wrong pig. Or they would get into less trouble if I killed a pig that was already dead." Doug rubbed his temples. His head hurt. "I don't know."

"How did you know which one was which? I assume you'd never seen either boar before, so how could you know someone was trying to dupe you?" Hades looked genuinely curious.

Doug leaned forward and let his legs dangle over the wall as he evaluated the pig again. "The Calydonian Boar came from Greek black pig stock that'd been domesticated and bred in the region for several thousand years. He's the ultimate product of a well-documented family line and pedigree. Some of the most excellent ham stock in all of Greece, in my opinion. Erymanthian's male was wild from the beginning. No one in his family history ever fed at a trough or slept in a pen. If you were to eat Mr. Erymanthian or one of his kin, you'd find the meat gamey and tough, only good for grinding into sausage. That wild spirit is why Artemis has such an affinity for him."

"I'm amazed at your depth of understanding and genuinely interested in your insight. I had no idea domestication could change so much in an animal," Hades said.

Doug turned to look at the god. "Generation after generation, those who farm and ranch notice the changes in the living things they practice husbandry over. Chickens, sheep, cattle, pigs, horses, any animal you might find used in a society, really. Sometimes we help direct the changes, sometimes we're pleasantly surprised or taken aback by the results."

Doug looked away from Hades and back to the magnificent creature calmly supping before him. "Pigs are different though. A couple thousand years of domestication, selectively breeding for all of the best qualities, and you think you have a completely different animal. Turn 'em loose, though, and in six months the pig will have reverted so much that even its bone structure will go back to that of a wild hog."[8]

"So the domesticated boar, once turned free, took on the traits and spirit of the wild boar." The god looked at the beast with more enlightened eyes and marveled. "And yet, somehow you can look at the one and definitely distinguish it from the other."

"The Erymanthian Boar is said to have a hide black as a starless night, rich and dark and lustrous, but still just a variation on the color of our common pig. The Calydonians bred for generations to get a particular trait, one that sets their stock apart from the rest of the

---

8. This is almost true. Probably triggered by epigenes, if you turn a domestic pig loose in the wilds, they actually undergo morphological changes in order to better survive in the new environment, while not quite completely reverting into a wild hog. There might be cognitive changes as well, though all pigs only really have two thoughts that run on a loop through their mind. "Can I #$%@ this?" and "Is this edible?" and not necessarily in that order. They're also not very discerning if the answer to either of those questions is remotely close to a yes.

land. Black denotes common, while our Calydonian friend here is a redhead." Doug reached out to scratch the pig behind the ear.

The pig raised its head for a minute, gave a happy grunt in acknowledgement of the attention, then immersed its snout back down in the rapidly vanishing mash.

"A red pig or a black pig. I've seen them both and I never even noticed the difference." Hades chuckled. "I'm amused at your knowledge and appalled by my own apparent lack of observation."

Hades's face grew grim again quickly. "This particular choice of animal may have been made in an effort to reflect poorly on me. Someone seems to be going to great lengths to discredit my work as of late."

"I'm not really completing the task I was given," Doug said. He felt a bit guilty about trying to pull one over on Teutamides. "But I don't see the point to killing a boar who's doing nothing to harm anyone."

"May I see the list the task is written on?" Hades asked.

Mod handed the scroll to Hades.

Hades let his eyes scan over the writing. He took in every nuance recorded by ink and quill as he did so. He waved his hand over the scroll and the ink rearranged from the word *Erymanthian* to *Calydonian.* "The lists held by Teutamides will be changed as well, along with any other occurrences in any records or documents pertaining to your tasks.[9] You have returned my lost deadstock to me,[10] let the pardoned Erymanthian animal live and breathe for another day. His life this day is spared. You have completed your given quest, so says Hades, god of the underworld." With that statement, Hades handed the altered scroll back to Mod to watch over.

Hades made a couple of strange gestures in the air, and he suddenly held a quill and scroll. He scribbled a few lines on the

9. Hades heartily endorses Spell Check. "The Find and Replace in all linked documents feature is a godsend. And I should know. I'm a god."- Hades

10. You can't call it livestock if it's dead, can you?

parchment, sealed it with an impression of his thumb, and handed it over to Doug. "Proof of delivery of the requested animal to me. If they wish to dispute the claim or say you captured the wrong animal, they will be granted a personal audience with me to do so. I'll talk to Artemis about this. I'm sure she'll be happy to play along."

"Personal audience?" Mopsus asked.

The lord of death grinned and nodded. The temperature in the area surrounding the god cooled noticeably.

Mopsus gulped. "I shall pass along the warning to anyone foolish enough to question your word."

"I trust your discretion on this," Hades said to Doug.

"You'll see me personally in your realm before I would ever utter a word about it," Doug said truthfully.

The god inclined his head ever so slightly in acknowledgement of the oath.

"So we're done with this task?" One asked.

There was a dinging from Mod's pocket in reply.

"Guess so?" Mod said. "Anyone want to look at the next and final task?"

"Why not." Doug motioned for his brother to open the scroll.

Mod pulled out the device and unrolled the scroll. "In the palace of Larissa, Teutamides will give the final challenge to the one called Doug." Mod shrugged. "That's all it says."

"Guess we have to go back to where it all started," Doug said.

Hades scanned the skyline surrounding them before he returned his gaze to the boar. "He's so calm. As one of the more spirited beasts ever to cross my borders I'm surprised he behaved so well for you. How did you capture him?"

"I'm the son of a pig farmer," Doug explained. "I know the things a big guy like him wants. I can't help with the one he thinks is first on the list, but I can certainly help with the second item. I've had my people gathering the best acorns we could find to make feed mash for a week. It worked. The scent is bold and rich and something he couldn't resist."

"He looks happy," Hades observed.

"I'm pretty sure he is." Doug pulled his feet up on the wall and rested his chin on his knees. "If we threw a pretty Mrs. Pig in there with him, I bet not even death could drag him away.

Hades smiled. "I like you, Doug. May you succeed in everything you do."

Doug bowed as best he could in his awkward seated position, kind of a spastic but gracious nod. "My thanks for the blessing, my Lord." He pointed his chin in the boar's direction. "You need to take him now?"

"It is so rare that I get to experience or witness moments of simple joy," Hades explained. "Let him finish his lunch. I'm in no rush."

"Good call," Doug agreed.

Off in the distance the dogs started barking again, first the closest dog, and then one much further away.

The sound immediately drew Hades's attention.

Doug listened to the barking as well. "It happens a lot wherever I go," Doug explained. "Almost like something is following us that doesn't want to be seen."

"That must be mildly disconcerting," Hades said. "Similar things have also been unsettling me as of late."

Doug shrugged and shifted about in an effort to get a bit more comfortable. "Why worry about things you can't change?"

"Sage counsel," the god observed.

"Yeah, sometimes." Doug sighed, dropped his chin back on his knees, and wrapped his arms around his legs. "It'd be great if I was dumb enough to take my own advice."

Hades laughed at that, possibly in agreement, but he said nothing to clarify.

It wasn't long until whatever the dogs barked at passed beyond their territories, and the valley was once again filled only by the sounds of the contented pig.

Chapter 34

Warning from a Friend

Doug woke up in the dark of night. Stars twinkled brightly high above.

He shifted and was surprised to see he'd slept on grass, not on the boat where he'd drifted off. He propped himself up on his elbow and looked around. Mod, Medusa, Mopsus, and the others weren't there. He wasn't panicked, rather curious as he tried to figure out where he was. He could make out trees off to his right, their leaves rustling in the soft night breeze.

"Are you awake?" Anthea was sitting on one of the lower branches of one of her trees a couple of yards from Doug.

Gargantua. Doug smiled as he looked at the girl, the slight worries building in his mind suddenly banished. "I'm awake, thank you. It's nice to see you again, Anthea."

"You remember me." The girl blushed and shyly twined her hands behind her back.

"Of course." Doug sat up and crossed his legs in front of him. "You're my friend."

"I'm glad." Her face perked up, then her smile dropped just as suddenly. "I'm also sorry. I thought it might scare you to bring you here, but Papa said it was important."

"I'm fine," Doug assured her. "And I trust your papa. What did he need to see me about?"

"Papa is everywhere. He hears things. He hears things and some of those things made him worry about you."

Doug sat forward, wide awake now. "What has Erebus heard that concerns me?"

Anthea took a deep breath and swallowed hard. "Bad things. People want bad things to happen to you."

"Teutamides?" Doug knew the king didn't like him.

"Poor King Teutamides." The girl shook her head. "Bad things will happen to him too."

Doug came closer. "Someone is going to hurt the king?" Then he realized what else a threat to the king might mean. "Is Larisa in trouble?"

Tears welled in the corners of Anthea's eyes. "Maybe. I know you love her, so I hope not. Papa isn't sure about her. Papa was sure about the king, though. The palace in Larissa will soon be without a king."

Doug didn't want Larisa's father to die if it was something he could stop. "Can I do anything to help him? What if I don't finish my tasks?"

"It doesn't matter what you do," Anthea said sadly. "The king started something bad, and now it's no longer under his control."

"And Larisa?" Doug was panicking now.

The small slip of a girl choked back a sob. "You can't see her again."

All the life went out of Doug. He somehow managed to ask a bit more. "My brother? My friends?"

"Anyone who stays with you will probably die." She was crying freely now. "Papa doesn't know who's behind it. Some people have gone missing. Some gods have gone missing too."

She was silent for a moment as she listened to something in the night. When she started to speak again the words weren't her own. "The king has allied himself with a dark force that will scour the royal blood from the kingdom. Teutamides erroneously believed he directed the course of events. He is not in control and will pay for his lack of foresight with his life. If you succeed in the final task, the phantom will take you as well, but not before it forces you to witness the life ebb from your precious ones. Larisa will be killed before you are able to triumphantly pass the threshold of the palace. Your brother will fall before he has a chance to flee."

Something beyond nausea and disbelief held Doug now, an inevitable fear so abhorrent he'd not even contemplated it. "What can I do? If I stop, will Larisa and Mod be okay? My friends?"

"The threat to Greece is larger than your tasks. Only by completing your tasks will the threat to the palace be revealed, so the larger threat to Greece may be dealt with. If the girl you love, if those you love, are sent away, they will be out of the path of immediate danger, but the threat will grow until it can no longer be contained. They will be safe for the now if they are not in the palace. They will be safe for the now if they are not with you."

Anthea leveled her intense eyes at the young man. "You can speak to no one of what you have just learned."

"No one?" Doug couldn't even talk about what was happening. How was he supposed to do that? He hadn't kept anything from Mod since they were both three years old.

I can't go back to them. Any of them.

Another thought struck him. *I don't have the last task.*

I have to go back to Teutamides whether I want to or not.

There was no way around it. He'd have to set the final meeting up through a messenger and be very careful about what he asked or said.

"The ears of a servant or messenger may overhear a thing spoken in confidence," Anthea said cryptically as if she just read his mind. "The earth and sea, the winds and sky may overhear and bear a record to those who would cause you harm."[1]

---

1. Due to a curse, Midas was given the ears of an ass. Only he and his barber knew of his shame. The barber kept the absurd fact hidden until he thought he would burst. Ribs cracking from restraint, the poor cosmetologist dug a hole in the dirt, stuck his head in, and whispered the secret in a safe spot free of eavesdroppers. He refilled the hole and felt much relieved by his clever solution. Later a patch of reeds, urged to grow by newly turned earth and fertilized by juicy gossip, sprouted on the spot. Now Aeolus just had to put his lips together and blow, and the thing Midas wished hidden was

Doug was silent for a moment as he processed what he'd just heard.

"Could you get a message to the king for me? Just set a date for me to pick up the last task?" Doug asked.

"Servants and administrators will know, and word will spread," Anthea said in a voice sounding deep and concerned, "but the meeting must be. I shall ask for you to meet the king on the date of Thargelion."[2]

Doug knew all about the sacrifices of Thargelion. It seemed fitting to meet on that day.

"If you want, you could stay here," Anthea said, her eyes losing that faraway look and her voice returning to normal as Erebus left her and went about the task given him by Doug. "Papa could keep you safe here."

Doug rose to his feet, walking over to the girl sitting on the branch. "I'd like so much to stay here safe with you, but if I stay—"

"You're worried about your brother and friends and your beautiful young woman friend. If they go looking for you?" Anthea wrung her hands in frustration. "I'm worried about my friend." She looked at Doug and sobbed.

Doug came close and held her until her crying stopped.

"You're so sweet, Anthea. But I can't stay. My family and friends could be in danger," Doug explained. "They'll be in danger if I stay here. If it's as bad as your father says, we might all be in danger if I stay here." He reached out and took the girl's hand. "Thank you."

She started to cry again. "I just told you something bad. How can you thank me?"

He squeezed her hand, then reached up to brush her tears away.

---

blabbed by gossipy reeds to every plant, animal, and rock in the general area. A long explanation but written to illustrate a point: someone or something is always listening.

2. About May 6th or 7th in our calendar. Thargelion was a date of thankfulness for agriculture where sacrifices were offered to appease the gods and grant a good harvest. Erebus did not suggest the day lightly.

"I can take care of the people I love because of what you told me. Thank you."

"What are you going to do?" she asked through a veil of tears.

Doug smiled and shrugged. He had no idea.

All he knew is he would protect those he loved, even if he had to die to do it.

CHAPTER 40

DOUG AND THE KING

LARISA, CLOAKED AND HOODED, SLIPPED IN AND AMONG THE people crowded into Teutamides's inner court. It was hard to do so unnoticed, but somehow she managed.

There was quite a crowd gathered in the court of the king that morning. Many of the officials returned in the hopes that this business with Doug and the quest would be concluded and the king would return to his more normal, workable self. Or if not, then maybe a coup would happen and Doug would claim the keys to the kingdom. Many of them didn't care which outcome happened. They were just tired of treading on eggshells in the kingdom of Larissa, and almost everyone believed any change would be better than what they dealt with now.

Larisa had heard their whispers with growing concern in the past few weeks. But the nobles and administrators weren't the only one's present.

Doug's band added only a small number to the total of people present to see the historic issuing of the final task to the boy who would woo the princess. Larisa inched a bit closer to them to see if she could learn why Doug wasn't with them. Mopsus and Aesimus were just off to one side, their hands a flurry of motion. They were communicating in court handsign. Larisa eavesdropped on those two first, or rather, read their hands.

"*There are hundreds of people here,*" Mopsus marveled. "*I had no idea the exploits of Doug and company had garnered such a following.*

Strange that the man of the hour is not here yet. Doug is unusually thoughtful and punctual."

"*I have a couple of trusted men shadowing him. He'll be here presently,*" Aesimus responded. "*As to the crowd? It's been big news. The boy has become somewhat of a hero to the common masses. Many a boy aspires to be a man such as Doug.*"

"*I'm told he tried to keep the meeting with the king a secret, but the walls have ears, and once the date and the time of the meeting were set, more and more people had to be here. And justly so.*" Mopsus beamed. "*I'm encouraged that a young man such as Doug should be revered.*"

Not much to learn there. Larisa shifted about until she could hear Mod talking to a woman Larisa had never seen before.

"Any sign of your brother?" the woman asked.

Mod didn't answer right away. It looked like he searched the faces about him in a jumpy manner that gave the woman and Larisa an answer.

"He wouldn't talk to me." Mod was unable to keep the concern from his voice. "I figured he just needed time to process, so I let him be. He left camp three weeks ago in the middle of the night, and I haven't seen him since." Mod turned to the woman then. "I'm scared, Medusa."

After she heard the emotion in Mod's voice, Larisa was scared too.

She made her way to an alcove off to the side of her father's throne.

That Doug wouldn't talk to his brother was one thing, but no communication to the girl he did this for was quite another. A bad feeling grew in Larisa's stomach, and she felt sick.

She dropped her cloak and let Mod see her looking at him as she walked to stand beside her father's throne. She pleaded with her eyes for any reassurance he could give.

Mod wilted under her eyes and dropped his gaze to the floor.

No one knows what is going on with Doug. Larisa hadn't even seen the scroll containing the last task before her father had sealed it away.

The level of noise generated by the people enclosed in the hall continued to rise. To top it off, Ergos, the king's ancient dog, began to howl as well. Larisa could see the king's blood pressure elevating in step with the volume.

Just as Teutamides looked as if he were about to burst a blood vessel, a wave of silence swept the hall.

Doug strode boldly in through the palace gate in the quiet's wake.

Now hooded, Aesimus slunk forward to take his place behind the king.

Doug didn't look to the left or right, his focus turned solely to the throne and its occupant.

Larisa tried to catch his gaze, but he concentrated only on the king.

"King Teutamides." Doug bowed down before the king and all assembled. "All the tasks given have been completed, as I'm sure you're already well aware."

"There was a discrepancy." Teutamides took out his scroll and glared at it. "What is on the last scroll is not what I was told to wri—is not what I wrote." The king corrected, frustrated.

"I did my best." Doug bowed low. "I don't know what else I can say."

The king looked embittered, but he was unable to argue.

Teutamides held his hand close to his chest, clearly unhappy the young man stood before him. "So the tasks given have all been completed. And only one remains?"

Larisa could hear her father's sneer without even seeing his face.

"One final task," Doug said cautiously.

The king grumbled and fell into a sulk.

When all was quiet, Doug spoke, "The challenges recorded on the scrolls are accomplished, my king. I would like to ask for a boon in return."

"Chaos and the demons he spawned! You cheat me in one task

and now you wish to cheat me in another!" The king rose up and thrust a finger at Doug. "Knowing twelve tasks were agreed upon and sworn to the gods, you seek to make a liar out of me and still claim my kingdom and my daughter as your own!"

Doug didn't lash back, instead remaining calm and quiet. He waited for the king to finish.

"Well? What say you, boy?" the king demanded.

Doug took a step forward. He planted his feet and squared his shoulders. "I committed to the tasks the moment we agreed. Live or die, succeed or fail, I am promised to the final challenge."

Doug lowered his voice and continued. "Would it help, my king, if I said the boon I seek shall benefit your people whether I accomplish the task given me or not?"

Teutamides looked trapped.

How could any king deny something good to his people? Larisa thought.

"On my life I swear it will be for the good of the people of Larissa." Doug promised.

Larisa's father didn't seem convinced.

"I know you don't like me, that some of the tasks were meant to be a danger to me, to defeat or kill me."

Doug turned from the king to his brother. "I may have succeeded on some of the quests by myself, but most certainly would've been lost without those who follow me."

Larisa watched Doug shift his gaze to each of his followers. She saw him wink at Mod before he turned his attention back to the king.

Doug still wouldn't look at her, though. Larisa was feeling even more confused and hurt now.

He's going to do something stupid.

Doug smiled, his arms sweeping to indicate those who had helped him. "I've succeeded because of those around me. I admit this freely. So to prove my heart and my intent, I will take up the last task alone."

At Doug's statement Teutamides gave a wicked smile. "Stupid

boy, you've just delivered me my victory. Go find your fitting end." He took a flattened scroll from the pocket in his robe and tossed it to Doug.

Doug caught the scroll with one hand and tucked it away without even looking at it.

"Your resolve pleases me," Teutamides said.

"As I had hoped it would, my king." Doug gave a stiff, formal bow. "With that in mind, may I ask for you to grant the favor I ask?"

Doug could see Larisa was trying to get his attention, she was sure of it. She moved behind her father until she was in his line of sight. No matter where she moved, Doug wouldn't meet her eyes. He purposely avoided her gaze.

"Fair enough," the king said. "Though there is nothing you can ask for that will help you now."

"Whether I live or die, Larisa is free to do as she will. Her mind will be her own. Her choices her own. Her life her own. Swear this and your final task I will attempt with my whole life."

"No!" Larisa shouted. "How dare you ask for such a thing!"

The echo of the slap as the king brought his hand down on the arm of his throne reverberated across the hall. "Silence!"

Larisa felt as if the king had just slapped her instead of his throne.

"Foolish boy, I grant your request. The princess is free. Get her out of my sight." This drew gasps from the crowd, but the king didn't seem to care.

Teutamides had his guards escort Larisa from the room. She struggled at first. The look her father gave her made clear this was not the time, and the time would never come.

If I'm free, then why are you forcing me from my home like this, Father? Larisa thought. She wisely held her tongue and left.

There was nothing else she could do.

If Larisa had known it would be the last time she'd see Teutamides before his death, she might have reconsidered.

CHAPTER 41

FREEDOM

"DOUG!" LARISA CRIED AFTER HIM AS SHE CHASED DOUG through the back alleys of Larissa.

Doug took a quick left down a narrow path, then a right, then a left.

He's trying to lose me. The realization made her angry. *Not going to happen in my hometown.*

There were only three possible paths out of town from this point. And Doug would take the one that was most likely. Larisa cut through a back alley, jumped a wall into a yard that made roofing tiles, then hurried across the small wagon path between two warehouses. She got to the small market square about half a minute before Doug.

The square was empty. Everyone was at the agricultural festival or at the palace for Doug's meeting with the king.

Doug skidded to a stop in the empty square just short of running into her.

Out of breath, Larisa folded her arms over her chest and glared down at him. "What was that? Do you realize what you just did?"

Doug didn't raise his head to look at her. He said nothing.

"I might not be the princess anymore because of you. Is this the freedom you wished for me?"

Doug swallowed and shook his head. "I'm sorry," he whispered.

At least that's what she thought he whispered. He was speaking so softly she couldn't hardly hear him. "You waltz in, demand the last task, and leave. You didn't even talk to your brother," she said. "How long has it been? Three weeks? I bet he's worried sick.

"Why didn't you speak to us? Why didn't you look at me in the throne room?"

Doug shrunk down a bit at that. "I'm sorry." He shifted about like he was uncomfortable. "I've got to leave."

That was the wrong thing to say. Larisa was about to lose it when she noticed the tear running down his cheek.

Her hard heart melted, and she reached for him. "Doug?"

He started to blubber. "Tell Mod I'm sorry. Tell him I love him." He wiped his nose on the back of his arm. "I have to go."

Larisa put her hand on his shoulder, and he jerked away. He dropped his head lower, if that was even possible.

This wasn't the same man that had just boldly stood before the king.

And all Larisa wanted to do now was hold him and make him stop crying. "Doug, are you all right?"

He looked up at her then, and his eyes broke her heart. "Erebus will let you know, when everything is done." He looked away quickly, as if he might say too much or his resolve might falter.

There were gods involved. That explained a lot.

"I can help," Larisa said.

Doug shook his head. "Take care of Mod. He won't understand."

"Of course." Larisa reached for him again, but once more he shied away.

"I need to go now," he said, pausing for a second. "Please."

Please meant that he loved her.

Please meant that he didn't have a choice.

Please meant that he couldn't explain.

Larisa stepped aside.

Doug nodded, took a step, then straightened his back and strode out of the square.

Larisa collapsed to the ground once she lost sight of him.

She wasn't aware of how long she had cried before a gentle hand touched her on the shoulder. "Larisa?"

It sounded so much like Doug she wasn't sure whether to be angry or relieved.

It was Mod.

"He's gone," she sobbed as she rose and hugged Mod tight. "I don't know where or what, but he's gone and he's scared and he won't let us help him."

"I know," Mod said as he awkwardly tried to comfort her. "We have a boat, and the owner may be able to help us all help Doug."

Larisa didn't even ask whose boat it was. If there was any chance to help Doug, she would take it.

Chapter 42

Doug and the King (Part Two)

Doug had a lot of time to think about the last meeting with Larisa as he walked from her home to Taenarum. There were so many things he wished he'd done differently.

"I should have told her I loved her." It would have changed nothing, but then at least she would have known.

Regrets, might-have-beens, and doubts weren't as important as keeping her safe.

He was here, where he needed to be, and he could only move forward if he wanted to keep her and all the people he cared about safe.

The cave at Taenarum, on the southern tip of the Peloponnese, wasn't nearly as impressive as Doug had imagined it to be.

There were lots of doors to Hades's realm, this just seemed to be the best option for someone who was still breathing.

Doug unrolled the scroll and looked at it again. *In the realm of the dead, stop that which cannot be stopped.*

He stuffed the scroll back in his pocket. There wasn't much point to finishing the task for him, but if it helped his family and friends, he was going to see this through.

Doug paused before he stepped into the dark maw of the earth, acutely aware of the line that separated the light of the sun from the dark interior beyond. He looked back the way he'd come once, made sure no one followed him, then stepped over the threshold of the cavern into Hades's realm.

It still felt like someone was following him anyway.

It made sense. This was supposed to be the path of the dead, after all.

But who would follow him into the realm of the dead?

Doug stopped from time to time and looked over his shoulder for whatever trailed him, convinced he saw something he couldn't quite make out in the corner of his eye.

Something was following him.

The deeper he traveled, the more the thing following him became real.

"Doug?"

The echo of the whisper would have been too quiet to be heard in the land of the living, but here the uttered word was loud enough it stopped the young man in his tracks.

Disembodied spirit: one. Freshly laundered undergarment: zero.[1]

"Who's there?" Doug tried to search the area, but he could see nothing and nothing tangible fell within his reach.

"One who should have interacted with you differently in the past, it would seem," the voice said as it moved closer. "You come to this place on your own?"

Doug was relieved at the answer. "I do. I swore my pledge to a nobleman, and the gods witnessed and would that I should keep my word."

"And you do this for your own glory?" the shade asked.

"Heh." Doug couldn't help but laugh. "The truth? I'm here because of my own stupidity, mostly. In the beginning, I just wanted to impress a girl. Things have changed a bit since then." Doug felt about for a place to set down his pack to sit and rest a while.

"To your left," the shade said. "About a pace and a half from where you stand is a shelf of rock. Set down your burden and rest your feet."

"My thanks," Doug scooted to the left in halted, little steps. His feet probed the floor of the cave for the promised bench. It was right

---

1. Doug was just kidding himself. He wasn't wearing underwear.

where the ghost said it would be. Doug plopped down with a weary sigh. "How did you know where this was?"

"I belong," the shade said. "The way is bright before me. I see everything clearly."

"In any other circumstance I would have brought a light," Doug said about his apparent lack of preparation. "Someone gave me a warning about being seen, and I may have taken it a bit more to heart than I should have." His shoulders slumped a bit as another thought occurred to him. "Besides, Mod usually took care of those kinds of things."

"You're deep enough into the underworld that anything to aid your sight and passage would be preferable to being spied upon, and kinder to your extremities. I am fated by the gods to partake this final journey," the shade said. "As such my surroundings do not confound me as they do to one who doesn't belong."

"Dead, huh? My condolences to you and those you loved for their loss."

"Not many will mourn my passing, I fear," the shade responded.

"Every life lost is felt," Doug said. "You probably judge yourself too harshly."

"Not harshly enough. Should you know who I am and what I've done, you of all people would probably agree."

Doug knitted his brow, perplexed.

The shade continued to speak. "By revealing myself, your true feelings will be exposed. You knew me in life by the name Teutamides."

Shock, disappointment, and sadness bore down on Doug. The young man's shoulders slumped, and he let his head hang.

"I'm so sorry," Doug said. "I'd hoped that if I acted quickly enough, whoever was doing all these things would've left you alone, so you'd be able to take care of your daughter and she could take care of you."

"You truly feel sorry for me?" the king sounded shocked.

"I love your daughter," Doug explained. "How can I have hard feelings for you that don't reflect on her? You acted like a jerk to me. But a part of you made her who she is, so there's something in you that I have to respect and care for too. At least, that's how it works in my head."

"How refreshing and utterly naive," Teutamides said. "You would've made a terrible king."

Doug was forced to laugh at the naked honesty. "Probably. I was just in it for the girl. I would have let the ministers and advisers run things if I'd come back triumphant." Doug bent over and picked up his bag. He slung it over his shoulder and stood in one smooth motion. "Not that there's any chance of that happening now."

"My apologies for that," Teutamides said.

"I guess your plans didn't turn out the way you expected," Doug said.

"About that . . ." Teutamides paused. "A god influenced and directed me. Promises of power and glorious legacy proved too much of an enticement, and I went along with it far too willingly."

"You got snookered, huh?"[2] Doug took a few hesitant steps deeper into the cave. "Happens to everyone at one point or another."

"Hermes spoke with a honeyed tongue, and I was too eager to believe his sugared words," Teutamides confessed.

"Hermes? He's one of the smarter, better-spoken ones. His would be a hard voice and intellect to resist," Doug consoled.

"I should've known I was being played. A fool for ever being misled," Teutamides said. "If I might ask, why do you insist on completing the final task. You could go home, marry my daughter, rule over my kingdom in my absence."

"I'm pretty sure you disowned and disinherited the princess in our last meeting," Doug said.

"Ah. Yes, there was that." The king sounded ashamed.

"Sorry. That was a bit insensitive," Doug said. "I promised you

---

2. Snookered: synonym for duped, bamboozled, and smeckeldorfed.

and the gods that I would accomplish this task, and now it seems that if I don't, the fate of Greece hangs in the balance."

"I've inadvertently put Greece in danger?" Teutamides sounded aghast.

"Erebus thinks so. He's not sure who's behind it, but the signs are all there," Doug said.

"How could I have been so blind?" Teutamides took a deep breath and let it out in a slow sigh. "My apologies for having drawn you into the god's tangled web as a result."

"I accept your apology," Doug said. "I try not to be one to hold grudges, though I wish you'd shown a little more discernment in who you believed. Sorry you had to learn a lesson the hard way, and that it turned out like this for both of us."

"You have no idea the depth of my shame," the king said.

"Water under the bridge. Nothing we can do to change history. Whatever lesson we learn, whatever good can come from it, lies somewhere up ahead." Doug shuffled his feet down the path and tried not to trip in the dark.

"You speak truth." The king started after the youth. "It's just hard to reconcile and pinpoint how and when it went so wrong."

"Yeah, I do that too, thinking too much about things I can't change. Maybe we're not so different. All I can do is keep moving forward." Doug took several longer steps into the dark and rammed his shin hard into an outcropping of rock.

"Are you all right?" Teutamides asked.

Doug sucked in his breath. "Just waiting for my brain to assess the damage." He hopped about for a few moments, finally exhaled, and spit through clenched teeth. "Of course, I have to get to the end of the path before I can be properly condemned to the afterlife."

"I'm standing to the left of you. Please, take my arm." The king extended his hand. "The least I could do is get you there with a minimum of contusions." The king gasped in surprise as Doug stretched out his fingers and gripped Teutamides's wrist.

"Lead on, Macduff."[3]

The king shook his head at Doug's casualness. "I'm not getting the reference,[4] yet I swear to guide you true."

Once he touched the robe of the dead king, Doug began to discern shapes and outlines of the path before them. Those shapes and outlines clarified, and his vision improved the longer he was in contact with Teutamides. "I'm beginning to make out details ahead. That's a good thing, right?"

"I'm not sure," Teutamides said. "Do you feel a compulsion to head in a certain direction?"

"The cave floor has a sloping descent. Aside from the obvious effects of gravity compelling me downward, no."

"Let us hope that continues to be the case," the king said.

"Here, let me try something." Doug let go of the king's arm. He could make out the tunnel behind them with clarity. The cave ahead opened into a huge hall, leading to a larger void beyond. Doug saw the striations of the stone arching above his head, colors and variations dimmed but still visible. In the distance, gold and silver veins streaked through the rock. Gems twinkled in darkness like stars. "It's actually kind of pretty down here."

"The fact you no longer have to be in contact with me to see this realm does not set me at ease." Teutamides nevertheless let Doug find his own way. "I'll be nearby if you require further assistance."

Doug heard the sound of running waters somewhere in the distance.

"I believe we're getting close to the first barrier of the underworld," the king said.

---

3. It's, "Lay on, MacDuff," from the play *Macbeth* by Shakespeare. Doug got it wrong because he never did well in high school English because he's Greek and because high school English hasn't been created yet.

4. See previous footnote. Said previous footnote's explanation is also applicable to the king's understanding of the quote.

CHAPTER 43

BOOKING A RIDE ON THE RIVER STYX

DOUG COULD SEE THE DARK WATERS OF THE RIVER STYX. IT WAS so wide he couldn't see the other side. There was a small, somewhat ramshackle, driftwood ticket booth paired with an equally haphazard dock just ahead. Velvet ropes moldered on tarnished silver poles and created a maze in front of the building. A sign that read *queue here* was strategically positioned at the opening in the ropes.[1] Inside the shack, a ruddy-cheeked man snored, perched precariously on a leaning chair balanced on its back legs, his feet propped up on the desk before him.

"Hello?" Doug called out. "Is this where we hire a way across the river?"

The man inside the shack jolted awake at the inquiry. His arms pinwheeled and his foot caught on the upper drawer of the desk and threw him off balance. A series of vulgar swears hung in the air as he fell backward into a stack of empties large enough to do proud the most accomplished of boozers. Sounds of glass breaking and high-pitched screeching garnered the attention of everything living or dead within a several-hundred-meter radius.

The man emerged from the shack, dusted off his robes, and flicked off a few errant shards of glass. "Oh, bloody hell. Look what you gone and made me do."[2] The man examined a fresh tear in his

---

1. Queue: in British English it means a line or sequence of people awaiting their turn to be attended or to proceed. Neither Doug nor Teutamides understood the sign. Refer to the two previous footnotes for explanation.

2. Imagine an inebriated, redhead Tortuga bar rat from the Johnny Depp pirate

company uniform and probed the rip with several wriggling fingers. He tried his best to track down who'd caused such offense before he finally zeroed in on Doug and the king. Kind of. He blinked and shifted his gaze like he couldn't quite focus his eyes.

"My apologies," Doug said sheepishly. "First time visitors. We don't really know the lay of the land yet."

The man produced a non-empty bottle from somewhere and proceeded to take a long pull on the amber liquid inside. He wiped his mouth on his sleeve with an audible smack. "No harm done, luv, you just took me by surprise is all." He belched and sniffed the eddies his exhalation created in the air. Consoled by what he had or hadn't detected, he blinked hard and turned his attention back to the men who stood before him. "Now, what is it I can do for the four of you?"

Teutamides took a step back from the man's breath. "There are two of us."

The man squinted. "As of this moment I am currently unable to verify your claim. So I reckon another belt couldn't hurt." He took another drink and studied Teutamides and Doug with a sidelong glance.

The drink seemed to do the trick. "Well, two there are. What can I do for you gents?"

"Passage," Teutamides said as he pointed out over the river. "Across that."

The man's face split in an expression of profound understanding. "You be looking to hire a ferryman!"

"As it were," Teutamides said. "I'm not particularly impressed with the outfit here so far. Would you be so kind as to tell us our options?"

The man laughed and pointed back over his shoulder. "Options? To get over that bloody big river? Ain't no options but one." He pointed at a shoddy looking boat tied up to an even more unstable

---

movies and you should get the audio and physical tics of this particular character pretty close to what the guy writing it envisioned.

looking dock. "You gots to hire Charon! He'll likely get you across, lickety-spit!"

"I think the term is 'lickety-split,'" Doug said.

The man eyed Doug with suspicion. "It's lickety-spit,[3] as in, you trod on a gob of mucus and your foot 'bout shoots out from under yer arse fast as a pat of butter skittering across a hot griddle."

"Your gift for verbal elucidation boggles the mind," Teutamides said.

"Vivid," Doug chimed. "And subject heavy. Combining phlegm, posteriors, and cooking terminology all seamlessly in the same explanation? With oratory skills like that, you could do anything you want. You'd make a fine unemployed philosopher or an incorrigible military dictator or maybe even a position in public administration or services, like a garbage collector."

"Aye, I'd be surpassing fine as a leader 'o men, but tis not me callin'. I'm a company man through and through." The man pulled off the rag hat covering his head and revealed a mop of unruly, curly, bright red hair. He held the hat tight over his heart and rose up to his full height. "Puttin' pole to water, shiftin' the souls o' the damned from the memories o' the past to the now o' master Hades's land, traversing daily across the realm o' my pater, Erebus. That's me calling. And I's intends to do it 'til the day I dies."

"Such dedication," Doug observed. "An impressive show of loyalty to your employer. You should get a company discount on your final trip across the river."

"Alas, I ain't anywheres close to retirement." The man shook his crimson pompom head. "And Hades, gods bless 'im, ain't much on employee perks."

"Ferrying souls to the afterlife. Son of Erebus." Teutamides gasped, incredulous as the pieces fell into place. "Dear lords above, you're Charon."

---

3. Doug is right on this one, although the ticket-booth operator does make a powerful argument.

The red mop bowed a deep bow. "Guilty as charged, sor!" As he righted himself, the bottle again appeared in his hand, and he took a mighty swig.

Teutamides read the label on the bottle before Charon whisked it away. "Bacchus's Best Brandy,"[4] he muttered. "I think I've seen that label for sale on the lighter fluid aisle of the local Piggly Wiggly."

Charon pulled the brandy back out and gazed at it lovingly. "Tis a fine vintage," he said. "Imported, of course." He took another long pull on the bottle before he offered a swig to the king.

"It's obvious the quality of your choice of liquor would be wasted on one such as I. I must respectfully decline."

Charon looked a little crestfallen to have his offer to share refused.

The dead king, drawing upon his many years of diplomatic maneuvering, managed an ambiguous compliment as a deflection. "You're surely blessed with an exceptionally discerning palate."

Charon beamed at the supposed accolade and directed the praise to his liquor of choice. "A finer brandy you'd be 'ard pressed to find. Pity when me coin purse gets thin at the end o' the month and I 'ave to subsist on the cheap stuff." He stared at the bottle for a second, his eyes going wide and out of focus.

"I'm pretty sure he just lost consciousness," Doug said, thoroughly amused by the man. "Not quite the grim specter I was expecting. I like him."

Charon came back to somewhere during Doug's statement. "Aye, they want me to be grim, but I just cain't. It's me rosy cheeks and lively hair." Charon shook his head in sad wonderment. "People expect a toothy-jawed skull, not a childful, pinkish cherub to be the driver o' the skiff whisking them on to judgment. Try as I might, I can't hide me youthful nature and glow."

"Must be hard," Doug said.

"I handle it in me own way." Charon tipped the bottle again.

---

4. Bacchus Brands: the go to Italian brand for cheap booze and aggressive degreasers.

Teutamides choked back a cough as Charon exhaled in his direction. "I'd hazard a guess this man's blood is at least fifty proof."

"So, back to the matter at hand." Charon blinked hard at the two men. "What can I do for you fine gents on this fine day?"

"We needed a trip across, but perhaps we can find another option," Teutamides said.

"Hermes could skip across, but he's been doing a foul job at his job as of late," Charon said.

Teutamides frowned. "Hermes seems to be preoccupied with another endeavor."

Doug patted Teutamides on the shoulder. "It's okay. You can't win them all."

"You don't care that Hermes is neglecting his duties?" Terutamides asked.

"Lodging a complaint with HR is a nightmare,[5] what with the nepotism and whatnot. Everyone's related to everyone, or sleeping with the boss, or both. Who's gonna listen? Not like it's their problem." Charon waved his arm in a broad sweep, indicating all the floodplains stretching away from the river, dotted here and there with random smatterings of the dead, some solo, and others in large groupings. "Dead as far as the eye can see and beyond, wandering lost. None o' them in the right place to proceed onward." He indicated the queue sign. "Usually Hermes drops 'em right here, at the sign what tells 'em to line up, and they lines up and I takes 'em over there." He pointed across the river. "I can't go round 'em up 'cause who would I leave in charge o' the ticket booth while I chase that bucket o' wild cats? Business has been slow because they wander all willy-nilly 'stead of waiting all nice and orderly in the batting cage right here."

"So they can get to Hades by just walking around?" Teutamides sounded hopeful.

"Nope. Ringed by a moat of ghastly rivers is the land o' the dead.

---

5. Dionysus is actually the one in charge of hiring and firing. He's terrible at his job, but so much fun at parties that the bosses fear a mutiny if they get rid of him.

You need a boat or a piggy-back ride on ol' Hermes to get across the rivers. Hermes is off doing whatever he wants with his feathered-slippered toesies. That leaves travel by boat. Only one boat in all of the hells." Charon pointed his thumb at his chest. "Only way in is with ol' feather-toes or with meself."

"We'll take two," Doug said. "Does the cruise have a drink and snack service?"

"Maybe we should think about this," Teutamides cautioned.

"Shore, shore," the ferryman confirmed to Doug. "I have sodas and those little nuts that come seven to a bag."

"Pea?" Teutamides offered.

"If you need to pee, do it afore we get on the boat, otherwise you'll have to do your business over the side, and that makes me antsy because everything gets tippy."

Teutamides looked as if he felt swimming appeared to be a better option, so Doug hastened up the transaction. "How much?"

Teutamides put a finger in his mouth and felt around for a bit, disappointed to find nothing but teeth and tongue. What he was expecting to find was beyond Doug, but the king suddenly looked embarrassed. "I seem to have misplaced my purse."

"It's all right," Doug said. "I'm paying."

"Two obol apiece," Charon said.

The king looked taken aback. "Two? There should only be one!"

"We all gets to deal with rabid inflation in our own ways," Charon said, nonplussed. "You don't like my prices, get yourself an Uber."[6]

"I have no idea what you just said." Doug wanted to get going and wasn't going to waste time as he haggled over a boat ride, though one obol apiece would be better than two. Perhaps he could get a group discount for paying the king's fare as well. "How much?"

Charon's brow furrowed in deep concentration. "For the two of yous—well that would be—two coin apiece—adds up to?"

---

6. Not available in rural areas. Or at times one thousand years bce.

So much for the hopes of a discount.

The tip of Charon's tongue licked the corner of his mouth, and he started counting on his fingers. "Carry the seven . . ." Charon still calculated when he looked at Doug. "I just realized something. You're alive!"

"He is." Teutamides pointed at Doug in confirmation, then clarified things further as he pointed at himself. "But I'm dead."

"A live one! Well ain't this special!" Charon looked extremely pleased. "Ain't had a live one since Heracles. Or was it that singer? Was 'is name? Orion?[7] Onion? Ophilia? No, twernt Ophilia, I'd remember someone with a name that pretty." He scratched his head for a moment. "No matter. You'll be the latest mouth breather to cross the Styx now. That's quite a thing, that is." He smiled and pursed his lips and nodded. "Course, I'll have to charge the live one double."

"Double?" Teutamides was aghast. "This is outrageous! I'd like to lodge a complaint!"

"Talk to me manager," Charon said smugly. "You want a boat ride, you pay. And you," he pointed at Doug, "pays double. Round trip, innit?"

"Let's just focus on the here and now." Doug looked at the five coins in his hand. "Two coins per means that I owe you four."

"Is that all you have? Five obol?" Teutamides leaned in and whispered to Doug. "That means you'll be shy for the return trip. I forbid you from doing this!"

"My thanks." Doug ignored the command of the dead king and tried to hand the four coins to the ferryman.

"Uh, sorry." Charon shied away from the clenched coins. "I know it's weird, but I have a hard time taking money from someone's hand."

"You never know where that money might have been, right?" the king said flatly.

---

7. Orpheus. His name was Orpheus. I'm pretty sure he was the lead singer for Queen at one point. He was going by the name Adam Lambert by then.

"Oh, pay is pay. So it ain't that." Charon grimaced. "I'm a little embarrassed to have to explain. It just don't feel proper, being handed cash like I was peddling to the living."

"He is living!" Teutamides indicated Doug.

Charon just raised his eyebrows. Waiting.

Teutamides let out a weary sigh and turned to Doug. "He expects you to give the money a brief laundering first."

Doug stared blankly back at the king, not understanding.

Teutamides explained. "The dead, having no pockets or purse, might lose whatever coin is given them to pay the ferryman. Therefore the family of the deceased attempts to put the money in the place where the decedent is least likely to lose said cash."

Doug's eyes widened visibly as the king explained. He could think of several possible destinations for said coins, and most of them were unpleasant. "This is going to be another one of those instances where one of my naive and comfortable suppositions is going to be mangled and disposed of ignominiously, isn't it?" Doug turned to Charon and pleaded with his eyes. "Couldn't we forgo any more explanation if I just toss the cash to you?"

"Ah don't like tossed things. Reminds me of a bird that pecked at me head once," Charon said in way of explanation. "Sorry to be so peculiar about the pay and all, just seems off to me if I ain't taking coin that ain't presented a certain way."

"He wants you to put it in your mouth," the king clarified. "The coins of the dead are usually placed in the mouth under the tongue."[8]

Doug was young enough he didn't often think of death and all the little things associated with it. The bit with the coin under the tongue was new to him. He looked from the king to the ferryman like they were both pulling a prank on him, although an orally inserted coin

8. Pay for transport into the land of the dead was placed under the tongue. Under the tongue is important. Coins were fairly secure under the tongue. If you just put the money in the mouth all willy-nilly there's a chance that getting the coin to Charon will take something more invasive than a finger in the cheek.

was preferable to some of the other options he'd imagined. "So to pay for the boat ride I have to put the obols in my mouth first?"

"'S a weird proclivity o' mine," Charon apologized. "If it don't get done a certain way—"

Doug looked to Teutamides just to make sure.

"He's the weird one," Teutamides said as he pointed back to the ferryman. "What could I possibly gain from making up something like this?"

Still unsure, Doug raised his hand to his face and popped four coins in his mouth. He was pretty sure he got one of the coins from a sketchy food cart with funky goat cheese. As he moved the coin with his tongue, he was certain of it. A lot of flavor had been preserved under the deep ridges and the recesses of the pressing. The coin tasted more of fetid goat than curdled currency.

"I can take the obols out of your mouth if you'd like." Charon stretched forth a finger.

Doug took one look at the state of Charon's nails and rejected the offer. He would've rejected it anyway because it was creepy, but the unmistakable grime on Charon's appendages sealed the deal. The ferryman, apparently, was unaware of the invention of manicures or of the hygienic benefits garnered by regular applications of soap and water.

Doug gagged a little bit and almost swallowed his boat fare. "Just stick your hand out." Doug mumbled around the currency in his mouth. He leaned forward and spat the obols into Charon's open hand.

Teutamides furrowed his brow. "How come you didn't have to take two obols from my mouth?"

"He paid for the both of ya." Charon nodded toward Doug, then pushed his hand toward Teutamides. "But if it'll make you feel better?"

Teutamides looked at the glistening money and looked as if his dead stomach lurched. "I retract my inquiry. I'm good if you are."

Charon shrugged. The ferryman counted out the moist coins in his palm. "There are indeed four obol here." His fingers sealed the obols in a slow, tight fist.

Charon spoke again, his voice now deep and dark. His words chilled the blood and came across as very professional. "So the bargain is struck." Charon was suddenly taller, a very appropriate and cavernous hooded cloak shaded the red fires that replaced his eyes. "My services have been engaged. The meter is currently running." A skeletal arm slipped out of the sleeve and invited the men to the boat. "Gentlemen, if you would?"

Both Doug and Teutamides had to suppress a running-down shiver, Doug in his spine and Teutamides in the place where his spine used to be. They quickly commenced down the gangplank. Both looked as if they attempted to power walk with a potato held between their thighs.[9]

"I think I liked the other version of Charon better," Doug said.

9. The involuntary constriction of certain muscle groups can have an effect on the proper execution of a stride, which in turn affects the gait. You can't really do anything about it. Nobody could blame Doug for his sudden, silly walk. Not sure why Teutamides, who no longer possessed muscles, felt the same constrictions. It wasn't very graceful, but with the sudden and unexpected change in the transaction dynamics, who could blame them?

Chapter 44

The Good Boy of the Underworld

"It's been a pleasure," The bottle of brandy disappeared into Charon's robes and his hand reappeared with a business card. "I don't get much repeat business, but this here gives directions if ya needs me for an unscheduled pickup."

Doug took the proffered card from the ferryman's calloused hand. It had an impressive heading in a Gothic typeface. *Charon, The Ferryman What Cares*, Doug read.

"Aye. That'd be me." Charon beamed.

There were addresses given to admonish those reading the card to follow Charon's exploits on social media.[1] The more pertinent information for Doug was spelled out on the bottom. "It says if I need you, I come here, to the ferry landing, and I yell your name."

"That'd do it." Charon extended his hand to clasp Doug's. He shook it energetically. "A word o' advice in partin'. Don't upset the dog. 'E gets testy a'times."

The significance of the statement eluded Doug right now. He tried to narrow it down slightly. "The dog barks, or does he bite?"

"Yes'm," Charon said as he pushed the skiff away from the dock. "But not with more than two heads at once, lessen he's truly riled."

"Thanks for the warning." Doug waved at the ferryman as the

---

1. Charon was an early adopter and was ready for the rush of clients once the internet was created. He used his foresight as an ageless creature that existed outside time and space to plan ahead. Social media hadn't been invented yet, which is why Doug hadn't heard of Twitter and Facebook. Charon didn't plan on using Friendster. *Nobody* was going to use Friendster.

boat zipped away from the shore. The craft put a clean, razor-thin slice on the water's surface. It moved neither left or right, straight as an arrow as it was swallowed up in the distance.

A bit of mist from the river Lethe was making it hard for Doug to concentrate.[2]

"Dog?" His current canine conundrum continued to confound him. He knew he'd thought about dogs before he'd come to the underworld, but he couldn't quite remember *why* a dog or dogs in general were important at the moment. Doug shrugged his pack higher on his shoulder as he turned from the dock to proceed into the land of the dead.

He hadn't gone more than a few steps before he stumbled into the back of Teutamides.

"Sorry about that," Doug said as he still tried to decipher what Charon had mentioned. "Why'd you stop? Just a bit ago you seemed so eager to be off."

The king trembled and pointed a finger up ahead. "There's something not right here."

Doug couldn't see what the king was worried about. He took a few steps forward and something launched itself at him from the shadows.

The mastiff of Tartarus lunged at the live boy, three massive chains attached to three massive spiked collars around its three massive necks stopped it just short before it would have crushed Doug in its three massive jaws.

"Oh, that dog. I feel silly for forgetting something like him," Doug exclaimed as soon as he could feel his heartbeat again.

Cerberus settled into a quiet judgmental set of stares focused on Doug and the king. One head focused on the king, the other on Doug, while the third pair of canid eyes alternated between the two.

---

2. Five rivers run through and surround the land of the dead. Drinking or touching any of them come with different consequences. The Lethe makes one forget, Acheron gives one sorrow, Cocytus causes lamentation, and Phlegethon is the river of fire. Styx is the biggest of them all, separating the surface of Gaea from the underworld.

"Funny," Doug said.

"How can this possibly be funny?" Teutamides asked.

"It's just, well, look." Doug turned his back to the giant canine to face the king. "There was Snickers at the beginning. Then there've been dogs barking at whatever in the realms of Zeus they barked at everywhere I went." He pointed over his shoulder to Cerberus. "And now a three headed monster dog wants to rip my flesh from my bones. This has been a dog-heavy experience from start to finish."

The king gaped at the boy. "This is seriously your takeaway from what you've been through?"

Doug shrugged. "Just an observation."

"Hrrm." The king arched an eyebrow. "Your observation of this final dog may have also made you aware that said dog is barring your way from proceeding any further along the path of your task."

"Oh, I'm not worried about that." Doug dropped his pack to the ground and started to undo the drawstrings. "This last little bit of the trip has been a tad disconcerting, and I kinda forgot what I'd planned for a while. There was a reason I've been lugging this heavy pack down into the underworld." Doug reached into the bag and pulled out a substantially meaty bone from inside.

Doug now had Cerberus's full attention.

"That might distract one of the beast's heads for a bit, but . . ." While Teutamides continued talking Doug pulled another two bones from his bag.

Cerberus sat back on his haunches and panted heavily. He fully expected a treat.

"Who's a good boy?" Doug asked. He tossed one large bone to one slavering mouth, a second bone to another, with the final bone being snatched from the air with a snap by the third.

The dog wasted no time as he dropped down and began to chew happily away. His front paws moved from this bone to that as the mouths and teeth in question deemed the extra paw stability was necessary.

Doug walked right up to the giant canine and scratched each head right behind the ears.

The king watched it all happen, slack jawed and aghast. "I truly believe any other being in existence would have been ripped to shreds just for approaching such a beast."

"Really?" Cerberus rolled over to let Doug scratch his belly. "He seems like he's a pretty approachable guy to me." Doug leaned in against the dog, using both arms to cover as much belly area as he could reach.

It wasn't nearly the full tummy of the dog, but Cerberus didn't seem to mind.

The king acted as if he might attempt to pat the dog on one of its heads, but just one tentative step closer elicited a deep growl and bared canines from the head immediately closest to him.

Doug gave the huge dog a final pat and stepped back.

Cerberus righted himself and stepped aside to clear the path. The dog panted and smiled at Doug with two heads while its third head snapped at Teutamides as they walked past.

Chapter 45
Hermes

"Dogs don't like Hermes." Teutamides offered out of the blue.

"Hmm." Doug grunted. "Good to know, I guess."

"My dog didn't like him," Teutamides said. "I should have trusted in Ergos's loyalty and discernment more during those visits."

"Visits?" Doug was intrigued. "You and Hermes must have been on pretty good terms."

"I didn't know it was him," Teutamides said defensively. "At least, not until it was too late."

Doug arched an eyebrow but said nothing.

"He was always invisible or in shadow. He didn't reveal himself until we were both standing over my dead body."

Doug's eyes widened in shock as he looked over at the king. "That's a hell of a way to find out you've been manipulated."

Teutamides clenched his hands into tight fists. "He was gloating. He manhandled my corpse before me. It took me quite a minute to realize what I was even looking at." The king was shaking.

"I'm sorry, Teutamides," Doug said, shocked that even a god could be so cruel. "No one should ever be exposed to such a horrifying thing."

Teutamides shut his eyes. "And then he told me my death was just a glorious beginning of something better yet to come." His eyes popped open again as he stared at Doug. "How can a glorious thing spring forth from the death and manipulation of a king?" Teutamides was quiet then as if imagining his figure slumped at an unnatural angle at the base of a stair.

"He said he'd used others, but I was his . . ." Teutamides stopped, and swallowed before he continued. "I brought him closer to his goal than any he had used before.

"He told me Larissa would fall, and my kingdom's absence would bring about the end of Greece and the gods themselves.

"It made me so angry that I struck him." Teutamides raised up his fist and shook it. "With this ghostly fist, I bloodied his godly lip."

"Well that's a bit of a victory right there." Doug said. "Who'd have thought such a thing was even possible. Have hope. Your daughter might still be able to salvage what was left behind," Doug encouraged.

The king looked stricken at the words. Teutamides slowly shook his head from side to side in shame.

"Oh, yeah." Doug had forgotten about the king exiling his daughter. "Sorry I brought that up."

"You say sorry quite a bit for someone who is not responsible for the mess you're dealing with," Teutamides growled.

Doug shrugged. "Sorry."

The king shook his head, a slight smile creasing his lips. "There's just no hope for you."

"You never know, do you?" Doug said brightly. "I was told by a reliable source that if I completed the task, we might be able to stop some of the bad from happening."

"Reliable source?" the king sounded as if he weren't convinced. "The task was meant to be impossible," Teutamides reminded Doug.

"Yeah, and man wasn't meant to fly," Doug said, "but my cousin Icarus still managed to escape from Crete on wings made of feathers and wax."[1]

---

1. There are differing versions of Icarus, some flying, others with him and his father escaping imprisonment on a boat with sails. In all the versions Icarus drowns. And then there's my version: Icarus falls, survives, and now passes his time building kites for kids on the island of Samos. I like my version best.

"Didn't Icarus die from drowning?" Teutamides narrowed his eyes.

"He still flew," Doug said. "I can do an impossible thing, no matter the cost, if it gives everyone else a fighting chance."

He sounded so determined that Teutamides didn't press it any further.

As long as I'm stuck doing the impossible task, it isn't over. Hermes can't go through with his plan. Doug reasoned to himself.

Chapter 46

Minty Fresh Tour

"Well. Hi there!" A cheery, chipper voice greeted them as they passed beyond the reach of Cerberus's chain. A positive and perky young lady waved at the pair and smiled.

Doug returned her greeting with a wave of his own. "Hi. I'm Doug, and this is Teutamides."

"Oh, wonderful! Wonderful! You just answered my first questions." The woman wrote their names on a couple of stickers on her clipboard. She cheerily pulled off the temporary name tags and handed them to the men. Doug's sticker read *Dug* and Teutamides was spelled out partially phonetically as *Toot-ah-mighties*.

She beamed at the pair until they both put on their tags.

Doug put his on with a grin and played along with the game.

Teutamides sighed wearily. "Everyone in the underworld is a moron, and I'm now stuck in a place where my intelligence being factored in raises the bell curve of brainpower dramatically."[1]

He placed the misspelled label on his lapel when the woman gave a quiet and impatient "Ahem," as she covered her mouth with a dainty fist.

"Oh, thank you so much," she chirped. She brought the clipboard down in front of her and bounced a little dramatic hop where she

---

1. So called because the common shape of the equation laid out on a graph looks like a bell. It should be the Gaussian Curve because it was discovered and first used by Karl Friedrich Gauss, but Teutamides didn't know Gauss, who won't be born for a few thousand years, so we'll give the king a pass on using the common term for the graph.

stood. "Oh, I almost forgot. I'm Minthe,[2] and I'll be giving you a little walkabout tour as you learn the hows and whys of the wonderful land of the dead!

"Are you all familiar with everyone in the group?" she asked the large, mostly unpopulated, area.

Teutamides glanced around. "I have no idea who she's referring to." He arched an eyebrow at the guide. "There's two of us. And we came here together."

"It looks like we might have the makings of a few new friendships here." Minthe smiled and winked in their general direction, and in a couple of other directions as well. "So just to make sure we keep all of our new friends with us, I think we should choose a tour buddy. Come on, everyone. Partner up with someone. We wouldn't want to get separated from the group, and that works best if you have a buddy to keep an eye on you."

"There's just two of us," Teutamides growled and indicated himself and Doug. He gestured broadly to point out no one else was there, then turned back to Minthe exasperated. "How the hells do we get lost in the crowd with only two of us?"

Doug gave the former monarch a forlorn look complete with big, puppy dog eyes. "Toot-ah-mighties, you don't want to be my tour buddy?"

"If we weren't already in Hades, I might kill you right now, just for that," The king growled.

Doug laughed and reached out to grab the king's hand. Teutamides was quick, but Doug was faster. "Miss!" Doug yelled, louder than he needed to. He gripped the king's hand tight by the

---

2. One of Hades's former girlfriends. Persephone wasn't too keen on keeping an old flame of her husband's around, so she just happened to turn Minthe into so much dust. Hades thought the punishment a bit harsh and changed Minthe into a mint plant instead. Then Charon pointed out that with Hermes mucking up the works, the dead weren't really getting to the correct places of judgment or eternal rest anymore, and he could use a bit of extra help. A compromise of Minthe becoming the underworld's welcoming and orientation specialist was struck and grudgingly agreed to by all.

wrist as he raised it over his head and waved their arms frantically. "Miss! I think I found my buddy!"

Teutamides let his hand and arm go limp. "All I can do is just wait the whole thing out."

"I know this is the first time any of you have been here, so I thought I might ask if there is anything you'd like to see? Does anything in particular really pique your interest?" Minthe clasped her hands together and beamed at them.

"Well, I've seen the river Styx and the big puppy, and those were two of the things I really wanted to check out before I stand before my final judgment." Doug gave Teutamides's limp wrist a shake. "Anything in particular you wanted to see, buddy?"

Teutamides yanked his arm away from the young man.

Doug chased after him and grabbed his garment by the sleeve.

"I swear an oath that I will kill you," the king glowered.

"Waste of effort," Doug pointed out. He shifted his grip so the king couldn't tear the fabric from his grasp. "You're dead, and I'm already in the underworld."

"You could visit the courtyard of the godly palace or walk along the viewing path on top of the main gate," Minthe offered. "There's also the fields of Asphodel, quite lovely, or we could go by the imposing pavilion of judgment." She still hadn't gotten any reaction from the dead king. "I don't often suggest this, but off to the west we have the fields of punishment."

"Much as I hate to do this . . ." Doug let go of the king's arm. The time for fun was over. "We should probably check out the fields of punishment. It's where we have to go after all."

Minthe cocked her head to the side. "I'm not sure how to interpret that. Is there someone in particular you were hoping to see being punished? I don't know about showing off souls in agony, but since the young man expressed a preference. It takes all kinds, right?" She paused. "If you tell me who you're looking for I might be able to swing you by."

"We'll know what we're looking for when we see it," Teutamides said somberly. "Why don't you just take us on a tour of the most inventive?"

"I'd love to," she beamed. "I'm sure you'll find many of the punishments created here to be on the cutting edge of emotional torment, irony, and deterrent measures."

"The emotional toll of punishment I understand, along with a healthy dose of the ironic to drive the point home. However, deterrent measures?" Teutamides asked. "The punishments deter further atrocities by those being punished? And the punishment of the tormented ends?"

She shook her head. "Oh, if they've offended the gods, they still get theirs," she clarified. "The deterrent is more directed at everyone else in general."

Teutamides stopped mid step. He blocked Doug, and the tour as a whole, from going forward once Minthe noticed the men no longer followed her.

Teutamides glowered. "I don't see the logic in any of what you just said. Sounds rather like having a set list of punishments and durations of said punishments is unnecessary when all of this is just carried out according to the flighty whims of, oh, I don't know, whoever is most pissed off at the one being punished?"

"While it is good to pontificate on such matters, it really works better for everyone involved if we keep the tour moving." She gave a smile meant to placate the king and made little come-along gestures with her hands. "We're walking." She beckoned them on. "We're walking. We're walking."

Teutamides rolled his eyes and begrudgingly took a step in Minthe's direction. "If I understand you correctly, people have no idea of the punishments being carried out, and from the randomness of most of the methods executed, have no way of guessing what those punishments may be."

"Exactly!" Minthe beamed. "The punishment you can't expect is the punishment to be feared."

"No wonder they call this the age of reason," Teutamides said with a sarcastic scowl. “If I had my way, I’d have a thing or two to say to the gods about this whole system.”

“I’m not sure you want to talk to management about this,” Minthe said in a warning tone. “Complaints like this need to be handled in a certain way.”

“Oh, I bet they do.” Teutamides shook his head. “Sadly, we’re probably about to experience their unfathomable, unreasonable, ineffable justice firsthand. I’m saying the word ‘ineffable,’ but in truth I’m thinking of another word that starts with the letter *F* often used in conjunction with the word *up*.’”

“Well, you’re a feisty one.” Minthe looked a little worried that the tour wasn’t moving along.

Doug could see the dead king’s blood-pressure rise and thought it might be best to shift his focus to something else for a while. A palpable collection of pleasant scents wafted by. Doug moved in that direction. The smells grew stronger with each step he took.

“Something smells good.” Doug sniffed at the air. “Does the underworld have a concession stand?” He might be able to banish the lingering taste from the goat coin he’d stuck in his mouth earlier. The snacks he got from Charon weren’t enough to cleanse his palette.

They all headed in the direction of the smells.

A sumptuous feast appeared. So much food was spread over several tables it spilled down onto benches and the ground in some places. Cakes, candies, wines and punches, the finest of fruits and vegetables, the feast lacked for nothing. It even had a young ox being turned on a spit over a bed of glowing coals. The whole affair was circled by a ring of stone seats.

Doug felt his mouth fill with drool. “Anything I can get for an obol?”

Minthe shook her head and smiled at Doug like he was a moron. “The food isn’t for sale. It’s a test and torment of a man cursed by the gods.”

“Poor fool,” Teutamides said.

"Hey, that voice sounds familiar," one of the stone seats said. "Is that little Toot?"

"Wait a minute. Phlegyas?" Teutamides searched the area.

"Oh, man, are you looking in the wrong direction!" the voice went on. "Look down, my beloved cousin! My kingdom has been reduced to the confines of a rock."

One rock had a face, three fingers, and a thumb of a right-hand protruding from it. Phlegyas wiggled his index finger in salutation.

Teutamides stared at the stone. "This is my cousins' final prison? You're in a rock the size of a footstool, Phlegyas. Not how I expected to find you, well, ever."

"How'd you wind up here?" Doug asked.

Teutamides explained before his cousin had a chance to answer. "Apollo killed his wife, so Phlegyas set fire to Apollo's temple. Apollo couldn't take vengeance himself, because, well, that would mean he had some kind of responsibility for the situation. So he sent Phlegyas here to be taunted for all of eternity imprisoned in a rock the size of a footstool."

"Of an ottoman," Phlegyas corrected. "It is the breadth and width and depth of my new empire! My Ottoman Empire![3] Ha! Get it?" The man in the stone snorted at his own joke. "I crack me up! At least I hope I do?" He grunted and stretched. After about a minute of effort he gave up. "Damn. No fissure," he sighed. "So, what brings you here, Toots? You finally kick it?"

"In a manner of speaking." Teutamides indicated his companion who gave a little wave to the man trapped in the rock. "This is Doug. He's still among the living."

"Wow!" Phlegyas appeared impressed. "That'll be the talk of the town for a while. Welcome, Doug! I bow in greeting to you!" With his

---

3. The Ottoman Empire spanned much of Southeastern Europe, swaths of Western Asia, and a good portion of North Africa starting in the fourteenth century ce. It was established well after our tale, but Hades has a newsletter full of history's up and coming attractions circulated down below once monthly.

current state of constriction, the bow came out as more of an eyebrow spasm.

"Pleased to meet you, sir." Doug gave a slight nod and bowed in return.

"Polite," the man in the rock said. "I like that. Toots, you should totally hook this guy up with your daughter."

Doug cleared his throat and arched a judgmental eyebrow at the king.

Teutamides looked more than a tad embarrassed. "That small reproach is no more than I deserve."

Phlegyas strained against the rock again and tried to shift himself closer to the food.

"You seem determined," Doug said.

"Can you not smell that?" Phlegyas marveled at the feast. "I salivate just being near it, which is pretty much all I can do, but I'm so close." He flexed his fingers again, his ring finger stretched to its fullest. "If I can just manage a bit more reach, I'm totally getting a biscuit."

Doug walked over to the table and grabbed a biscuit.

"I don't think you're supposed to—" Minthe tried to object.

Doug shrugged. "Anyone directly ever said not to?"

"No," the woman admitted. "But—"

Doug turned his attention to Phlegyas now. "Butter?"

The man in the rock nodded his eyebrows.

"Honey?"

Phlegyas started to blubber. "Yes, please."

Doug took a knife and cut the biscuit in two. The bread steamed like it'd just popped out of the oven. He slathered a generous portion of butter on each side, then smothered both halves with clover honey. "Here you go, man." He knelt down beside the rock and broke off bits of the biscuit to feed to the trapped man.

"This really isn't part of the task. I'm really not sure you're supposed to be doing this—" Teutamides started.

The look Doug gave back told the dead king that: A, he was

already in the land of the dead. B, what greater punishment could he garner if he fed the damned. C, Teutamides, personally, was a coward. And D, he should be the one down here caring for his beloved cousin.

"Carry on," Teutamides said.

"I'm just helping a guy out." Doug grinned and gave Phlegyas another bite.

Phlegyas smacked his lips. His eyes rolled back in ecstasy. "Oh, this is so good. I mean, I remember liking biscuits. I remember 'em being wicked tasty, but this?" He took another bite. "Buttery and a bit dry both at the same time." He wrapped his tongue around another hunk of cooked dough. "I'd forgotten just how divine a good, flaky biscuit could be."

A crack suddenly appeared in the rock around him.

Minthe yipped in shock. "If he gets out, Apollo could be really angry."

"Does Apollo ever come down here?" Doug cut a thin slice off of a loaf of bread and put a bit of the roast beef on it.

She shook her head. "Not really, but—"

"So what's the problem?" Doug waved the bread in the general direction of the heavens. "He's too busy bleaching his hair and flexing in the mirror to worry about us helping someone snack on a bit of succulent roast beef." Doug paused then and studied the meat on the bun with an odd, quizzical expression. "I thought even animals got to live out their afterlives lazing in emerald fields, far from danger or harm. So how do we explain what's happening to Mr. Bovine here?"

"I rather enjoy being useful and desired." The calf on the spit turned his head to look at Doug, grinned, and nodded approvingly. "Just doing my part.[4] Enjoy!"

"I'm totally going to get turned back into a plant. I hate aphids."

---

4. A tip of the hat to ol' Douglas Adams, or was it Eoin Colfer? Anyway, the cows that want to be eaten are from *the Hitchhiker's Guide to the Galaxy* books. They're good. You should read them.

Minthe nervously wrung her hands. She paused now and then to scratch at imaginary microscopic bugs.

"Oh, you'll be fine," Doug said. "Just tell anyone who says anything about it that I was very insistent. Or blame it on Teutamides. He's a king, and he ordered you to let us make snacks for the exhibits."

"So I will bear the brunt of punishment for your impetuous action?" Teutamides chided Doug.

Doug turned his head slowly to the dead king and once again arched an incredulous eyebrow. "Really?" he said after a long, silent pause.

"Ah." Teutamides realized what he'd unthinkingly spoken. "Point taken."

Doug turned his attention back to Phlegyas. "Mustard?"

"Gods, yes!" The man in the rock cheered.

Doug finished a few flourishing touches on the meal and knelt back down by Phlegyas. "How're you doing?"

Phlegyas smiled so broadly that the rock around his face sprouted new crevices and a few shards actually sloughed off. He flexed and his pinky finger appeared. "Can I hold that sandwich?"[5]

"It's open faced."

"I'm good with that." Phlegyas wiggled his hand as he begged for it to be filled.

"Fair enough." Doug handed the sandwich over, and Phlegyas promptly dropped it. Luckily it landed face up.

Doug was about to kneel down to grab it when Teutamides stepped in. "Allow me. If I'm to take a portion of the blame, I may as well go all in."

"That's the spirit, Toots." Doug smiled as he went back to the table to make another snack. "Hey, Minthe, which way is Tantalus from here?"

---

5. Sandwiches haven't been invented yet, but they didn't know what to call it otherwise.

CHAPTER 47

A GOD, TWO WOMEN, A NERD, A SOOTHSAYER, AND SIX MECHANICAL PEOPLE WALK INTO A BAR

Larisa felt she didn't belong in the kingdom anymore. Luckily, Mod and the others had found her, so at least she wasn't alone and was with people who cared about Doug. With Mod and the crew's help Larisa had been trying to find a way to aid Doug, but no one knew what the last task given to him was.

Larisa was sitting on the *Nyxy Business*. She tried not to despair as she waited for any inspiration to strike. None was forthcoming, when out of nowhere, she and the crew welcomed a visitor.

The cloaked man walked up to the ship. "Hello. I may have some information about a lad named Doug and the circumstances currently surrounding him. I'd like to be of help, if I may?"

Mod rose to greet the man. "I would very much like any information you might offer."

Larisa stood up next to Mod and gave the man a visual once-over. "We're currently speaking to a god," she said.

The man looked startled by the observation, then smiled at Larisa.

"How could you possibly know that?" Mod asked.

Larisa pointed down at the water of the Aegean Sea. "We're five kilometers from shore."

The god laughed. "Athena said you were smart." He pointed at the deck of the ship. "Mind if I come on board?"

Larisa, Mod, and the others welcomed him.

The god did a double take when he saw Nine.

"Is there a problem?" Nine asked.

"You just look like someone I wasn't expecting to see." The god's voice trailed off. The god shook his head and looked at the others. "Larisa, Modifixeus, Mopsus, and Medusa. It is good to see all of you, my children." The god then turned to One and her siblings. "I knew the children of Kestibios and Talos accompanied Doug on his quests, yet I'd hoped to meet you under different circumstances.

"I am Zeus," the god said.

Everyone on the boat was shocked. They hadn't expected this.

Larisa came to her senses first and bowed. The others all followed suit.

"None of that now," Zeus said. "I came here not for worship but to try to help Doug."

"We all want to help Doug." Larisa came close and pleaded with the god. She almost started crying at even the thought of hope. "Any way you could aid us would be greatly appreciated."

Mod did start to cry. Medusa put an arm around his shoulders and tried to soothe him.

"I can see the burden of worry weighs heavy on all of you." Zeus looked up at Apollo following his path across the sky. "I think you all could use a drink to help you cope with all of the things we're about to discuss."

"Drinking? This early? It's just past noon." Nine pointed out.

"It's five o'clock somewhere." Zeus waved his hand,[1] and a passage to an inviting, well-kept bar appeared.

As she stepped through the portal, Larisa recognized many of the patrons as gods and goddesses. Larisa didn't know if she should be excited or terrified. Gods and goddesses were unpredictable, and there was no way to know what to expect.

Zeus must have sensed her unease. "It's alright. This is a safe place, and you're with me."

Across the bar Hephaestus and Arktos were sharing some mead

1. Jimmy Buffett had divine inspiration when he wrote this one.

during a break from the work at the forge. They waved at Mod, and he gave a small wave back.

Larisa's group took the corner booth away from everyone else. It was just big enough to fit all of them.

Once they were settled with their drinks, they discussed everything they knew. It was the news from Zeus of who was behind everything that got the biggest reaction.

"Hermes? I wouldn't have expected it," Mod said. "Not in a million years."

Larisa had suspected him. Zeus only verified who'd been manipulating her father. She pulled out her list of gods responsible for thought. "Knowing it was Hermes just doesn't seem to be the final answer I was looking for. Something is still missing."

"I never liked Hermes." Medusa looked at Zeus. "How did you manage to figure it out?"

Zeus smiled. "Actually, it was Mopsus who figured it out for me."

Mopsus looked perplexed. "Me? How?"

"My messages weren't getting through," Zeus explained, "Hermes made the connection spotty for a while, but then he gave up his pretenses and stopped taking messages to Mopsus altogether. Didn't take much deductive reasoning to parse it out from there."

Mopsus nodded. "That does explain why I've been having so many problems."

Everyone at the table was quiet for a moment.

"We have a slight conundrum," Zeus continued. "Hermes, in all his machinations and scheming, really stacked the deck when it came to the kingdom of Larissa. The city will be cursed if Doug takes the throne. The city will be cursed if Larisa takes the throne. The city will be cursed if a usurper takes the throne. The city will be cursed if it has no monarch. The city will be cursed if it is conquered. The city will be cursed if it has a regent. The city will be cursed if it is occupied. The city will be cursed if it is razed and laid fallow."

"That's a lot of cursing. How in Hades did he manage that?" Four asked.

"You've just got to know which oracle to bribe," Zeus said, which garnered shocked glances from everyone at the table. "A grievous flaw in the system, I agree."

"Which ones did he bribe?" Medusa asked.

Zeus blinked hard and shook his head like he couldn't believe the answer. "All of them."

Mopsus asked the obvious question, "And in all of these varied scenarios, the unhappy fate of the kingdom of Larissa leads to what?"

"The downfall of Greece. The fall of the gods." Zeus sighed, rubbed his eyes with the tips of his fingers, and shook his head. "Makes me wonder if things might have turned out differently if I'd spent more quality time with Hermes when he was a child."

At the counter Satan dug through the bar mix for a pretzel. "Or had you applied the rod a bit more liberally," he murmured to himself as he chewed on a salty bread nub.

"I swear to myself, don't make me come over there, Morningstar." Zeus pointed a sharp, accusatory finger in Satan's direction. "Don't you have a holy man's shoulder to sit on while you whisper sweet nothing-doings in his ear?"

Satan picked up the bowl of snacks in a huff. "Well, excuuuse me! I didn't know I was intruding on a private conversation." The Morningstar snorted in self-righteous justification and moved to the far end of the bar. Halfway along, he made a wide berth around Arktos and Hephaestus.

Larisa glared at him. Her head tracked Satan's path as he left. "He totally knew he was intruding."

"The weaselly little man with the bar nuts appears not to like the bear," Nine grumbled.

"Maybe the bear doesn't like tricksters and liars?" Zeus looked at Hephaestus and his companion. "Smart bear."

"Is there a code of ethics for attendance that precludes patrons from rending the flesh from the bones of other customers?" Nine asked.

Everybody at the table ignored Nine.

"It's a legitimate concern," Nine defended himself.

The bear noticed Zeus and tipped a jewel-encrusted grail toward the Olympian. Zeus acknowledged the gesture and returned a libation salute before he turned back to those at his table.

"Unusual guests aside, it is a bar," Larisa defended Satan for the overheard earlier bits of the conversation. "And we're a pretty large group. Someone is bound to overhear something."

"It's a very exclusive club," Zeus tried to correct.

Larisa raised an eyebrow and set her jaw.

Zeus admitted defeat on the point. "I suppose you're right about the privacy issue. Someone was bound to be listening. It's just that the whole situation requires a bit of extreme reckoning to be resolved, and I do some of my best thinking here."

Mod furrowed his brow. "Without Teutamides, the fall of Larissa leads to the end of everything. Teutamides isn't coming back?"

Medusa squeezed Larisa's hand. "Have they found your father yet?"

Larisa had to choke back a sob. "I hadn't really understood how much I wanted Father until he wasn't here. No one saw him leave the palace. Not one person. No one's seen him since the day he yelled at Doug and threw me out."

Zeus grew somber. "I'm afraid, young Larisa, that Modifixeus's question should be stated more as if it were a fact. Your father will not be coming back. I am so sorry, my dear."

The faint spark of hope faded from Larisa's heart. "I expected as such. Father was many things, but he'd never leave his people without a leader."

"So we're stuck, and we need to figure out how to deal with the fallout from the fall of Larissa," One said.

"There's no fallout to deal with." Zeus sounded weary. "I've consulted all the oracles and the Fates themselves. This is the beginning of the end."

"I'm not so sure. We're still missing something." Larisa's anger acted as an antidote to her sorrow. She was mad, and she wanted a solution to help release the tension that had built inside her.

"I was just getting my life back," Medusa lamented. She didn't sound too surprised. "Maybe we could have stopped Hermes earlier had we not all been looking in the wrong direction."

Larisa froze at the last word.

What was it Athena had said?

"Direction?" She turned to the king of the gods. "Where's Athena? I need to ask her something."

"Busy." Zeus poked at a peanut on the tabletop with a finger. He flicked it absently as he stared blankly ahead. "Things have been chaotic lately. I've been having a hard time keeping track of her because she's in so many places."

"No Athena. We'll just have to figure it out ourselves," Larisa said.

Nine, apparently unenthralled by the whole situation, laid his head on the tabletop. After a minute he quietly started to snore.

Chapter 48

You Can Lead a Soul to Torture, but You Can't Make Him Eat

"Holy cow, man. What are you, a three-year-old?" Doug was clearly frustrated as he tried to hold the rapidly disintegrating sandwich together. "It's food. The way you keep reaching for the pears I just thought you might want a bite to eat."

Tantalus kept his mouth shut and avoided looking at Doug in the eye. He shifted his head from left to right like a stubborn pet avoiding taking medicine. "It's probably poisoned," the man snarled through bared teeth.

"You're dead!" Doug felt silly as he explained, then realized it was almost as odd to shove food at the mouth of someone whose mortal body currently fertilized daisies. The realization didn't stop his attempt to help the condemned man. "It's not poisoned! Even if it was, what's a poisoned sandwich going to do to you? Kill you again?"

"It's yucky," Tantalus pouted. He squashed his lips shut in defiance, his face sour. "Don't want it."

"Oh, for Pellas's sake." Doug dropped the beat-to-death, well-traveled dagwood to a plate. "I'm just trying to be nice."

"Maybe it's the filling on the bread," Teutamides said. He eyed the squished sandwich. "Particularly the exposed cuts of meat. Perhaps the texture is too similar to—Tantalus's meals of the past."[1]

"What was it he ate in the past?" Doug asked.

---

1. Pulled Pelops sandwich, anyone? Goes great with hickory BBQ sauce and a bit of creamy horseradish. Tantalus is not the poster boy for *Greek Good Parenting Monthly*. He chopped up his own son, Pelops, and tried to serve him as a dish to the gods on Mt. Olympus. I didn't say all the people punished by the gods were undeserving.

"Oh, I heard about this one," Minthe said perkily. "Tantalus fed the gods a meat dish. The gods knew something was off, like maybe he'd dropped it on the floor or the dog had eaten out of the bowl, as soon as Tantalus showed up with the crock-pot. None of the gods would touch it. Only Demeter, distracted from worry for her abducted Persephone, made the mistake of eating any of the tainted dish. Demeter said the roast was really good. Tender. Juicy. Full of flavor. But when she found out what it was, she felt bad about eating it." Minthe stopped for a second. "Now that I think of it, no one ever said what kind of meat was in the dish."

Teutamides pointed at Tantalus. "It was his son. He killed and cooked his son and tried to feed the boy to the gods."

"Really? I never knew that." Minthe went a bit green in the gills. "No wonder Demeter didn't have seconds."

"That's why he won't take the sandwich, Doug. He's had time to think about how wrong he really was, and he wants to be punished," Teutamides said.

"Some of them do," Minthe concurred. "Several examples spring to mind.[2] Tantalus suggested a few of the fruits he's currently being denied because he wanted them more. He has other hang ups too. The guy might just be a bit mentally unstable."

"He roasted his own son as a snack for the gods! Of course he's mentally unstable! Hence we should punish him more?" Teutamides said. "I'm disgusted someone half a bubble off plumb should be punished and won't conceal my disapproval that the gods allowed this kind of treatment. We should be counseling and teaching, not condemning! I have a hard time believing someone sick in the head should be fully responsible for the acts they commit."

"Punishment is the ultimate deterrent," Minthe quoted the company line. "Counseling and teaching would just be a waste of time and resources."

---

2. Minthe had seen quite a lot, and not all of it painted people in the most flattering of lights.

"How very bourgeoisie of you."[3] Teutamides scowled.

In the distance, Cerberus launched into a barking fit.

Something or someone just passed the boundary into Hades's territory.

Doug made note of the frenzied barking but was more intent on the dead man who stood beside him. "Not what I expected you to say, my king." Teutamides truly looked disturbed by the plight of Tantalus. The dead king seemed pretty upset by just about everything they saw in Hades, now Doug thought about it.

What else should I expect? We are in the land of the damned, after all.

"You think me unfeeling and aloof? I care about all the people of Greece. I don't desire to see any of them suffer so. Would that it were in my power to do something about it." Teutamides knelt down beside Tantalus and cupped the condemned man's cheeks in his hands. "Here I am dead, powerless to do anything but mourn and show them my pitifully inadequate empathy. Such a woefully deficient gesture will not aid or comfort here."

Doug watched as Tantalus looked up into the other king's eyes, imagining a deep communication of the soul silently conveying a message the condemned man could not utter.

A momentary flash of hope, of redemption, worked its way into Tantalus's gaze. The emotions in the tortured man's eyes shifted and flittered from one to the next before Doug was even able to register what they might be.

"Doug has shown me that even in death I must be proactive. The manner in which you reach your final task has meaning." Teutamides leaned closer. "Now I search for any way I might aid my fellow man."

And that was when Tantalus bit him.

"Son of a *motherless goat*!" Teutamides snatched back his arm

---

3. If you don't know what the bourgeoisie is, then you're probably a member of the proletariat.

from Tantalus's snapping horse teeth. "If I still had fingers, that would have hurt!"

"Still want to save him?" An unintended smile creased Doug's lips. "You examined your extremities and counted your fingers twice. A bit unnerved?"

The dead king cradled his hand close to his chest. "I would still help if I could," Teutamides replied. "Though being masticated by the focus of my good intent would likely complicate matters."

"Well, we'll both have plenty of time to figure out something, I expect." Doug noticed a small hill that raised sharply to a point in the distance. It beckoned him forward.

Teutamides looked in the direction Doug was staring.

Minthe turned that way too.

There were a lot of eternal punishments in Hades, but only so many where Doug might be able to step in and stop the punishment or take the place of the accursed.

He knew the last place he had to go.

To Doug there was a feeling of finality in the sight of that small rise.

"Or at least you'll have time." Doug looked away from the hill. "I'm probably going to be busy."

Doug turned to Minthe to apologize. "I didn't mean to upset you earlier. If anyone says anything about what I did with the snacks for the, uh, inmates? Guests? Exhibits? Whatever you want to call them, I want you to tell the powers that be I'm totally responsible for any hiccups in the punishment routine."

"I totally get it," Minthe said. "I still believe the gods know what's best in these situations, but I can see why you'd object to what's going on."

Doug nodded that he understood where she came from.

He turned to the dead king. "Thanks for being my tour buddy. I wouldn't have made it this far without you."

Teutamides's face fell. "I feel there might be multiple meanings to that statement, but knowing you a bit more intimately now, I'm inclined toward the best possible interpretation. It has been a pleasure." He paused. "We can all agree 'pleasure' is an odd thing to say, especially considering our current location and circumstances.

"You've shown me a small way I might find redemption, by the offering of aid and comfort to those trapped in this place." Teutamides paused, as if contemplating the depth and commitment of his words.

The king looked at a loss for what to say for what he had done to Doug.

Teutamides took a deep breath as if steadying himself and started again. "You are a tolerable, even acceptable, travel companion.

"Whoa, hold back man! I might get all weepy if you get overly emotional." Doug teased Teutamides and chucked him lightly on the arm. Teutamides looked rather uncomfortable until Doug winked. "It's all good, slick. I totally get what you mean to say." He nodded and gave Teutamides a warm smile. "Keep up your good work here in the land of the dead."

"I shall try to do as you would." Teutamides bowed.

Doug took a deep breath and let it out with finality. "Welp, that about wraps it up. I think we've just about reached the end of Minthe's fabulous Hades's realm introductory tour."

Minthe looked as if she was about to object to leaving them unaccompanied.

Teutamides put a hand on her shoulder and smiled sadly at her. "Thank you for your time and assistance. We've got it from here. I'm resigned to my fate and the living youth is here for a purpose."

Minthe seemed to understand. "I should probably go see what the dog was barking at. Someone else might need a tour." She bowed to the two men before excusing herself so they could be about their business.

"In the realm of the dead, stop that which cannot be stopped." Doug repeated the words of the final task as he watched Minthe walk away. He pivoted back to face his intended destination. "I guess I could've asked her to take us by one last notable site, but I have a pretty good idea of where I might find Sisyphus and his boulder."

Teutamides suddenly looked stricken. "I should go with you. See if there is some way I might assist?"

"I swore to the final task being mine, and mine alone." Doug took a deep breath and steeled himself. "I'm glad we were able to spend this time together." He reached out a hand to the dead king. "I wish we'd met under different circumstances. May the judgments of the gods favor you. May your land prosper despite your absence."

Teutamides clasped the young man's hand firmly. "I wish for so many things to have happened differently . . ." his voice trailed off.

"We deal with what is," Doug said, more sure than ever Teutamides didn't deserve whatever was coming to him. "I hope you're given a good judgment. You shouldn't be held accountable for what Hermes influenced you to do."

CHAPTER 41

ARE YOU FAUX-KING KIDDING ME?

Larisa could see the mood of everyone at the table was grim. She wondered what to do about it as Isaac walked up to their table, a glass gleamed under his polishing rag.

"Figuring it out without your best thinker here to help? Seems like a hard one, Mr. Z," the bartender said in a low voice as he eyed that one patron at the end of the bar.

Satan turned away and pretended like he hadn't just strained to hear what was being said.

"That's about the gist of it, my friend," Zeus admitted.

Satan seemed distracted as something buzzed about his head, so Isaac continued, "The bad guy wins unless Teutamides is still on the throne?"

"Yes." Zeus said a bit testily. "As we've already clearly established."

"Seems to me, then," Isaac said with a smile, "you just need to find a way to get the king back on the throne."

"He's dead." Zeus slammed his fist down on the table.

Nine's head bounced. An ear fell off and his nose skittered off the end of the table. A bit dazed, Nine raised his head up out of the small puddle of drool. A stringy little loop still connected his bottom lip to the tabletop. He blinked hard and didn't even notice his eyebrows were on upside down and his schnoz was missing.

Larisa and everyone else at the table stared at Nine in disbelief for a quiet moment.

At the other end of the bar Satan caught whatever had flown around his head and started to pull off its wings.

Isaac paused his polishing rag mid wipe, rag and glass held still while he squinted to see what Satan had caught a bit better. He didn't like what he saw. "Seems to me, if Teutamides residing on the throne is so important, you just might find a way to make it happen, however improbable that may be. Now, if you'll excuse me, I have to go rescue someone from something," Isaac said as he hastily departed.[1]

Isaac snapped the back of Satan's head with the whip crack of a wet bar rag. Satan yelped, let go of the bug in his hand, and the elder gods ceased their rumblings far below the bottom of the ocean floor.

Larisa frowned. "How could we replace my father with my father?"

"Interchangeable king." Mod's eyes went wide. "Interchangeable parts?"

"What was that?" Larisa asked.

Mod now stared hard at Nine, a weird glint in his eye as he watched the disheveled automaton, like he couldn't believe what he now thought or considered. "You know, he's about the right size. And judgmental to boot," Mod said to the others as Nine felt about below the bench for his nose. "Does it have to be Teutamides for real or just someone who looks like Teutamides sitting on the throne?"

Larisa followed Mod's gaze as she tried to figure out what he'd just said.

Nine reattached his nose and twisted it into the almost correct position.

Medusa clued in. "Right build, and hair, and quite a few of the facial features are already similar. Plus, he thinks he knows better

---

1. Satan is currently tugging on the wings of the Lord of the Flies, Beelzebub. If the Fallen One actually goes through with what he's currently thinking, it'll kick off a conflict that will make the dilemma in Greece look like a YouTube influencer's ill-conceived baby gender reveal in comparison.

than everyone else, so ordering people about would look totally natural."

Everyone else seated in the booth slowly turned and looked at the mechanical man.

The automaton looked almost, but not quite, like the deceased king. It'd only take a change of one or two minor features to make him an exact doppelganger.

"It's absurd, I'll admit. We didn't see it before because we didn't need to before," Mod answered everyone's unspoken question. "This might give us a possible solution to the current crisis."

Nine, clueless, noticed he was being studied. "What?" He demanded of the group.

"Interesting." Zeus stroked his beard in contemplation. "Not a direction I'd have thought to go but might have a few possibilities. I'll have to ask for a bit of clarification from a soothsayer or two on the restrictions we're facing."

"Expert advice would be helpful," Four said to the god, nodding his head in agreement. "He can't even keep his room clean, and you might be putting him in charge of running a kingdom and holding back the tides of war? This is not the sort of thing you take chances on." He gave a good long stare at his brother. "Power in his hands could be chancy."

Larisa had pretty much decided if they needed to go ahead with the plan they would, expert advice be damned. "And this? Our current situation? You don't see this as worth taking a chance? It could solve issues that would affect every creature living, dead, and immortal in Greece."

"Point taken," Four acknowledged.

Nine shook his head. "I still have no idea what any of you are saying. And the stares are making me self-conscious."

"On to another matter." Zeus let the question of the king and kingdom hang unanswered as he addressed a separate important issue. He turned to Mod. "Your brother was determined to accomplish the last task by himself. I will honor his wishes."

"He'll die." Mod knew it was true as he said it.

"I think you give him too little credit," Zeus said. "Doug would not throw his life away for nothing, yet I also feel he worries about other people's welfare far more than his own. Let him accomplish the task on his own. I don't know what the task is, but once accomplished it'll begin to undermine some basic fundamental principle in the laws governing everything in our universe, and then we might have a chance to halt it."

"Wow. That sounds so promising." Nine rolled his eyes. "Let Armageddon kick off. No biggy. We'll stop it before it gets up a full head of steam. Come on, guys, we'll be late to the party but with a 'can-do' attitude we can make this work." He mocked everybody else for being hopeful.

"My dad could also be a dick to people around him," Larisa said to everyone while focusing on Nine. "Nobody would think twice if you treated them like this."

Nine eyed her coolly. "I still don't know what any of you are talking about."

Chapter 30

Back to the Fundamentals

Larisa paused for a second, then turned to Zeus. "Wait, you said Doug would do something that would undermine the fundamental laws of the universe. What laws are we talking about?"

"Laws," Zeus said, as if it should be obvious. "The rules that govern everything, set in place since before the gods occupied Mount Olympus and began rule of everything above and below."

Larisa's brow furrowed and she dropped her head. She shifted from left to right as she thought and whispered to herself. "Laws. Gods. What was it Athena said? I was close to the mark but searching in the wrong direction. What does that mean?"

Zeus cocked his head to the side, listening. "It's beginning. I can feel it." He closed his eyes and concentrated. His face scrunched up as he focused harder. "Doug moves toward fate. He's not in the Heavens nor somewhere on Mother Gaea." A pause, as he clarified and reconciled what he was sensing. "Doug is somewhere in the realm of my brother, Hades. Hades has some autonomy from me, so my control and abilities within his realm are somewhat limited. Finding Doug will take me some time." He opened his eyes and met the gaze of everyone sitting at the table one by one. "We must now find out what we're to do if we're to save him."

"We all stand ready to do whatever it takes to help him," One said, garnering nods from all of her siblings.

Zeus shook his head. "You are all crew pledged to his service. None of you could help without violating your oaths."

"They weren't really oaths, per say—" Nine started until the king of the gods shot him an incredulous look. Nine dropped his gaze and agreed reluctantly. "Okay. They were totally oaths."

Zeus made sure. "There was no doubt about this. Hermes has violated trust after trust in his machinations, and we will not give any reason for him to argue before the cosmic forces that we dealt unjustly in this silent war he wages."

"Cosmic forces." Larisa tapped her finger on the tabletop and bit her lower lip. "Gods. Wrong direction."

Zeus looked over at Mopsus and Mod. "No one pledged to Doug shall be able to accompany me in this endeavor to save him. Not a person urged to follow him by a god, nor a person bound to him as a sibling."

The talk of pledges pulled Larisa's attention from the main subject she worked over. "I haven't pledged to him yet. I was thinking of it, but he's been so busy running around taking care of Hermes's stupid list that I haven't had Doug alone long enough to pledge anything," Larisa said sadly.

"Sure. You're saving that for the third date." Three gave a conspiratorial wink to Nine and snorted when he bristled.

Nine glared at his sister. "From your manner and tone, I can only assume the word pledge is a euphemism for something unholy."

Larisa bristled. "I would shut my trap while I still had genitals were I you." The look she gave the mechanical man had no jest in it.

"Always threatening emasculation. What is it with you people?" Nine's hands dropped protectively to his lap, and he purposely avoided Larisa's gaze.

Four grabbed his brother by the back of the neck. "Words and implications have consequences. You're out of line, and you know it." He forced Nine's head toward Larisa. "Apologize."

"Ow! You're hurting me!" Nine growled.

Four tightened his grip.

Nine swallowed and lowered his head. "Sorry, Larisa," he muttered.

Four released Nine's neck.

"Apology accepted, I guess." Larisa cleared her throat, narrowing her eyes and folding her arms in front of her breasts. "I can save him without *violating* anything," she said the word with pointed emphasis toward Nine. "But I might end up smacking him in the head with a club for him being such a putz."

"I've got a reset club you could borrow if you need," One suggested helpfully.

"Thanks for the offer, but we'll pass." Medusa put a hand on Larisa's shoulder and gave her a knowing smile. "I'll just tag along to make sure Larisa doesn't do anything to the man she loves." She turned to Zeus. "I owe Doug but am not beholden to him by oath."

Over at the other booth, the huge bear cleared his throat.

When everyone at Zeus's table turned, Arktos raised a huge paw and volunteered his services. "Doug brought about the circumstances to free me from bondage. How may I assist?"

"You've been listening this entire time?" Mod asked, slightly offended.

"It is a fairly public place to have such a discussion," Arktos said.

"Ha! I knew it!" Satan sneered from the other end of the room.

Zeus ignored the devil on the barstool and nodded his acceptance to the huge bear as a broad smile spread across his face.

Arktos and Heph lumbered over to the table. "This god messing with things, what does he look like?"

"Slight. Quick. Winged sandals and a soup-bowl like helm with chicken-sized wings adorning the sides of it," Zeus said.

Arktos furrowed his brow. "Sounds unsettlingly familiar. I have a suspicion I've met him before." Arktos rubbed a claw through the fur where the necklace of Harmonia used to sit. "Now I must insist that I accompany you. I'd like to meet this Hermes in person.

"Pity Heph destroyed the necklace Hermes gifted me with. I'd love the chance to let him borrow it for a while." A calculating look spread over Arktos's face, and the bear leaned over and whispered something to Hephaestus.

The god of the forge smiled and clapped his friend on the shoulder. "I'll see what I can whip up for you." He nodded to everyone at the table. "I've got a bit of anvil-smashing to do. I'll catch up with the rest of you later." With that he winked at Arktos and headed to the door.

Having a god from somewhere else offer to help save Doug and all of Greece made something click. Larisa's eyes went wide. "Oh. My. Gods." Her jaw dropped open and it took her a minute to speak. "I just figured it out! What Athena meant. Going in the wrong direction!"

Zeus arched an eyebrow. "Well, you certainly have our attention."

Larisa was so excited she flipped her hands in front of her and took a bunch of quick shallow breaths. She turned to Zeus. "You said Doug would be forced to violate something that will break the eternal laws of the gods."

"Yes. I did," Zeus said calmly as he waited for her to continue. "And?"

"The gods. They put the laws in place after they came to power!" Larisa repeated. She couldn't believe it had taken her so long to figure it out. "But the gods worked with what they found. There were other things that came before the gods."

Zeus blinked hard. "I hadn't even considered this. Well done, child. Very well done. You know, suddenly I have a good feeling about all this. Hermes will have no idea what hit him."

Chapter 51

The Boulder at the End of the World

Doug looked at his task one final time before he took the scroll, wadded it up, and tossed it to the ground. "In the realm of the dead, stop that which cannot be stopped."

The constant rolling of the stone of Sisyphus fit the bill. There might be other punishments that fit it as well, but this one stuck out in Doug's mind. He made his way up behind the man struggling to push a boulder up an impossible slope and placed his hands against the stone and rolled it upward.

Sisyphus had probably never conceived that someone could touch the stone but him. Without the weight of the boulder pressed against him, his strength failed.

Doug caught the man with one arm before Sisyphus could fall and bore him up. "It's okay," Doug said. "I've got you."

"I've got to get the stone." Sisyphus clawed the air before him. His raw fingers grasped and clutched at nothing but empty air. "You don't know what will happen if I don't keep rolling the stone."

"Will it be worse than what happens because you roll the stone?" Doug asked.

Sisyphus fell over himself mentally. "I didn't know the answer, though I suspect much from things intimated to me in the past."

"Rest a minute," Doug said. "It's okay."

"I've offended the gods. I've used my wife in a way that earned her the ire of the gods and our people. My family and people suffered because of me, because of my foolish desire to avoid death." Sisyphus's muscles in his back, arms, and legs started to jerk and spasm.

He tried to move forward, and his legs and feet went out from under him.

"Whoa. Easy fella." Doug helped Sisyphus to the ground. "Lie here for a bit. Take it easy."

Sisyphus tried to roll over, insistent as he attempted time and again to get back to his feet. "I have to get back to the stone. You don't understand."

Doug tried to hold the man on the ground, but Sisyphus was lean and wiry, and had done nothing save labor with the stone for an eternity. Doug simply wasn't strong enough to hold him down.

"Can you rest a bit while I tell you what I need to say?" Doug tried to get in the man's way. Sisyphus shoved him aside and put his shoulder into the stone to push it back toward the top of the hill.

"The gods gave me the task of stopping the boulder!" Doug shouted at the man's back. "Are you going to deny the will of the gods?"

Sisyphus kept to a steady, tortured pace as he rolled the stone upward. He looked over his shoulder at the youth who stood behind him, a cold and determined gleam in his eye. "I couldn't give a flying %$#& about the gods. And their will! And you!" He returned his focus to the hill before him. "I've got to keep this boulder moving."

"Why?" Doug shouted at him.

"Because if I don't, it's my wife the gods will punish!" Sisyphus yelled back. "The only way, *the only way*, to stop them from ever hurting *her* is for *me* to keep this boulder moving!"

"But if you get it to the top of the hill?" Doug asked.

"I never will. The gods won't let me finish this task," Sisyphus cried. "Don't you understand?" Sisyphus shoved a bit harder, his desperation now clear to Doug. "I do this for her!"

"You're protecting your wife?" With that revelation, Doug felt unsure about how he should continue.

The air above him sparkled and shimmered. Hermes burst forth from the ether like a thousand sparklers going off at once.

Doug gritted his teeth. "All flamboyance and show now that you're out of hiding?"

"It's called showmanship. My acolytes will come to expect it once I rule everything." Hermes flitted about in the air behind Doug. "Quite the conundrum." The god mused. "If you stop Sisyphus from his task, you condemn his wife. If you condemn his wife, you condemn an innocent. By doing so, you condemn yourself."

"Take a long walk off a short pier," Doug said to the god. "Get out of here and leave us alone."

"Oh? But I haven't finished," the god went on. He sounded smug and secure in how everything was going down. "You pretty much lose whatever you do. I'd go into the details, but I'd rather see the look on your face when you make the wrong choice and find out what kind of punishment you've won."[1]

Doug could hear the god, but he paid more attention to the man who fought to push the boulder up the hill. Doug made his way up the incline toward Sisyphus, while Hermes hovered close behind. Doug walked up beside the condemned man and put his hands back on the boulder.

"Back off!" Sisyphus shouted and struggled to keep purchase on the sweat-slicked surface of the boulder. "Only one person can touch the stone at a time. And It gets harder to control the closer it gets to the top."

"And if it rolls back down?" Doug asked.

"Listen, this is more difficult than it looks. I don't have time or energy to devote to your stupid questions." The rock whipped back and forth in Sisyphus's grasp, almost as if it were possessed.

---

1. Contestant: "I'll pass on the guaranteed payout and risk it all on Door Number Three, Smiling Bob."

Smiling Bob, Host of *Embarrass Your Family for Money*: "Are you sure that's what you want to do?"

Contestant, nodding violently: "I'm feeling lucky!"

Smiling Bob, "Well then . . . Door Number Three!"

Sound FX: Whaa whaaa whaaaaaa! (You chose poorly!)

Doug said nothing. He followed close by, insistent, and stepped up beside Sisyphus for every inch the other man pushed the boulder.

"That's very distracting," the condemned man growled about Doug's lockstep presence. "Kratos's beard! Give it up man. I don't want to talk to you."

"How long do you have to return to the boulder when it rolls down the hill?" Doug was polite in the way he asked it, yet something in his manner indicated that the answer mattered more than Sisyphus realized.

"If it rolls away, I don't have time to take a leisurely stroll down the hill to retrieve it," Sisyphus snapped. "No time for a nap. No bathroom break."

"You're dead, so I figured you wouldn't be fertilizing the vegetable patch anymore." Doug couldn't help but be amused. "It'd be hard to push a rock up a hill with legs crossed while you danced to relieve bladder pressure at the same time."

Sisyphus paused for a second, blindsided by the comment or the manner in which it was delivered. "Are you high or something?"

"Or something, that's for sure," Doug said.

The boulder tried to wrest its way out of Sisyphus's grasp. He fumbled with it, and it changed direction again. The man's fingers searched for purchase and couldn't find enough.

Doug was nearly bowled over as Sisyphus lost his grip, but the youth caught the stone and held it.

"You fool! I already told you, only one person can hold the boulder at a time!" Sisyphus was frantic. He stumbled and rolled several yards down the hill. "My wife—"

"Will be punished if the boulder ceases to move," Doug said as he wrestled with the huge stone. The young man dug in the tips of his sandals to get enough leverage to shove the stone back in a generally upward direction.

He struggled with it for a bit longer and started to make some progress.

Sisyphus sat on his heels down below and gaped. "What are you doing?"

"The will of the gods." Doug grunted and cursed under his breath as the boulder changed direction three times. It rolled over his toe in the process. "Technically, the task given me only said I had to stop the thing that cannot be stopped. The scroll might have been referring to you. As long as I keep the boulder moving, you and your wife are safe."

"But then you're stuck rolling the boulder for eternity," Sisyphus explained.

"Not the outcome I'd hoped for, but what'cha gonna do?" Doug pushed the boulder higher up the hill.

Sisyphus sat there for a moment, speechless. "And you're doing this why?"

"Why does any guy do something so far beyond the spectrum of moronic that it defies rational explanation?" He thought about that for a bit and was actually able to come up with plenty of stupid things he'd done without a second thought about impressing a member of the fairer sex. There were a lot of instances when he'd played the idiot for idiocy's sake.

"Scratch that. Guys do dumb things for lots of reasons. Not that helping you and your wife is a stupid thing." He felt the explanation was going on a bit too long, and it had become slightly convoluted. "It started with a girl, but now I'm doing it for everyone I love," Doug sputtered and tried to wipe his brow.

This rolling the boulder work is harder than I expected.

"Course, keeping the boulder rolling to keep you and the missus safe means I probably won't be seeing any of them for a while. It's not a perfect solution, but—" The stone struck Doug in the knee, and he almost went down. The youth righted himself quickly and moved upward.

"I—I don't know how I feel about this." Sisyphus was at a loss. "I should take the boulder from you. This isn't your task."

"Looks like it is now." The boulder was bucking back and forth.

The lively stone now attempted to escape so hard it even rolled uphill in its movements. "I take it the boulder is magic?" Doug asked as the rock did a figure eight move and smacked him in the sternum, hard.

"Magic or supernatural," Sisyphus said.

"Is there a difference?" Doug asked rhetorically.

The man watched the youth struggle and grapple.

The rock was doing its best to roll over the top of Doug.

"I usually lose my grip on the boulder by now," Sisyphus said. "How are you keeping hold of that?"

"With some difficulty," Doug managed. He averted a breakaway attempt as he blocked the stone with his knee. The same knee the boulder had smacked before. It hurt. He was going to be nothing but a mass of bruises in pretty short order. "Ever wrestle a greased pig?"[2]

"Can't say I have." Sisyphus stared down at his empty hands. "This feels odd." He weighed his empty hands and took a couple of experimental steps. "It feels odd, but I think I like it."

"Glad to oblige." The rock did its best to climb onto Doug so it could roll over him and escape. It worked. Doug was left dazed. He searched the sky for the boulder as he lay sprawled just shy of the top of the hill.

"I'll go get the boulder," Sisyphus sighed. "Any freedom for me was destined to be short lived." He started to make his way to catch the stone when something above grabbed him by the shoulders and restrained him.

"It's not your task anymore!" Hermes cackled. "By allowing the boy to wrestle with the stone long enough, the task has been pulled from you and thrust upon another!"

"My wife?" Sisyphus clutched at the god hovering above him. "She is safe though? The stone's still moving, so she's safe, isn't she?"

"Your wife? I don't know. Who cares? Can't you see I have bigger things to be about than wasting time on some old hag?" Hermes put

---

2. Should be "greased piglet." There isn't a man alive that could wrestle an oil-slicked, full-grown boar.

his foot on the shoulder of Sisyphus and kicked him down the hill. The man rolled head over heels until he crashed into the lip of the trench at the bottom.

Doug raced down to where the dazed man lay. "Are you all right?"

Sisyphus blinked hard. He tried to focus and failed. The man struggled to get to his feet. "The stone. If it doesn't move soon, my wife will be—"

Doug gently pushed the man down. "I'll make sure the rock keeps moving. I'll make sure your wife is safe."

Sisyphus smiled and nodded. He passed out against the wall of the ditch.

Doug looked up at the god. Hermes was unaware of what he'd done, or he just didn't care. He floated in the air patting himself on the back and cackling.

Nobody was pushing the boulder and Doug had committed himself. He took a deep breath and started pushing it back up the hill.

Chapter 52

Hermes Triumphant

"I've done it!" Hermes screamed as he beat his fists against the air. "The keystone is pulled, and the arch will soon fall! Gods, I am so awesome! And everyone will soon know it!

"What's going on?" Sisyphus looked dazed, like his eyes wouldn't focus. "Why is this floaty guy so loud?"

"He thinks he's just executed the perfect plan to take over all of creation," Doug explained as he caught his breath and gave the boulder another shove.

The stone rolled much easier at the base of the hill than when it was at the top, not that it mattered. The effort still made Doug tired fast. "Mad respect for you, Sisyphus, for having fought against this task for as long as you did," Doug said.

With a clap of thunder, more people were there to see the downfall Hermes had just wrought on the Greek Pantheon.

"Fitting you should be here, Father," Hermes started.

Doug saw Hermes do a quick double take when his father arrived. The messenger god was putting on a brave face, like his success was not as assured as he played it to be.

For a second Doug actually felt empathy with Hermes. It's hard to impress a father.

Of course, Doug hadn't betrayed and tried to overthrow his dad.

Doug saw Zeus wasn't alone. He had Larisa, Medusa, and Arktos with him.

Doug felt a cold flush run down his spine. Larisa was here, with gods and bears and the end of the world.

What if she got hurt?

Doug wanted to run to her. To get her out of here. But that would mean he'd have to leave the boulder, and then he wouldn't be keeping the end at bay.

"Doug!" Larisa called out.

Doug sobbed, choked back his desire to reply, and put his shoulder to the rock and pushed. It was so much harder to do this with Larisa here.

"Not yet." Zeus put a restraining hand on Larisa's shoulder as he looked up at the bedrock.

Arktos sniffed the air, grimaced as if something were unpleasantly familiar, then glared up at Hermes. "Recognize me?"

The flying god glared back at the bear. "Why are you here, dog?" Hermes asked Arktos.

"I'm disappointed you were right about meeting my son before," Zeus said to Arktos.

"As I told ye, I suspected we'd met; I was just unable to verify it until now," Arktos explained.

"I see you're missing your collar, beast. No matter," Hermes sneered. "You can either bow before me or suffer my wrath."

Arktos arched an eyebrow and said nothing.

Zeus cast about and surveyed the underworld. "I can feel it, son. Pretty powerful. I'm sure you feel you've got a nice start to the fall of, well, everything. Too bad it's not going to end the way you think."

A giant crack appeared in the dome of rock that hung over the underworld. The sound of the fracture hit them a few seconds later.

Doug pulled his attention from the boulder and everything else for that. He panicked as he saw the great pieces of stone shifting within the crevice.

This shouldn't be happening if I'm still doing the task? Was I wrong?

Doug doubled his attention on the boulder on the hill and pushed harder.

The boom of the crack above was followed by another fissure racing through the vaulted bedrock.

Then another.

Doug ignored them and kept pushing the boulder higher on the hill. His fears were now giving him strength.

But that idiot Hermes sapped at Doug's resolve every time he opened his mouth.

"You see, Father!" Hermes flung his arms wide to indicate the scope of what he'd begun. "The very mantle of Mother Gaea is rent! The foundation of everything bears witness! It's only a matter of patience for me now."

"He has a good point," Arktos said to Zeus. "It makes a great deal of sense if ye look at it from his childish understanding and limited perspective."

Zeus pursed his lips before he nodded and stroked his beard in agreement with the Arktos. "Taken as such, you're probably right. Too bad."

"He's young," Arktos said. "He'll probably gain insight when he's older."

Larisa and Medusa looked at each other as if that weren't very likely.

Zeus shook his head at the comment that Hermes might see more clearly with age.

"Pity," Arktos said. "I was willing to give him the benefit of the doubt."

Doug could see Hermes didn't like that.

"Don't talk down to me," Hermes growled. "No one, not my father or his two trollops of the hour or an overfed mastiff have the right! I'm going to be the king of the gods, don't you see?"

Medusa whispered something to Larisa.

"Don't you dare talk unless you speak to me!" Hermes roared. Hermes rose higher in the air, his arms spread wide to point out what was in process as it happened. "Take a look around and tremble. The foundation of everything you built is crumbling! You've already lost to me!"

Everything in the underworld was silent but for the sound of breaking stone and the quiet scrapings of the boulder as Doug pushed it up the hill.

Arktos, Zeus, Medusa, and Larisa glanced up at the granite and basalt that cracked and fractured.

The effects of the disaster were sure to have dire consequences if they progressed.

Doug kept rolling the stone.

"Eyes full of greed, the lost sees victory that was never theirs." Arktos pointed his nose in the direction of Hermes, then he turned his head to Doug. "Meanwhile, the unwitting hero saves the day doing something simple and pure with no thought of reward. Doug is one full of deep magic."

Doug missed a step at the mention of his name. The boulder tried to take advantage of it, but he caught it and wrested it back to his chest.

What in Hades is Arktos talking about? There's nothing special about me?

But the words made Doug feel hopeful, even though he didn't know why.

Let the others keep talking. Doug didn't understand, but if rolling the boulder gave them the time to figure it out, he would never stop.

Chapter 23

Deep Magic and Superficial Illusion

Larisa had never heard the phrase Arktos just said before. She looked at Doug and knew the god bear was right that Doug carried it with him.

"Deep magic?" Zeus asked.

"The rules that govern everything," Arktos explained. "The laws set in place before any of us were even considered."

"Deep magic. The base upon which everything else must be based." Zeus nodded and smiled at Larisa for her brilliant intuitive work. "Just like you figured out."

"Well, now we know what to call it," Medusa said.

"All truth springs from the same source," Arktos said.

"And given a chance, even the most lost of souls might recognize such grand truth," a shade said from behind the group.

It was the one voice that could pull her attention away from Doug. "Dad?" Larisa turned around, shocked.

"I was drawn by the commotion. Hi, Lala. I've missed you." Teutamides held his arms open as he smiled at her.

Larisa threw herself at her father.

"Dad!"[1] She hugged him. "You haven't called me Lala in forever. How did you find us?"

"I've been accompanying Doug for the past few days. When I felt

---

1. How do you hug a shade? The same way a shade interacts with a rock or is bound inside a footstool or drinks from the rivers in the underworld. Certain physical bounds and characteristics had to have existed in Hades's realm or many of the physical punishments and interactions wouldn't have happened.

your presence, I had to see you." He put his face in her hair. "Ah, my daughter's warmth and her smell and the rightness of holding her." He pushed her out to arm's length. "I'm sorry for how difficult I've been of late."

"Doesn't matter." Larisa pulled him close and buried her face in his chest. Then her eyes opened wide, and she pushed back from her father and started dancing up and down. Her feet moved in quick, excited little hops. "Oh, have we got a surprise for you!"

"What in the world kind of surprise could you give to me?" Teutamides looked a bit shocked. "All I need is to know you are safe and my people are safe. I truly desire nothing else."

"Oh, just wait! It's gonna be a good one!" Larisa said, then paused a bit. "Or at least, I hope it will be a good surprise. I'm sure you'll get along. Or not. Now I'm nervous."

"Do not fret, child," Arktos said to Larisa. "It will be a day of wondrous revelations. Loss makes ye realize what's important and makes ye value the price paid for what truly matters." Arktos spoke with a sense of wistfulness. "When something has served its purpose, when everything represented has been replaced by something nobler and grander, there can be no sorrow." The bear looked around at the chaos Hermes had brought to pass. "Even Hermes's folly plays a part in the grander plan."

"Are you kidding me?" Hermes sounded livid and frustrated and confused. "I'm destroying the universe and remaking it in my image, and you're all talking about joyful reunions and ineffable purpose?"

Zeus looked up to where Hermes flitted above them. "Heh. For a moment I'd almost forgotten you were there." Zeus turned to the women. "Is everything ready?"

"As ready as we can be." Medusa held up a box with a few items in it.

"You had to put it in a box?" Zeus asked.

Medusa shrugged. "I'm a woman. In this unenlightened day and age, fashion for the female form doesn't include pockets."

"I hate to break it to you." Zeus leaned in and spoke somewhat apologetically. "It doesn't get much better in the future."

"Ready?" Larisa asked everyone.

Medusa stepped forward with her box, Zeus nodded, and Arktos smiled.

"Then let's wrap this up." Larisa led the rush forward.

Chapter 34

An End and a Beginning

Doug watched as Zeus and the women stepped over the berm of the ditch at the bottom of Sisyphus's hill and started up the incline toward him. Erebus' warning was still in his mind. He tried not to engage with them, which was hard when they could move so much more freely. They didn't have to contend with an ensorcelled boulder.

Zeus took to the slope in several long strides and quickly closed in on the young man wrestling the rock. "How are you doing, Doug?"

"I think I'm getting my second wind," Doug said as he tried to focus on the boulder. The boulder pegged him in the crotch. "Second wind gone," he said in a pained whine.

Zeus winced in male solidarity with the youth.

Larisa and Medusa reached out to help Doug steady the rock.

"Don't!" Doug panicked and averted his eyes from both of them. "Only one person can roll the rock at a time."

The girls stepped back and waited for a signal from Zeus to proceed.

"I've got this. You all should just leave." Doug pushed and slid a bit. He tried his best to hold onto the smooth stone as it attempted to wrest itself from his grasp. "I almost made it the first time." He managed through clenched teeth, inch-stepped to the side, and the boulder shifted to the right just like he anticipated. "I think I'm getting a handle on this."

"Thank you, Doug. You've done more than enough." Zeus reached out and placed his hand on the boulder. He palmed it hard enough the pressure created a divot in the hill below, so the stone sat immobile and trapped in a little depression.

"I swore!" Doug shut his eyes tight and trembled. "And if I don't complete the quest, Erebus said—" Doug tried to twist the stone from its seat. "I need to do this!"

"Doug, I hold your oath fulfilled. The danger foreseen by Erebus is averted—or will be soon enough." Zeus gently pulled Doug back from the stone. "Your quests are over."

"But Sisyphus and his wife?" Doug protested. "All the people I love?"

"Are fine." Zeus still held down the boulder as Doug continued to attempt to roll it.

"I wouldn't be so sure about that, Father." Hermes scowled from up above.

Zeus ignored Hermes, and patted Doug on the back. "Sisyphus is done with his torment, and his wife is safe thanks to you and your stubborn insistence on trying to help others. Your family and friends are safe. You've completed your quests. Well done, lad. Well done."

Doug looked to Larisa for confirmation. She nodded. and he almost couldn't contain his emotion.

"*No*! Not well done!" Hermes snarled at Doug. "You only accomplished something that broke an unbreakable law." Hermes then turned to Zeus. "And you, Father, have just violated your own decree, breaking your own law and everything your universe is based upon!"

Larisa reached out a hand to Doug. He looked at it like taking her hand might hurt her or him or both. After a moment he slid his hand into hers anyway. Just touching her made him lightheaded.

He swooned a bit, suddenly unsteady on his feet.

Larisa held onto Doug like she would never let him fall.

"You're wrong," Larisa said to Hermes. "The moment when you decided to use Doug, you'd already failed. You made it so Doug would have to do something that broke the laws set in place by you and your fellow gods, but Doug is good, and wouldn't do anything to go against the foundations that uphold those laws."

Hermes paused in the air for a second, his brow furrowed as he tried to make sense of what the young woman had said.

Doug gave her hand a reassuring squeeze and Larisa continued, "All you succeeded in doing was threatening the kingdom of Larissa and killing my father. The other parts of your plan never had a chance."

Hermes's lip trembled and his whole body shook.

"Poor child," Arktos said as he swung his head sadly from side to side. "He still doesn't understand."

Zeus nodded and sighed.

"I am not a child!" Hermes roared in defiance. "I know the law. You broke the law. You will be punished because of it. The idiot girl's talk of deeper foundation stuff is utter crap!"

"Hermes, my boy, come down here." Zeus extended his hand up to his son. "Please."

Doug could see it was something in the *please* that unnerved Hermes, possibly more than anything else he'd ever encountered. The wings at the god's feet momentarily stopped moving, and he dropped a few yards in the air before he caught himself.

"It is true," Zeus said. "I'll confirm some of what you knew, Son. I set a series of punishments in place, eternal and irrevocable. Your machinations have caused me to rethink and reevaluate many of the rash decisions and declarations I've made in the past."

"You admit, with your own mouth, that you're violating something unbreakable and eternal!" Hermes rose again and flitted back in defiance.

"Freely," Zeus agreed. "What I've put in place cannot be ended or rescinded, even by me." The king of the gods extended his hand to his son again. His face fell slightly as Hermes pulled back in revulsion. "What you don't understand is what I put in place can be superseded by something greater."

"The deep magic," Arktos whispered. "He that lays down his life for his brother."

"Or for someone he's never met," Zeus said to Doug. "You were given opportunities to save yourself. You didn't take them."

Larisa gripped Doug's hand tighter.

"So the task?" Doug asked, still uncertain what was really going on.

"You put the needs of others above yourself. Like you just did for Sisyphus," Zeus pointed out. "Like you did for your friends and family. Like you did for all of Greece. Well done, boy."

"No," Hermes said in a disbelieving whisper. He clenched his fists and rose higher in defiance. "I set everything up and you played out your part and now look at what I've done!" He flung his arms up at the cracks in the bedrock above him, only no new cracks had formed.

"He still can't see it," Arktos said. "Even with all our talk about sacrifice, he still doesn't get it."

"I told you." Zeus regarded his son with a bit of pity. "Slow learner."

"I'm winning! The foundation of the universe is breaking," Hermes now sounded like he was begging. He stumbled over the words coming out of his mouth. "The changes I started are coming to pass." Hermes's face twitched and trembled and he looked as if he were about to cry. "I broke the bedrock."

"No." Zeus shook his head sadly. "You didn't break the stone above us. He did."

"Who?" Hermes said guardedly.

Zeus turned from Hermes to focus on Doug.

"Greater love hath no man," Arktos said.

It sounded to Doug like Arktos had just quoted something old and powerful.

"Are you freaking kidding me?" Hermes gasped.

He jerked about through the air in such an erratic manner Doug was afraid he was going to lose control and hurt himself if he hit the roof of the cavern or slammed into the ground with a crash.

"Are you freaking, *freaking*, kidding me?" Hermes screamed.

One hand still on Doug's shoulder, Zeus extended the other hand up to his son. "Hermes. Please come down."

"He broke the rules!" Hermes spat. "And it doesn't matter what you say about that, anyway. I had a backup plan. Larissa is going to fall, and it's going to take everything down with it!"

"Ah, about that," Teutamides said. "Dreadfully sorry to have caused such a fuss."

"Yes, you were fairly thorough about that, weren't you, Son." Zeus nodded in the direction of the dead king. "Only the true, and now previous, king would be allowed to sit on the throne. With Teutamides here in the underworld, pretty much all the options left put Greece and the gods in quite a bind."

Zeus nodded for the girls to go ahead with the plan.

Medusa stepped forward, pulling a loop of wire attached to a control panel out of the box. "Just give me a second to find a flat spot to put it." She positioned the portal and turned it on.

A second later Teutamides stepped through the portal.

One divine, one ghostly, and one mortal jaw figuratively dropped to the floor.

Doug narrowed his eyes and studied new Teutamides. He had a pretty good idea of what he was looking at, but he couldn't quite be sure. The shock was enough that he let go of Larisa's hand just so he could touch the automaton to make sure he wasn't seeing things. "Nine?" he asked.

The king brushed Doug's hand away. "Just call me 'your majesty,' if you don't mind," the mechanical man huffed.

"Yeah. it's Nine," Doug said with a grin.

"We did a pretty good job, didn't we?" Larisa clasped her hands in front of her chest as she looked at her father. "Do you love it?"

"The likeness is uncanny." Ghost Teutamides leaned in. "Examining myself, I'm certain this is me. It's unsettling."

"Still not sure how I feel about all of this either," Faux Teutamides, aka Nine, grumbled.

"Hermes set your body aside in a dark, quiet place," Zeus said. "I wasn't able to find you in time to undo the damage made to your vessel of clay."

"So I just, what, inhabit it?" Teutamides reached out to touch his replicated cheek with an ethereal finger.

"Not inhabit. Cohabitate," the mechanical man said as he grabbed the finger and held it just shy of its target. "Shared accommodations. It benefits us both. You get to have your life back, and I get to lord it over those lesser than me."

"May I?" the ghost asked.

"I didn't get all dressed up for nothing," Nine said flatly.

For a second, Ghost Teutamides and Faux Teutamides tried to take the space of the other, then they were just fuzzy around the edges for a bit as they snapped into focus. Doug didn't have a word for what he saw,[1] so he just called it a thing that gave you a headache in the eyes.

"Feels a bit cramped—Don't touch that. It's mine," Teutamides said as he spoke over himself.

"It might take a bit for the two of you to work out the rough edges," Larisa said as she gave her father a hug.

"I was hopeful, but it is a relief to see it all pull together." Zeus clapped the once and future king of Larissa on the shoulder. "I'm sure there is to be a learning curve and some give and take for a while," Zeus said. "But it averts the coming crisis and lets all of us live and learn for another day."

"That's not fair!" Hermes whined. His altitude dropped with his attitude. "I planned for so long. I thought of almost every contingency."

"If more thorough planning is the only lesson you learned from all of this, you need to grow up more than I believed," Zeus said to his son. Then he turned to Arktos. "I guess we'll have to do it after all."

Arktos's chest rumbled, emitting a low, infrasonic purr.

---

1. For a second Ghost Teutamides and Faux Teutamides looked like a special effect from a John Carpenter movie. You know the one.

Doug wondered what the god might be doing.

Arktos walked in a slow circle, pulling the attention of everyone, Hermes included, away from the still open portal.

While everyone was focused on the bear, the large, hairy person Arktos had signaled came through the doorway.

Arktos stopped his rumble, sat back on his haunches, and smiled.

"What was that all about?" Hermes asked.

A huge pair of hairy arms pinned the flying god from behind.

"Peekaboo!" Hephaestus said as he clasped the newly reforged chain of Harmonia around Hermes's neck.

The necklace shrunk tight against Hermes's skin. "How dare you!" Hermes gasped. As Hermes struggled to get the chain off, the bells went crazy. There was a tinkling of bells every time he moved.

"Just for a while, until we can be sure you aren't up to any mischief," Zeus said. "You understand?"

Hermes sneered at his dad. "Jerk." And he was gone, leaving the receding sound of tinkling of bells in his wake.

"At least he won't be able to sneak up on anyone now," Zeus said.

Doug's eyes went wide. "Uh, are we sure that was a wise thing? The necklace had a bad effect on Arktos, and I think Arktos is a way more stable person than Hermes."

Heph brushed it off. "I destroyed the original necklace, remember? And I had to make this one in a hurry. The necklace is unbreakable, and he can't take it off. It should alert anyone of Hermes's presence. The compulsions, bad effects, and assorted other poisons are missing from this particular creation."

"You think that will be enough to keep him out of trouble?" Arktos asked.

Zeus sighed. "Maybe? As I think of the father-son talks sure to emerge from this, the first few will not be pleasant, but I hope in time Hermes will come around. He misunderstood his place in the universe. It will take a while for him to reconcile many things. Time will tell."[2]

Larisa stepped away from her father and back to Doug. "So you finished your tasks, and wound up saving the world."

The doubts about everything going wrong crept back into Doug's mind.

It couldn't be this easy, could it?

Okay. It wasn't that *easy.*

Once again It was hard for Doug to look at Larisa. He looked down and closed his eyes. "Anathea and Erebus sounded so sure. I don't—I don't want to hope that this is all over and find out I messed up."

Larisa reached out and pulled his face up so he would be locked in her gaze if his eyes weren't screwed shut.

"Doug," Larisa said his name in a soft, soothing voice. "Sometimes the hero wins."

"Did I win?" Doug whispered, his voice quiet and guarded.

"You give yourself too little credit." Larisa said. "If you aren't a hero, I don't know how to define the word. If you ever doubt your heart or your abilities, ask me and I'll remind you of your worth. I'll be right beside you."

He held onto his fears so tightly the last words spoken by Larisa took a moment to register.

"You'll be right beside me?" he asked. "After how I ignored you in the throne room and tried to run from you. I thought you'd never want to see me again."

"I love you," Larisa whispered so quietly he barely heard it.

"I-I love you," Doug whispered back. His lips trembled and he sucked in a sharp breath. "I'm scared."

"Oh, my sweet Doug." Larisa's face was right in front of his. "You're over thinking things. Open your eyes."

---

2. Chronos ain't telling nothin'.

A single tear ran down his cheek as he decided to trust her. He opened his eyes.

"There you are." She brushed the tear from his cheek.

He felt he needed to say something then, but she shook her head no. Larisa looped her arms around his neck and pulled him close.

Doug let her.

Their first kiss was perfect.

Join the Cursed Dragon Ship Newsletter

Want more just like this one? Sign up for our newsletter so you don't miss out on the adventure. You'll get:

- A free book for signing up
- Advanced notice of new releases
- First word of books on sale
- Opportunities for free books
- Most up-to-date information on author appearances.

We're busy and know you are too. We won't send more than one newsletter a month.

Register below.

ACKNOWLEDGMENT

I have to give to give thanks to my family—those who came before and those here now—for their creative tendencies and bravery to use them. Thanks to my wife, Churstan, who has learned over many years how to deal with my sense of humor. Thanks to my mother, Sharon, who taught me and so many children in my hometown to love reading. Thanks to my brother, James, who encouraged me to keep writing and helped point me in the right direction to make my book a reality. And thanks to my children, who think their dad has a good sense of humor. And I would be totally lost without my editor Kelly, who has been patient as I learn, and who has the good sense of when to rein me in and when to let me run.

About the Author

Jeremy Brundage has worked as a stone mason, a carpenter, an artist, an animatronics engineer, and more. He is working on several projects with his brother James A. Owen for Coppervale Studios and assists in creating armor for the SCA at Windrose Armory.

Jeremy writes comedy, fantasy, and science fiction, sometimes combining all three.

Join his newsletter to keep informed.

Not Quite Legendary Book Two

Two friends, who could be more than friends if they'd actually communicate, must put all that aside to fight their way to the center of the universe through literal layers of hell to fix the machine that keeps it all running. If they fail, the teetering universe will crumble and any possibility of a future will end—for everyone.

Other Titles from Cursed Dragon Ship Publishing

Stealing the cash box of your mercenary unit as you run away probably isn't wise, but it sure is funny.

www.ingramcontent.com/pod-product-compliance
Lightning Source LLC
Chambersburg PA
CBHW031004190726
48285CB00004BB/1471

* 9 7 8 1 9 5 1 4 4 5 5 5 3 *